The

Keeper of Her Heart

A Romance Novel

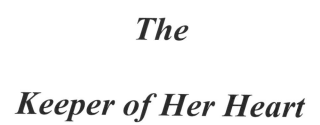

By

Marion R. Hunter

To my husband

Jeffery A. Hunter

Thank you for all your support and being there when I need you.

Thank you to my editing team
Kimberly Cefaratti
Heather Dyne

From my son Beau, 12/6/10
We were practicing Beau's spelling words. He had to spell the word "writer." He looked at me and said "Mommy you're a writer. You go to your writing class." My seven year old said I'm a writer. A treasured moment in motherhood.

Other Novels
by
Sharon R. Hunter

The Rancher's Wife
Love On The Ranch

Happy Hooker's Bait & Tackle Shop
A Romantic Comedy

Available on Amazon and Kindle

Chapter 1 - The Unwanted Trip

Hawke's overheard phone conversation seared at my heart, branding me with a new burning scar. The fire fueled, edging at the anxiety he caused me. It wasn't beneath me to listen in on any of his phone calls. I had done it for years. My blood boiled, filtering the newest of arguments that would soon be up for the attack. The inkling thought of another woman, his perfectly laid plans, his web of a story that he'd weave around me, only pissed me off. Jealously of another woman would be far easier to swallow than what Hawke had put me through. So the rush of jealousy wasn't needed, but it surfaced. No other woman ever mused his thoughts. His eye they'd catch, but never his heart. He made sure it belonged to me, no matter how torn he had left mine. A hand held on the doorframe steadied my hate-filled rage as I deceptively and deliberately eavesdropped on his phone call. Just hearing his electrified voice, only his side of the conversation lashed through me with anger and crushed my soul. My shadowy figure loomed outside the bedroom doorway, he knew I was there. Hawke always knew my presence well before my appearance. Even the warm rays of sunshine that played on my back couldn't spoil my darkened, ugly mood. Silencing the pain, I nearly bit through my bottom lip hearing his simple words. "Hunt" and "bear" set my rage into motion.

"Bastard," I'd never say it to his face - maybe I was a little afraid to. But then again, he knew my heartfelt feelings towards him. "How could he? He promised me." Huffing, I'd made sure he heard me as I headed for the steps mumbling with a spiteful stomp down each one. "Promised. Never ever would he leave me again." Barefoot and stomping on wood steps, I soon found that to be a tad bit painful. Still engaged, better yet engrossed with his hunting conversation, I glimpsed at him on the landing. My presence made known, he made sure I felt his surly grin as I staked toward the kitchen. With my mission nearly accomplished, my heart swelled with this past years' reality. "Damn him. Damn, damn, damn him. How could he do this to me?"

From the kitchen window I spied Emma and Amelia playing in the backyard garden. They were the only bright spot in my lifeless marriage with Hawke since the miscarriage. After a year my wounds still festered with open pain. Would they ever heal? Just hearing the word "hunt" sent me spiraling into a sickening flashback.

With my mind held prisoner, a visual memory of a hospital room reappeared. White walls as pale as my icy cold skin clouded my thoughts. Empty and alone, I desperately waited for him. Echoes of sobs and praying to die were absorbed by those same heartless walls. My time had run thin and every medical avenue had been exhausted in trying to save our baby. Nothing, nothing could save her. The baby was gone by the time Hawke got to me. Wrapped in Aunt Maude's arms of comfort instead of his, I had awakened to the next round of nightmares.

There was no possibility of reaching Hawke in the remote area of the mountains he had been guiding, along with hunting. He learned the horror of his unfortunate fate when he returned to the base camp. Word had come into the hospital, Hawke was on his way. Aunt Maude reassured me over and over he'd be there. Tears pricked at my eyes remembering that scornful day of why I hated him. We once held a bond, a connection of tangled love that wove our spirits close to the heart. On that day, at that moment, my devastated heart felt every step he had taken. From landing the plane, to the eerie echo of his footsteps racing down the hallway of the hospital. Our twisted bond of love had been shattered, chocking the life from my heart. They had drugged me heavily for the pain and my hysteria, but I knew when he arrived on the floor, well before he appeared at my side. Hawke had finally made it, but it was too late. Aunt Maude had tried to pass me, his sobbing wife, into his waiting arms. Not wanting him near me, I could only scream, hating him. My drug induced weakness left me helpless to fight his sympathetic, loving embrace. How could he have done this to me? He knew. He knew all too well that this pregnancy registered high risk. So high risk a minor problem could become life threatening. But he still left me. A single tear slipped through my shattered thoughts and rolled down my cheek rushing me back to the present. My hurt, I wore it like a badge. It was and still is crushingly visible.

His chosen profession as a skilled hunting and fishing guide came well before me and our two young nieces. The business grew, and we grew apart. The thrill of the hunt, he lived for it. Pulsing in his veins, he thrived on it. It was our livelihood. "That's what keeps us living comfortably." His reminder, a mere slap of sarcasm for being a stay at home mom to our nieces, even cooking at Maude's diner didn't rate. Oh, how he reminded me. We were lucky if he was home for a week out of a month. The day brutal reality snapped at him, the miscarriage stopped him cold. The core of his hardness completely smashed. It changed Hawke. Kept him closer to home. Kept him tentative and closer to us. For me, forgiving him was a different story.

"Dove, pack your bags. You're going to Michigan with me." Too much excitement bounced in his cheerful voice.

"Michigan? Did hell just freeze over?" My sarcastic delightfulness he brushed it off. "NO!" The air we breathed chilled by my nasty statement of "no." "I'm not about to go anywhere with you." My eyebrow arched in disgust, Hawke blew off my sarcasm. The glare I delivered, it only pleased me to see I could still rattle his chain.

"Uncle Ralph and Aunt Ruby, they want you to come with me, Dove." He spoke softer, pulling my attention back to him.

"Why?" No way was I going to let up.

"Got a nuisance bear with my name on it." The gleam in Hawke's eye soured me. "Dove they want you to come. First thing out of my Uncle's mouth. We haven't seen them in years."

"We don't travel anywhere because you're always hunting." Another glare of annoyance cast from me to him.

Easily, Hawke tossed my negativity aside for his own convenience. "Come on honey, give it a chance."

"Give you a chance is more like it." I snapped in fury at him. "It's a hunt. That's why your Uncle called."

"Dove," The sharp tone of his voice advised me to watch my step. My point had been made. "A little time alone with me might just thaw your frigid mood." He retaliated back at me. His patience, I wore it thin.

"Frigid?" We both ignored the comment with a truthful meaning as I ranted on. "Why? Why should I go with you?" My new victim, the coffee pot, it got slammed back on the burner.

"Did you ever stop to think, I want you to? You need..." his express softened toward me, "...we need some time alone together."

6

"Ha," the cattiness in me flourished, "Alone? With you? No!" Not being charmed by his smile, my glare heated. "Let me guess, Fred and Lance, they'll be tagging along. Besides, I'm not about to leave the girls this summer." My retaliation didn't take him by surprise, Hawke had learned to live with it. The girls were a valid reason and he knew it, but then again, I'd make any excuse not to be alone with my husband. I plopped down at the kitchen table, slopping my coffee everywhere.

"Jane would love to keep the girls. You know it." With confidence no longer hiding in his back pocket, Hawke chiseled away at trying to melt my icy emotions for him.

Not only did he chisel and chip away at my "Ice Queen" mood, he weaved his charming smile and tenderness around me. He could ground me with his simple calmness. Irritating yes, but he knew how to stand his ground peacefully. He played me with a wave of velvety smoothness, dancing around my agonizing emotions. My protective instincts kicked in. Stay strong, I can fight his attempts. Who was I kidding? I just wasn't ready to forgive Hawke, yet. A rambling of unspoken thoughts raced in my head as he sat down next to me. The kitchen clock became my focus, tick-tock-tick-tock, the hands mindlessly bounced around the numbers. I wouldn't acknowledge him. Daringly, he touched the ends of my hair, playing with a loose curl, twisting it through his fingers.

"Dove, it's been a year. Your body is more than healed." He inched closer to me, "Let me heal your heart." Begging wasn't his style. He's never desperate, did he mean it? "Come with me Dove, please?"

For the first time in months his touch didn't make my skin crawl. Still, I cringed. I know he felt me shutter. It showed in his eyes. Knowing that touching me was next to forbidden, Hawke pressed his luck kissing my cheek. As his own long sleek hair brushed over my shoulder, he felt my trembling at his closeness. Lightly tugging, I let my fingers thread through the ends of his hair.

Again, Hawke dared to inch even closer to me, "I need you. I need, no, I want my wife back." His truthful feelings for me came out.

Why was I falling for his game? I knew all of his tricks, but this, this felt different. Riding on my erupting emotions, he gently took my hand in his. On my palm, Hawke circled his fingers in a calming attempt. I felt the light touch warm over my ivory skin. Still, I wouldn't look at him. Overwhelmed with my own feelings, how I craved his touch. Even desired it. He caused a stirring I thought had all but died in me. The sigh on my lips, just a remembrance of how tender he once was. Quickly, I suppressed the long ago memory, not letting it surface. Somehow, Hawke was winning. I couldn't let that happen. Or could I?

"Dovey, it's summer break. Jane loves having the girls. You know we can fix this." He continued to calm me with his simple touch to my palm. "If you'd just trust me enough to let me back into you life. Say you'll go, Dove. Please."

Persuasion without bargaining. He dealt his case well and I felt my heart caving to his not so unreasonable request. Did I dare go with him? Could I leave my girls? Hawke had kept every promise he made. Maybe I could move on. But was I able to forgive him? True, it had been a year. It was me, my body refused the pregnancy and he never held that against me. Everything healed, but my mind. My emotions were left raw and stinging. He wasn't there when I desperately needed him. I studied his face with gritted teeth. My tears threatened. Those eyes of his, they never lied, Hawke meant what he said.

"Fine," I snarled my answer at him. "Fine. You win. I'll go with you." I yanked my hand from his in protest, "But just remember, I'm not happy about it."

My snarling "yes" left him erupting in laughter. Just hearing his laughter, knowing I was caving into him, burned at me. Hawke had just won over my iced and broken heart. His bear hug of a squeeze left me gasping for my next breath. Another kiss stolen from my lips this time, Hawke dialed up the phone and celebrated his success with his Uncle Ralph.

The coffee cup sat quietly at my finger tips as I watched him gloating about the news to his uncle. Me on the other hand, I struggled with the dampening thought of being alone with him. Reality surfaced that I didn't want to face. We hadn't shared the same bed in nearly a year.

Chapter 2 – Hawke

Displayed in the open gun safe was Hawke's own private arsenal of weapons. He took pride in all the top brands of steel that graced the ironclad safe. He needed power, but not the kind he used when hunting in Alaska. A box of 180 grain solids for his 300 win mag, would do. Extras, there would be no need for an extra box. But for good measure, he carelessly tossed a second box of ammo on his desk.

The smoke smoldered at his fingertips as he crushed out the end of the cigar. Reeling at his triumphal win, Dove was really going with him. Satisfied with his accomplishment he laid two more pieces of his favorite hardware out on the desk. Cold hard steel, stocks hand made by his own hand. His father had taught him the craft of woodworking. At times he felt his father's presence, always wishing he could see him again. Speak with him just one more time. Patience, one thing his father had instilled deeply into him. What he really needed now was his father's wisdom and guidance. How he could've used the help of the old man today if only he were still alive.

Hawke ran his hand roughly over his coarse hair. He knew the battle still wasn't over with Dove. She fought him hard over this trip, used every excuse under the sun not to go. She loved him, he knew it, but he had broken her heart. He'd already started to stir her reserved emotions for him. Hawked mused over the ways to rekindle the fire in Dove and bring her spirit back to him. His attention pulled back to the three guns that would handle what needed to be done in Michigan. Gently, as if the gleaming steel guns where fragile, he placed them in separate gun cases. Secured and locked, the guns were ready for the airport.

The flight from Portland, Oregon to Sault Ste. Marie, Michigan would be over four hours by commercial carrier, with one layover in Minnesota. How he'd love to have flown her to their destination. Just the two of them. Years had slipped by since Dove had been flying the sky line with him.

Hawke once enjoyed his own personal co-pilot. The float plane had once been used for their secret weekend adventures. He'd fly them high into the endless blue horizon, setting her mind and soul free. After landing in an isolated bay on a sheet of clear water, he'd take her deep into the backwoods. The great outdoors never suited Dove, but she'd campout for a weekend of pleasure with him. Under a blanket of stars he recalled how he'd make endless love to his wife by the firelight. Dove turned her body over willingly to him, his shy wife flourishing into his passionate lover. At one moment in their life, she'd have done anything for him. The present played out a whole different story with his wife.

His mind grayed over as he eased back into the leather chair recounting his memories of how he'd lost her. His heart still ached with knowing how he had not been there when she lost their third baby. A frown of sadness creased over his brow reliving the doctor's words. "If she conceives again, the odds are high that Dove will die before she could deliver." The final blow came when he chose her life over attempting to have another child with her. Riddled with guilt, he took matters into his own hands, not telling Dove until after the fact. Hawke made sure his wife would never suffer a miscarriage again. His decision left their marriage spiraling into disaster. With his choice made, he wounded her deeper, and Dove loathed the sight of him.

Obsessed by his work, it became an outlet, a refuge of sanity for him. The Cessna had turned into his primary business partner. Hawke's priorities shifted as Dove secluded herself from his touch. He became rated in the top five for hunting and fishing outfitters in Oregon, leaving little to no time for his wife or their drowning marriage. Another tortured memory for the files, he sighed, relieved knowing Dove was upstairs packing. The intensity of the trip over the last few weeks had weakened her hatred towards him. Dove's affections became something she offered warily and rarely to him.

Dove, she dreaded the trip, mostly the part of the upcoming hunt. To make things worse, the evasion of Lance and Fred's presence, but he needed them for scouting. A nuance bear only caused trouble. Finished with his packing Hawke brought the gear up from his basement office, tripping over the pile of Dove's packed bags scattered over the kitchen floor. Actually surprised that Dove had listened to him, even more impressed she was still willing to go.

Last tally over all the bags, he admired her from the doorway, watching her fuss over every little detail for the girls. Her babies, ten and twelve, their nieces craved Dove's affection. The unreachable dream of a baby still haunted them both. She'd mother anyone or anything. It was her talent, in her nature, and she was good at it. The girls clung to Dove, absorbing all of her love. As for that damn cat cradled in her arms, it replaced the baby she'd lost. The girls brought it home beat-up and starved. He hated cats, but Dove had begged to keep it. Nothing like competing with a bastard cat for Dove's attention now.

"You going to be able to live without that fur bag?" Sarcastically, Hawke asked.

"I'll make do," Dove couldn't give up the cursing glare. "Why does he bother you so much?"

"You named it Ebony for one. You love that damn animal more than me." Crap, the truth just fell right out of his mouth, and Hawke watched as the hurt filled Dove's eyes.

"Don't go there, Hawke. I could easily change my mind," she whispered. No sarcasm, just jagged pain.

"Dove," his anger elevated. "I'm really putting an effort out here. Least you could do is give me your attention." It was a low blow, he should've known better, but Dove needed to hear it.

"He's a cat, just a cat," she pouted, protesting, and kept stroking the purring animal.

"You packed?" Hawke snapped, clearing his throat, subject changed.

"Yes," she hung onto the "s" with a hiss, "I have one more bag. The girls are ready for Jane." Dove clutched that cat tighter, tears edging into her eyes. "Hawke…I…I don't know…I don't think…I can…" Her voice teetered with reluctance as she struggled to even glance Hawke's way.

"Dove, Dovey," Her tears streamed. "Don't back out on me now. You'll be fine. The girls, you can call them everyday. Morning, noon, and night." His reassurance didn't calm her.

Hawke was completely astonished by the fact she actually let go of the menacing animal when he reached for her. Dove allowed his hands to wrap around her, drawing her into his embrace.

"Dove you need to be with me," smoothly his hand stroked through her endless auburn curls. "We need to be alone for a while."

Dove's body sculpted, forming into his. She clung tightly to him. Dove hadn't been willing to let him touch her in months. Relishing in her soft scent, Hawke felt her vulnerability under his touch. All these months of waiting, wanting to hold her, comfort her. Finally she let her guard down, letting him in. Dove would never admit defeat, but her wall of icy emotions fell to him. Hawke felt her surrendering. Still aware, he knew it wasn't enough yet to let him back into her bed, but she was warming.

The back door swung open biting deep at the wall. No knocking, just an outburst of demands echoed through the quiet house. Jane arrived in her own style towing Fred by her side. That woman could lecture a person to death with her endless barking of orders.

Fast to halt, Jane didn't expect to see the fresh tears stained on Dove's face. Let alone the shock of Hawke cradling Dove tightly in his massive arms. As if Jane's mouth had been unhinged, it flapped wide open in surprise. In a blink, she shut it tight. Her untimely presence only pissed Hawke off even more. Jane skated on the thinnest of ice around him. Shifting Dove closer into him, Hawke's glare heated Jane's fury.

"Ya know Jane…" he snarled, ready to strike her down with his forth coming words.

Jane fired back before he could execute another syllable. "Shut it Hawke. I'm not impressed." With another glare from Hawke and before Dove could intervene, Jane decided to redirect her attitude. "My girls…where are my girls?" She glanced around the kitchen before grabbing Dove from Hawke's secure embrace. Jane whisked her away, heading for the privacy of the living room. Toting Dove by her arm, Jane barked more commands at Fred and pointed to the pile of duffle bags and suitcases. The low whisper of female conversation had been concealed to the walls of the living room.

"Take it you've been counting down the days until you're out of here?" With disgust in his voice, Hawke asked his long time friend. "Have you ever just wanted to pop that broad?"

"Now Hawke," Fred rolled his eyes, "don't forget, Jane's my wife. I'll admit, yep, I've thought it over a few times." A little gleam sparked in his eyes. "Think she could beat both of our asses." Fred let out a low humorous chuckle. "That woman won't shut her yap. Mouth just a flapping all the way over. Got her panties all up tight in a wad. Worried about Dove." Another deep eye roll flitted over Fred's face. "Do you know how fragile your wife is? She's needing Jane's guidance. You know that, don't you?" Fred sneered, hauling up three bags from the floor.

"Dove? My Dove?" Hawke smirked in amusement. "Sure you've got the right woman?" Hawke shook his head still amused. "Hell, Dove can back me down with one of those damn evil-eyed glares of hers. There's nothing fragile about Dovey." Maybe just her heart, and he kept that thought to himself.

Fred puffed out his chest, "And what does Hawke think he's going to do to her? Alone for a month?" Fred mocked his wife's pitchy voice. "Can't stand the fact she ain't going to have her nose up your business for an entire month."

"Small relief, I'll take it. Good thing I'm taking you with me Fred." Hands full of bags, Hawke stopped to survey the drama of Jane and Dove's conversation in the living room. "You know Jane, she'll be burning up the phone lines to Dove every single day that we're gone." With an elbow, Hawke held the backdoor open for his buddy as they hauled the ample amount of luggage out to the truck.

"Now, seeing we're out of ear shot, how did you get Dove to say yes?" Fred asked to serious of a question while he tossed in another bag. "Can't see you down on your knees begging Dove to go. If you didn't beg her, what did you promise Dove this time?"

"Charmed her," Hawke grinned and gave Fred a sly wink, "just some old fashioned charm. You should try it on Jane sometime."

"You're so full of shit." Another over rated eye roll flew from Fred. They both knew Hawke lied. "There's no way you could've unruffled Dovey's feathers. Had a little help did you?"

"Unbelievable that I got her to say yes in the first place," Hawke blew out a sigh of relief, "Maude, she sealed the deal for me. I owe her big time. You know Maude, she kept talking to Dove about going. And you know Dove, she'd do anything for that woman. Loves her like a mother."

"Jane said they had some long girly talk with Dove. That girl, woman shit, it scares me." Fred shuddered at the thought of the three females lost deep in conversation as he tossed in the last bag.

"Whatever they said to her, I hope it lasts." Hawke checked the time on his watch and headed back to the house. "Dove, let's go." The tone of his gruff command had the women's heads snapping.

Hands firmly placed on her pencil thin hips, Jane retaliated, "For crying out loud Hawke, don't get so bossy. Let Dove say goodbye to her girls."

"One of these days Jane," Hawke bit his tongue as dirty looks were exchanged between them. How he would love to pop his wife's best friend, just once or just get the last word in.

"You better take care of her Hawke," Jane snarled, "and bring her back in one piece. That's an order." With all her demands, Jane should've been a drill sergeant.

"Dove, honey," calmly, Hawke asked, "time to go." He offered his hand to her. "We've got a plane to catch."

Reluctantly, she weaved her fingers through his, letting him lead her out the backdoor. "Everything will be fine, Dove."

Bouncing along beside them, their two preteen nieces giggled from excitement of staying with Aunt Jane and Uncle Fred. Dove was quick to spat out another lecture about behavior, but the endless shower of hugs tugged at her aching heart. Dove didn't want to go, but deep down she knew it was their only hope. One last hug good-bye from her girls and Hawke helped her into the truck, shutting the door tightly behind her. One hurtle down, his sigh of relief went without notice. Regaining his wife's emotional loss towards him would be his next challenge.

Fred and Lance would be joining them by the end of the week. One week alone with Dove. One week to win her heart back. Would it be enough time? He started the engine and pulled down the paved driveway. The girls had already raced through the yard standing in the middle of the quiet side street waving and yelling their good-byes. It was as if they were afraid they'd never see Dove again. They'd miss Dove, miss her more than they'd ever miss him. Dove, she is the life support of the family. She couldn't pull her gaze from the bouncing figures. Arm stretched out the window still waving good-bye, Hawke pulled onto the main road. The silence in the truck was broken by Dove rummaging through her purse for a tissue. Tears, he expected it, should've been used to them, but they still shattered him.

"Didn't you say they lived close to here?" James asked, keeping the conversation alive.

"Yes. His Aunt and Uncle owned a cottage down the lane from here. They lived here year round. Don't know if they still do." Chloe sipped her coffee while slipping into yesteryear.

"You ever stop down to see if they're still there?" James lightly pushed for more details.

"No, I'm sure they wouldn't remember me. Plus, how do you go up and say, 'Hi, I'm the kid who played with your nephew…how many years ago?' She laughed at her own joke.

"Wasn't this the kid who tried to teach you to fish?"

"Yes. Him and his uncle. As you can see," she tapped the photo with a painted nail, "they were not successful." Chloe's giggle of obnoxious humor filled the air. "They always included me in on all their fishing trips. Lord knows they tried."

"Poor kid. You ever find out what happened to him?" Still interested, James asked.

"No, I sure don't. You know, he kissed me on my birthday." Chloe's eyes turned into pure puppy love mush.

"Kissed you? How old was he?" With humor, even trying to be jealous, James played along.

"Just a couple of years older than me. I don't remember. I never saw him after that summer."

"And here I thought you saved your first kiss for me." James knew how to entice his wife back to the present. He captured her lips with his. Slowly James had her eagerly accepting more. Easily, Chloe draped her long, model like legs over his. James skimmed his fingers over her creamy skin. Chloe clinched her favorite coffee mug tighter at the warmth of James' lips nibbling down her neck. The old swing swayed with their shifting positions.

"Get a room." Jason, the mastermind behind interrupting his parent's romantic romp on the swing, bellowed. He'd rallied his cousins and continued on with a bash of wild cat calls from the sandy shore.

James relaxed deeply into the comfort of the swing's cushions, "Just great," he steamed, "How am I ever going to get you alone with this bruiting crowd?" His glare of annoyance heated at the four boys bobbing in the water. "Chloe," this time James took his sweet time sharing another kiss with his wife. Another round of hoopla echoed from the boys. "Whose idea was it to bring all these kids?" He knew his kiss left her lightheaded. "Take this matter up later," James blocked the boy's view of Chloe with his body. As he stripped off his jersey style t-shirt, he shucked it from his hands and into his grinning wife's hands. His hands skimmed over her oversized cat print t-shirt covered breast. Chloe's chilled fingertips seared down his washboard abs. She didn't resist him or his last kiss. "Be back." He joined the group of boys splashing in the water. James played monster-of-the-sea with the crowd of youngsters aging from eight to fourteen.

She tapped the side of her mug and sighed, "A month long vacation with four boys under foot. Guess we'll be doing a hell of a lot of sneaking around."

Chloe glanced back at the old photo still in her hand. The nameless, but not forgotten playmate still captured her mind. His long, shiny, poker straight hair hung loosely below his shoulders. The color picture had faded over the years, but the young boy's eyes still held the radiance of honey amber. Two awkward kids, tall and skinny stared back at her. Compared to her friend, Chloe had been the princess of fair skin and freckles, accompanied by her wild flowing auburn curls. Her mom had told her that her 'summer crush' was of Native American heritage, which explained his dark reddish brown skin.

"Wonder what ever happened to you?" Chloe whispered as she ran a finger over the yellowed photo.

"What did you need her for? Or should I ask, how can I help?" Ruby could hear his relief over the end of the line.

"Want to take her for a little ride." Hawke replied with hope. "Found an inlet with a beach she just might like."

"You scouting? Or are you planning on spending a little time with her?" Aunt Ruby didn't hesitate to make her comment direct.

"Feel like I'm talking to Maude here, Ruby." Both Aunts would do anything to keep this marriage afloat.

"You do the asking. I'll back you if she won't budge. Besides your Uncle and me, it's our weekly poker night at the Hoffman's. Got the house to yourselves. Make it count boy." Aunt Ruby, still a true romantic at heart, giggled.

"Aunt Ruby, I'm blushing." Hawke played innocent with her.

"Bullshit boy. I know you," her chuckle of laughter echoed over the phone, "I'll put a bottle of your Uncle's homemade wine in the fridge to chill. I think luck just might be on your side tonight." Aunt Ruby laughed harder and clicked the phone off.

A quick stop at the smoke shop fulfilled his smoking habit. One thing about Dove, she enjoyed the smell of a good cigar. He only bought the best to tickle her fancy. Hawke never noticed the same SUV parked at the "Sunshine Cottage" as he drove down the shaded lane. The mystery woman at Ginger's Market didn't even mingle in his mind anymore. She faded away as he planned his mission of an evening swim with his wife.

xoxoxoxoxoxo

Persuasion came easier than he anticipated. Armed and ready for Dove's assault of defensive answers, she halted him in his tracks when she said 'yes' to his evening offer. She'd go for a ride with him. No protesting. Not even a defiant eyebrow lift from her usual glaring eye. Hawke wondered what lecture Ruby had handed down to Dove. Lovingly, of course. He wasn't about to butt in on a female conversation. He'd learned that lesson the hard way.

Ruby and Ralph rattled past them. They didn't have to assume what had just taken place. They were pretty sure of Dove's answer by Hawke's surprised expression.

"Here honey," Aunt Ruby handed Dove two fluffy beach towels and a bottle of wine. "Now go. Keep in mind what we talked about." She patted Dove's cheek. "Just enjoy yourself." The older couple shuffled around with a tray of food and quickly moved toward the door.

Before it closed behind them Uncle Ralph ducked back in. "Going to be a late night kids. Don't wait up. See you for breakfast."

Security became the two thick beach towels clutched in Dove's arms along with the chilled bottle of wine. Her eyes trailed from Ralph and Ruby's escape out the door to her husband's pompous winning grin. Hawke watched as hopelessness and abandonment showered her at the sound of the door clicking shut. All along, Dove had had Ruby and Ralph to intercept being alone with him. He could only imagine how her heart thumped to a beat that had to be bouncing in her brain of "what the hell is she going to do now." The way Aunt Ruby edged at her all afternoon about spending more time alone with him, he'd thought would have been a ringer of a giveaway. A few batted eyelashes towards him in wonderment, Dove left him standing alone in the living room as she silently strolled into the kitchen. Only the clicking of her sandals on the tile floor spoke to him. Hawke smirked to himself as he watched the eyelet flowered sundress sway from his view. A game Dove played with him. She knew he'd follow her. Tonight, there would be no way he'd let her off the hook and Dove knew it. Hawke played the game of toying with her emotions. When he appeared in the doorway, he found her rummaging around a kitchen drawer. Her gifts from Ruby lay on the butcher block countertop as she tried to hide her glance to him.

"Dove?" In her full view, she jumped at the sound of his voice.

"Guess we need this." Dove whirled the corkscrew around her finger. "Where do you think Aunt Ruby keeps the paper cups? I don't want to take her good wine glasses." Her act of pretending, as always, obvious to him. Like clockwork he could predict her swinging moods.

"Try above the stove," he answered her, then waited for the fit of protest to kick in. Dove's new trick she played on him, her calmness. He wasn't used to seeing this side of her.

From under the sink, Dove grabbed an empty shopping bag. Ignoring Hawke at all cost, she went about her business. Towels shoved in the paper bag nestled the wine bottle securely. Next up, two large plastic cups. From the refrigerator, she retrieved a plastic container filled with cheese, pickles, olives and a sleeve of crackers. Dove carelessly plopped the container in the bag, grabbing it by the plastic handles. She passed by Hawke to the backdoor without a word. No glance of happiness to him.

"Dove, you get into Ruby's stash of feel good meds or something?" Her disapproving glare back lashed him as if she slapped him in the face. He rubbed his jaw at the pain she inflicted by using just her eyes.

Propped with the toe of her leather sandal, Dove held the door open, "I said I would go. That's all." She left Hawke standing in the kitchen with all its accessories.

He couldn't say she was being bitchy, not even whining. She just moved, keeping her secrets of emotions to herself. He heard the slam of the truck door as he locked and pulled the cottage door shut behind him.

"Damn woman. Can't make heads or tails out of you," he mumbled to the evening air as he walked down the sandstone sidewalk.

The brown shopping bag glossed with "Ginger's Market" in lipstick red print, sat between them as an unofficial referee.

"What the hell kind of protest are you throwing at me now?" Confused, he egged her on and turned the key to the engine.

Dove's so-called "female signals" left him at a loss. No reply. He'd gotten used to that as they headed down the lane under the canopy of green foliage. Like clockwork her expression turned to a twist of a lip. Or could it possibly be a pout? Nope, just the "don't speak-to-me-you-idiot" glare that flashed through Doves eyes.

"I'm not fussing, protesting you, or whatever else you think it is that I do. I'm here." A bitter edge clung to her words. "Little sick and tired of hearing how I'm supposed to be, from both your Aunts." Dove's hostile glance bounced out the window and not at Hawke for once. "I just don't want you to think..." A new pattern shifted in Dove's emotions. She smoothed the skirt of her dress over her legs. Her voice melted into silence as the breeze rushing through the open cab windows twirled her hair around her stilled face.

"You don't want me to think what, Dove?" He took advantage of her restlessness.

"Nothing...just." She let out a heavy sigh. "Don't be expecting me to do..." Dove snapped her mouth shut. The urge to attack reeled in her. Another one of her spiraling emotions caught his attention.

"Not expecting anything, Dove." Hawke wanted more. Painfully, it showed in his eyes. His plan for this evening, push Dove to her limit, emotionally and physically.

"Where are you taking me?" She snapped in hopes to change the subject.

Before she could get an answer, Hawke had turned off the main road. He followed the twisting, overgrown dirt trail. Tree branches slapped at the side of the old truck as they bounced along. Finally, the overgrowth gave way to a refreshing sandy beach with its own private dock. The lush greenery of summer sprawled to the water's edge. The old truck hissed to a stop. Hawke grinned at her openly shocked expression and grabbed the bag off the front seat. Before Dove's door could slam shut with disapproval, he had already stripped down to nothing but his bare, russet skin. Clothes scattered on the dock next to the grocery bag, he plunged into the glassy blue water.

"Come on Dove. The water's great," he coaxed her with a warm smile as he laughed.

"NO! NO! NO! I'm not. NO!" Dove screamed her disapproval from the front side of the truck fender. "You dragged me out here to go skinny-dipping with you? You really are crazy."

"Come on Dove. You know you want to." He could see the fury burning deep in her widened eyes.

He had pissed her off and enjoyed her sulking, surprised mood. She couldn't even escape him if she wanted to. If she wanted to leave, Dove would have to fish the truck keys out of his jeans pocket lying on the dock.

Perched on the end of the fender, Dove contemplated wandering over to the wooden dock. The agony of him winning eased while she watched him swim. No one was around for miles. Just the two of them. The sun's descending rays rippled over the splashing waves he made, antagonizing her. Deep breath in. Deep breath out. With a grudge holding for Hawke, Dove kicked at the pebbly sand while she inched her way over to the edge of the dock. She contemplated the thought of taking the truck keys along with his clothes and driving off. She smiled at the devious plotted plan as she walked her sorry-self across the dock. Sandals freed from her feet, she sat herself on the edge of the dock dangling her feet in the cool lake water. In a routine motion, out of habit, she folded Hawke's rumpled clothes. Placed neatly behind her, Dove then raided the bag she'd packed. Plastic container of cheese in hand, Dove slapped it down on the wooden dock. The force of her anger only made it bounce back at her.

"Lucky for you you're plastic," she took her frustration out on the container. In one hand the bottle of wine. Corkscrew in hand, she worked it over the wine bottle, imagining how she wanted to ring Hawke's neck for bringing her out here. Cork yanked free from the bottle, Dove scowled. Her eyes didn't hide the pending threat as he swam closer to her.

"Do you want any of this?" The bottle chugged and wine spilled into her cup. Before he could answer, she nearly dumped the wine on him with a crooked grin of repayment splattered on her lips.

Payback, to Dove it was like the cherry floating on top of the whipped cream. He didn't bite at her little spat of revenge, only massaged a wet hand over her legs.

"Swim with me Dove. Like you used to do. You remember?" His voice sultry. Even inviting. He had her fidgeting and enjoyed the moment.

"Yes, I remember. Remember I was too naïve to know better. I let you talk me into way too many things back then." With another sip of wine she sympathetically recalled the fun they once had. Countless upon countless times she'd been more than willing to sneak off skinny dipping with him. Dove tightened her lips in an attempt to conceal her growing grin.

"You weren't that naïve, Dove. You were willing to because you trusted me. Do you still trust me?"

The sting of her batted eyes landed on his. She didn't answer right away, leaving him in an uncertain limbo. "I never lost trust in you. Just lost…"

"I know, Dove. You don't need to relive it. You're here. Let go of what happened to us in the past. Live today, tomorrow, and the rest of your life with me."

"You promised me you'd take care of me forever. Love me no matter what." Dove's soft voice whispered around the tranquil lapping water.

"Believe you made the same promise to me, Dove." His wet hand roamed up higher on her bare legs. "I'm not giving up."

With his slippery hands roaming over her bare legs, Dove closed her eyes. She replayed the comments they'd just delivered to each other in her head. Not out to prove a point, she knew Hawke was right.

Hawke tossed his empty cup back on the dock. He knew he had an advantage over her. He had Dove's heart thumping to a timely beat of wondering nerves. Hopefully, he'd awaken her lost emotions. In front of her, he rested his chin on her knees, playfully bouncing his head from one knee to the other until a giggle escaped her. Hands planted to the side of her on the dock, he propelled himself from the water landing a kiss on her lips. His thick muscular legs surrounded her thighs. Her sudden protest of surprise didn't stop him. With a gentle force, he pushed the weight of his dripping wet body onto to her. A tempting struggle from Dove, he covered her body with his as he laid her back on the rough wooden slats of the dock. Hawke's naked body dripped the evening's warm lake water over her. Beaded droplets fell from his hair and pooled on her chest. Little rivers of water ran down the sides of her neck. Conveniently, Hawke had drenched the entire front of her cottony sundress. Another droplet of water splashed on her cheek as his finger teasingly pulled on the skinny straps of her dress. Hawke took advantage of his daring, trapping move. He lowered himself fully down on Dove and blocked her squirming. He enjoyed the way Dove's breath caught in her throat when she felt the hardness that only she could arouse in him. Under the thin layer of cotton, he felt her legs tighten closer together. Between the tangles of soft material he slipped his hand up her bare thigh. When Dove arched her back, he tugged at the zipper of her dress. She flattened her body on purpose. One hand trapped beneath Dove's trembling body, he pressed himself harder into her tightening thighs. With his free hand, Hawke roamed up her bare thigh until he found the curve in her fleshy hip. Dove worked her hands up his bare back occupying his mind with her touch. He missed the sudden surge that fired in her eyes as she fisted and yanked a handful of his tangled wet hair.

Anger boiled deep from in his throat. "Damn it, Dove! Let go!" His annoyance met the spiteful depths in her eyes.

As requested, Dove unclenched her hands. In an unsuspecting swipe, Hawke grabbed her by the wrists. "Hawke, no." In retaliation, he slammed her hands flat to the wooden dock pinning her arms above her head. Inches from each other, he hovered above her. "Stop it." Helpless to him, her heated denial flared. "Get off of me." Dove's demand dismissed, Hawke only made himself comfortable on top of her. "This isn't funny. Please, get off of me. You," she grabbed for any words, "you got me all wet." With the full weight of his lean body resting on her, Dove pretended to play nice and attempted to conceal her growing panic.

"Plan is Dove, I'm going to get you more than wet."

"You're what? No, no, no, no, no." Pinned under her husband, his bare skin to her clothed body, she couldn't move. "Hawke, I can't."

"You can't or you won't?" He caught Dove by surprise. He knew every single line of protest, heard them for a year. Hawke's lips crushed down on hers, exerting his impatience in a hard, rough kiss. Held firmly under him, he felt Dove's body quiet. Her demand to be free, soften for his wanting touch. One of his hands loosely wrapped around both of her wrists with little fight. "Tell me Dove..."

"Hawke, please. Just let me up." Flustered at not being in control, she surfaced for a breath of well needed air. Before she could protest or even think clearly, Hawke consumed her in another maddening kiss.

Dove's body stirred, possibly awakened by his touch. She trembled as he found his way back to the curve in her hip he liked to touch so much. Hawke broke the connecting kiss between them. He enjoyed the startled expression in his wife's crystal blue eyes. Her heartbeat matched each pounding beat of his. She panted for a breath as he slowly ran a finger over her supple lips.

"I still love you." Dove whispered, a tear tumbled from the edge of her eye.

"I never stopped. I need you back Dove, all of you. Every crazy inch of you." He'd given in and let Dove wiggle her hands free of his locking grip. Her fingers traced the edged lines of frustration in his face.

"Hawke," she searched his eyes, "I'm, I..." Did a little fear escape from her voice knowing he'd just won her heart back?

"Dovey, there's nothing to fear. Just keep opening your heart to me." He waited, not sure of what Dove's next move would bring. Her long fingers circled his face. A painted nail tapped on the side of his check. It could've been worse. Dove could have completely rejected his persisting advances. But she didn't. Instead, Dove drew him closer. In an awakening hunger for him, she brushed her lips lightly over his. She repeated the kiss he'd pinned her down with.

"Here," Hawke slipped the pile of his neatly folded clothes under her head, "Comfortable?"

"Not really. This wooden dock isn't comfortable." Protest rose in her eyes, but quickly drained away when his hand skimmed the lace edge of her panties. The feel of his fingers gliding between her thighs sent her heartbeat skyrocketing. Her breath quickened from his massaging touch. Hawke was no longer blocked by Dove's year-long obstacle of hate. What blocked his happiness, the damn dress she wore. He rolled his body taking her with him. Zipper down, he pulled the dampen eyelet dress over her head.

"Hawke, no..." Words of a scared protest circled in the evening air as he flipped Dove onto her back with him securely keeping her from getting away.

"The word "No" doesn't' exist in our relationship from now on." Hawke prayed she hadn't slipped backwards into her life of darkness.

"No, I mean, here? What if someone comes?" From underneath his warm body, Dove scanned her surroundings. Only the setting sun met her worried eyes.

He didn't answer. Nor did he hesitate in stripping her panties down her long creamy legs. Tossed on top of her rumpled dress, he covered her fully with his body. He wanted to kiss and touch every inch of her exposed ivory skin. "Hawke, really, we..." her innocent worries didn't stop him. There'd be no detour for the safety of four walls and a bed. His hands overfilled with her smooth silky breasts, he suckled both. His tongue flicked roughly over her soft sensual skin.

"Hawke," Dove moaned his name in a whispering breath. She gripped his shoulders with each and every pass he made over her. "Hawke, please..."

"Dove," he massaged his fingers deep into her fleshy breasts, "Don't deny me now."

"I don't want you to stop." Her fingers lightly threaded in his thick hair.

Comfortable between his wife's legs, Hawke heard her breath catch as he entered her. Slowly, controlled, just like the first night they'd ever spent together. Again, she willingly accepted him. Her hips rose to meet his, taking all of his thickness. Hawke didn't flinch when Dove's razor sharp nails raked down his back. He only applied more pressure with each thrust deeper into her. Dove's moaning of sensual pleasure slipped into words of begging for more of his attention. Fully aware of what she secretly longed for, he filled his own needs with hers. Hawke collapsed on her bare chest. The pounding of Dove's wild heartbeat mirrored his heavy panting of fulfilling exhaustion. His desire to have all of Dove back, conquered. His sexual appetite for her would never be completely fulfilled. He'd always want and need her. Exhausted, their bodies laid quietly on the surface of the rough wooden dock.

"What did you do?" Dove searched his swirling honey amber eyes.

"Reminded you of how much I love you." He felt her tamed body tremble under his. "Come with me Dove." From her warmed body, Hawke slipped back into the lazy lake water. He'd left her lying naked on the dock, dripping wet in places that hadn't been heated in a long time.

Left in a daze of renewed passion for Hawke, Dove curled her body to the side. Her fingers crept to the balled-up sundress she'd worn. Tugging it over to her, she clutched it tightly to her chest as she sat up. On the old rickety dock, Dove soaked in her glowing moment. She had just made love to her husband. No bed of fluffy comfort. Just his clothes as a pillow. She knew Hawke had put everything on the line for her. A flame rekindled brightly in her healing heart. In the shadows of the setting sun, they had made love. Finally, she freed herself from the devastating past.

From the edge of the dock, Dove dangled her 'weak in the knee' legs in the refreshing water. She admired Hawke's sleek, toned body as he swam out deeper and deeper. Wine cup in hand, she gulped down the last few swallows. She caught the trickle of red candy running over her swollen lips. The taste of his kiss lingered deep in her. Not waiting any longer, Dove dumped her crumbled dress on the dock and slipped into the water. Within reach of him, Hawke pulled her through the water into the safety of his arms. Her legs wrapped around him, her breathing heavy from the short swim. She nestled her face into the crook of his neck.

"Hawke."

"Hmm," Water rippled between them as he murmured into her ear.

"I'm not saying you won." She pulled her head up looking him squarely in the eyes. "I admit, I've missed you. Missed your touch. Missed the way you love me. I want...I need you back in my life and..." he circled her around in the water waiting to hear just one more thing, "I need you back in my bed."

"You've made me wait too long of a time to hear this, Dove." His forehead bumped into hers. "You've always had me, Dove." Relief breathed from his lungs. He'd won the battle he came to fight. Hawke had put the pressure on Dove, in the right ways. Dove didn't cave into his demand. She willingly wanted and accepted him.

Chapter 7 - The Walking Path

"I'm on vacation. Why am I awake?" A silent moan escaped Chloe as she shuffled the bedcovers and tried not to wake James. Kicking free of the covers her feet finally hit the floor. The cool cold wood floors woke her even faster. "This is early. Too, too early." Even mumbling under her breath Chloe knew she wouldn't disturb James and his freight train snoring.

Bed pillow in hand, she grinned at her snoring husband. "Just one smack," she whispered at him lovingly. "It would be funny."

Instead of her planned pillow assault, Chloe, being a 'sweet' wife, chose to stumble down the hall to check on the other four sound sleepers. The men in her life were pleasantly lost in their deep sleeping slumber. The microwave in the corner of the kitchen beamed its florescent blue numbers of five am, adding a sting to her blinking eyes. From the cozy kitchen window she could see the thick, grey clouds looming low in the sky while a dewy mist covered the ground. The early morning daybreak still covered in darkness, had Chloe wishing she could sleep in, just like the sun decided to do.

With no sleep left in her, she stopped by the remodeled bathroom to freshen up before she went for her morning walk. Unsuccessful with running a comb through her wild mess of endless curls, she tied her hair up in a dangling ponytail. Another round of snoring ripped from James, scaring her as she crept back into their bedroom to grab her walking gear. Favorite shorts and ragged purple t-shirt in hand, she had yet to make any kind of fashion statement. A must for walking, she swiped the hot pink IPod Jason had given her for Christmas from the dresser. The amazing little piece of electronics held all of her favorite eighties music and more.

Dressed and ready for her daily stride, she turned a plain white napkin into a scribbled note for James. After slipping into her walking shoes, Chloe drew him a short map of the path she'd be taking. Her detailed art work would have him laughing over his morning coffee. Secretly, she knew James would breathe easier when he found her detailed map of directions.

The creaky backdoor didn't give her exit away as she slipped into the early morning coolness of July. Surprised by the chill, she quickly worked through her morning stretches. In this tiny vacation town, at this hour of the morning, you would barely find another soul up, let alone out and about.

IPod in hand, she messed with the small controls until she found one of her favorite songs. A snappy dance tune from Billy Idol vibrated in Chloe's ears. She started down the one lane road to the opening of the paved walking path. Even as the sun tried to break the grey mist of clouds, the lakeshore still shimmered with beauty.

James and Jason had thought of every walking gadget she would ever need. Her pedometer determined she had successfully and briskly walked a mile. Unfortunately for Chloe she had left her bottle of water sitting next to the detailed napkin on the kitchen table. A little parched, she rested against a weathered bench to catch her breath and enjoy the view out over the lake.

Mist crept and spun its way along the surface of the water disappearing into the clouded sky. Chloe drew in a deep breath of the morning freshness and stretched her aching muscles while she enjoyed the beauty of nature waking. The summer landscape held a breathtaking view even with the clinging mist circling around. The peaceful scenery had her relaxing against the old wooden bench. She yanked the buds of the IPod from her ears. The ringing of the last song escaped her ears as she tuned into nature's morning melodies.

xoxoxoxoxo

Hawke crept along the soft, pine needle covered floor of the forest. The thick carpet of nature concealed his footsteps from the deer he'd been trailing. He silently wove his way around the entire north end of the walking trail checking for any evidence of a bear, early morning scouting for the gnarly perpetrator who haunted this region. Hawke came upon the evidence he needed to continue on. Black fur rubbed on the thick bark of an oak tree. Stripped clean, a decaying beaver carcass along with a trail of dried droppings. All the signs, at least a week or so old. The beast in question had moved on to find a better feeding ground. Pleased with his findings he stepped from the depths of the forest into a grassy meadow leading to the trail. This is the area his Aunt and wife couldn't wait to walk on. Now the trail would be safe to navigate.

At the top of the trail Hawke's steps stopped suddenly. The woman by the lake had captured his full attention. What the hell was she doing out here? And how the hell did she reach this part of the path before him? Fading in and out of the early morning mist, his eyes focused on her shapely silhouette. His eyes glazed with annoyance. He'd specifically asked Dove not to walk on this particular part of the trail. It had been the last section he needed to scout. Did she know this would be his route today? Or did she have another game to play with him? He'd left her in their bed, fulfilled, content, even glowing. His annoyance slipped away as fast as it came. All Hawke could think about, was Dove. With silent footsteps he stopped only yards from her. Still she didn't notice him. Her ragged purple t-shirt sculpted close to her curves. The plum shorts she wore exposed her long, creamy legs. Those same legs had been wrapped tightly around his torso several times through the night. Hawke smiled at Dove's image standing with her back to him. Auburn hair, tossed in a half-attempted ponytail. Curls dripped to the side of her head nearly touching her shoulders. How'd he love to firmly grab hold of her. Try to scare some sense into his favorite stubborn redhead for being out here. Just whirl her around to see the unexpected surprise flare over her face. Then, just devour her body in the misty morning with the backdrop of the rising sun. His body craved for her touch. The smile on his lips, only a reminder of how she wanted him, needed him.

"Dove, what are you doing out here?" Only steps from her, he waited for Dove's attention.

xoxoxoxoxo

"Dove." Directly behind her, Chloe heard the deep rasp of a man's voice call someone's name. In her sanctuary of peacefulness, she realized she was no longer alone. Startled by his intrusion, she spun herself around to face him. The forceful spin left her grabbing for the edge of the wooden bench. Praying for the support of the old rickety bench, she dug her fingernails into the weathered wood. The splintery wood didn't let her down. Unnerved by the stranger, Chloe steadied herself against the whirl of dizziness from the sudden turn. She held her place only a few steps away from the stranger.

"Dove, you just see one of those ghosts that reside in our house?" An inviting smile warmed Hawke's face.

"Ghosts?" As if she appeared to have seen one, Chloe's mind instantly flashed to the childhood photo. "Where did you come from?" Her communication skills got stuck on hold as she remembered this could be the man from Ginger's Market. "You." Startled, her heart skipped a beat. So much for always being aware of her surroundings.

"You all right?" A hint of concern rang in his husky voice.

"I...sorry, I didn't hear you." Rattled by his presence, Chloe twisted the cord of her IPod around her fingers.

In the stillness of the misty morning they stood motionlessly fixated on one another. What was it about this stranger? First the old photo. Then the grocery store. And now...here. Her mind tap danced around with a mysterious desire of wanting to know him. Just his presence caused an arousing aura to flood her entire body with warmth.

The call of a soaring red tail hawk had Chloe scrabbling to regain all five scenes. Quickly she analyzed everything about him. His height, definitely taller than James by a least a good four inches. His build, strong and rugged with sharp features that enhanced the smile he offered her. His long poker straight black hair shined even in the grey of the morning light. She caught herself being captivated by his deep, warm brown eyes and his dark reddish bronze tanned skin. The pale blue t-shirt he wore clung to his sculpted muscular body that rippled through the thin cotton. A pair of faded blue jeans that should've been trashed years ago, finished his outdoorsy rough attire along with some kind of scaly reptile that had been made into boots. The mystique of this stranger had drawn Chloe into his smooth velvety eyes. Her analyzing fantasy had been shaken when he spoke to her again.

"Dove what are you doing out here? You agreed to wait for me." His grin of annoyance tighten as Chloe noticed the calmness in his husky voice.

She shook her head lightly, "No. I'm sorry, but I'm not Dove." A voice of control rolled from her. She wondered who Dove was as she steadily fixed her eyes on his.

"Okay," Hawke played along with her game, "Didn't mean to scare you." He cocked his head to one side and eyed Chloe over. He noted the slight tremble in her hands. Still a little annoyed at her, he waited for her to answer his original question. "You didn't answer me."

"Answer you?" Even more rattled by him, Chloe held up her IPod half smiling. "I don't hear much with these in my ears." She shrugged her shoulders, "Kind of obvious...I've been out for my morning walk." She announced clearly and calmly to him. On the other hand, Chloe's fluttering heart finally slowed to a somewhat normal palpitating beat. "You've really mistaken me for someone else. I don't think I'm the person you're looking for." She pushed enough air through her lungs and managed to keep her sentence direct.

His smile broadened as he closed the small gap left between them. Chloe's safety net of distance from the unknown stranger left her leaning heavily on the back of the wooden bench. Realization engulfed her in a rush of new tension. Within one step, she stood only a hands reach away from him.

Chloe drew herself up to full height. She squared her shoulders. Intimidation was her best trait. "We're not from around these parts." She griped her hands tighter onto the old bench.

"Okay, Dove, I'll play along." He smiled contently at her. "So you're not from around these parts? You sure? I know I've met you before." His eyebrow rose mixing with a pleasingly questioning smile. Then he let a long low deep chuckle erupt out of him.

"Like I've said, I'm not this Dove person. My name is Chloe." She half-heartedly returned the smile. "I don't believe we've ever met." Maybe, just maybe, he really was the man from Ginger's Market.

"Love the way you're full of surprises, honey." Hawke stopped his lusting desire to reach over and tug one of her many dangling curls. "Love the way you surprised me last night too, Dovey."

Chloe nearly toppled backwards over the bench. This man really thought she was a woman named Dove. "I'm not Dove." Composure quickly regained, again Chloe attempted to inform him.

"Okay, honey. Like I said I'll play your game."

A ray of morning sun interrupted the graying mist. Chloe could see the charm surrounding his tough ruggedness. Under all of his external appeal, he appeared amazingly handsome. Someone she'd never look twice at. Clean cut and well groomed fit her needs. But this man, whoever he was, held her interest and entertained her thoughts.

Boldly showing in his deep dark eyes he seemed to be on a mission. His mission rallied around her or who he thought she was. Still leery of him, she teetered on the edge of her instincts. A touch of fear surfaced when he shifted his gaze over her. Chloe suppressed her feelings of panic. She had no intentions of running away from him. Nor did she feel any threat from him. An unexplainable bond had formed between them in minutes. His mistaking her for someone else played an emotional role in the game. Chloe refused to break eye contact with him. Still hanging onto her reservation of him, she cleared her head of the wild roaming thoughts.

"I'm on vacation with my family. So I don't think I'm this Dove person you've been referring to." Chloe returned a hesitant smile. Fully aware of his closeness, she shifted her weight from one foot to another. "Speaking of my family, I really have to be getting back to them. I'm sure they're wondering where I am." She glanced at her watch, then quickly back to him. "Enjoy your morning."

Without any hesitation, Chloe stepped aside from Hawke. The walking path waited to take her home. In a single fluid movement, he reached for her swinging hand. Rough, leather like fingers gently wrapped around her perfectly manicured fingers. He massaged the palm of Chloe's hand with a gently tenderness she'd never felt before. Every last one of her five senses exploded. The tingling sensations ran through her body like a ramped fever. Chloe's eyes flickered wildly from the mysterious warmth that generated from his hand to the coolness of hers. He grinned at seeing the fine hair on her pale freckled arm stand on end. The same rush of tingling flared along to her now rosy cheeks. Gold specks mixed into the depths of his pooling brown eyes. Again his smile deepened at her unexplained sensitivity.

Hawke enjoyed the rosy glow over the cheeks of who he thought was his wife. The uncanny but yet unique feeling they shared didn't rattle him at all. He'd known it for the last ten years. Chloe's hand, so delicate, had been swallowed in his as he wrapped his fingers tighter around her trembling hand, steadying her. Gently he pulled her hand towards him. Lightly he kissed the back of her soft pale skin. Another tingling array shot through Chloe's quivering body.

"You're playing with me, Dove." Hawke softly whispered and rubbed his thumb smoothly over the back of Chloe's shaking hand.

"I told you, I'm not Dove." With a firm tone, Chloe shielded the panic in her voice. Quickly, she yanked her hand back from Hawke.

But this time Hawke let a low deep chuckle of laughter out as he let Chloe's hand slip away from him. Openly, her confused expression rose in her flushing cheeks.

"Who are you?" She managed to ask.

"You all ready know my pretty dove." Hawke's reply, simple but yet somewhat arrogant. He lightly tugged at one of the many loosely fallen curls surrounding Chloe's flushed face. Then, he simply ran a finger down the bridge of her nose. "I'm so glad you opened your heart to me again."

No warning. No goodbye, no nothing. The mysterious stranger, who had appeared from nowhere, turned and started to walk down the path. Left in complete astonishment, Chloe wondered what had just taken place on the edge of the lake. Her body trembled and her eyes trailed after him.

Before his foot hit the payment of the trail, he turned to her one last time. "I'm really enjoying your game. Love the way you toy with me. Happy Birthday, Dove." His charming smile broadened. "Don't keep me waiting long." His deep chuckle echoed in the silence of the surrounding forest. "See you back at the cottage." Amused by who he thought she was, Hawke kept grinning. He lit what Chloe thought was a cigarette. But the foulness of a scented cigar filled the fresh morning air as he walked out of her life.

The brief, mystifying encounter Chloe just had left her in shock. She felt perplexed and lost in disbelief. Her thoughts and emotions had never once strayed from James in their ten years of marriage. Chloe's jaw dropping encounter left her head spinning. Lost in her private world of turned upside down emotions, she kept wondering who this man really was. His statement of she already knew him, but Chloe knew she didn't know him. Not in the way he insinuated. His last quote, 'Not to keep him waiting,' those few words had her heart fluttering. Her heartbeat bounced to an unfamiliar rhythm as she replayed those words out loud.

"Don't keep me waiting. Waiting for what?" Chloe's eyes popped wideopen. "Whoever Dove is, she's in for a real surprise." Her silly laugh echoed over the tranquil morning air. "Better yet, how did he know it was my birthday?"

With the palm of her hand Chloe pushed her dropped jaw shut. She watched intently as the eye catching stranger disappeared down the path. A cloud of nasty cigar smoke trailed behind him. Her eyes still glued to him until she could no longer see the mysterious stranger. A sigh of relief escaped her. Chloe knew this situation could have turned disastrous. So much for the self-defense class James had signed her up for. She'd forgotten everything they'd taught her. With a stumble, she plopped down on the old wooden bench that had supported her. Wincing in pain at how hard she'd dropped, she babbled to nature's creatures asking the same questions over and over.

"Who is he? An explanation would be good." Chloe's still shocked voice filled the empty silence around her.

Lost in her wild wondering thoughts, she kept replaying the whole bazaar, but yet enchanting encounter. The IPod wire twisted tightly around her finger, she blurted aloud. "Who is he? How could I possibly know this man? I've never met or seen him before." She focused her disarray of thoughts out over the calm lake relaxing to the brilliant rays of sun that glistened with each ripple.

The unknown stranger had stirred a hidden sensitive emotion that Chloe didn't know existed in her. It wasn't even obvious to him that he had mistaken her for someone else by the name of Dove.

xoxoxoxoxo

"Aunt Ruby." Annoyed, Hawke growled at her, "Did Dove get back yet?" He stomped up three steps landing in front of his Aunt on the deck. "Damn woman. Never listens to me."

"What's the matter with you?" In hopes to calm him, Aunt Ruby offered Hawke her own mug of coffee.

"Told her not to go on the walking path until I scouted it." He accepted her luke warm cup of coffee. "Is she back?"

"Calm yourself down before you wakeup everyone on the lane." She took her mug back from him. "Dovey isn't out of bed yet. Not like her to sleep so late. What did you do to her last night?" Aunt Ruby blew him a playful kiss. She already knew what they were up to. The singing of the squeaky old bed in the kid's room woke her up more than once throughout the night.

"Sleeping? No way. I just saw her down by the lake." The "peace" mug of coffee switched back to his hands.

"Just peaked in on her a few minutes ago. Little worried about her." Aunt Ruby winked at him. "Your girl has a glow about her this morning. Glad to see you two patched things up."

"Ruby, she's been here the entire time?" Hawke shook his head in dismay.

"Yep. Go check for yourself. Dove's still sleeping. She didn't even wake up to the smell of brewing coffee. I know your wife loves her morning coffee."

"Ruby, if Dove's asleep" he glanced back to the direction he'd just come from, "who the hell was the woman I just saw?" Hawke shoved the empty mug into Ruby's hands.

"What woman?" Ruby glanced into her empty mug, "Who did you run into?"

"A woman who could pass as Dove's double. That's if my sleeping wife isn't playing another game with me."

"And I'm telling you, Dove's been here. Go see for yourself." Aunt Ruby held the backdoor open for him. "Take her a cup of coffee ya crazy fool."

The bedroom door, just the way he left it, shut. He turned the handle waiting to find an empty bed. Curtains still pulled, he made out the shape of Doves curvy figure under the fluffy quilt.

"Dove." His hand trailed over her body as he called her name. She rolled to her back making room for him to sit down.

"Hi," sleepily she answered him. "Did you just get back?"

Hawke skimmed the draping curls from her face, "You weren't out walking this morning."

"No. Too tired. Think I got enough exercise last night." Her sleepy smile met his. "How many times did you wake me up last night?" Dove feathered her fingers over an old scar on his bicep then playfully ran her finger down his tanned arm. "I had the weirdest dream."

"Really? Tell me about it." Hawke skimmed another dangling curl from her face. He noted Dove's walking clothes. Freshly laundered, folded in a neat pile on the dresser. She shifted around in the bed, sitting up. The comforter and sheet tumbled down revealing her bare, freckled shoulders. Not a single sign she'd been out for an early morning walk.

"You were rubbing my hand," another yawn escaped Dove, "in you know, the magic circle pattern." Hawke nodded in agreement knowing how it calmed her jittered nerves. "The tingle, intense. It pulsed through me. You were so warm. But me, cold, so chilled. The dream, all misty. Foggy. Like the lake in the morning." She yawned again, "You brought me coffee?" She happily accepted the steaming cup, but her nose crinkled as she smiled. "You had a cigar for breakfast?" By Hawke's smoky scent, Dove had been fully awakened.

"Yeah Dove. Habit." Hawke ignored her question and sternly asked one more question of his own, "You playing games with me?" He pulled his ragged t-shirt off and eyed his wife's body barely hidden by the cotton sheet. Biceps rippled as he pulled his age old jeans off and tossed them across the room.

"It's seven in the morning," she answered, puzzled by his question. "The only game I want to play is getting you back in this bed." Dove pulled back the quilted comforter and sheet revealing what Hawke knew had been true. She'd been here asleep waiting for him. Her grin only enticed him back into the warm bed they shared. "My first cup of coffee," she sat the half full cup of coffee on the night stand, "you know I can't function without it."

Every inch of Dove's body, completely naked. Not one obstacle of clothing to stop him. The old bed squeaked as he climbed under the covers with her.

"Could you please oil this bed or something? Annoyed by the squeaking, "Every move we make, your Aunt and Uncle will hear it. I'm sure they did last night."

"Yep, they did Dove. Need that pillow?" He yanked one of three pillows out from under her head. "This should work." Straddling over Dove, he jammed the feather pillow between the wall and the brass rail headboard.

Whoever Hawke encountered earlier this morning, wasn't Dove. His wife had been sound asleep in their bed while he scouted the forest. One thing Hawke couldn't dismiss, this other woman, she could easily pass as his wife's twin.

Chapter 8 - Chloe's Birthday Surprise

Memorized by the dancing sunlight bouncing across the rocky shoreline, Chloe's fleeting mind snapped back to reality. For an extra half hour, she'd sat on the weathered bench replaying her intense but bazaar meeting. Her present feelings ranged from delightfully intrigued, to 'who the hell could this stranger be?' One particular man, possibly the same one from Ginger's Market, stirred emotions in her that she didn't even know existed. Alone with her thoughts, Chloe twisted her silver elastic watchband around her finger. She flipped the cheap but reliable watch over, only to be shocked at the time.

"Great. Just great." She glared at the watch. It only told her the truth. "Talking about making myself late. Surprised James hasn't sent the National Guard out to look for me." Chloe blurted out her annoyance to the chirping birds. "Seven-fifty-two. I'm always back by seven. At this hour of morning, I'm sure my zoo-crew will be up." As if someone poked her with a heated iron, Chloe bolted from the wooden bench.

While she sprinted along the paved path, Chloe couldn't shake the mysterious man from her mind. The faster she moved, the faster her mind obsessed. She'd never been exposed to a man of his distinct caliber. Rough, raw at the edges, but his eyes hinted at how tender he could be underneath his tough mask. His captivating smile had her heart racing as she now ran toward the cottage. Her heart pounded harder from the accelerating run. Or did the mystic attention of the dark haired stranger make her heart race? Her life, complete with James. Everything she'd dreamed of James delivered, plus more. Chloe's heart and soul totally belonged to James. No one ever tempted her thoughts, or even dared to play with her emotions. But the rugged stranger had done exactly that. Finally, she popped out on the lane that led back to the cottage. The hard sprint left her puffing as she walked down the road. Each calming breath she caught filled her lungs with the fresh air, relaxing her, soothing her every footstep.

"Just a harmless mistake in identity. Really, that's all it was. Surely it won't happen again. No. It won't happen again." Chloe reassured herself as she continued her one sided conversation. "This man, he truly and obviously thought I was, what was her name? A bird. A dove. That's it. Dove. I'm sure I won't ever see him again." In a hopeful attempt, she tried to brush off her morning encounter. But she couldn't let it go. Her spine tingled. Her thoughts still ran freely for the dark haired stranger. She slowed her pace, letting her breathing return to normal. In front of her she could see the neon yellow sign that glowed from the base of the driveway. Home away from home, The Sunshine Cottage awaited her return. Relief and security filled her as she slowly walked up the gravel drive.

Giggles of laughter seeped from the open cottage windows as she approached. The morning air lingered with the delicious smell of sizzling bacon. A grumble gurgled from Chloe's empty stomach as she sneaked in through the front door. Her pack of five males were on the move. The morning's entertainment had to be James at his best. One of her many 'mom skills', she could enter a room without anyone noticing. This morning was no exception. Another spree of giggles echoed from the kitchen's direction. From the shadow of the living room, Chloe secretly spied on James. The one man culinary show kept the boys entertained.

All hands on deck, James manned the stove like a pro. For an apron, he had tied a beach towel around his waist. His favorite Cleveland Indians baseball cap, turned backwards, dubbed as a chef's hat. A spatula waived high in the air as he told the boys a tale from his college days of flipping burgers. One hand on his tailored hip, James flipped the scrambled eggs in one skillet, as he kept an eye on the crisping bacon. Grease splattered high up and over the top of the gas stove as he commanded one of the boys to butter the freshly popped toast. The coffee pot chugged another groan and alerted him to its finishing drips.

Motionlessly, Chloe stood in plain view of him. She enjoyed her private ogling of her husband. Coffee cup in hand, James checked the clock on the stove with a frown. He turned the blazing flame to simmer. Breathlessly, she waited for him to find her. A simple turn on James' part and his sheer blue eyes tangled with hers. Their connection made.

"Boys, need some help." He winked an eye at her and motioned her to move from sight. "Let's surprise mommy with breakfast on the patio." James casually handed plates and utensils to the boys, then ushered them out the backdoor. No boys in sight, he left his greasy post in the kitchen, "Chloe. You worried me."

"Sorry." Any and all thoughts of the mystery man cleared from Chloe's mind. She ran her cool fingers over James' sun tanned cheek. "I lost track of the time."

Her tattered appearance only enhanced his mood of play. A clump of spiraling curls dangled around her neck. Auburn tresses dipped low into the v-neck of her favorite purple shirt. With a zigzag pattern, James ran his fingertip through the moist droplets that beaded between her breasts. He navigated her backwards, well out of everyone's view. James enjoyed pinning her adrenaline pumped body between him and the weathered front door.

"When did you sneak in?" His bacon flavored lips teased hers. "Thought I'd have to send a search party out for you."

"Sorry. I just lost track of time." Not only time, but a little of her own mind. James brushed his tasty lips over hers again. "You taste heavenly," Chloe didn't hesitate in licking the hint of coffee from his salty lips. "How much bacon did you cook?"

"Chloe, did I ever tell you," preoccupied with running his hand under her top, James tugged at her refining jogging bra, "I really hate this padded bra." The firmness of the material didn't slow him down. He stretched the form fitting elastic and slipped a hand under the obstacle he hated. His fingers played deeply into her tender, soft flesh. The old door supported both of them as he rubbed her thighs with his.

"James, the boys." She tugged at the makeshift apron around his waist. "We can't…" but her hand brushed over his stiffened arousal. "Bedroom," she panted harder when James' hand slipped over her hip to pat her curvy bottom, "the door locks."

"Love the suspense, Chloe. Will they catch us? Or won't they?" Chloe's finger tips dug deep into his t-shirt covered shoulders. "Just a quickie." He tugged at her cotton shorts, "just wrap the towel around us. But you'll have to keep quiet." He grinned and kissed her protesting lips before any other words slipped out.

"James," her fingers tousled through his thick hair, "the doors wide open. We're in plain view of anyone who passes by." Surveying the corners of the tiny cottage for any signs of life, she protested again. "What if…"

"Chloe, you worry too much." He had his wife joining his adventure. In seconds her panties and shorts were bunched at her ankles.

"You're putting the meaning of "quickie" to the test," she yanked at his boxer style shorts, freeing him, "you better hurry up."

"Just hang onto the towel," He propped one of her long legs over his thigh as he slipped inside of her.

"James," Chloe whispered, trying to remain quiet with her arousal from him and the excitement of not getting caught. Their rocking rhythm had the door bouncing back and forth into the wall. One last thrust and he pinned her body hard to the door.

"Really hate quickies." He relaxed his body on hers, "But the adventure," swooping down he replaced her panties and shorts back to where they originally started. Clothes arranged to somewhat normal on both of them, "Just one of many birthday surprises." James kissed the tip of her sunburned nose.

"How in the world did you come up with this one?" Chloe asked as she dropped the towel that shielded them and made a final adjustment to her clothes. Sniff, sniff, she turned her head toward the odor coming from the kitchen, "I smell smoke."

"Oh shit!" Roughly, James tucked himself back into his shorts, "the bacon!" The burning odor had them both scrambling to the kitchen.

"Thought you turned the burners off." Chloe grabbed for a potholder, "bacon's good." She removed the first skillet. "Hash browns…well," flame turned off, she flipped them around the skillet, "crispy, not burnt. Think breakfast is salvaged."

"You know you shouldn't distract the chef." With a playful wink, James scooped the scrambled eggs from the last skillet. "This is all your fault birthday girl."

"From now on, behind closed, locked doors mister. My heart is still pounding. Thought for sure we'd get caught."

James watched the boys from the kitchen window, "think we could go another round." He playfully nodded his head toward their bedroom.

"Mommy's back!" Jason flew into her waiting arms. "Happy Birthday!"

"Thank you." She'd been surrounded by all four boys and a handful of birthday cards. "Breakfast is ready, who's hungry?"

"Patio is all set up for you Aunt Chloe." Paul, her oldest nephew announced.

Neon yellow and green patio furniture decorated the wooden deck. A matching umbrella shaded the preset table. Dishes of piping hot scrambled eggs, crisp bacon and hash browns waited to be served.

"Now can we celebrate Aunt Chloe's birthday?" Mason shoved his homemade card into his Aunt's hand.

"Hope you're ready to celebrate in style, Chloe." James delicately kissed her lips. "Today it's all about you. We've got a huge surprise for you."

Chloe glanced around at all the beaming grins not sure what to think. "Let me guess? You booked a fishing charter?" She laughed at her own answer knowing better.

"No way Aunt Chloe," Paul scratched his head, "Everyone knows you're bad luck when it comes to fishing."

James rippled with laughter, "The boy's right, honey. I can't imagine you on a fishing charter. Seriously," he pretended to cast a line, "you with a fishing pole in hand? You touching bait?"

"Don't think that would happen." Chloe sipped her coffee, "with my luck, I'd fall overboard."

"Did consider it." James enjoyed his bite of jelly toast, "but we voted. Fishing lost out."

"So what's the big surprise?" Scooping the last bit of eggs from her plate, Chloe asked.

"Remember you saying how you and your mom would go to the Grand Hotel." James slid a shinny brochure across the table to her.

"How about this year, the five of us accompany you?"

"Really? I don't have to go alone?" Chloe beamed, "You'll give up a day of fishing to spend it with me?"

"And, we'll all be perfect, refined gentlemen for the entire day." James winked at the boys. "You only turn thirty once."

Chloe's eyes lit up with excitement. "You're serious aren't you?" She smiled at the men surrounding her.

"All day. For as long as you like." James, with coffee pot in hand, seated himself next to her. "Here," he offered her a slim box wrapped in shiny pink paper. "Happy thirtieth, sweetheart. Open it."

"James, you're full of surprises this morning." She smiled at him, remembering the 'quickie' adventure they'd just had. The pink blush on Chloe's cheeks matched the neatly wrapped gift box. Box in hand, she gave it a shake. "What could be in here?" For fun, she placed the pink package to her forehead, "Oh great Swami, tell me what is hidden in the box." With a wink to James, her boys broke into a giggle.

"Open it Aunt Chloe." Matthew cheered her on.

She tore the pink wrapping paper leaving it crumbled on the table top. Chloe held the slim black jewelry box in her hand. She slowly eased the case open to find laying on the white velvet lining, an emerald bracelet sparkling up at her.

"James. Oh, James. This is," tears of happiness filled Chloe's eyes, "it's beautiful." She ran the gold trimmed emerald bracelet through her fingers. Lovingly, Chloe embraced her husband, "James, you really shouldn't have."

"Chloe, you're my angel. Just wanted you to have something nice for your birthday." James caught one of Chloe's many tears on the tip of his finger, "Here, let me help you put it on."

She offered him her right wrist, "James, thank you." Fastened tightly, the dazzling bracelet dangled on her thin wrist. "Thank you. Thank you. I still can't believe you did this." Chloe sealed her "thank you" with a kiss to his lips. She held her wrist up to the morning sunbeam. An array of glittery sparkles jetted from the bracelet. "How can I ever thank you?" She ran her finger along his sturdy jaw line then softly kissed his lips again.

Chapter 9 - Life Will Never Be the Same

As she rolled to her side, Chloe's eyes focused on the bright digits of the alarm clock sitting on the nightstand. Filled with glowing cheer, four in the morning boldly announcing itself. She ran her hands through her wild, unruly main of curls. After the passion driven night with James, she couldn't figure out why her body wanted to be awake at this ungodly hour? Still cozy under the covers, she stretched her aching muscles and tried not to wake James.

Chloe's eyelids couldn't be convinced to surrender to sleep. She relaxed a few minutes longer, enjoying the closeness of James's warm body. She giggled knowing why her muscles felt worn out. James had turned her body in every imaginable position. They enjoyed an evening of exploration. Not only in the bedroom, the cushioning comfort of the back patio lounge chair, and the soft leather seats in the back of the SUV. But the most riveting, an evening swim followed by the tranquil romantic encounter they'd shared in the warm evening lake water. She basked in the after glow of how he made her feel. More awake than before, she decided to sneak out for an early morning walk.

Chloe had already tossed her thin cotton night gown to the floor. Left only in a pair of pink lacey panties, she sat on the edge of the bed while James gently rubbed her back. He connected her numerous decorations of freckles with his finger. She felt the tip of his finger trace down her back until he stopped to outline the brown flowered like birthmark on the edge of her lower back.

"Can't believe you're awake." James tugged at the stretchy lace on her panties. "You sure you want to go for your walk this morning?" She sensed his arouse as he woke from a deep sleep.

Lifelessly, Chloe let her torso fall back on James. Her auburn tresses scattered over his bare chest. Her full, curvy breast completely exposed to his waiting touch. She sighed as his fingers outlined her erect pink nipples. Chloe rolled to her side facing him, brushing her bare chest over his. She pulled back the bed sheet not surprised to see how stiff James's erection had become. She straddled over him and eased herself down on him.

"Why are you awake," she playfully asked as his fingers brushed over the soft skin of her thighs.

"Can't get enough of you." James gripped his hands tightly into her hips as they rocked their bodies in unison. "My kind of morning workout." He grinned and sunk his fingers deeper into her fleshy cheeks.

"I appreciate the warm up before my walk. Can't believe no ones knocked on the door." The emerald bracelet dangled from her wrist, as Chloe stretched her long arms up along James's muscular chest.

"Don't jinx us. I'm not done with you, Chloe." James flipped her backwards landing on top of her and finished what she'd started. Exhausted, he rolled off her warm body trailing his fingers down the center of her stomach.

Fully awake, Chloe sat on the edge of the bed, "I won't be long. Promise." She felt the heat of his body filling in behind her.

"Chloe," his lips showered her shoulder with affectionate kisses. "Take your time," his smooth warm kisses trailed to the base of her spin, "you've worn me out."

"James." She giggled and pulled the pale blue sheet over his naked tan body. "I'll be back in less than an hour. Love you." One last kiss left her lips to rest on his.

Her favorite jogging shirt and shorts in hand she slowly opened the creaky bedroom door. Carefully, she double checked the short few steps to the bathroom. No boys stirring, she clutched her clothes to her still tingling body and tiptoed toward the bathroom.

She tripped over an assortment of sandals belonging to the boys as she reached the safety of the bathroom. Securely locked in the bathroom, Chloe switched on the overhead light. Brightness could be unkind in the early morning. But her beautiful glow of happiness greeted her in the mirror. No denying it, James had an affect on her that would last a life time. Washed up, teeth brushed, walking clothes and shoes on, one last thing to tackle, her hair. The usual, her hair yanked up in a swinging ponytail, she glanced in the mirror again and groaned at what she saw. A pattern of pale purplish 'love bites' had been fluttered down her neck, a loving gift of artwork from her husband. She cringed at her reflection. He knew how she hated to be decorated with the so called "hickeys." But in the heat of the moment, she didn't stop him.

IPod in hand, Chloe stopped to check on the boys. In double sets of bunk beds, she found her boys still in a deep, sound sleep. Arms and legs tangled around the sheets and blankets. She grinned at her perfect sleeping angels.

Metal screen doors had a way of making it impossible to slip out of the cottage. The squeak echoed in the stillness of morning. IPod switched on, the music blasted a pulsing beat in her ears. She practically skipped down the dew covered lane to the walking path. Aware of the early dawn's beauty, she kept up her fast paced steps. The early morning rays of sun glittered over the lake. The lingering chill of the night air refreshed her as she walked along. The bounce of happiness in her step had led her halfway around the paved path. Openly, she sang along to her favorite songs. Chloe knew she should be aware of her surroundings. But what harm could it do? No one was out here this early in the morning. Her body beaded with droplets of sweat while she kept up the ridged pace. A glance to her watch and she'd be back to the cottage in less than a half hour. James would no doubt be surprised to see her back so soon. She felt alive, energized, and couldn't wait to return to him.

xoxoxoxoxo

In the dusky morning dawn, hungry for breakfast, the loan bear lurked along the tree line. Just yards behind, the creature trailed Chloe's scent of sweet honey that mingled with her dripping perspiration. Her ponytail teased the animal as it swung from side to side with each step she took. The game of chase aroused the black bears senses and pulled it away from the depths of thick woods. The animal's massive paws gripped solidly into the dew covered grass. Its slow, rambling pace down the hill, behind Chloe, picked up into a full sprinting charge.

Completely unaware of the trailing predator, a full set of claws swept down and over Chloe's back. The sharp slicing pain felt as if a thousand knives pierced into her left shoulder. Chloe tumbled aimlessly to the ground from the force of the bear's huge thrusting paw. Her head bounced off the black pavement of the walking path. Fear flooded her wounded body as she tried to get to her feet and run. Attacked again, her shoulder took another massive blow of rampage from the enraged bear. Forced to the ground again, the bear's powerful claws shredded her leg into bloody slices of flesh. Chloe's dripping blood spilled heavily over the pavement. Screams of her horrifying pain and fear were absorbed by the empty woods. The only one who could hear her pleas for help, the ragging bear on its attack.

She rolled to her side trying to avoid its brutal assault. The sweet smell of the early morning fresh air vastly filled with the gagging stench from the huge, shaggy bear as it towered over her. In another attempt to escape, she actually felt the bears sickening moist breath on her torn skin. The coarse hair of the bear rubbed through her bloody, oozing, open wounds. As if the bear were tenderizing her exposed flesh, it continued to paw her over.

With still some wit left, Chloe realized she just became the main dish on the bear's breakfast menu. The bear batted her body around like an old rag doll with its massive front paws. It's snarling hot, revolting breath poured into her blood stained face. Her screams of excruciating pain didn't even phase the dangerous animal.

For an agonizing second, the bear toyed with Chloe and acted as if it had terrorized her enough. The beast seemed to be done with her nonstop wiggling and continuous howling of painful screams. She lay motionless, curled into a tight bleeding ball. Openly she prayed the bear would leave. Not a single grunt of hate came from the bear. With what little strength Chloe had left, she forced her battered body to stand...and run. Not even a few steps taken, the bear tackled her. The deranged animal tossed her toward the forest line. Like a rubber ball, she flew through the air. Her already wrecked body became up close and personal with a tree that didn't want to bend to her injured, bloody frame. Chloe's slashed body helplessly wrapped around an unforgiving massive oak tree. Her injured shoulder and head took another blow as her body parts hit simultaneously.

The horrific sound of her own bones cracking and crushing as she fell to the ground rang inside of what was left of her battered skull. Still clinging to life, Chloe pictured the true loves of her life, James, her devoted husband, her son Jason, and her three adoring nephews. A mangled heap of raw, ripped flesh and blood was all of what was left of Chloe. The remains of her favorite purple t-shirt hung in shreds loosely over her body. The bear's jagged claws ripped into her soft ivory flesh and left it bloodily, torn, and slashed wide open. A continuous steady stream of crimson red blood trickled down her face, over her neck and pooled on her chest. The freshly sliced claw marks down her legs turned into a burning fire of agonizing pain that sent an uncontrollable shiver throughout Chloe's entire body. Her warm blood dripped from every rip and tear the bear had gashed into her. Lying there she marveled at the thought of still being able to breathe. In a mangled broken heap she gasped helplessly for another breath to keep living. She focused her eyes on the powder blue of the morning sky. The pounding in her head slipped into a dizzy spin. The warmth of her blood drained from the open wounds covering her battered body. She subsided to the wrenching pain and steady loss of her free flowing blood. Slowly, her body commanded itself to shutdown filling her with numbness. The huge black bear moved closer to make its final kill. Its snarl echoed through the woods as the beast stood on its back hunches. Each step the bear took, it growled with a sickening pleasure, sloughing its way to Chloe.

A thundering loud crack from a gun shot rang out. The single shot silenced the bear's unruly growls. Right beside Chloe, the massive bear dropped dead from the gun shot. Its lifeless carcass lay parallel to her ravaged body. A lone giant paw landed with a thud on her bloody chest. Barely clinging to life, Chloe could still smell and feel the foul stench of the bear.

The thought of death filled what little consciousness Chloe had left, but her body continued to pump air through her lungs. The blue sky, which she'd focused on, disappeared into shards of darkness. Uncontrollably and violently, Chloe's body shook. The black haze of death cradled Chloe in its arms, wanting and waiting for her to take the last breath of life. The lush green grass that cushioned Chloe's crumpled body now had turned crimson red.

xoxoxoxoxo

"Oh my God! No! Dove! No! Don't you leave me! Don't you dare leave me now! I just found you again!" Chloe's eyes flickered open. She could barely see the image of the man behind the agonizing voice that shouted at her. His deep raspy voice, almost familiar to her was filled with a tormented fear that brought her back to a semi-conscious state of mind.

"You?" Chloe's voice hung beneath a whisper of life.

"Dove. Don't talk. Save your strength." Hawke kept his alarm at bay as he checked over Chloe's battered and beaten body.

"No. Not, I'm..." She tried to speak again.

"Dove. I'm here. Don't move. You've got to stay still." Panic sliced over Hawke's rugged features.

"Not Dove." She whispered the woman's name to him.

Chloe focused her gaze on the stranger's haunted golden brown eyes that blazed with fear. She could read the torturing pain on his weathered face. Once again, Chloe flirted with the angel of death. She fought to stay alive. But the web of darkness beckoned her, offering her a comfort from the pain.

"Fred! Help! It's Dove. Grab a blanket!" Hawke yelled in agony to his best friend.

Hands twice Chloe's size gently wrapped a wool blanket around her lifeless body. Like a feather, he lifted her crumpled body from the blood stained ground. A breath escaped from her lips as she tried in vain to tell him she wasn't Dove.

"Hang on Dove. She's barely alive, Fred. We've got to get her to the hospital."

"My name...Chloe," she whispered to him. "Chloe." Her paper thin voice trailed off to nothing.

Hawke's rapid steps toward the truck only inflicted additional pain into Chloe's battered body. "Dove, I love you. Please, Dove don't you die on me now."

"Not Dove." Chloe mouthed the words to him. In pain, confused, and plus the lack of life left in her, she couldn't convey who she really was.

"Watch your step with her, Hawke." In fear, Fred directed Hawke as he ran ahead to open the passenger's door of the pickup truck. "Lance radioed in. He's got the Rangers over with him. They found another woman. Said she's been mauled pretty bad. Not looking good. On their way to the hospital with her now." Intense fear, even anger oozed from Fred's voice. "For Christ sake, Hawke, be careful with her." Fred stepped back from the open door, "Watch her head. You've got to curl her up so I can get the door closed." Panic flew from his voice. "Please, Dovey, hang on. For God's sake hang on. Jane will kill us all if you die."

"Just drive Fred. She doesn't have much time." Hawke cradled who he thought was his wife closer to him.

"Lance, he notified the hospital. They're waiting for us. We'll get her there, Hawke. She's going to make it."

The trucks engine screamed in its own mechanical pain. Gravel and dirt flew high into the air as Fred gunned the engine and pulled out onto the main road.

xoxoxoxoxo

Unaware of even being carried in the muscular arms of the stranger, Chloe slipped back into the living world. She flinched at the overhead brightness of the hospital lights. Each step he took with her, she felt like a chewed up rag doll in his massive arms. Delicately, like a fine piece of bone china, he laid Chloe's damaged body on a gurney. People buzzed beside her. They opened the blood soaked blanket she used for security. Eyes open wide, Chloe met the horror of pain in the stranger's worried brown eyes. So much of her crimson blood had smeared across his white t-shirt and down his tanned arms.

"Dove. I'm here, Dove." He stroked the matted hair from her face. "You're going to make it."

"Mr. Hawthorne, you have to let your wife go. We need prep her for surgery. Please step back." A nurse gently touched his arms. "We'll keep you updated."

"Dove, I love you. The girls, they love you. We need you. I need you." The winching pain of his voice rang in Chloe's ears as they rushed her to the waiting trauma unit.

She tried to speak. Tried to let them know she wasn't Dove. Her name was Chloe. The horrific pain, the trauma to her body, her voice wouldn't surface.

Before the doors closed behind her and the trauma team, she caught one last glimpse of the mysterious stranger who risked his own life to save her. The man who called her Dove.

xoxoxoxoxo

"Hawke you've got to sit down. Sit down buddy. Sit down before you fall down." Fred steadied his long time friend by the shoulders. "She's going to make it. Woman's as tough as nails. Come on, she's been married to you for what ten years?" Fred tried to lighten the paralyzing moment with idol chatter. "She survived living with you. Dove will make it." He led Hawke to a waiting area, "I'm going to call Ruby and Ralph."

"Mr. Hawthorne!" An ER nurse burst into the waiting room, "Come with me! Now! Your wife, she," Tears darted in the woman's eyes. "We don't have much time, but she said your name. Please hurry."

Hawke flew from the chair Fred had settled him into to follow the woman in surgical scrubs. A dark blue curtain separated Dove from the other victim of the bear attack in the trauma unit. Machine's buzzed. People dressed for surgery called out commands as they ran back and forth to each of the critically injured patients.

"Dove," Hawke softly spoke as he took her bandaged hand into his, "I'm here, Dove. Hang on. You're one hell of a fighter, woman. Don't let me down." Tears rolled uncontrollably down his rugged face.

Terrified and frightened, Dove met his eyes. Her lips tried desperately to form words that she couldn't speak. Her hand wrapped in his, she squeezed tightly with what life she had left.

"Mr. Hawthorne," a firm hand gently touched his shoulder, "we're waiting for Life Flight. We have to finish prepping your wife for the flight into Grand Rapids."

"I can't leave her." Hawke wiped the blinding tears from his eyes only to stay focused on Dove's.

"Sir, we've done everything we can for your wife. We have to prep her for the flight. I need you to wait outside." The ER doctor pressed sympathetically.

"Dove, I love you." He kissed the hand he still held before a nurse led him out of the trauma unit.

xoxoxoxoxo

In the bed next to Dove, separated by the heavy blue drape, "Can you tell me your name?" A surgical nurse begged Chloe to speak. "If you can hear me, squeeze my hand."

Chloe responded by clinging to the woman's hand. Unable to speak, the commanding voices echoed in her head. So many hands touched at her torn and battered body. The same nurse who asked her to speak her name, desperately tried to get her to say it. Her blanket of comfort, which still held the spicy smell of the stranger, was abruptly cut away from her body. The remains of Chloe's tattered jogging clothes, walking shoes, pink IPod were all removed and placed into a plastic bag marked "Bear Victim #1." Only the emerald bracelet remained on her wrist. She kept fighting to stay awake as a number of doctors and nurses ran between two trauma units. Her desire to slip into unconsciousness kept tugging at her.

"Dr. Remington!" A nurse shouted from the adjoining unit. "Life Flight has landed. We need you over here."

Chloe's body subsided to the heavy does of pain medication. As her eyes closed, she drifted into the waiting light. Numb to everything that existed around her, she reassured herself that James would be waiting for her.

"We're losing her!" A nurse shouted as the monitor wailed the dreaded flat tone.

Chapter 10 - An Unexpected Visitor

Devastation took its toll on the sleepy vacation town. One menacing bear had met its match with a hunter who pursued it day and night. Unfortunately, the word spread fast that two young, vibrate woman had been attacked by the nuisance animal. Sheriff Meyer's hand shook as he reread the typed report.

"Jim," He stopped by his dispatcher's office as he pulled his hat from the shelve, "I'll be on my way over to the Sunshine Cottage." The grim realization reflected on his tired face. "Toughest part of the job."

"Ray's waiting for you. Said if it is Mrs. Morrison, someone will need to stay with her boys while you take James over to the hospital. You don't want him driving."

"Thanks Jim. I hope to the high heavens it's not her. Nice family." The sheriff caught one of his own stray tears with the tip of his finger. With a heavy heart he left the police station knowing the drive would only take minutes. He knew this family well. The Sunshine Cottage had been rented year after year by the Morrison family. He remembered Chloe, as a child, coming summer after summer with her parents. He'd watched her grow into a beautiful wife and mother. "Please don't let this be happening," he said a silent prayer as they pulled into the driveway.

The cottage hadn't changed much over the years. There it sat nuzzled safely away in the woods looking out over the lake. The morning sun reflected up off the smooth glass like lake as the cruiser slowly pulled into the sandy pebble covered driveway. The crunch of the gravely mix could still be heard as the sheriff turned off the ignition glancing apprehensively over to his deputy.

"How am I going to break the news to this family?" The sheriff's heartsick voice filled the silence around them while both men sat motionlessly deep in their own thoughts. Sheriff Meyer stepped from the cruiser and rehearsed in his head how he would be delivering the heartbreaking news to James Morrison. A tear filled his eye. He'd have to describe with care the sensitivity of the death to James of his beautiful young wife.

"Sheriff, you okay?" Ray gently patted his shoulder.

"Truth Ray, no. No, I'm not." He whisked the tear away. "Hope you never have to do this." The horrific happening of the early morning attack weighed heavily on his mind as he subconsciously pushed the car door shut. His heart already breaking for the family inside the cottage, he paused in the driveway not wanting to walk up and knock on their cottage door.

"One of the hardest part of the job, Ray. Makes you question the justice." He removed a white handkerchief from his hip pocket. He wiped the cotton cloth over his moist brow and slowly started to walk up the sandstone steps of the cottage. "I've known these folks for eight years. Known Chloe longer. Eight years they've come up here and vacationed. Just ain't right." He shook his head as he lightly knocked on the metal screen door which seemed to echo over the calm lake and the surrounding forest. In no time a little curly haired boy appeared in the open doorway with a bright toothy grin.

"Good morning little man. Is your daddy here?" As cheerful as he could, the sheriff smiled back at the freckled faced boy.

"Yep, my daddy's here. We're waiting for mommy. She went for a walk. Do you want to come in and see my bug collection?" The boy's eyes mirrored his mothers.

The sheriff's heart sank deeper as he heard the happiness in the youngster's gleeful voice. His news would surely shatter this family into a million pieces.

"Well my little man, how about we look at those bugs another day. Like to speak with your daddy. Would you get him for me?"

"Okay, I'll get him." The boy's curly hair bounced as he let out a glum sigh of disappointment and he politely screamed at the top of his lungs for his dad. "Daddy! Sheriff Meyer and another man are here." A small stampede of noisy feet and chattering voices could be heard racing to the front doorway of the cottage.

"Sheriff Meyer, what a surprise. We were going to stop by this afternoon to see you." James stepped out onto the little stone steps with all the boys pushing out behind him. He extended his hand to the sheriff as the delighted smile on James face slowly faded. He noted immediately, the forced smiles and the shadow of sadness over the sheriff and deputy's faces. "Sheriff Meyer, I take it this isn't a social call?"

"I wish it was James. Is Chloe here?" Sheriff Meyer could barely stammer out the words while he removed his hat to wipe his brow again.

"We're expecting her any minute. She left early this morning for her walk down by the lake." James checked his watch. "Figured she'd be back by now. You know Chloe, sure she's just enjoying the peace..." His voice trailed off as he focused in on the two men's tormented expressions. "Did something happen? What, what happened?" Intense worry rose in James's eyes. Panic twisted his mouth as he tried to ask the next questions. "What is it? Did something happen to her?"

Four sets of wide with worried eyes drew their focus to the middle aged sheriff, who mopped his entire face with the damp handkerchief. "James you might want," he ruffled the hair of the young boy standing close to him as his heart sank. "Might want the youngsters to step back inside. Like a private word with you."

"Guys, why don't you finish up breakfast while I'll chat with Sheriff Meyer?" James pulled the screen door open, "Paul, keep them inside."

"But Daddy, we wanted to wait for mommy." Jason, the last in the doorway, "Please."

"How about you finish your breakfast and we make mommy a hot one as soon as she gets here?" James barely could turn his lips into a smile for his son, but somehow managed. He waited until each boy had disappeared into the cottage. "Sheriff Meyer, did something happen to my wife?"

"James, I'm so sorry to be the one to have to tell you this. Might want to sit down, son."

"No. Just tell what you came here for." Panic swept over James. "Where is Chloe?"

The sheriff inhaled a ragged breath, "There were two bear attacks this morning. One happened over on the far side of the walking path. The other, about quarter of a mile away. Same path your wife," he stopped short to mop at his face with the cloth, "we found two victims. Two women. Both women, they both have a very uncanny resemblance. So many features the same."

"Two women, are they, they..." James stuttered.

"James, I'm so sorry, but we need you to come down," Sheriff Meyer's drew another agonizing breath in, "James," he paused and meet James's worried eyes, "we think, possibly, it could be Chloe."

James leaned hard back into the old metal screen door. It squeaked in pain, the same pain that was rippling though him. "You think it's Chloe?" Out of disbelief he stuttered.

"James, we're not sure. There was no ID on her." The sheriff mopped over his brow.

"No. No, it can't be her. No! Not Chloe! It's not possible!" Frustrated, James mumbled. His shaking fingers vigorously raked at his thick wavy blood hair. "No. It just can't be."

"Easy Mr. Morrison. Sure you don't want to sit down?" The sheriff's deputy asked as he steadied James's swaying body.

"Not Chloe. It's impossible. She was just here. Just a few hours ago." He took a moment to collect his jolted thoughts.

"James, I'll drive you to the hospital. My deputy can stay with the boys. You don't want them to be there."

"I'll go, but I'm telling you Sheriff, this is all a mistake. Paul," James contained the fear in his voice as he called for his oldest nephew.

"Uncle James, you don't look so good." Paul stepped out on the step next to his uncle. At age fourteen, the teenager knew that something was terribly wrong.

"I've got to go with Sheriff Meyer. I need you to look after the boys."

"Why? Did something happen to Aunt Chloe?" The boy grabbed for his Uncle's arm, "Tell me."

"I, we don't know yet. Don't say a word to the little boys, promise me." He hugged his young nephew tightly.

"Yes. Okay." James turned back to Paul, "Listen to me. If Aunt Chloe shows up, you call me immediately. Do you understand?" He gripped Paul's skinny shoulders, "Do you understand?"

"Yes, Uncle James. I'll, I'll keep the boys busy." Not knowing what to do next, Paul relied on the three men for guidance.

"I'll take care of the boys for you, sir." The deputy offered, "If your wife shows up, we'll call." Ray held the door open and ushered the young boy inside with him.

Again, James frantically raked at his tousled hair, "I've, I need my shoes. My phone." He followed his nephew into the cottage and returned within seconds. "Sheriff Meyer, you don't really think?"

"James, I wish I could give you an honest answer. But I just don't know." In silence the two men walked toward the cruiser. As he heard the crunching sound of the pebbled driveway under his feet, James stopped to stare back at the cozy cottage before he slowly sank down into the front seat of the cruiser. Sheriff Meyer slipped his seat belt on, and politely pointed to James to do the same and turned the ignition over.

"James lets just pray that this lady isn't Chloe. I'm really sorry to have to put you through this." The sheriff radioed his dispatcher to notify the hospital that he and James would be arriving shortly.

Bewildered in silence, James sat quietly as the cruiser pulled out of the driveway onto the one lane road to their next destination, the hospital.

In silence, James held tightly to his crushing emotions. "This can't be happening." He didn't even look at the sheriff. He kept his gaze straight out the window. All the motion in James's life moved in a circle of slow motion. The sheriff sped along, but the cruiser didn't seem to move fast enough for James. Every few minutes James ran his hand through his thick hair and tried to control what emotions he had left. Over and over he repeated out loud, "It can't be Chloe. God, please don't let it be Chloe. Please."

The view to the entrance of the hospital came into their sight. Sheriff Meyer pulled the cruiser to a halt in the brightly red-stripped area clearly marked "No Parking." Any other day, he'd be more than happy to write a ticket for the fool that parked there. But today those florescent strips didn't hold any meaning. James barely waited for the cruiser to halt as he threw open the passenger's door and darted to the entrance of the emergency room. The nurse on duty motioned Sheriff Meyer and James to the side. A few steps from where they waited another panic of commotion played out.

"Mr. Hawthorne, I'm sorry but you can't go on Life Flight with your wife. There isn't enough room. We have a team of four people flying with her. She's in the best hands possible." Dr. Remington tried to reassure Hawke. "Grand Rapids General is waiting their arrival. We have a State Trooper to escort you."

"Hawke, honey listen to me," Aunt Ruby's arms cradled her nephew tightly, "Dove needs you to stay in one piece. You've got to stay strong for her. Just get in the truck with your Uncle and follow the troopers. They'll get you there."

"I can't leave her alone. What if she..." Hawke clung to the tiny woman who supported him.

"She's alive, Hawke. For once in Dove's life she needs you. Now go." Aunt Ruby whisked the tears from his eyes. "The boys and me, we'll pack up everything. Be right behind you."

"I've got to call my girls." Hawke fumbled for his phone.

"We've already called Maude. She's taking care of them along with Jane. Now go." Aunt Ruby kissed his cheek. "Dove really needs you."

"Son," His Uncle Ralph hugged him. "The troopers are waiting. Let's go." He turned to his wife, "I'll see you in Grand Rapids, Ruby." With a peck to her cheek, he mouthed I love you.

"Good luck son. God bless you and your wife." Sheriff Meyer patted Hawke's shoulder as they passed. Not knowing the terrified man standing beside the sheriff, Hawke found his own eyes reflecting the same agonizing pain as the stranger's.

"Clear the hall." A commanding loud male voice demanded. Dressed in blue jumpsuits, the four crew members of Life Flight pushed the gurney along the hallway.

James and Sheriff Meyer stepped aside as the gurney with a woman covered in heavy white and bloody red bandages passed by. Her head, wrapped like a mummy's, bled through the white gauze. A hospital blanket wrapped securely over her midsection and legs were surrounded by beeping medical equipment that kept her alive. The team from Life Flight escorted the critically injured woman to the waiting helicopter.

"Dove!" Hawke's voice echoed in pain.

"Mr. Hawthorne, we have to move." A female doctor in scrubs pulled him out of the way. "We're doing everything in our power to save your wife. We will see you in Grand Rapids."

Ralph Patterson, the sheriff's long time friend, held onto his helpless nephew, Hawke. The day's tragedy edged over their drained faces. Mr. Hawthorne, the man they'd brought in from Oregon to silence the ravaging bear had done his job, but not before the bear mulled and attacked two women.

Sheriff Meyer bowed his head and said a silent prayer as the gurney passed by. Sadly, the sheriff realized that the woman who clung to life was Mr. Hawthorne's wife, the same battered and torn woman he had carried into the hospital.

The emergency room doors slid shut with a loud thundering thud. The drumming sound of the helicopter lifting off with the Life Flight team and the woman who struggled to stay alive held everyone's attention.

The silence was broken by the soft voice of a nurse. "Sheriff is this Mr. Morrison?"

"Yes, Nicole." Sheriff Meyer nodded his head and gently reached for James's arm.

"Please follow me." Her bright smiled dimmed as she walked with them to the elevator.

In deafening silence, they were escorted to another part of the hospital. There would be no waiting room for when someone came out of surgery. No one to take James directly to the ICU. No recovery room. The waiting ended when the glossy elevator doors slid open.

"It's just down the hall." Without meeting James's eyes, the young nurse kept walking.

A chill of numbing, cold pain rose up and over James's body. The group stopped in front of the double wooden doors. Etched on the diamond pattern frosted glass, the words "County Morgue" nearly crumbled James.

Sheriff Meyer caught James before his body buckled. "James, we don't have to…"

"I'm fine. Please, can we please get this over with?" Not wanting to believe what he read, James memorized the letters on the glass.

Slowly, Sheriff Meyer pushed open the right side of the door and gently guided James in. Behind the desk a man in a blood stained lab coat met them with a grim smile.

"I'm Dr. Roberts. We're terrible sorry Mr. Morrison. We haven't had time to prepare your wife's body properly. If you'd like to wait…"

James grew pale with every ticking second of the wall clock, "Please just let me see her."

"Certainly, Mr. Morrison. All I ask is that you please look carefully. Take your time. The injuries she's suffered are extreme."

"James, I'll come with you." Sheriff Meyer guided James through the next set of doors.

Four walls of the grey sterile morgue sent piercing chills into James. There in front of him, on a metal table laid a body under a blood soaked sheet. His eyes fought back the sting of tears. No words formed in his dry mouth. A swirl of truth rocked in his head as his heart crumbled in pain.

"When you're ready Mr. Morrison," Dr. Roberts walked over to the draped body.

James prayed as he approached the side of the table. "Please, please God don't let this be my Chloe."

Without warning, an arm slipped free from under the bloody cover. A sparkling emerald bracelet dangled around her blood stained wrist and reflected brightly under the overhead florescent lights.

"No." James left the support of the sheriff. With trembling hands he removed the sheet from the victim. Another gasp of horror echoed in the empty room. "No." Now exposed, James found long auburn hair matted with clots of blood and chunks of torn flesh. "Oh my, God! Oh God, no!" His screams filled the silent morgue. "Chloe! My beautiful Chloe!"

"Mr. Morrison, I'm so sorry," Dr. Roberts began to cover her body with the sheet, "we'll take proper care of your wife."

"I need to see the rest of what's left of my wife."   With trembling hands, James stopped the doctor. "Let me see her."

"Mr. Morrison, you've already identified her. You don't need to go through anymore. Please, it's best to remember your wife the way she was."

James yanked the bloody sheet from the doctor's hand. What once used to be his vibrant beautiful wife, James found her torn and mauled naked body. Shades of purple and black bruised patterns were splattered over her ivory white skin. Claws from the devil animal had ripped into her freckled skin. Jagged teeth marks covered her shoulder and arm. Her upper torso had sustained the worst of the hellish attack.

Clearly in shock, James no longer chose to see the damage to Chloe's mangled and bloody body. He lifted her left hand to his lips and kissed what was left of the chewed on hand. The remnants of dried blood were smeared over the soft shade of lilac nail color. Carefully he laid her battered hand over her torn stomach. Delicately, James picked up Chloe's other hand, the one she wore her birthday gift on and removed the emerald bracelet. "This is my wife." His hand still on hers, a deep heart-wrenching sob echoed from James. "No! No! This can't be happening! Why? Why did this happen to my Chloe? Why?" His cries of anguished pain echoed through the silent room.

Dr. Roberts carefully started to cover Mrs. Morrison's torn and battered body when James stopped him. "No. No, not yet." Ever so softly he stroked her matted auburn hair, "Chloe," he leaned down to her blood stained face and gently kissed her lips for the last time as he lovingly said good-bye. With the soiled sheet in his hand, "Chloe you were the one. The only one for me. I'll always love you." Before he completely covered her, James leaned down and kissed her forehead.

Sheriff Meyer, only a step behind James, quietly stood there with his own tear stained face.   James welcomed the waiting embrace from the sheriff as Dr. Roberts slowly wheeled what was left of his wife out of the room. Once again Sheriff Meyer gently guided James by the arm. The coolness of the morgue had been left behind as he took James to a nearby waiting lobby. James paced the lobby like a lost child looking for his mother as Sheriff Meyer made a phone call into the station.

"James, Division of Wildlife confirmed the bear that took Chloe's life has been killed." James had stopped pacing.   His ghost like appearance alarmed the sheriff. "James, please sit down." He guided James over to a comfortable leather chair and sat down next to him. "We had some trouble further up north with this particular bear," not sure if James was listening, the sheriff rattled on. "Brought an old friend's nephew in, one of the best at taking care of dangerous animals. I'm so sorry we didn't get him here sooner. Lives way out in Oregon. Here James, try and drink some coffee." He put a cup of warm coffee into James' trembling hands. "You know, I remember the first summer you and Chloe came here. You were having a baby in the fall. Every summer after that you always came back. James, I'm so sorry." The sheriffs' words of comfort seemed to float in the air past James. The horror of the day had settled into reality for the man who just lost his beloved wife. "The doctor should be out soon. He'll help you with everything."

James's head snapped up, "The other woman. The one that left in Life Flight, did she make it?" He stared at Sheriff Meyer through swollen, blurred eyes.

"I don't know. They said she was hanging on by a shoe string. They were hoping she'd hang on until they got her to Grand Rapids. Much bigger, better equipped hospital than ours. I don't know if you noticed, but the man who was across the hall from us, he's her husband.

"Yeah, I saw him. He was waiting for his wife with the others. I hope his wife makes it." James barely sipped his coffee.

"Fish and Game brought Mr. Hawthorne in to hunt that savage beast down. Killed that damn bear with one shot." Sheriff Meyer calmly patted James on the arm as they sat silently waiting for the doctor.

The tears from James's eyes ran heavily down his pale white face. Reality had harshly surfaced. The agony of the day pulsed over and over in his brain. He had just lost his love, his best friend, the mother to his son and the aunt that three little boys desperately needed.

A creaky lobby door slowly opened as the doctor appeared holding a clear plastic bag labeled "Bear Victim." Offering his condolences, he handed James the clear bag that held Chloe's remaining blood stained life processions. Through the plastic he saw a neatly folded but ripped bloody purple t-shirt and shorts, the blood stained little pink IPod, one walking shoe and her wedding rings. James could no longer hold his emotions in, he burst like a dam, the sobs of pain flowed from him.

"That's it? That's all that's left of my angel? How am I going to tell the boys? What am I going to do without her?" He clutched the bag of Chloe's remaining treasures close to his broken heart, sobbing harder now. "She can't be gone! She just can't be gone!"

"James, is there someone I can call for you? Someone to help you?" Sheriff Meyer asked.

James pulled his cell phone from his pocket. He thumbed through the list of names and stopped at his brother-in-law's name. He stared at the number while his finger pressed the green button and handed the phone to Sheriff Meyer. For once, James called in an overdue favor from his brother-in-law. He flopped himself down in the leather chair unaware of the sheriff's conversation. James could barely stand the pain of losing Chloe, he wanted to die himself. He felt as if his heart had been ripped from his chest and stomped on with spikes and handed back to him. He couldn't remove the images of Chloe's naked, bloody and torn body. The grisliness of the attack would stay with him forever.

Hours passed before the arrival of his brother-in-law. Together with the hospital staff they helped James with all the necessary arrangements. James wanted everyone to remember Chloe as the beautiful wife and mother she had been. He decided it would be in the best interest to have what was left of her body cremated.

Later that day, James would be faced with the painful task of telling his young son that his mother was gone. She wouldn't be coming home. Chloe's life had been taken by a vicious bear attack.

A hospital social worker assisted him in telling his son and the three nephews who loved her dearly. Along with her grim task, this kind lady also helped get them packed to go home, without Chloe. It was a vacation that James would never forget.

A few weeks after the Morrison family had returned home, Sheriff Meyer checked with the hospital to see if anyone knew what happened to his friend's nephew's wife, the other victim of the bear. The details were sketchy. After stabilizing her in Grand Rapids, she had been flown to a larger hospital in Chicago. After going through several life threatening surgeries she was kept in the trauma unit and placed in an induced coma for several weeks to hopefully let her body heal. There weren't many details from that point. The family moved her to the local hospital in their hometown of Seaside, Oregon, where they hoped somehow she would recover and come back to them.

Chapter 11 - Dove's Awake

"Hawke, she's awake!" I heard the excited, but gentle voice of a woman as I awoke from my deep coma of sleep. Startled by her, my blurred eyes followed the woman as she suddenly ran from my bedside to find the owner of the name she called out to.

Left alone, I frantically searched the unfamiliar surroundings with clearing vision. The maddening thought that pondered in my mind…what happened to me? My eyes were wide open to the daylight that filtered into the room, but yet I felt lost in the misty belief of my reeling dreams. This couldn't be real. Or was it? Minutes seemed to pass since the older woman dashed from my side bouncing with excitement.

Pretty sure I was wide awake, my eyes fluttered with the haze of sleep as I tried to focus on my stilled body. Someone had taken on the task to make sure I'd been kept incredibly comfortable. My entire body had been strategically placed on several cushy pillows. A once over inventory of my battered body only scared me. My left hand and forearm were completely covered in a mummy like wrapping of white bandages. My left leg rested on more pillows and was neatly wrapped in the same mass of gauzy whiteness. An excruciating pain rippled throughout my entire body with the slightest movement I attempted to make. Unable and unwilling to move, I let my eyes scan the surrounding room I'd been placed in. From what I gathered, I was definitely in a hospital. But why?

From my cozy nest of a hospital bed, I could see the flashing red lights on the monitors and hear the humdrum beeping of all the machines that were attached to me. The unknown woman who'd been sitting by my bedside had left me alone and the sudden fear of being forgotten began to overwhelm me. The woman with the soft spoken voice had yet to return.

My mind darted in a helpless direction of fears. Family, I had a family. Why weren't they here? My left hand showed no signs of a wedding ring under all the bandages. But yet I knew I was married. Where was my husband? My children? Where is everyone? Or were they only the family from my intense and vivid dreams? A fog swirled about my head as my mind continued its game of playing tricks on me. I let my eyes scan over the empty room, was I dreaming? Or was this really happening?

From the far end of the hall, heavy footsteps picked up in pace. Someone moved swiftly toward my room. My family, it has to be them. Someone had to be coming for me. Please let it be the family who appeared in my obscure dreams. Anxiously, I stared at the empty space in the doorway waiting for the approaching footsteps.

My wish granted, a man I didn't even recognize filled my anticipation fully when he halted in the open doorway. Standing boldly, breathing deeply, his presence saturated my room.

Rocked gently by my dreams, his warm smile captivated me as he cautiously walked closer to my bedside. Thick, shiny black hair fell loosely over his shoulders. Sharp, well defined features covered his ruggedly but handsome face. Velvety brown eyes focused on me. The intensity of them pulled me into his surrounding mystic aura.

Who is he? Why is he here? Am I dreaming? Yes, I'm dreaming again. This is just my imagination deceiving me. He's beautiful. No, he isn't real. Carefully, I forced my stunned eyes to focus on him and concentrated on the man who stood by my bedside. He's not real; I heard the words in my head tell me. I'm dreaming, only dreaming, but I knew my eyes weren't playing tricks on me. Or were they?

The stranger hovered close to my bedside. The surprise of reality assured me I was definitely wide awake when he spoke to me. The silence of the room filled with his clear, deep husky, yet tender voice.

"Dove." Relief, shadowed by panic showed in the smooth silkiness of his voice as he carefully sat down on the bed beside me. "Thank God, you're finally awake."

Helplessly, I lay there searching his eyes for answers. He dared to inch closer to me. The warmth of his body soaked through the cotton cover half draped around me and my bandages as he made himself comfortable beside me. Careful of my injuries, his lean, muscular arm crossed over my broken but recovering body. Lightly, he rested his massive sun weathered hand over top of my uninjured hand. The warmth of his hand penetrated deeply into my chilled fingers. Neither of us said a word. Only my eyes spoke question after question to him. Desperately I searched, even racked every corner of my empty mind to remember this man who came to comfort me. Confusion, maybe even happiness erupted inside of me for this unknown man who held my hand.

"Dove, you've finally come back to us." Warmth and love flooded from him as he caressed my hand.

A startling question perplexed itself to me. He called me Dove. Who's Dove? My name? Is that my name? Why can't I remember my own name? Sheer terror flooded me as the spinning wave rushed through my head like a horse racing on a track. Snapping my eyes tightly shut, confusion once again circulated. My own fears didn't help me in any attempt to process my current state of dilemma. I willed my mind desperately to drift back into the safe shelter of deep sleep. Instead, the gentle voice of my bedside stranger pulled me back into his world.

"Dove, honey do you remember anything?" Worry tipped in his voice as he picked up my only bandage free hand. On the palm of my right hand he slowly rubbed a soothing circle pattern.

My fingers wiggled as I cautiously wrapped them around his warm hand. Tightly, I squeezed his hand and opened my eyes to find him again. I stared back into the deep mysterious eyes as I realized I didn't remember him. My findings only sent a tear down my cheek.

"Is she in pain? Maybe we should get the doctor?" She'd come back. The older lady who only wanted to help me, waited patiently for him to answer.

With his free hand, my unknown stranger gently wiped my unexpected tears. His secure but gentle touch comforted my sorrow. "Dove you're going to be okay." His reassurance only left me clinging to his hand.

From down the hall a chatter of excited voices rose. "Dr. Thornton, Mrs. Hawthorne is awake." A friendly, upbeat voice of another unknown woman rang out.

"It's an amazing day. Let's welcome Mrs. Hawthorne back." Bellowed the doctor's voice, a voice I'm sure I'd soon be getting acquainted with.

The swiftness of another flurry of fast paced footsteps and chatting voices could be heard rushing down the hall. Three people in white coats appeared along with a nurse. Adding to the parade of visitors, two little girls, with glowing smiles, clutched the hands of the gentle faced lady.

"I'm sorry Hawke. The girls heard she was awake. They've waited so long to see her." She whispered to him, apologetically.

His eyes left mine to smile lovingly at the pretty little pixies by her side. Could this be my family? My eyes drifted back and forth from him, to the older lady, and then back to the pretty little girls. Still admiring them with wonderment, a booming voice grabbed my attention away from who I could only hope was my family.

"Mrs. Hawthorne! Welcome back home. You're one hell of a fighter." Delighted by my awakening, the loud doctor continued his exam over me.

Not moving a sole from their places beside me, the team in white coats began their work. Machines checked, notes scribbled in an extremely bulging chart, they talked amongst themselves and smiled at me in amazement.

"Dove, let's start with something simple, can you use your voice?" The bubbly doctor waited with anticipation along with everyone else.

Like a croaking frog my voice broke, "What happened to me? Why are you calling me Dove?" My eyes meet the startled stranger's sitting on the bed. "Am I Mrs. Hawthorne?" My raspy questioning voice stopped the entire happy party dead in their tracks.

Each tug I made to free my hand from the man beside me, he only resisted in letting me go. By the fourth pull I'd freed my hand to wipe at my own tears. An uncomfortable silence hushed over the room as everyone's focus turned directly to me. A silent alarm dinged in panic along with pain from my abrupt movement. An exchange of worried glances filtered over each and every person's face in my now crowded room.

"Mrs. Hawthorn, I'm Dr. Thornton. Let's see what you remember?" He edged closer to my bedside knowing I was fully aware of the distressed look of concern he'd given the man called Hawke, but the doctor continued. "Can you tell me what month and day you were born on?"

"July 13th." The number immediately popped into my mind.

"Favorite color." He snapped the everyday question off quickly.

"Emerald green."

"Favorite music?"

"Jazz." My voice croaked the word right out.

"Your house address."

"House address?" Stumped, I quickly looked to this person called Hawke for help, "Numbers? Street? I...don't know. I can't remember them." My eyes glued to the doctor, I hoped for another easy question.

"Dove, can you identify any of your family? Can you tell me their names?"

From face to face, I studied each member of this family who I hoped was mine. From the smiling pretty girls, to the older lady, to the man they referred to as Hawke; I couldn't remember a single name. "No. I don't know...just him." My eyes darted and fixed perfectly still on the man sitting beside me. "Just you..."

"Me? Dove, tell me what you remember." As if he and I were the only ones in the room, "Dove tell me." Fixated on my answer, he waited.

"In the night," I coughed clearing my throat, "you were here."

"I've been here every night since we brought you home." Smooth, silk like, his voice tried to calm my panic.

"I don't know any of you." That panic, it just erupted. "Please, someone tell me what happened. I can't remember. I hurt, I hurt all over." Weakened by my own emotions, I could only cry.

"Dove," Dr. Thornton stepped in, "you have to stay calm. Try and focus. You said you remember seeing Hawke through the night. Can you tell us about that?"

"You," through my own tear filled eyes, I found Hawke. "You watched me sleep. Held my hand." I slightly moved my right hand that he'd be clinging to. "When you covered me with a blanket, I could feel the warmth of your body. I felt every touch of your fingers when you massaged my feet."

"You knew I was here? Why didn't you speak to me?" Caught by surprise, Hawke searched my tearing eyes for an answer.

"Dreams. My dreams, they were so vivid, I thought you were only a dream." This time my fingers tighten around his.

"Hawke, you forget to tell me something?" Dr. Thornton's eyebrows perked in question. He'd known that Hawke kept a vigil over his wife night and day.

"Doc, her eyes fluttered from time to time. Dove you never fully opened them." His attention turned back to me, "you never responded to my touch, or when I spoke to you."

"I don't remember you. I don't know what happened to me. I can't even tell you what day it is." This man, the one I assumed to be my husband, never once did he let go of my hand as I struggled to remember my family.

Perplexed by the rising situation, Dr. Thornton touched the white bandage I wore like a hat wrapped around my head. "We're going to take every step calmly, slowly. You're in pain, aren't you?"

"Movement doesn't help. My head feels like someone hit me with a baseball bat. I can wiggle my toes, but a line of pain shoots up my leg. And well my left hand, I can't even see it. Is it still there? What happened to me?" A spunk of demanding questions jumped from me.

"Dove, do you remember anything from the day you were attacked?" Dr. Thornton quietly questioned.

"Attacked?" Again, my eyes went back to this Hawke person for answers. Again, nothing. "What attacked me?"

"Dove, you don't remember anything of the bear attacking you?" The silence and tension became so thick in the room, I swear I could have cut it with a butter knife.

"A bear? I'm in this condition," my eyes swept over my broken body, "because a bear attacked me? How? When?" My haunted whisper kept my captive audience silent only momentarily.

"Easy Dove," his voice feather thin, but he held my attention, "we're lucky to still have you." Why did his gentle touch calm me? "Dove, it's…you…we…"

"What happened to me?" Pain filled into his eyes as I asked for my distressing question to be answered.

"Dove," Dr. Thornton regained control of the conversation. "You were battered badly by a bear." The good doctor went into clinical mode. "You sustained the major amount of the injuries to the left side of your body and your head. Multiple broken bones." He pointed to my leg and arm. "The majority of your wounds were from tears and punctures from where the bear ripped into your skin." He pointed to my still healing wounds. "Your skull took an unbelievable beating. I can honestly say you've got a hard head, lady." He chuckled in hopes to lighten the details, "From the x-rays, your skull is healing perfectly."

I started to squirm at the doctor's light description of my accident. "But my memory…it's been wiped away from me." I cringed with pain when I attempted to move my left hand. "I don't remember getting attacked by a bear."

"I'm sure Hawke will fill you in on all the details. But for now, lay still Dove. I don't want you excreting any unnecessary energy. You need to rest. Nurse Jenkins, let's up the dose of morphine, add another ten cc's, please. That should alleviate the pain and let you sleep, Dove." He pulled a pen light from his pocket and shined it into my eyes. "Just focus and follow the light, Dove."

"Think I did that several times before. Not too long ago. Bright light. Tunnel." The sarcastic wit flowed from my mouth.

"Very good Dove. Glad to see your verbal skills are intact." Dr. Thornton winked at Hawke. "Let's stay focused on this light. You see any others, let me know." He gave me a wink of the eye and continued his exam.

As instructed, I let my eyes follow Doctor Thornton's pen light all the while he kept pushing on my throbbing head. My hand gripped tighter to the man who I presumed to be my husband until the torturing exam of my head ended.

"This has been a monumental day. Welcome back Dove. You're showing great signs of improvement, but you've also exhausted yourself. It's time for you to rest."

"No, I don't want to rest. I can't sleep. Please, I need to stay awake. My family…I don't know…I don't remember any of you." Desperately, I pleaded with them as the nurse made her way over to my dripping IV.

"Dove, honey, the medicine, it will help you rest. Let you keep healing." There she was, tissue in hand, drying my eyes. "No more talking. You need to rest. We'll be waiting for you." Her soft voice matched her heartwarming smile. This gentle woman, who I couldn't remember, made me feel as if I were her own daughter.

"Please tell me…you're my family. You're really them?" My panic collided with the horrified stares of the people surrounding my bed.

"She doesn't remember us? Why doesn't Aunt Dovey remember us?" The younger of the two whimpered.

"Oh sweeties she will." The soft hearted older lady kissed the top of the child's head. "She'll remember us," her lip quivered in question as she repeated the words, but her eyes held her heartfelt pain.

"Doctor Thornton, why doesn't Aunt Dovey remember us?" The other brown eyed beauty asked as she clung tightly to the arm of the dark haired man.

In all the unpleasant excitement of me not knowing my family, Dr. Thornton temporarily held off on my feel good medicine.

"Everything will click in time, girls. Your Aunt has had a combination of several life threatening events hitting her body all at one time. First off, we have the bear. A two hundred pound bear attacked her. Your Uncle just happened to be in the right place at the right time. He shot and killed the bear before the animal could do any more harm."

"You were there?" A little surge on adrenaline kept me wanting to know more. "You saw what happened to me?"

"Easy Dove. It's over." His touch not only calmed me, but so did his presence. "You're safe."

"Okay little ladies," Dr. Thornton continued his detailed descriptions. "How about a little more information on why Aunt Dove can't remember anything? Let's start with all the white bandages wrapped around her head. Not a very pretty hat now is it?"

"Is the hat thing holding Aunt Dovey's brains in?" Quick to ask, the voice of the youngest girl bubbled aloud.

"In a roundabout way, yes." A soft chuckle escaped from Dr. Thornton. "The bandages have been helping the outside of your Aunt's head to heal as well as the inside. The bandages keep everything in a nice neat order."

"But why can't she remember any of us?" The older of the two blinked back tears as she inquired.

"Your Aunt Dove suffered a massive head injury. So lots of things in her memory got scrambled like an egg. Your job will be to help her put all the puzzle pieces back together."

"Aunt Dovey, we get to be your nurses. You know like when we get hurt, you always fix us up." The two girls giggled out a smile for me.

"Just a little more information girls. Then we have to let your Aunt Dovey rest." The good Doctor continued, "The bear did major damage to your Aunt's skin," again he pointed to wounds that had been healing, "I'm sure when the rest of the bandages come off, she'll have plenty of scars. She lost a lot of blood from where the bear clawed and bit at her. All this trauma to her body caused her to have a seizure."

"What's a seizure?" When the youngest one said seizure, it sounded as if she sneezed, "Did it hurt her?"

"Good question Amelia." Dr. Thornton had the girl's undivided attention and I just learned one of their names. "Let's see, how to explain a seizure." He tapped his finger to his lips, "Remember when I said Aunt Dove's brain got scrambled like an egg? All that scrambling caused her brain to short circuit. It's like when you get static on the TV, honey, and everything goes fuzzy."

"So, Aunt Dovey's brain got scrambled, then fried like an egg in the skillet?" In the eyes of the oldest girl, I could see the wheels of knowledge trying to figure it all out.

"Emma, Aunt Dovey can't cook her own brains." Amelia giggled at the thought.

My two beauties had names, Amelia and Emma. From all the fear that flooded my heart these two little beauties had been able to put a smile on my lips. "Well it would explain why I can't remember anything." I muttered aloud.

Dr. Thornton explained my trauma to the girls in a simple down to earth version as he kept a very close eye on me and my reactions. "Anymore question ladies?"

The dark haired beauties glanced back and forth to each other. Finally, the one named Emma spoke, "When can we take her home?"

"Not for a while girls." You could see the brightness fly from their eyes. "Your Aunt is lucky to still be alive." He smiled and gave a wink of an eye to the girls. "We've got to get her mind and body completely healed before I can send her home."

Tears tumbled down from their eyes as they clung to the older lady's hand.

"But we want her home." Amelia choked on her words.

"Now girls," the older lady gently interrupted, "we've got to get Aunt Dovey healthy. She'll be home before you know it." She kissed them both on top of the head.

"I think we need to wrap our visit up here ladies. Your Aunt really needs to rest. Nurse Jenkins." Dr. Thornton pointed to the medicine in her hand then to the IV bag.

"Dove, I've ordered something called a PET scan. The digital images project a deeper scan of the brain. Gives us a better image of what your brain is registering. Amnesia is very common when you've had a bad head injury like this."

"Will I be awake for it?" The druggy effect of the medicine began to show.

"You'll be sedated, Dove." Dr. Thornton smiled back at the girls, "Okay my little doctors-to-be, I'm going to need your help." The girls clung to every word he spoke. "My suggestion, bring some pictures in. Just show them to your Aunt over and over. Tell her everything about your lives."

"Aunt Dovey, we thought we lost you." The little one named Amelia crawled up on the bed with me. She clung to my good hand as the teardrops fell from her eyes. Gently squeezing her little hand back, I offered her a smile of reassurance. My natural motherly reactions had stepped in.

"Amelia, no. You might hurt her." The older lady reached her hand out to the youngster.

"Maude, she's fine." Hawke gently smiled back at her.

Finally, a name went with the gentle faced lady, who seemed to take so much care of me. She had a name, Maude.

The rugged stranger, who they called Hawke flipped Amelia's long black hair over her shoulder. Wrapped closely to his side, Emma's sad brown eyes couldn't keep her worry from me.

"Maude," he handed her a tissue. "We've got her back."

"I know. I know, Hawke, just happy tears. Sat here many of afternoons waiting for your eyes to open Dove." After she dabbed at her own tearing eyes, she securely locked her arms around Emma. The pain and sorrow welled in my family's eyes as they all tried to keep skeptical smiles of encouragement.

While the medicine pulled at me to go back into the depths of sleep, I memorized each of my family member's faces and rehearsed their names over and over in my scrambled brain as Dr. Thornton put it. I couldn't pull my eyes from the two beautiful girls who called me Aunt Dovey.

"Dove, Dovey you need to rest honey. Close your eyes white dove. I'll be here when you wake." Worry shook the soft edge of Hawke's voice.

My eyelids refused to stay open. I demanded them to let me see my family just one more time.

"Aunt Dovey," the little one kept me awake only for one last moment. "I'll be here when you wake up. So will Emma, and Uncle Hawke, and Auntie Maude. Please get better soon. We want to take you home." The little girl named Amelia was the last thing I heard as my body chose to give into the medicine.

My eyes could barely focus on her tear stained face as I drifted off into my sleepy world once again. Even with the high doses of morphine my sleep became restless. The reoccurring nightmare had come back to haunt me even in my resting moments. Two figures continued to search desperately for someone. I didn't recognize the man with wavy blond hair who held a little boy with wavy curls. Their features came in shades of sadness. His distraught voice echoed throughout my dream as he kept calling a woman's name while hopelessly searching for her.

xoxoxoxoxo

"Hawke, honey you stay with Dove. I'll take care of the girls. Take all the time you need." Maude pressed a gentle kiss to the top of her nephew's head and by their hands, tugged the girls away from their Aunt's beside. "Come on girls. We need to find those pictures."

"She's going to be out for a while," his eyes never left the sleeping figure. "I'll walk out with you." Hawke shifted his weight from the chair that held his tired body. The day filled with so much excitement had also drained him. "I'll be back in a few white dove," he stroked his fingers along her pale ivory check and followed his family from the hospital room.

Hawke waved his last good-byes to the taillights of Maude's car and stopped short of returning to Dove's bedside. From his t-shirt pocket he pulled the pack of Kent cigarettes. Bad habits return in bad times. Wooden match in hand, he struck it along the brick wall igniting a tiny glowing flame. A deep inhaling puff of the slim stick caused its glow of red to brighten. He laughed smugly at the sign posted in front of him. "No Smoking." Boldly, its letters hit him in the face and he just didn't care. Dove had returned to him, but her memory didn't follow. His mind raced with the overwhelming thought that Dove had awaken, but would she still be the same loving, sassy woman he'd married? He recalled how he'd fought so hard to get her back into his life. Their reuniting moments on the wooden dock when she ended her grudging war against him. He'd regained her trust, her love, everything. She was his life. He held his gaze on the window of the fourth floor that had become a second home and pulled in another deep breath from the cigarette.

"If there is a God out there, please let her come back to me." He said his heartfelt prayer between puffs. "I need you back Dove."

"We all need her back." The shrill voice Hawke grown to hate over the years inched up behind him. "Heard the good news. Dove's awake." Jane gently placed her hand on his shoulder. "How are you holding up? Fred told me Dovey doesn't remember anything."

Hawke shook off the tears that brimmed in his eyes as he slowly turned to meet Jane. "Don't give me any of your shit Jane. I'm in no mood to go toe-to-toe with you over Dove."

"Not here to bury the hatchet in your back. Sure I'll have plenty of time to do that at another date." Jane smirked and took the smoking cigarette from his hand and drew in a long breath, "Just come to check on you. Fred said you sounded bad."

How he hated his wife's best friend, but in the end look who had shown up to offer a temporary olive branch, Jane. "She woke up. Doesn't remember any of us. Nothing. She thought I was a damn dream in the middle of the night." Hawke accepted the cigarette they started to share between them. "She knew her date of birth, favorite color, and music. She couldn't even remember our house address."

"Hawke come on. She just woke from that damn drug induced coma. God only knows what's been circulating in her brain. She's alive, Hawke, alive. Somebody upstairs," Jane pointed to the cloud covered sky, "they're not ready for Dove. You've got a second chance. Make it count."

"You got a motive here, Jane? Plan on filling her head with the hell we went through over the last year?" Hawke lit another cigarette, chain smoking had become a habit over the last month.

Jane blew off his sarcasm and stepped back into the memory of time she had shared with her best friend, "Dove tell you she called me?"

"About?" He tried to shake off the negative vibe Jane always casted at him.

"She wanted me to be the first to know that the two of you patched things up."

"Not surprised. You two have been joined at the hip since what sixth grade?" A thin smile cracked across his face.

"God Hawke, the excitement in her voice. Swear she was walking on air. Next thing I knew, Fred, his call dropped me to my knees. Still can't believe this happened."

"Relive it every time I close my eyes, Jane." He'd eased back against the posted "No Smoking" sign on the hospital wall, "Not sure what to do from here."

"You love her like you've always loved her. Face it Hawke, Dove held an independence that pissed you off. Now's your chance, she needs you."

"What's in it for you?" Hawke could usually read Jane's alternative motives, but not today.

She cocked an eyebrow and grinned, "I get my best friend back."

He handed Jane the remainder of his third cigarette, "Things will kill ya. I'm going back up, you coming?"

Surprised by his offer, "No, she needs you right now." Jane started toward the parking lot, "I'm going over to relieve Maude. Sure the girls are off the hook with excitement."

Hand held on the entrance door, "Jane," Hawke paused and studied the woman who could give him pure hell, "Thanks."

"Like I've told you before...you better take care of her." As she hurried toward the parking lot, Jane tossed him a wave good-bye.

Chapter 12 – Recovery and Discovery

My days in the hospital passed quickly as I dozed in and out of my unconscious state of mind. When I'd surface from the coma like sensation, I'd always find a seemingly old, but still unknown member of my family waiting. I'd become quite accustomed to opening my eyes to find the brown haired beauties giggling by my bedside. The soft spoken older lady, who the girls fondly referred to as Auntie Maude, had been quick to shoe them away so she could spend time with me. A comfort I'd become accustomed to, having Aunt Maude by my bedside daily. Her gentle manor was as calming to me as her nephew's, my husband that I struggled to remember…I struggled to remember all of them.

Several times, to their surprise, my beauties were delighted to find me awake when they arrived. The excitement of finding me with my eyes open to greet them only caused Aunt Maude to fly into a tizzy of worry. Her fear, the girls would over exert me or hurt my already mangled, but healing body. My two nieces took full advantage of their short visiting time with me. They took it upon themselves to help me with my hair and nails. Even with the heavy layer of gauzy bandages around me, it didn't stop them in their attempts to make me look pretty.

One particular afternoon, Aunt Maude, with a cup of coffee in hand, found me admiring the girls' handy art work in a mirror. My budding artists designed a neon purple and yellow flower, complete with a bright green stem. Slightly to the right side of my head, the gauzy bandage turned into a fashionable hat of sorts. It didn't hurt, their touch mirrored there Uncle's. Gentle. Aunt Maude never left my creative beauties alone with me again.

My round the clock visitors enjoyed sharing the family photo albums with me. I learned a lot about me, my husband, and my two nieces in a short amount of time. Even Aunt Maude, with her gentle mothering ways, beamed with joy when she showed me the years upon years of pictures. All my family memories kept me wanting to stay awake to learn more about them. The photo books had become a daily ritual, all in hopes something would trigger my memory. This close knit family of mine certainly showered me with a great amount of love and devotion.

My husband, the man they called Hawke, or as the girls referred to him, Uncle Hawke, at any given time, would appear in the doorway of my hospital room. His movements were fluent, stealth like, so unbelievably quiet. It seemed to match the name he'd been given. While lost in sleep, day or night, I wasn't even aware of his presence until I felt the warmth of his hand touching mine. My mind was continually boggled by this stranger who called himself my husband. My biggest question still went unanswered, 'Why couldn't I remember him?' Everything about Hawke's constant presence mesmerized me. His outer ruggedness continually caught me off guard. He definitely didn't fit into the suit and tie world. He held a mystery in his velvety eyes that begged to be unlocked. Along with his heart warming smile, he kept me eagerly intrigued to learn anything and everything about him.

I found myself becoming dependent on him when I woke throughout the night. Always by my bedside, hand in hand, his touch comforted and settled me. Unofficially, I had appointed him the guard of my hellish nightmares. Fortunately for me, several times through his 'night watch,' he'd awaken me from my disruptive nightmares. Didn't matter what night, the haunting dreams always found their way into my sub consciousness to frighten me. I didn't want to acknowledge or even talk about the replaying nightmares. The hidden fear behind the saga only meant one thing to me, something bad was yet to happen. Grateful to be awakened by Hawke and the soft rasp of his husky voice reassured me how safe I truly was with him.

My fast paced recovery had Dr. Thornton's mind twirling. He had gladly reduced the daily amount of morphine and finally weaned me off it to a low dose pain medication. My strength improved thanks to the slow 'baby steps' as my team of therapists called it. I graduated from 'bedside' therapy for my left arm and leg to 'land' therapy. They'd wheel me to a larger gym-like therapy room to continue my tortuous healing routines. Daily therapy left me with a full body workout and entitled me to a few hours of sleep.

Each day I discovered more about my old yet new to me family. They kept a regular visiting schedule allowing one of them to be with me. Lunchtime had become a daily routine with Aunt Maude and the girls. Hospital food had been completely removed from my diet. Aunt Maude, who claimed I was the reason her diner was so successful, supplied a delicious lunch everyday.

Expecting to see the usual glowing faces of my girls and Aunt Maude, Hawke appeared in the open doorway. In his hand, he held a fresh bouquet of pink and yellow carnations tied with a white ribbon around the stems. I had slowly become accustomed to his typical everyday ruggedness. Today was no exception. His 'look' appealed to me. Long thick black hair pulled into a loose ponytail. Faded blue jeans, a few rips here and there, I wondered if the man owned any jeans without the added flare. Added to this mix, a well loved green t-shirt. He was impeccably clean, but had a love for his worn and tattered clothing. Another amazing thing I learned quickly about Hawke, his distinctive footsteps. The click clack steps he took while wearing those unusual snake skin boots generally gave me notice of his arrival. Today I expected the females of my family, only to be surprised by him.

"Dove," I swear his eyes glowed a shade of honey amber, "look at you. You, you're sitting up. By yourself." Hawke couldn't contain his surprised reaction to me sitting up without the aid of a dozen or so pillows. His contagious smile caught with mine as he crossed the threshold to my bedside.

"Huge progress," I patted the one pillow under my left leg, "they're nearly all but gone." I boasted a bigger smile and ran my hand over my tangled mess of free hair.

"Your hair." Another pleasant shock about me, my hair freed from all the gauzy white bandages. "Can't believe I can actually see your hair again, all those curls." Before I could run a hand through my mass of messy curls again, Hawke's fingers gently threaded over my long missed locks. Not only did Hawke notice my free flowing hair, he easily felt my unsettling vibe of nervousness all due to his closeness to me. Making life a little comfortable for the both of us, Hawke eased a step back from me, "Bet you're happy they didn't shave your entire head."

"How they managed to spare all this mess of redness," I flipped a strand of my hair over my shoulder, "I'll never know, and they kept it all wrapped up in a neat package of gauzy bandages."

"Mind if I check the healing of your scars?"

"Which ones?" As I glanced down and over my body, I wasn't sure where he was going to begin. There were so many wounds healing on my body.

"I'll start here," Hawke's fingers flipped another long loose end of my hair as he started to examine the tender sides of my skull. "Let me know if..."

"Hawke," I flinched in pain, "think you found the wound." His fingers stopped abruptly as I tried to jerk away from him. "You see any left over teeth marks?" I kind of giggled one of those nerves laughs.

"No teeth marks, just some jagged lines. You okay, Dove?" He threaded his fingers through the loose ends of my dangling hair.

"Peachy," My reply didn't come out sarcastic, just pure nervousness showed, "it's just...when you touched," I pointed to my head, "it just tingled...really strange feeling." With the rapid blinking of my eyes, I'm sure it gave way to how uneasy I'd just became.

"I'm sure your entire body will be sensitive for a while. All your nerve endings are reconnecting." Feather like, his finger trailed along the neckline of my ugly paisley print blue hospital gown.

Why did I jump at his soft and warm touch? Fast to change the subject, "Smell me." I pushed my perfumed arm toward his nose, "I took a shower. A real shower."

"By yourself?" My arm still in his hand, Hawke inhaled another breath of my clean and polished skin.

"Of course not, I'm not that talented yet. Two of the nurses helped me. Do you know how nice it was to just stand up under the hot water?" Silly, I know, but it was another accomplishment and a step closer to going home.

"Take it, it felt great."

"Unbelievable." He still hadn't returned my arm to me.

"Dove you're starting to smell like your old self again." He did it again, just took in a deep breath of me and my scented skin. "Even starting to look like your old self."

"Really now. My old self?" My smile turned into a frown at hearing those words. "I wish I could remember something about me. Even if it was just one thing." Disappointment clouded my accomplishing moment.

"I do know one thing," he reached for the wrapped flowers he'd left at the foot of the bed, "you love flowers. All kinds, any kind. Me, I don't have a clue about this blooming stuff. Only thing I know, it always made you smile. Even when you were mad at me."

"Did I get mad at you a lot?"

"Oh yeah." His chuckle captured my wonderment. "At least once or twice a week, I'd bring flowers home for you."

"Whether I was ticked off at you or not?"

"Yes. Most of the time you liked me." He snorted another laugh, "Can't wait to get you home."

"Home? You? The girls? Aunt Maude?" The world 'home' had my eyes flying wide open. Where was this home of ours I'd studied in all the pictures? Silently, I panicked as that one word rattled in my already nervous mind.

"Dove, you okay? You're getting a little pale." Hawke picked up easily on my silent change of moods.

My emotions were a wreck, but hearing his voice I found my way back to his peaceful eyes. Composure somewhat back, "Um, yeah. Yeah, I'm okay. No doctor needed." I sheepishly grinned and waved my hand as if I just shooed Dr. Thornton out the door. "You said home. I can't even remember anything about our home." I whispered, trying to hide another sudden growing panic attack. "Just the photos."

To rescue my uneasy feelings, his calming voice attempted to settle my now obvious nerves. "The girls told me that Maude brings them by for lunch."

"Yes, yes she does." That brought a smile back to my anxious face, "And," I pointed to the pile of photos, "we spend a lot of time with the photo albums."

"Girls tore the house apart finding every photo album we had. Had to finally stop them when they used up all the colored ink printing off pictures you had stored in the computer." There it was again, his warm gaze that surrounded me and kept me safe. "Dove?"

My puzzled stare into his eyes gave way to more questions. "You keep telling me, you're my husband. You really are? Aren't you? I'm mean, you, were in all the pictures." My nerves got the best of me as I babbled on and on. "It's...I can't remember you." This time I fought the tears back, "Or these beautiful girls that you say are our nieces. And Aunt Maude. Nothing, nothing at all is coming back. I don't understand why nothing is clicking."

"Dovey," he said my name with patience, "you've got to give yourself more time. You've only been awake for what, a month? Look at everything you've done in this short amount of time. Let your mind finish healing."

"But I want to know and remember everything about you, about us, even about me." Another disappointed sigh escaped me as I began to ramble on. "I just want to be able to remember the first time we met. Our first kiss. Our first date. When I fell in love with you. When I said yes to marrying you." A little relief lifted from me as I let the words of worry tumble freely out of my mouth. My slipping mental crisis of tears and twisting panic plunged to a new high and it didn't even phase Hawke. My heart tugged with a highly emotional sensitivity to the entire package of unanswered questions. All the while, Hawke's eyes glittered with a reflection of happiness, but still they were clouded by concern for me. He took everything in stride, and rode my emotional outburst like a gentle wave rolling into the shoreline. His finger stained, with something black slipped along my jaw and under my chin. As if I were the pet cat, he rubbed my chin, and then chuckled at me. Not what I was expecting from him. "You're amused by me?"

"Mum hum." His reply, the same sultry chuckle again. "Well that hasn't changed in you."

"What hasn't changed?"

"Filled with so much sentimental emotions." He stopped petting me and held his thumb on my chin. "It's what I love about you. When I look into your eyes I see your soul, feel your heart."

"Oh." My mood brightened by his tender and touching words. Slowly, I pushed his hand from my chin, only to have his stained fingers wrap around mine.

This rugged man, with who knows what stained on his overworked hands, kept me wondering what hid behind his grin that instantly made me blush. Hawke definitely wasn't afraid to show me the tender, compassionate side to his exterior roughness.

"Doc's surprised you survived at all." Our tender moment of bonding had just been whisked away when Hawke's mood for details switched. "Bear took one hell of a toll on your body." He glanced at my damaged but functioning body. "You were nothing but a bloody heap of human flesh when I got to you."

"You...you?" My questioning words staggered from my lips as Hawke's eyes filled with tears. Then in the next breath our conversation switched.

"They were bringing you out of the coma when your body went into a full grand mal seizure." His dazzling smile that kept me captivated disappeared into an expression of twisted sorrow and pain from the memory. "Can honestly say no one, not even Doc was prepared for that. You didn't have anymore, just the one." He toyed with the edge of my fingertips, "Never knew how damn scary a seizure could be. Appreciate if you'd refrain from surprising us with those." With his candid joke made, Hawke took a moment to wink an eye of reassurance at me.

"I'll give it my best shot to keep all seizures at bay." I cracked a tiny smile at him while I tried to process the key words from our short conversation. With my eyes fixed on Hawke, I replayed the words, seizure, bear attack, bloody heap of human flesh and my whole body shuttered. "Hawke," I blurted his name out as if searching for him. But he patiently waited for me to recover as if my outburst was an obvious trait that he expected from me. Eye contact still held between us, only my rapid short pants of breath could be heard. The shock of realizing what he just said mingled in my unspoken thoughts. My next question played at the tip of my tongue. As my fear absorbed me, I hesitated to ask, but did, "What bear? What seizure? My bloody body. This sounds like some ridiculous horror movie that we've lived through. But I can't remember it. And you witnessed it. I need to know every detail that happened to me." My emotions held tight as I fought the urge to break into tears, "Please Hawke, I need to know. You're the only one who knows."

"Dove," His usually reddish bronze skin drained to a paler shade, but he didn't come close to the pale shade of white I wore. Hawke reached for a nearby chair, the scraping sound it made as he pulled it closer to my bedside, echoed in the silence. Without a word, he planted himself in the stiff wooden chair. He exhaled several deep breathes as he collected his thoughts. "You don't remember any of this do you?" Hawke softly asked.

"Nothing." I focused all my attention on him as he ran his hand along his stressed jaw. "Hawke, I need your help. Please..."

"Do you remember anything about the day you woke up? You remember how Doc described everything to the girls about what happened to you?"

"Barely," I shook my head, "I don't remember much about that day, just a blur of total mass confusion for me. I didn't know any of you. The pain I was in, it was unreal. How worried everyone looked. The only thing that wasn't a blank for me was seeing you throughout the night. I really thought you were in my dreams. Nothing registered that you were real."

The chair moaned with a squeak as Hawke eased his frame back into it. The truth, we both didn't want to face, blinked like an overhead neon sign. My memory of our life together had been dissolved. Everything we built on love, trust, and honor disappeared into the black hole of the unknown. Would it ever return?

My heart stopping anxiety shadowed over me as I helplessly asked, "So, it's...its really true?"

"Afraid so, Dove." A heavy sigh of what I hoped wasn't disappointment or frustration which seemed to be wrapped in a lot of overwhelming sadness came from Hawke.

Subconsciously, my fingers toyed with the pretty bouquet of flowers as he gazed at me with desperate and serious eyes. The shattered expression on his well weathered face spoke volumes. He needed and wanted back the woman I used to be. The breath slipped from my lungs as I realized my husband was now a stranger to me. All I could do was hope and pray my memory of our life together would return.

Close enough to my bedside Hawke rubbed his hand across my bandaged leg. "You don't know how much I've missed you."

I blinked back my fresh tears as I read the sorrow in his eyes. In the awkward silence, I fidgeted with the flowers as we both searched for answers in each other's eyes.

"Will you please tell me what happened?" I managed to whisper.

Hawke drew in a long, deep and staggering breath. Carefully, he studied my anxious filled expression before he answered me.

"Dove, are you sure you want all the details? Honey, it's pretty…Dove think about it." He let out another long sigh as he crossed his arms over his chest and leaned back into the uncomfortable wooden chair again. "You had one foot in the grave. The details are grim."

"Give me every grim detail you can remember." I barely uttered above a whisper. "So I can heal mentally, I need all the awful details of what happened."

With apprehension, Hawke ran his hand hard over his tied hair. After another long drawn out sigh, he rested his hand, lightly, back on my injured leg.

"Okay, but at any time I feel it's too much, I stop. Understand?"

"Understood." I curled my fingers around the edge of the blanket that kept me tucked in and waited for Hawke to begin.

He didn't waste another breath. "We hadn't been spending much time together. Our marriage, it," he sadly glanced toward the window then back to me, "it was stressed. My work, I was barely home. Left you with the girls. We just weren't getting along."

"Why?"

"Dove, you," Hawke looked me square in the eyes, "you lost a baby. You had three miscarriages in a few short years and I made the decision that you'd never feel that loss again."

"So we can't have…"

"We've got the girls. Dove, I can fill you in on that part of life another time."

"Okay, I guess." The pain that filled Hawke's eyes had me agreeing to his request. So I made a mental note of another missing piece of my life to ask him about later. I waved the wrapped flowers like a wand over my bandaged body. "Then tell me about how I got into this shape, please."

Unbeknownst to me, Hawke held a secret that he wasn't about to share with me, "Dove, you sure you're up for this? You look really tired. Maybe…"

"Hawke, please tell me." My sharp reply was a pleading request, "Tell me what happened."

Uneasy with the upcoming conversation, Hawke shifted his body in the uncomfortable chair as he began to spill out the details, "It was your birthday. A biggie, you turned thirty. Thought it'd be nice for us to have a little get-a-way. Hoped we could reconnect again." There it was again, a wink from his honey golden eyes, "We fought a lot the last few months. Needless to say you were a pretty tough sell. Did my share of persuading…"

"You mean sucking up?" A spontaneous giggle from me lightened the moment, momentarily.

"Believe you me," Hawke smirked back, "I'm the king of sucking up to you."

"I take it all your sucking up worked?"

"You gave in." His smile broadened and I felt a sudden warmth flood over my cheeks. "We left the girls with Jane and Fred for the weekend. Took off down the coast. You always loved driving the coast line. Halfway into the drive we stopped at one of the state parks for lunch." His expression changed rapidly as he patted lightly on my leg in agitation. Hawke stumbled over his words as he tried to select them carefully. "You walked off to find the restroom." He hesitated and took a deep, almost cleansing breath. "Screaming. Blood curdling screams. They were coming from you. I followed your screams…found you. So did the bear that was attacking you." Hawke grew quite. His eyes mirrored the horror in mine. "The bear, apparently it came out of the woods behind you. Followed you. There was no way you would have seen it coming. You sure you're up to the rest?"

"Please, go on. You promised. Every detail." I whispered and reached for the box of tissues.

"By the time I got to you, the bear had already torn into your left shoulder. Left your arm and hand shredded." He ran his fingers gently over my bandage leg again. Hawke reached for my left hand and gently ran his fingers over my exposed finger tips before he returned to more of the hideous details. "In all my years of hunting, I'd never seen anything like this. Had to be something wrong with this bear, rabid, crazed, I don't know. Tossed you around like some kind of rag doll. Bloody gashes covered your body. There was so much of your blood everywhere. Damn animal even wore your blood."

My sickened gasp of fear wasn't the reaction Hawke had expected from hearing the point blank details of the attack.

"Dove, I don't have to finish this." Hawke, unaware of the deep pressure he had applied to my exposed, injured fingers had me flinching as his grip tightened.

I caught myself nearly choking and started coughing while trying to answer him. "Details." I coughed harder, "You promised. No matter how gruesome it is."

"Drink this," he handed me the water container that sat on my bed stand. "Ole Thornton finds out about this he'll…"

"He'll get over it." I coughed harder and like a good patient, I finished my water, "Thanks. I'm ready. Go on."

Hawke's body language read "No" loud and clear as he repositioned his weight on the uncomfortable chair. "Your leg became the new chew toy for the bear." He glanced down to my left leg that I still kept propped with only one pillow. "Only thing I could do…start yelling. I charged the sucker. Wasn't about to let a bear end your life."

As I dabbed my eyes, I whispered, "Thank you."

"Few other brave souls tried to help. By that point the bear just picked you up and flung you into the side of a tree. Still have my own nightmares over hearing your screams. Really thought you were dead."

I hung on every horrifying, descriptive detail he told me. Our fingers intertwined together as he relived the tormenting pain of seeing me dying right before his eyes. Distraught by the details, Hawke held himself together and again he took another deep breath, and slowly exhaled.

"You laid there. Lifeless. Not even a muscle twitched. Not a single sound came out of you. I couldn't even see you breathing. Thought you were dead." His tortured sigh filled the silent room. "Dove."

Nausea filled my empty stomach and churned at my insides. My body broke into a clammy cold sweat. Hawke regained his composure, as my shade of pale white slipped into an unflattering shade of greenish grey.

"Dove, you alright?"

Speechless, I barely nodded my head yes to answer his question.

"The hit you took. Probably explains why you can't remember anything. Dr. Thornton said you should've been dead from a blow like that."

"Guess the spirit world wasn't ready for me." My voice even appeared to be ghost like.

Hawke raised an eyebrow, "Still got it."

"Got it?" I perked an eyebrow at him, "Explain." We both needed a break from the gory details of my accident.

He tightened his lips into a smile, not a broad smile, and arched his eyebrow to match mine. "Your wit. You just come out with some of the most off the wall comments when things get rough."

"This is a good thing." It felt good to know something about me had stayed in tack.

Our break ended, "Take it you've seen most of your wounds?"

"I hear my back resembles a purple lined roadmap. Saw my arm and leg when they changed the bandages."

"Saw most of it when you were still in the coma." He traced his finger over my injured hand. "Don't know why the damn animal enjoyed chewing on your hand."

"Did I have wedding rings?"

"You did. Don't know if the bear swallowed them or not. Doc had one of the top orthopedic surgeons in Oregon flown in. He worked one heck of a miracle at reconstructing your left hand."

My fingers dangled outside the mass of wrapped white bandages. The tips of my fingers were still bruised and purple. "Not so pretty. But I've been moving them more." Unfortunately, I couldn't keep my tears away and the bed sheets just got used to catch a falling tear.

"Here," Hawked plopped another box of tissues in my lap. "As soon as your hand heals, we'll get you a new ring. Even let you pick this one." The ease of his smile comforted me.

"What if I liked what you gave me before? What did I have?" Brave enough, this time I reached for his hand.

"Simple gold band. Dove, you sure you're alright?"

"My head hurts. Certain parts of my body just throb. Will I ever be me again?"

"I'm counting on it. You have enough of this near death experience?"

"No." Then I boldly asked, "How did you not let it kill me?"

"Killed it with one shot." Hawke's eyes narrowed warning me not to ask another question. His point made clear, there would be no more details.

Packed with a punch, the anxiety of the attack hit me and I slumped back into the pillows behind me. "Hawke, I just can't believe…"

"Dove you need to calm down. You're alright now." Soothing, silk like, his voice flowed with calmness in his attempt to convince me to try and relax. "Yes, honey it's true. A bear, a very dead bear now, viscously attacked you. I saw it happen. I see it happen when I close my eyes. But Dove, you're alive. And I've got you back."

A passionate flare flew from his eyes to meet mine. In an odd way it was if he tried to say this is a sign. A good omen. A second chance at life and not to be taken lightly.

"It's just a lot to take in. Not remembering how I ended up like this. And then hearing the gruesome details of...of being a bears dining delight. At least I have you." My simple smile and teary eyes seemed to ease his heartache.

"Your bear,"

"My bear? I thought the creature was dead as a doornail?"

"Very dead, Dove. Took the rotten bastard's hide down to Tom's taxidermy shop. I'm having him make a rug out of it." A sharp laugh, almost evil, rippled from him. "You can wipe your feet on it any time you want."

"I'm sure I'll be more than happy to stomp all over it. I think I've heard enough of how I nearly died at the jaws of some beastly bear. You keep calling me Dove. Is this my real name? Or just a nickname you call me?"

Surprised by my 'as a matter of fact' attitude, Hawke's eyes lit up with my swinging attitude. "No nickname. Your name is really Dove."

"Just glad that I didn't remember the 'bear of deaths' attack on me. You think it had something against red hair?" Playfully, I pulled at a dangling lock, my sarcasm had Hawke smirking at my dry since of humor.

"Told you, you had a twisted since of humor." He laughed right out at me.

"Hawke, this really scars me." Drastically my mood changed. "I have two beautiful nieces. An Aunt Maude. And you. I can't even remember you. I feel so pathetic and completely dependent on you." My flare of sarcasm had broken me down into a drowning pool of self-pity.

"I shouldn't have told you all of this, Dove. Just too much at one time." He sympathized with me.

"But I needed to know. And no time like the present." Easily, I repositioned myself with the pillows tucked behind me, "Remember I'm the one who asked for the details." I cringed as a flare of pain and fatigue of the day sliced at my body.

"Knew this would be too much for you Dove." He stood and reached for the call button. "You're in way too much pain. Let me call the nurse."

"No. Not yet, I'm fine. Just need to wrap my scrambled brain around the truth. What are you doing?" Skillfully, even with care, Hawke slid onto the bed next to me.

"Dovey, if I could, I'd fix this. I'd have you back to who you used to be. But I can't fix it. All I can do is help you rediscover who you are."

Hawke's arms cradled around me and in a way it almost felt right. The closeness of Hawke and being able to feel his hard, rippled chest muscles through my thin hospital gown nearly sent me into an anxious panic. My overstressed emotions hesitantly found comfort in his gentle touch. Slowly, I tried to enjoy his charismatic tenderness and allowed myself to burrow deeper into his warming touch. With extra care, Hawke engulfed me in his massive arms of protection. His heavy sigh of relief filtered over my shoulders.

"Hawke, tell me what you're thinking."

"Dove, this is the first I've held you in my arms since," his heart picked up an extra beat. "this happened to you. I'm just remembering your affection, your love. How life, our life changed in one single day." He held me closer, tighter, "I'll never leave you."

Overly cautious, I tried not to resist his tighter, loving embrace. This man, my husband, his closeness caused me to struggle with my emotions. Barely struggling, I tried to free myself. My uneasiness only made the way for no escaping his secure embrace. My rugged outdoorsy man, completely devoted to healing me, only wanted and needed me back. My overwhelming fear of his closeness fed into my unstable emotions.

"Hawke, please I...I...I'm not..." I couldn't complete my sentence. Fear of the unknown just won. "Hawke this is too much for me." The man who held me so tenderly in his arms had become a stranger to me because of a freak accident. In my mind I reassured myself to slowly accept the comfort and safety he offered me.

"Dovey, you're safe now. Nothing will ever take you from me again." His voice flowed with silkiness.

Hawke, very aware of my new emotions, slipped his hands gently over my shoulders. His fingers weaved through my tousled hair as he pressed his forehead lightly on mine. I tried to hide my new found fear of him behind closed eyes. So close to me, I felt his warm breath circle around my tear stained cheeks.

"Dove, please look at me." Gently, he rested his hand along my quivering chin.

A few seconds slipped by before I opened my eyes to him, "Hawke, you're new to me, I can't...I have to relearn everything about you. About me...about our life."

"I know, Dove."

Desperately, I searched his passionate eyes for answers, only to catch my own reflection shining back at me. A rosy glow of blush brightened across my pale checks from his warm closeness.

"We're going to get through this. We've had our hardships and survived. Each one just made us stronger."

"But I knew you. I knew how your mind worked. I knew your touch. Everything we built, it is gone." We both knew the truth. As uncomfortable as I was, Hawke didn't move away. His love for me was real.

"Dove, the worst is over. I've got you back."

Completely caught up in his velvety eyes of reassurance, his fresh air scent, as if he just stepped off an ocean wave, I could barely keep my focus on what he was saying. Both of his warm hands cradled my still blushing checks. Unexpectedly, his lips brushed lightly over mine. From a feathery light kiss, he pressed his luck and deepened the kiss. My spine tingled from the rush of our sensual contact. Breathless, I grabbed for his hands and stared wide-eyed at him. Hawke easily read my intensely tangled panic as he let me slip gracefully from his tender grip.

An unsettling awareness just posed itself right in front of me as my shaking hands still clung to his. This loving stranger, my husband, suddenly made me very aware of the deep love and passion he held for me. A passion I couldn't remember sharing with him. To make the intensity worse, I couldn't remember how to return the same loving affection back to him. Slowly, he eased back from me flashing that charismatic smile as he lightly ran his finger down the bridge of my nose chuckling deeply.

"Don't worry my pretty dove, you'll remember me. I have no doubt about that."

"Everything, it's just a lot to take in all in one day." I felt the fatigue and pain flex in my body.

"Do me a favor, Dove. If and when you remember anything, you've got to tell me. Good. Bad. I want to know. We've been through a lot over the past ten years."

"Promise." I couldn't help giving him a reassuring smile this time. "I'm sure I'll have a good hundred or more questions for you. No matter what, you have to be honest with me. I'm completely dependent on you."

"I know it doesn't seem like it now, Dove, but we've always had a unique bond. Believe me, it's still there."

We both knew it would take me a while to readjust to the emotional affection we had once shared. The road to recovery and discovery had just begun. Hawke definitely held a calming and comforting affect over me. He made me feel safe and wanted. But not knowing him and our past only left me afraid of him in so many ways. The whole story of our lives wiped out and now needed to be rebuilt.

My favorite nurse appeared with a grin. "Mrs. Hawthorne, I tried to push this back as far as I could." She held in her hands my daily dose of magic medicine. "Dr. Thornton keeps close tabs on you. You need to rest." She handed me the paper mini cup containing a pill that would hopefully let me drift into a deep undisturbed sleep. "Mr. Hawthorne you should really…"

"Maggie, you know I'm not leaving her until she's sound asleep." Hawke winked at the afternoon nurse.

"Seeing the girls didn't get to visit me," I washed my 'sleepy time' pill down with a gulp of water, "I bet they'll want a full report. You should go home. I'll be okay." Protesting with Hawke didn't get me anywhere. He just wrapped me tighter in his arms.

"Left them with Jane on my way in, they're fine. Close your eyes white dove." He kissed my cheek and gently placed my injured hand in his.

As much as I had recovered, my body still demanded rest. But my mind couldn't follow the simple instructions. My favorite medicine relaxed me enough so I could actually curl in closer to Hawke. With my head resting on his broad shoulders my panic slept. He had become my own personal security blanket with the warmth from his body surrounding me in a safe haven. Hawke's deeply summer bronzed arms held me securely as I faded off into my land of dreams. For once, lost in the deep slumber of my dreamless sleep, the nightmare of the blonde haired man and young boy stayed asleep deep in my memory bank of dreams. Peacefully, I rested.

xoxoxoxoxo

As Dove rested in Hawke's arms Dr. Thornton appeared in the doorway.

"Hawke, need to see you for a moment." He nodded toward the hallway.

"You find something out, Doc?"

"Did you tell Dove everything?"

"Gave her enough details to get her through."

"Hawke, you've got to tell her about what happened in Michigan."

"Gave her the details of what happened, not where."

"Why the hell not? What are you trying to hide from her?" In the doorway of Dove's room, Dr. Thornton's whispering voice grew to an agitated anger at Hawke.

"Doc, I'm just not ready to relive every detail. I gave Dove what she needed to know at this moment."

"She's going to find out."

"I'll deal with it then. I need her to recover before I tell her that our marriage was a complete mess. Do you really think she needed to hear that she was ready to leave me?"

"Fine, Hawke, fine. But sometime in the near future you're going to have to fill her in before someone else does. You've been here every single day. Have you noticed anything different about Dove?"

"Other than her memory is shot to hell?"

"Amusing Hawke. Now think about it, Dove's grayish blue eyes. Did you notice how vivid blue they are? When did she develop all those freckles?"

"Thornton, that's nothing. Dove's eyes change with her moods. Freckles, the woman has endless marks all over her body. You got anything medical that I should be worried about?"

He scratched his head, "Just amazed how she pulled through. All vitals look great. She's healing. Just worried about her memory. Don't be playing games with her. You tell her what she needs to know or I'll tell her."

"Doc, just because Dove and I were living in a sham of a marriage doesn't mean I ever stopped loving her. I'm taking this second chance with her and running with it."

"You know Dove better than anyone. You need me, you know where to find me. I'll be checking on her later."

xoxoxoxoxo

Alive and returning to my so called 'same old self' had my family along with the medical professionals pleased. Progress, they said I was above average for their target goals.

The remains of all the gauzy bandages disappeared practically on a daily basis. As for my left leg and back, there was nothing much that could be done for the horrifying scars. On the other hand, everything had healed perfectly from all the muscle and tissue damage. Grateful that my left leg had full function again, I would always have the reminder of being sliced and diced by a bear.

As the days passed I had finally healed enough to start the even more demanding therapy treatments. With all my open wounds healed, Hydrotherapy became my best friend. Physical therapy exercises in a heated swimming pool allowed my muscles to regain their strength. My left hand lagged behind in progress, but I had regained full motion of my left arm with the help of a detailed occupational therapist.

Aunt Maude, accompanied by my two junior nurses visited daily. The physical and occupational therapists had given the girls easy tasks to help with my physical recovery. Basically, the girls and I turned our extra therapy into a game of who could help Aunt Dove. Anything from massaging my hand, to helping me walk down the hall, my nieces stayed right by my side.

The subject of the diner always popped up with Aunt Maude. She couldn't wait to have me back in her kitchen cooking again. She'd rattle off a list of the regulars who continued to ask about my recovery.

My mind bounced all over with at least a dozen or more questions a day. Puzzle pieces barely started to fit as I gripped a small handle on what my life used to be like. Everything about me kept improving except for my memory. I described it as if my brain were a block of swiss cheese, so many empty holes that needed to be filled. Dr. Thornton worried that it could be permanent, but always reassured me it might only be temporary. Only time would tell.

My adjustment when it came to Hawke was an understatement. Over and over I reviewed every photo album of him and me. With each page I flipped, I saw two people who built a loving life together. But none of it sparked my memory.

Life rolled passed me while I had been unconscious. I missed my thirtieth birthday along with our ten year wedding anniversary all compliments of a bear with a bad attitude.

Details of our life together, I noted and remembered. We adopted the girls after Hawke's sister and brother-in-law died in a car accident. They were still in diapers, not quite toddlers yet. Now they were eleven and twelve, pre-teenagers. Aunt Maude, my blessing of inspiration, had been here for every step of my recovery. No matter how down I'd get, she'd be there to pick me up. I found my best friend Jane to be a real treasure. She kept me laughing with all kinds of wild stories about Hawke and his two buddies and business partners, Fred and Lance. They all popped in to say hello and would give Hawke a break from the craziness at the hospital.

The days were dwindling down to when I would soon be leaving the hospital for good. My husband would soon be taking me home, but yet I still barely knew him. My own unsecure feelings left me intimidated by him and he felt it with every visit. Hawke made it very apparent how much he loved me and the girls.

News flashed through the hospital the day Dr. Thornton announced that my recovery had improved so much he'd be sending me home. The next challenge in my life would be home. Where was home? And what would home life be like when I finally got there?

Chapter 13 - Home

The time had come for me to take the next step in life. Leave the security of these hospital walls and reunite with my past life and continue to build a future with my family. Today, all that was left in my hospital room, rumpled sheets on an unmade bed. All the pictures, handmade artwork, flowers, and cards had been packed up and sent to the place called home. The words "going home" did send a delighted but scary shiver up and down my spine. Thankfully, my mind had retained all the new and updated information I'd gathered from everyone. Every detail of our home life, I placed in my current memory bank. Our home, located on the outskirts of Seaside, Oregon, a quaint tourist town, where Hawke also had a prosperous hunting and fishing business. Even better, just a few streets over from our house, you could find the sandy and rocky shoreline of the Pacific Ocean. From all the photos, the house I'd soon occupy again was a picturesque Victorian style that had a spacious yard and beautiful flower gardens. A small light bulb went off when I saw the lush gardens in the pictures. Gardening, I knew it like I knew cooking. Vegetable garden to flower gardens, Hawke verified that I had two green thumbs.

Relieved to be leaving the hospital, I wouldn't miss the stale white walls, all the ongoing therapy sessions, and the noisy beeping machines that kept tabs on me. As I put on a brave front, with the memories of my past thirty years wiped clean by a deranged bear, my nerves had taken another toll on me again. Hard for me to accept at times, but I learned to, I had become totally dependent on a man who I couldn't remember. This man, my husband of ten years, completely devoted to our relationship, held a tremendous and affectionate passion for me. Under all my erupting emotions, I tried to snuff out my terrified feelings of going home to a life I just couldn't remember.

Early fall had replaced the long summer days and my girls were back in school. They had spent nearly their entire summer vacation at the hospital. The countdown to my coming home started when the girls hung up a calendar and marked off each day with colored markers. A huge red heart circled the day Dr. Thornton set for my release. My pretty little girls weren't the only ones counting down the days; Hawke was also getting impatient for my release.

Scribbled on the big red heart, "Aunt Dovey's coming home." The date had finally come. I knew Hawke would soon be here to spring me. My goal, be dressed, bag packed, and ready by the time he arrived. My injuries still reminded me of the stinging truth. Pain, it would be with me for a while longer. I managed to pull and tug on my jeans along with zipping them. A little exhausted from tackling my pants, I plopped back down on the bed. With care, I slipped on the soft, long sleeved mauve t-shirt and when my head popped through the opening I found Hawke standing in the doorway of the hospital room, hopefully for the last time.

"You're beautiful, Dove." His beaming smile, those deep, velvety eyes that I tried so hard to get comfortable with greeted me.

All I could do was return the smile back as I continued to yank at the body of my shirt. What I didn't expect, Hawke helping me pull the rest of the shirt over my scarred body.

"Your scars are healing nicely." He stretched the cottony material around the top of my jeans, "You ready to come home?" As he twisted his fingers through my hair, I could feel his entire body vibrate with happiness.

"Home." The fear inside of me built as I attempted for the third time to tie my own tennis shoes. Annoyed and frustrated with the snug elastic bandage that cradled my left hand for protection when I wasn't practicing therapy moves. From the opening of the elastic material I let my fingertips flex and once again I tried to tie my own shoes, "I can't wait to get this thing off."

Of course coming to my rescue, Hawke, who had himself planted next to me on the bed, swiped up my legs and swung them onto his lap. "I got this for you." He didn't bother to hide his laughter at my small dilemma.

The fact I couldn't tie my own shoes and my legs rested comfortably on Hawke's lap, only left a flush of embarrassment washing over me. My being so self-conscious of his closeness alerted me to a secret he tried to hide from me.

"You smell," I sniffed at him and purposely drew in a deep breath of his unappealing cologne, "I never knew you smoked."

"I do on occasion."

I wiggled my nose at his lingering scent. "My sense of smell must be super sensitive today. It's not cigarettes," I sniffed him again, "Cigars? You smoke cigars?"

"Did you just remember that or are you guessing?"

I read the gleam of hope in his eyes, he wanted me to say "I remember." "Would you settle for familiar? There's something about the cigar's odor and the scent of you, the mix, it just smells familiar to me."

He relaxed into a smile, "Of all things for you to remember, Dove. It's a start."

"Do you smoke all the time? Or is that an occasional thing? Or just when you get nervous?" Pretty sure I wasn't the only one with a bad case of the nerves going on here.

"Small habit," Hawke held up his thumb and finger to indicate an inch, "every now and then. Started back up after your accident. Needed a little help to calm my nerves."

"Thanks for the reminder." My nerves kicked back into high gear when I realized my legs still sat happily on Hawke's lap.

"You never seemed to mind when I'd light up a cigar." Eye to eye with each other, Hawke took advantage of my weakness and sent my nerves into overdrive when he winked an eye at me.

"Makes me feel good that something is familiar." Rapidly, I swung my legs off his lap, "I'm just nervous…you know about…" I pretended to check the snug fitting bandage around my hand.

"About what, Dove?"

"Home." I fidgeted with the elastic, letting my fingers flex.

Hawke ran his hand softly though my hair again, "You have nothing to worry about, Dove. Waited a long time for this day to come." His fingers kneed softly at the tension in my shoulders.

"I'm scared. Worried. What if things don't come back to me?"

"Been through this before, Dovey, your body's healing nicely, now let your mind heal." Hawke had a love for touching me. From massaging my shoulders, his hand flowed down my back with a feathery softness. Through the thin cotton shirt, I felt the light pressure of his fingers outlining the new design of tender scars on my back.

"Did we always touch each other?" Blurted question up for discussion, I just kept my eyes focused on my wiggling feet.

If possible, Hawke inched closer to me, "We did." He had an obsession of constantly touching me and today was no exception. I could still feel his hand outlining the claw marks on my back. Something new I'd have to learn all over, his physical touching of me. "Would you prefer I stop?"

Agonizing under the heat of Hawke's eyes, he needed an answer. Ever so slightly, I lifted my eyes to meet his gaze. "No. I'm, it's," I gulped for a breath, "I..." that same gulp of air, I just released it. "I wish your touch was familiar to me. Not knowing my past...not knowing you," my hands trembled as I kept babbling on. "I'm really trying to be...you know, more...I...I don't mind...kind of even enjoy..."

"You're rambling, Dove." Hawke continued to twist a lock of my hair around his finger. "When you get nervous, you talk...a lot. Just babble on about everything. Nice to see that's still intact."

"I do?" I met his amused grin as he chuckled at me.

"Yep, you do."

"That's two things about my past." Pretty pleased with my "oh my gosh" memory, I flung my arms around him in celebration. "Go figure, babbling and your smelly cigars."

"It's a start, Dove." With arms wrapped around one another, I almost felt comfortable until Hawke had to mention, "Not only do I need to touch you, Dove, I enjoy the touch of feeling your body."

"Oh." My head kind of swirled, "we were, umm,"

"Emotionally connected to each other, with an added bonus, we enjoyed a healthy physical attraction to one another." Nicely put, I felt my cheeks burn, "we'll take it slow, Dove."

"Slow," my heart fluttered more than a jumping beat, "slow would be great." Just a light glimpse of what life had been like with Hawke, "I'm going to need some time to get reacquainted with you."

"Like I said Dove, we'll take everything slowly."

To avoid any further eye contact with him, I quickly turned to finish zipping the duffle bag beside me. Hawke had me flustered with all the "physical" talk about our relationship. He wrapped his arms around me and conveniently zipped the bag for me. Easily, he ran his hands down my cloth-covered arms. Hawke's mysterious warmth radiated from his body as he pressed his chest lightly into my back. Was he always this gentle with me? Or under the circumstance, did he need to take extra precaution when he touched me? Nonetheless, his deeply tanned muscular arms still surrounded me. In an attempt to adapt to Hawke's frequent touch, I bravely ran my fingers lightly over his rippled arm muscles. Several times I stopped to outline several fine scars on his arm. Finally, my hands rested on top of his. Lightly, I let my fingers drum nervously on the back of his hand. My body language explained it all, nervous and scared. Nothing about me got past him.

"You'll be fine, Dove." Hawked eased me closer into his embrace as he kissed the top of my head, "Made a promise to you ten years ago, I'd always take care of you."

"I'm sure I made you the same promise." My heart kicked into a racing beat, if I felt it, I'm sure Hawke was well aware of the timely thumbing in my chest.

"You did."

So close together, I felt Hawke's sleek black hair drape around my shoulder and tickle at my bare neck. Subconsciously, my fingers began to play with the loose dangling ends of his hair.

"Dove, there's so many things that haven't changed about you." His lips gently caressed along the edge of my cheek.

"Hawke," Lightly I tugged on the end of his hair, "do you always make me turn shades of pink?"

Before I could get my answer, "Dove, Hawke." The booming voice of Dr. Thornton broke in and had me jumping and Hawke laughing. "Time to spring you from this joint Dove." He tapped Hawke on the shoulder, "You'll have Dove all to yourself as soon as I do one last check. Want to give her a little space there buddy?"

Hawke barely budged, only allowing enough room for Dr. Thornton to do one last "look over" of me. "Hey that still hurts," I pushed Dr. Thornton's hands away from my still tender head. "Do you have to press so hard?"

"Yes. Now follow the light." He flipped a penlight from the top pocket of his jacket. Then he had me following the light up, down, to the right, and then left.

"Oh sure, now it's okay to follow the light. Remember you people yelling at me to stay away from the light."

"Dove?" Hawke's head snapped sharply, directly staring at me as Dr. Thornton and his dancing penlight came to an abrupt halt. "Mind explaining?"

"You yelled at me to stay away from the light."

"When?" Two sets of questioning eyes peered at me. "Who yelled at you?" Curiosity got the best of Dr. Thornton.

"Not you," I said to the dear doctor, "You."

"Me?" This time, Hawke slipped an inch or two back from me.

"Yes, you. Blood, I was covered in it. I was lying on a gurney, in an unbelievable amount of pain. All I could see were bright lights and shadowy figures hovering over me. People screaming about losing her. And then you, it was your voice. I heard it. You yelled at me to stay away from the light."

"Holy shit." Hawke's face nearly matched my everyday paleness.

"You okay?" I'm sure Dr. Thornton was as happy as I was that Hawke was sitting down. "Is this one of my wacked out dreams? Or did it really happen?" After a few moments for both men to recover, I got an answer.

"Yeah, Dove. It really happened." His color slowly edged back over his weathered face.

"Dove," Dr. Thornton stepped closer to us, "Take a look over this therapy schedule for me. Hawke." he motioned for Hawke to follow him.

"What's going on?" I asked as Dr. Thornton shoved a calendar like page in my hands.

"Doc," Hawke didn't bother to follow, "Happened when the ER staff was prepping Dove for Life Flight."

"Interesting, Dove. Anything else you remember from that day?" Dr. Thornton rubbed the bottom of his chin with his thumb and finger. His mind had to be racing like a hamster on a wheel.

"No, just when you shined the light in my eyes, it popped into my mind." I just missed the questioning glare Dr. Thornton past to Hawke. "This schedule is demanding."

"That it is Dove. You'll be here three times a week. As the therapists see fit, they'll reduce the time. I'll see you in two weeks. If I approve of your progress," Dr. Thornton shot Hawke another glare, "I'll see you in a month."

"She won't miss a single appointment, Doc." Hawke snatched the folder from his hand. "I'll bring her myself."

"Do both of us a favor Dove, every time you remember something, even if you feel it might have been in a dream, write it down. Keep a journal, we'll review it when you come for your visit."

"I can do that," I agreed as I tucked the calendar of my scheduled life into the folder Dr. Thornton gave Hawke.

"Dove, you've got my numbers. Call me if you need anything, or if this one gets out of line." Dr. Thornton smacked Hawke in the shoulder with another folder he'd been scribbling notes in. "I'm serious, you two need anything, call. Dove, you've made an amazing recovery. Good luck to you."

"Can't say it's been a pleasure, but I'm sure glad you were here." As he rose, Hawke shook Dr. Thornton's hand. "Can't believe I'm finally taking her home." He glanced back at me as I climbed to my feet without help, "You ready?"

"Thank you Dr. Thornton, for everything. I couldn't have made this recovery without you and my team of experts." My gentle teddy bear of a doctor didn't mind the hug of appreciation I gave him, "I'm sure I'll be calling."

My hand slipped into Hawke's and I clung to him like a lost child. Those dancing butterflies kicked up in my stomach like a soccer match in overtime. Our goal, get home without me having a nervous breakdown. The security of doctors, nurses, and therapists at a beckoning call, no longer existed. I had to rely on myself and the man who held my hand.

With my duffel bag flung over Hawke's shoulder, I halted us in the doorway to take one last look at the room that had been my makeshift home. A room where I'd gotten a second chance at life.

"Dove,"

"I'm okay. Just wanted to," I blinked back the tears, "sorry, didn't think I'd get this emotional about leaving. Learned a lot here."

Hawke squeezed my hand, "Your eyes give away your true feelings. Just saw it."

"Wish I could read you as easily as you've been reading me."

"I'm sure you will Dove."

"I'm ready. Could you please take me to our home?" I asked and took one last glance back at the empty hospital room.

After several well wishes and hugs goodbye from the nurses I'd become attached to, the elevator doors closed behind us. Once I stepped outside the hospital entrance I stopped short staring up at the brilliant blue sky and breathed in the fresh fall air.

"When was the last time I was outside?" I asked soaking in the warm sunshine.

Hawke, a little slow at answering, gave me an awkward sideways glace. "I'd rather not remember that day." He tugged lightly on my hand and led me toward the parking lot.

"Oh, that day." I whispered allowed. Last time I'd been outside, a deranged bear wanted me for breakfast. With me out of the hospital and on our way home, both our wishes had been granted.

"How are the nerves doing?"

"Not bad, not feeling a panic attack…yet." By the hand, Hawke lead me through the parking lot of cars, "Hawke, um what kind of car do we drive?" Something as simple as the make, model, and year of the car I drove, I couldn't even remember.

He snickered, as if I said something absurd. "There are no cars to be found at our house, honey." Parked in an end spot, Hawke stopped me in front of a deep navy blue, Ford pickup truck.

"Ours?" He snickered again as I pointed to the pickup that barely fit into the spot. "I take it I like to drive trucks?"

"Matter of fact, you do." He walked me to the passenger side, "Had a nice four door car for you and the girls. But you were always steeling this one from me to run your errands." His smirk came off sarcastically.

"Really? You're serious aren't you?"

"Ended up getting a Ford Crew Cab for you to tote the girls around in, you had to have your favorite color…"

"Green," As he held the door open for me, our eyes locked, "Emerald green."

"Did you…"

"Remembered." Filled with an overwhelming feeling of accomplishment, "Just had another one of those "pop into the brain" moments."

"Keep those memories coming Dove." Excited with my day of progression, he tossed my bag in the seat behind me and offered his hand, "Did you want to drive?" He cracked another smirk at me.

"Um, no." My shocked expression made him laugh again. "You really want to end up back at this place don't you?" I pointed back toward the hospital.

Comfortably seated, he grinned at me and tugged a lose end of my hair before he shut the door. My nerves worked overtime as I tried in vain to get the seatbelt around me. My left hand wouldn't cooperate with my needs and I kept letting the seatbelt slip out of my hand while trying to fasten it.

"How hard can it be to fasten a seatbelt?" I snarled after my fourth attempt.

By this time, Hawke had already seated himself on the driver's side and enjoyed yet another one of my many frustrations. "Need a hand?" Before I could answer him, he simply reached across me, with a click my dilemma with the seatbelt had been taken care of.

"Thanks." I really was thankful my color didn't turn rosy pink as he turned the key in the ignition. "Pretty excited about seeing where we live." My pulse surged as I glanced toward Hawke, the security of my hospital room now a distant memory.

"Let's get you home Dove." As Hawke pulled out of the parking lot, I took one last look at the hospital as it faded away behind us.

The view out my window kept my eyes fixated on the quaint town as we rolled by. My fascination held on the sculpted gingerbread houses, gift shops, and boutiques all centered in the main section of town.

"There's Maude's diner," Hawke pointed to the red brick building on my right. Pretty white lace curtains draped halfway down the full square picture windows. In bright gold letters trimmed in black the words "Maude's Family Style Diner" jumped out at me.

As my mind made mental snapshots of the place, "My other home?" I asked, wondering when I'd ever step foot into the charming eatery again.

"Mmm hmm." He nodded yes and kept driving. "Maude's been doing the happy dance about your home coming. Already started bugging me about you coming back to work."

"Should we stop in?" As the brick building reflected in the side mirror, I asked.

"Not today, but Maude will be over later today to check in on you."

"Can't wait to see her." My head felt like one of those dashboard bobble heads. I kept bobbing from window to window. "Hawke, you said I grew up here."

"Yep, lived here all your life."

"Feels like I'm visiting for the first time. Nothings "popping" for me. Can't say anything looks or feels familiar yet."

"Don't worry, Dove, I'm sure something will click for you."

"I hope you're right."

Like a tour director on a trolley, Hawke practically spoon fed me information as we drove towards home. I appreciated his detailed descriptions. As he drove, I kept track of my surroundings as we left the main part of town.

The houses we passed grew further and further apart. Then Hawke turned left onto a side road called Turtle Drive. The street had only five or six houses spaciously separated by lush, green manicured lawns. Half way down the street he pulled into what I presumed to be our driveway.

"Stop!" I shouted at him as we pulled into the driveway. My demanding outburst not only startled Hawke, but he slammed on the breaks jolting both of us.

Hawke's head snapped in my direction and he asked what seemed like a million questions, "What? What is it? You alright, Dove?"

"This house," my eyes grew huge as I took in the full view of the structure displaying itself in front of me. "Home? This is home? Our home?" Not in panic, I felt my heart beat wildly.

"Yeah, Dove. Me, you, the girls, we live here. This has been home for the last ten years." He tried to hide it, but I could hear the concern creeping into his voice.

"There's something, I can't put my finger on it." Through the windshield I examined the exterior of our home.

"Maybe the photo albums, you know all the pictures." Good suggestion, but there was something else.

"Yes, pictures, I do remember seeing them, but what is about this house..." Reality soaked into me like a sponge absorbing water. This was home. Before Hawke could reach for me, I flipped the seatbelt off, opened the door, and I slipped free from the comfortable seats of the truck.

"What are you doing? Dove, where are you...?"

Right in mid-sentence, I just shut the door on him and walked to the middle of the yard. I bent down to feel the lush green grass under my feet. It was as if I'd never touched the ground before.

The worry from Hawke's voice flowed through the open window. "Dove, what is it? You okay? You remember something?"

From the middle of the yard, "Hawke, there's something, I can't place it. We live here? We really live here?" Standing back up from petting the grass, mystified, I stared at him and then back at the house. "I just want to stand here and think. Please, just a minute. Go park, I'll be right here. I promise I won't go anywhere."

His expression turned from worry into total bewilderment with me, but he did as I asked. From the review mirror, I could see his eyes on me as he drove around to the back of the house to park. The engine went silent, a door slammed, and within a few steps Hawke walked back down the driveway toward me. He pulled his thick hair back into a tight ponytail while a puzzled expression crossed his face. I'm sure I left him clueless.

"You okay?" With a raised eyebrow he asked and walked into the front yard to stand beside me.

"Yes, I'm fine. Really, I'm fine. I just needed a moment to absorb all of this." I pointed to house. "I think I'm going to need lots of moments."

"Take all the moments you need Dove." Again, I got the arched eyebrows as he lit a cigarette. "Nervous?"

"Yes, you?" I motioned toward the puff of smoke he exhaled.

"Bad habit." His hand pressed lightly into the small of my back.

"I didn't mean to scare you when I jumped out of the truck." I knew I did and grinned at him anyways.

"You did." He inhaled another breath. "You're finally home Dove."

Just like the pictures I had committed to memory I viewed my home from the front yard. A two story Victorian home painted in two different shades of rose and trimmed in antique white paint. Wicker furniture sat neatly on the front porch, a brightly colored floral wreath on the front door, and flower boxes hung from each ground floor windowsill. A warm and inviting charm projected from the house. I felt as if it were inviting me to come in. Captivated by the beauty of the old home, Hawke's arms surrounded me. Instantly my body stiffened to his close embrace. I exhaled an anxious breath and tried to relax into his sculpted body.

"Let's see if I can jar your memory bank," Hawke swayed with me in his arms. "Do you remember helping me refinish this old place before we got married?"

Today had already been a revelation of my past, but as I tried to comprehend his question, "I did what?"

"You grew up under the eye of a well-known and reputable carpenter."

"I did?"

"You're a very handy lady thanks to your Uncle Joe." Hawke did it again. The wink of a smoldering eye and a wanting grin. My imagination shutdown on the possibilities of what he might want by his particular expression.

"I have an Uncle Joe?"

"Your Aunt and Uncle raised you. I've got some good stories later for you."

Lost for words, my mouth opened and closed several times. I didn't know what to say. But the questions mounted inside of me. I had an Uncle who taught me carpentry work. Hawke claims I helped him refinish our beautiful home. What else would I discover today?

"Come on, let's get you inside." Easily I let myself hold his hand as we walked up the paved driveway to the back of the house.

As we rounded the corner of the house the backyard view unfolded itself to me. The girls had a giant wooden swing set complete with double slides and an observation deck, and covered sandbox. Attached to the back of the house, a two tier wooden deck with plenty of blooming plants. On the first level, a complete outdoor covered barbeque with a granite topped island for picnic dinning. Several pieces of well weathered outdoor furniture were scattered over the rest of the deck. In the back corner of the yard, another small flower garden surrounded a beautiful two seated wooden swing. Even the clothes line off the right side of the deck had little flowers planted beside both poles.

Lost in the beauty of my own home, I found myself being scooped up in Hawke's arms, "What are you doing?" I yelped in surprise.

"Welcome home Dove." As Hawke carried me over the threshold, he jostled my body lightly in his arms. Pulled tightly into his chest, I swear I could feel every muscle ripple under his t-shirt.

Before I had time to panic over being in Hawke's arms, I laid eyes on the first room in the house. The kitchen was definitely the hub of this home.

"Wow" was all I could blurt out. "My kitchen?"

"Your kitchen, it's the command center of our home." He sat me down on my feet as gently as he'd picked me up. "You call it your go to place of comfort."

"I can see why." In front of me, a spectacular, well designed kitchen that could've been straight out of a magazine. My view nearly had me forgetting that my hands rested idol on his chest. The possibility of letting go of Hawke didn't even enter my mind. "Did you refinish the kitchen?" Hawke turned me in a semi-circle and centered me in front of his body and let his fingers knead into my waistline.

"Are you kidding?" He smirked, "Your kitchen became a battleground while we were working. Had several heated conversations over what you needed. Finally, you tossed my ass out and recruited your Uncle to finish it."

"Why would I do something like that?" I glanced over my shoulder to find Hawke grinning.

"Being the person who can look at a chunk of raw meat, then create a dish to die for out of it, I'd say you had the upper hand on the needs for the kitchen."

"So I take it, I'm pretty persuasive with a hammer."

"You are. Wish your Uncle was still alive to help me explain some of this to you. Great guy. I'll fill you in later about your side of the family."

Still wrapped snuggly in Hawke's draping arms, he wasn't about to hide the fact that physical contact was an important part of our relationship. I let my tense body soften as I examined the kitchen with my eyes.

Light oak hardwood floors were accented with deep multicolored green braded rugs. They were neatly placed in front of the stove, sink and under the old fashioned claw foot maple table. The deep forest green granite countertops had flakes of gold, bronze and black tailoring through it. Decorating the top of the counters, I found every imaginable kitchen appliance possible. All the cupboards, painted a bright white, reached to the ceiling. Some had inlays of glass, others completely open. Over the double porcelain kitchen sink an eloquent bay window with a white lace valance opened to a view of the spacious backyard and gardens.

"Hawke, this is amazing. We rebuilt this together?" He released his grip from around my waist so I could wonder freely through my kitchen.

His back turned toward me, he jotted something down on a piece of paper. "Not every room. Most of the house we did with the help of your Uncle. Here." He handed me a list of phone numbers and the portable telephone. "Thought you might like to explore on your own."

"You're leaving?" The panic teetered in my voice.

"Yes. I've got to get back to the shop. I'm only fifteen minutes away. These day's I man the office. I won't be out on any of the all-day charters for a while. You've got everyone's phone numbers there."

I scanned over his note, "Jane, Maude, the shop, your cell. Do you have to go?" This time the panic twisted in my voice.

"Yes. You'll be fine. Maude's stopping by a little later to check on you. I won't be gone long."

"Good. That makes me feel better." It was useless to even try to hide my fear from him.

Hawke leaned his long hard body back against the countertop and grinned as I curiously wondered through the kitchen opening and closing cabinet doors.

"Remind me, what is it you do again?" I laid the paper filled with phone numbers and the phone on the table and looked at him inquisitively.

"My job description?"

"Yes. I know I'm a cook at Maude's diner. And I remember you saying something about working in the outdoors?"

"Self-employed. L.H.F., Inc. Fishing Charters and Guided Hunts." By the grin on his mug, he knew he'd caught me off guard.

"So you hunt and fish for a living?" I cocked my head to the side and raised an eyebrow of question.

Hawke seemed amused by my antics. "Yes, I hunt and fish for a living."

"The L.H.F. code for?" I questioned.

"Stands for Lance, Hawke and Fred. We started our own charter business right out of high school. As it grew, so did the need for guided hunts. The fishing around these parts is best in the spring and summer. Most of the hunting, my specialty, is done in the fall, winter, and early spring. Pretty much year round employment."

"Hunting and fishing? You really kill things for a living?" My curiously puzzled expression seemed to strike a nerve with him.

Hawke's eyes narrowed, his lips tied into a smirk as he smoothly answered me. "It's a pretty fine living Dove. I've kept you very comfortable for the past ten years." His eyes scanned over me from head to toe. "I basically get to do what I want, when I want."

With the sarcasm hinging in his voice, I probed him with another question. "Was I not a big fan of this hunting and fishing business?"

"You were…you tolerated my work, most of the time."

"Tolerated?" I felt the tension in his voice. "What do you mean by tolerated?"

"I was gone a lot. Be up in the mountains for a good three to four weeks at a time. You," he cleared his throat, "didn't like it when I was gone for so long. You," he glanced toward the window not wanting to really tell me what was on his mind, "you hated it."

"I see." My nerves already frayed and Hawke's sudden seriousness on our marriage had me seeing him in a totally different character. I'd become used to the rugged but gentle man I'd woken up to over a month ago. "Is there something you're not telling me? About us?"

"Dove, this last year wasn't one of our best. We fought a lot." He waited for some kind of emotion, a reaction, any kind of response from me. When his jaw tightened, the tension in his eyes didn't leave. He exhaled a rough sigh and crossed his arms over his chest. "My line of work, it caused a nasty riff between us from time to time." Hawke's answer, direct to the point. More direct than he'd ever been with me. But was he telling me everything?

"Oh." The reaction he wanted from me didn't surface. "Well there's a memory that didn't "pop" into my brain." Had Hawke been checking to see if our conversation struck a chord with me? It never appeared. I couldn't say his change in moods didn't intimidate me, but it left me with questions for another day. "Now that I'm home," he met the worry in my eyes, "are you going to be gone for weeks at a time?"

"No, you're my top priority these days. After you're settled in and comfortable, I'll go back to the all-day fishing charters. Do a little of my own personal hunting."

"Good to know." As quickly as the tension filled subject appeared, it disappeared. "Everything is so girly around here."

"Ever try living with three women?" His body relaxed thankful for the change in conversation. "The three of you won out. I've been sentenced to the basement for all my 'manly' things."

"Manly things? What are you hiding in the basement?"

"A museum of taxidermy animals. Several bears, deer, elk, mountain goats, fish, even a bob cat or two."

"You've got walls of stuffed animals down there?" I asked, not really sure what to think.

"Yep, goes with the line of work. You'd get a little squeamish when you got the nerve to visit me down there."

"Really? I'll make a note to stay out of the man cave." I let a more relaxed giggle slip out.

"You don't have to." His flirtatious smile caught me off guard, "You'd get the girls to bed and enjoyed sneaking…"

"Enjoy what?" I jumped in before he could finish, "I enjoyed looking at all your dead animals hanging on the walls?" My words kept stumbling from my mouth. I knew what he meant, I just wasn't ready to hear it.

"Dove," His hands massaged the tension in my shoulder, "my basement office, it's another place where I could get you alone."

"Really," Hawke kept kneading my shoulders, "not sure I'm ready for…"

"Not to worry, all those eyes watching, they'll never tell anyone what we did on the pool table."

"Pool table? We have a pool table?" Lightly, I fell back into him resting my weary mind on his supportive body, "Hawke, I'm…I'm sorry. I wish I could say I remember…really, on the pool table?"

"Mmm hmm," his massive arms supported my entire body, "top of my desk too."

"You're not kidding are you?" I could see the red tint of blush washing over my hands as I padded my fingers along his arms. I didn't need a mirror to know my face was double in the color scarlet. There was no way soon I'd be recovering from this conversation.

"Like I said Dove, we'll take everything nice and slow…including the pool table." As if someone flipped a switch in Hawke, "Now listen. I've got to get down to the shop. I'm only fifteen short minutes away. Call me if you need anything. Maude said she be here around noon."

"What time will the girls be home?" Thankful for yet another switch in conversation, I followed his lead.

"Three-thirty." He checked over his cell phone, "What a racket trying to get them to school this morning. With you coming home today, I couldn't keep them in line. Surprised they didn't cook up some plan to get out of going." He chuckled at his hectic morning experience with the preteen beauties. "You call me for anything. I don't care what it is. You call me. Understand?"

"Understand." I grinned in agreement.

"Love ya white dove." Smack on the lips, Hawke kissed me and walked out the door. "Be back around five."

From the window of the backdoor, I watched Hawke happily walk to his truck with a smile that beamed practically to the sky.

"He just said I love you." Dazed, even dizzy, I sat myself down in an empty chair at the kitchen table. Hawke had made it clear on our physical closeness and his need to touch me. Unfortunately for me, his touch, no matter how gentle, sent me into a rigid stiffness. I hoped to overcome that fear soon.

I chuckled out loud at my own insecurities, "Well, guess it will be interesting getting to know my husband again." With that thought finished, I started to reexamine the kitchen. Thanks to Hawke filling in a few blank spots for me, not only was I pretty darn handy with a hammer, but I was an impressive cook.

No time like the present, I left my spot at the kitchen table and headed right for the pantry doors. Fully stocked, that didn't surprise me. In alphabetical order you name the spice or herb, I had it organized on the shelves. In a long row of bottom cupboards, I found an array of pots, pans, skillets, and an assortment of baking dishes. As I picked up one of the everyday dinner dishes, it brought me to a startling halt. Not what I expected to see, all the dinner plates, salad plates, bowls, cups, even the serving dishes had the faces of several wild animals on them. To my discovery, a wolf, elk, moose, even an Eagle soaring above the backdrop of mountains stared back at me. "This is kind of out of place in a kitchen like this. Where to next?" I returned the plate and went to see what else I could find.

Under an oval arched doorway, I stepped back in time to a Victorian style dining room. An antique cherry table covered with a white lace tablecloth along with matching chairs complimented the detailed hand carved buffet and china hutch. A fast peek inside the china hutch I found several pieces of stemware. "Look at this," I removed a plate covered in a delicate rose pattern, "Bavaria, I even have real china." As gently as I removed the piece, I replaced it and closed the glass door of the hutch. Placed on the buffet an assortment of wedding photos, several of just Hawke and I. Instantly, I recognized Aunt Maude, but not the couple standing next to me, "Wonder if this is my Aunt and Uncle Hawke mentioned?"

Hardwood floors flowed throughout the entire downstairs as I followed them into the living room. "Comfortable room," I mentioned out loud to the well-loved and lived-in room. An over stuffed brown leather sofa, loveseat, and a chair all squared around a wooden coffee table. An oval sized rug with Native American designs in reds, blacks, and browns covered most of the rustic wood floor. On the off white painted walls I found school photos of the girls and candid shots of the family. In the back corner of the living room, a roll top oak desk housed a computer and printer. Paperwork littered all over the top of it. We had our own media center in the living room. Surrounding the flat screen television centered in the middle of the wall, two massive deer heads posed as bookends. "Guess Comet and Vixen escaped the man cave." I even touched the now non-living deer heads. Under the well guarded TV, a stereo system sat on an oblong cabinet with glass doors and ample storage drawers. Inside, the cabinet had been filled with all types of movies and music.

"My music." I rummage through the CD's, "They played all these for me when I was in the hospital." Music, another thing that jarred my memory back to life. I knew every piece and artist that had been stored in the cabinet. I flipped the stereo on to a station playing jazz music and continued to explore my spacious home.

The last room on the first floor, tucked back away from the living room looked to be the girl's playroom. Filled practically to the ceiling with computer gadgets, videos, dolls, board games and girl stuff for two preteens.

I found myself standing at the base of a handcrafted oak staircase. The spiraling hand rails at the bottom opened half into the living room and half into the entrance of the kitchen. A side hall by the kitchen must have been the pathway to Hawke's man cave. I opted not to visit it and wandered up the polished staircase.

At the top of the landing, I found the bathroom, something that would come in handy. Making myself at home, I opened every cupboard door on the vanity to find the usual toothbrushes, toothpaste, and over the counter medications. The drawers under the vanity were filled to maximum with lotions, shampoos, soaps, hair clips, ribbons, bows, barrettes and my makeup. In the medicine cabinet, Hawke did have one shelve for himself. Poor guy, he really was out numbered here.

Each of the girls had their own room. Fancy hand painted name plates gave away whose room was whose. Emma's room decked out in shades of sunshine yellow and purples. Amelia's room, nothing but pink, from the walls to the bedspread, to the carpeting.

A third bedroom on the opposite side of Emma's served as a guest bedroom. A double bed with a blue chenille bedspread, a period dated dressing table and a comfortable looking rocking chair.

At the end of the hall, one last door stood ajar. With my hand resting on the glass doorknob, "This must be our bedroom." An anxious sigh escaped me as I pushed the polished oak door open and took in the view of the bedroom I shared with my husband. Another picture perfect room, it seemed as if no one, not even Hawke had slept in here during my absence. Not one single item out of place. A soft shade of mauve accented the flowery wall paper trim along the top of the walls. A glossy deep cherry chair rail separated the soft mauve and deep burgundy walls. Long flowing lace curtains draped the two floor length windows that faced out to the street. On each side of the room were matching light oak dressers, one mine and the other definitely Hawke's. It was the only masculine item to be found in our picture perfect bedroom. The romantic four poster king sized bed had lacey crochet curtains drawn back in a "V" that matched the cream colored canopy. Skirting around the bottom of the antique cherry bed a hand crochet dust ruffle matched the deep plum color quilted comforter. Several pink, cream, and sage green paisley printed throw pillows had been neatly arranged at the top of the bed. My fingers ran over the neatly made bed, I couldn't image someone as rough and tough as my husband sleeping under this canopy of romance. Another thought crossed my mind, not only would he be sleeping here, but he expected me to be sleeping next to him in our dreamy, cozy bed.

Startled by the ringing of the telephone on the night stand, I nearly jumped out of my own skin. Skeptical of answering the phone, I stood motionless waiting for my heart rate to settle to a normal pace. Alerted by few more rings, I finally answered, "Hello."

"Dove," Hawke's smooth voice answered me. "So tell me, how's the exploring going? Anything particular strike a chord with you?"

"I'm doing pretty good. As a matter of fact, music, I mean I found all my music. Hawke, I remember the kind of music I liked." The small amount of excitement in my voice had him chuckling.

"Excellent. Dove. You've got a wide range of favorites." His familiar voice had a way of calming me. "So what room are you in?"

Hesitation clung tightly in my voice and I wasn't sure how to answer him. "Our bedroom." I could hear his sultry chuckle as I attempted to ask, "So which one of us finished the bedroom? I can't imagine you sleeping in such a girly, girly room."

"I'd sleep anywhere with you Dove." His chuckle deepened at my growing shyness toward him. "Your Uncle helped me finish it for you. Kind of a surprise wedding gift to you."

"It's really beautiful. Did you sleep in here while I was gone? Everything is in perfect place."

"No, couldn't sleep there without you. If I wasn't at the hospital with you, I sacked out on the sofa so the girls could find me. Jane came over and gave the house a good cleaning before you came home."

"That was really nice of her. Are you two back to being friendly?" I kind of snickered.

"No. She's like a damn pit bull, always biting at my ass." Hawke snorted a laugh and ended any conversation about Jane. "I'll see you around five Dove. Call me if you need anything."

"Dinner at five then." I definitely heard the pleasure in his voice as we said goodbye.

As I turned from hanging up the phone, I'd planned on examining the bed I'd be sleeping in. To my surprise, perched at the foot of the bed, the household pet's eyes focused carefully on me. "Just whom might you be?" I asked the twenty or more pound black cat with eyes of minty green, thinking I'd get an answer.

While I perched my bottom on the side of the bed, I watched the sleek, shorthaired cat perform a display of deep stretching. In pussy cat fashion, the giant animal padded softly over the bed to where I sat. "You got a name?" A vibrating purr from my new friend greeted me before the animal rammed its square head into my arm. "You're black as midnight." Demanding my full attention, I stroked the cat's beautiful coat of silky fur. "You must be my cat for the way you want to be loved." The cat rolled to its back and offered me its tummy for another round of fuzzy therapy. "Any chance you might give me your name?" I asked as the cat rolled from side to side. "I could use some company, how about exploring with me? Any details you want to share, I'd appreciate it."

With my new buddy at my heels, we opened the door hiding the huge walk in closet. Built for two, on my side, I found a wide assortment of jeans, tops, colorful sweaters, even a few stylish dresses. "I must be an overachiever at organizing. First the herb cupboard is alphabetized and look at my side of the closet." The cat, who planted his chubby body in the middle of the doorway, hung on my every word. "Look what I do to my clothes, I color coordinate them." Hawke's side of the closet, not nearly as neat and tidy as mine. He was pretty much a jean, t-shirt and flannel guy. Not one suit, but I did find a few dress shirts and three ties, only three. My outdoorsman wore nothing but casual wear.

"Okay kitty," where I moved the cat followed, "let's checkout my dresser." My six drawer dresser was next on the list to conquer. Tucked around the edge of the mirror I found several playful pictures of Hawke and me. "What's this?" I pulled at one photo that had been tucked under another. "I see why I must've kept this hidden." The picture that had been tucked away revealed a couple cuddling. Hawke wearing nothing but ripped jeans, not even a shirt, "I must really trust this man." I stared at the picture of me nearly naked and in his arms. Concealed by his deeply tanned arms, he covered my bare chest. Shocked, but not surprised, I flipped the photo over. Scribbled on the back, 'Alone at Bayside Cottage' and the date marked on it was six years ago. "Mental note to self, ask Hawke about this picture." I returned the picture of us back to its hiding place.

On the left side of the dresser, the overgrown cat perched his tubby body, "So what's in the drawer?" The cat cocked his head to the right, "Oh look my underwear. Always good to have a drawer full of clean undies." I slid open the adjacent drawer, "Bras, and look I've got a nice assortment." Two drawers of pastel colored undergarments seemed to suite my every changing mood as I continued to explore. "Earrings," I said enthusiastically to the cat as I opened a thin drawer at the top of the dresser. "Okay, buddy, one last drawer to go." When opening another drawer, nothing could have prepared me for what I found. "Oh no," my hands skimmed over the silky garments, "There's…a lot…oh my." As my fingers picked through the pretty lacey clothes, "I really had no clue," I gave the cat a scowling glare, "you could've warned me."

The top right drawer, closest to the window left me practically speechless. Neatly folded, I found an assortment of colorful lacey garments that waited to be taken out and shown off. I had to pull out each and every lacey night gown, bras with matching panties, and a few items so sheer and revealing, I actually blushed from touching them. "Don't need to guess who I wear these for." My friend, the cat, walked over the assortment of pretty things and sat right on a bra, "No, kitty, don't think it's for you to wear." The cat saved my endless nerves as he rolled over the silky garments while I refolded and placed everything back in the drawer. The one thing I kept pushed far, far out of my brain…Hawke, me, and sex. I glanced over to the beautiful canopy bed as I placed the last nightgown away. The 'goose bumps' on my arms flared as I realized, Hawke and I had shared a very deep and intimate relationship before my accident. "Explains his affection toward me, it had to been mutual." I felt the butterflies turning in my stomach as I grinned at the cat and closed the last dresser drawer. "Guess I'll deal with this if and when it pops up." In my mind, I hoped it'd be much later.

"Well kitty, I think I've seen everything in the house, all but Hawke's man cave. Don't really want to go to the basement just yet." The furry ball of black circled around my legs, "How about we go visit the kitchen." Kitty's heavy padded footsteps trailed behind me as we descended down the steps and into the kitchen. "You know kitty," automatically I opened the cupboard where the cat food was kept, "The kitchen, it's consoling, you know comfortable." I filled the hungry cat's dish with dry cat food, "it really feels like home when I'm here in the kitchen."

Out of habit, I guess, I started planning dinner. I scanned the pantry and refrigerator. As I lined up chicken, sour cream, onions, butter, and a can of chicken broth another memory woke up. A recipe flowed from my brain to my hands and I began to create a meal. Everything about being in my kitchen felt natural, homey. I'd impressed myself with the fast wit to remember a recipe without looking it up.

On low heat the onions caramelized in the sizzling butter. I canvassed the spice cupboard in need of paprika. Of course I found paprika after the onion powder and before rosemary, because I had nothing that started with a "Q." After stirring in a large helping of Hungarian paprika, I placed the fresh chicken breast in the mixture. On low heat I let it simmer while I prepared the egg dumplings. Flour, eggs, a pinch or two of salt, extra paprika and milk, then I mixed the dough to the right thickness. By the spoonful, I dropped the egg dumpling mix into the boiling hot water. Not missing a step on my paperless recipe, I finished the chicken. Tenderly simmered, I removed the chicken breast from the skillet and added the chicken broth. On high heat, I added a flour and water mix for gravy. As it bubbled into gravy I added a pint of sour cream. The aroma of freshly made Chicken Paprika filled the entire kitchen. Shredded chicken and egg dumplings filled the gravy mixture in the heavy cast iron skillet.

Delighted with my memory of cooking, I wanted to share it with Hawke, but a soft knocking on the backdoor stopped me. He had said Aunt Maude planned on stopping by this afternoon. Cautiously, I peeked out the kitchen window. Patiently waiting at the backdoor, I found the soft faced lady who'd spent so many hours at my bedside.

Chapter 14 - An Afternoon With Aunt Maude

The backdoor swung wide as I opened it, "You're home." Aunt Maude beamed up at me. "Good God I thought this day would never get here. You're finally home, Dove." Another shout of happiness squealed from Maude as she wrestled me into a hug. Her hands pinched tightly into my arms as she pushed me back a step, "You're home." Then with all her might, she yanked me into another giant hug. "Oh dear, did I hurt you? Is everything healed? How's the head?" She ruffled my curly hair and squeezed the laughter right out of me. "Let me look at you." Again, she grabbed me by the shoulders and inspected me up and down, even turned me around once. "You're as good as new. You're radiant. You even glow, Dove." In the short time Aunt Maude gave me 'the look over' she hadn't even made it through the backdoor.

"That smell," like a bloodhound on a scent, Aunt Maude sniffed the aroma from the kitchen. "I know that smell." With one hand she pushed me out of the doorway and headed directly to the dish on the stove. "Oh my heavens. Oh my stars. You're making your signature dish. The smell," she inhaled deeply, "it's wonderful. So delightful."

"My what?" She ignored my question as I shut the door and hurried over to her and the simmering dish on the stove.

"Your Chicken Paprika, sweetie," Excitedly she answered me in awe. "Weekly special at the diner you know. None of us can duplicate your recipe. We try, but it just can't be done."

Skeptically, I joined her by the bubbling sensation on the stove and hoped she'd fill me in on some missing puzzle pieces.

"Spoon," she held her hand out like a surgeon waiting for an instrument, so I handed over the spoon. Before she dipped the table sized spoon in, she waved the steam of the simmering dish toward her and inhaled. "Ah, very good, very good."

Silver spoon in hand, she scooped up a large helping of the mix. As the flavorful dish coated her tongue, the corners of her mouth turned up into a broad smile.

"How is it?" To me it tasted great, but I waited for the expert's opinion.

"Ah, that's my girl. The cooking, you never lost your love for cooking. Thank the Gods above that this memory wasn't stolen from you." Aunt Maude folded her hands together as if she was praying and blew a kiss up at the ceiling. She smiled again at me and took several more samples of the simmering dish. "Dove, honey, this is unbelievable. I don't know what you do to it, but it makes my taste buds dance. Does Hawke know your making it? It's one of his favorites." Within the first ten minutes of Aunt Maude's visit, I don't think I managed to get a full sentence in. "You learned to cook on the apron strings of your Aunt Phyllis."

"So that's where it came from. Thanks for answering that for me."

"Sit. Sit." In her motherly way she tugged at my arm to join her at the kitchen table. "Tell me how you're doing. First day home, finding everything okay?"

"I managed to explore the entire house, all but Hawke's 'man cave' in the basement." I giggled as we sat down at the table together. "Things, it's still so new, hard to wrap my mind around everything."

"Hawke's down at the shop?" She asked. "You okay staying here by yourself? You should've called me, I'd been over sooner."

Her sweet smile easily put me at ease, "Hawke dropped me off a few hours ago. Gave me time to explore, you know, hopefully get a feel for my old life. The kitchen, I feel comfortable hanging out right here." I glanced over my kitchen that could've been a layout for some home magazine.

"Good, glad to hear that. See he left you everyone's number." She pointed to the list of names I'd left on the table.

"He did. Recopied the list and posted it next to the phone by the bed even."

The mystery cat appeared out of nowhere. The ruler of the house perched itself on an empty kitchen chair and glared at us.

"Aunt Maude," I pointed to the furry creature with glowing minty eyes, "The cat, he's huge. Well I assume he's a he." Knowing he was the topic of conversation, the cat twitched an ear. "What's the cat's name?"

"He's a he alright, big ole baby named Ebony." She chuckled and wiggled a warning finger at him.

"Ebony," I mentioned the cats name and the vibrating purrs flooded from him, "friendly guy. Follows me everywhere." I swear the cat just winked at me.

"Damn thing is in love with you. Fat beast worships you, don't ya?" Did the cat just scowl at Maude? "While you were laid up, he cried for you day and night. Thought he'd drive us nuts with his constant meowing. Girls finally gave him one of your shirts to sleep on." This time it was Maude who rolled her eyes at the cat.

"Really? I take it we've had him for awhile?"

"About five years. Girls found him pretty beat-up on the playground, drug his sorry ass home. And you," she pointed her pudgy finger at me this time, "you begged Hawke to keep him."

"He's not a fan of cats?"

"Hawke hates cats. Just despises them. You and the girls won him over." She chuckled as the cat yawned from boredom.

"He's a boy cat named Ebony, how did that happen?"

"Your girls named him. Thought it was fashionable." Ebony the cat rested his chin on the edge of the kitchen table as we talked.

"Maude, is the cat making goo-goo eyes at me?" Dreamy minty green eyes accompanied a soft purr as my cat tried to woo me.

"Like I said, damn thing is in love with you. Hawke walks by, thing hisses like crazy at him. Just to piss the cat off, Hawke, he'll walk by and take a swipe at him, then the fur flies. It's like a little boxing match between them." Maude had me laughing over the exaggerations of my new furry friend, Ebony.

Maude snickered at the cat and gave it a return glare. "Damn thing missed you as much as we did. So I hear you've had a few memories."

"Word travels fast in these parts." I grinned knowing she'd be the first one he'd call. "It wasn't much, not even sure if things really happened until Hawke verified it."

"Yep, yep, pretty exciting news. Sure you'll be having more as the days go on." I met Maude's motherly eyes of hope.

"Here's one I'm having trouble with. Hawke claims I helped restore this house with him and my Uncle." Conversation of picking Aunt Maude's brain was open.

"Do you remember anything about your Aunt and Uncle?" Her eyes beamed with a gleam of happiness.

"Nothing, I'm drawing a complete blank. Be right back." From the dining room, I retrieved the photo of the older couple. "I take it this would be them?" She accepted the picture frame and laughed out loud.

"Uncle Joe, what a piece of work that man was. Loved you and Phyllis like there was no tomorrow. Uncle Joe and Aunt Phyllis never had children so when they got you, their lives were complete. Not only did they think of you as their little girl, you were the son Joe never had. As hard nosed as that man could be, he proudly took you everywhere with him."

"When they got me? Aunt Maude it sounds as if they picked me out of the vegetable section at the local market." I snickered at my own joke.

"Oh my, sorry, honey," she chuckled at my silly joke. "Let me backup and start from the beginning. Your father and Joe were brothers, they even married sisters. Make a long story short, your folks left you with Joe and Phyllis when they visited some friends in California. They were out on one of those sight seeing planes," she drew in a deep breath, "it crashed and no one survived."

"How old was I?" My emotional state just bottomed out. I was left with no recollection of my own parents or my Aunt and Uncle.

"No more that four maybe five. Joe and Phyllis had been named your guardians. They took it one step further and adopted you. Dove, honey?"

With both hands, I rubbed my forehead, "So I have no family left here?"

"No, sweetie, I'm sorry they passed away a few years ago. Joe and Phyllis were both in their early eighties. Your father had been a good fifteen years younger than Joe. Everyone is gone except us." In an attempt to comfort me, she kept patting the back of my hand. "I'm sorry honey, but remember you've got us." The shock of hearing the only family I had left consisted of her, Hawke, and the girls, made my heart sink. "Let's make some coffee and I'll fill you in with some funny stories about how you and Hawke got together."

"That, I'd like to know about. Aunt Maude, I'm having a hard time connecting with him, again."

Not even looking in my direction, I saw her smile as she passed me the can of coffee, "Don't you worry, it'll happen."

"I hope so. I wish it was as simple as remembering how to use this coffee pot." One, two, three, and the coffee pot began dripping.

"Best advice I can give you...don't stress over it. Let it happen naturally."

The coffee pot perked and Aunt Maude settled into the high back wooden chair as she replayed my life for me. "You're one handy lady around a tool shed. Ole Joe, he taught you everything he knew about carpentry. When it came to rebuilding this house, you'd give Hawke a good fit if you thought it should be a certain way. Problem was, you knew more than him and well," she smiled a sassy grin, "his male ego got in the way. But got to say, with your knowledge on carpentry, you won most of the battles."

"Carpentry and cooking, what a combination. But what I really need is info on me and Hawke."

"Let's see if I can wrap your life up in a nut shell," Aunt Maude even giggled, "You started working at the diner for me when you turned sixteen. And did you ever catch Hawke's eye." Maude's smile just got bigger. "That boy was head over heels in love with you. He'd stop by every day you worked just to get of glimpse of you. Jane, she waitressed there and you and her would get the giggles every time Hawke and Fred came in. I could see the romance budding. Hawke, he kept saying he'd marry you someday."

"And, obviously, he did." I tapped the photo that held our wedding picture.

"But," Maude rolled her eyes, "Uncle Joe."

"My Uncle Joe didn't approve?"

"Not at all. Didn't want my wild nephew sniffing around his pretty girl."

"You're kidding me." I'd learned something new.

"He stopped Hawke dead in his tracks."

"Why wouldn't my Uncle let me date Hawke? He couldn't have been that bad of a guy." Again, Aunt Maude rolled her eyes in laughter, "Or was he?"

"Ole Joe, he knew Hawke well and the wild reputation that followed him."

"So I married me the bad boy."

"You did honey, but the kicker, your age." She drummed her fingers on the tabletop waiting for me to catch up with her.

"My age?" I questioned and tried to remember Hawke's age.

"Big problem for your Aunt and Uncle. You were only sixteen." She grinned, "Hawke was already twenty-one." She held up one finger at a time until she arrived at five.

"I'm five years younger than Hawke...and..." the wheels in my brain clicked, "Ha, I was jail bait." We both snorted a snickering laugh. "So what happened? How did we end up together?"

"After Joe gave him a piece of his mind about staying clear of you, Hawke let it go in one ear and out the other. When that husband of yours sets his mind to something, he'll do everything in his power to make it happen. He started showing up everyday you were scheduled at the diner."

"How'd he know what days I worked?"

Maude laughed, "He had full access to the diner, would memorize your schedule when you weren't around."

"Maude, it sounds like he was stalking me."

"In a loving way. Filled with determination to win your heart. He'd bring you flowers. Little gifts like earrings. When you turned seventeen your Uncle allowed him to come for Sunday dinner."

"Sunday dinner?" Wish that memory would've flashed into view.

"And he had to go to church with you or he couldn't come to dinner."

"That's a pure riot. I can't believe he did all this. There's got to be more to this. What happened when I turned eighteen?"

"The summer you turned eighteen, Hawke turned up on your doorstep with theater tickets. From that day on there wasn't much your Uncle could do. You were finally of legal age."

"Theater tickets...Maude," I stared her right in the eyes, "the show he took me to...a musical?"

"Yes, it was but..." Her brown eyes held an edge of hope.

"Cats, the musical was it Cats?"

"See Dove, if you just free your mind, it will come back to you." Impressed with my discovery, Maude beamed, "For as much as that man hates felines, he did take you to see Cats"

"My notebook," I flipped open the generic looking tablet and wrote another memory in it. "This is so frustrating. All I get is just the slightest of hints of my life."

"Dove, it will all come together. Ready for more?"

"More" my eyes must have brightened like flickering candles, "there's more?"

"Of course there's more." She gave me wink, "When you turned nineteen," she laughed out loud, "life changed. You had a ring on your finger and the two of you were inseparable." Glasses in hand, Maude dabbed the tears of laughter from her eyes with a tissue.

"From the way you're laughing...what aren't you telling me?"

"Honey, I've got a list longer than my right arm of the shenanigans you and him got into. Kept your Uncle up nights with worry. After the commotion of you two getting engaged died down, you bought this place as a fixer-upper. Keep ya busy and right where your Uncle Joe could keep an eye on things."

"You mean Hawke?" I suggested.

"Poor Joe, he wasn't too sure about handing you over to Hawke at such a young age. Here you were an engaged young woman, full time job at the diner, fixing this," she rolled her eyes around the kitchen, "this place up and ole Joe insisted you have a midnight curfew."

"Are you kidding me? Why? You're still laughing. Aunt Maude what trouble did Hawke and I get into?"

"Let's just say Hawke liked to sneak off with you and go skinny dipping. Disappear for a weekend up in the mountains with you."

"I'm still stuck on the skinny dipping part. I take it we got caught." Dumfounded, I stared at my husband's Aunt. "What else did he have me doing?" Wide eyed and wanting to know more about my old life I waited for Maude to spill it.

"Dovey, the stories I could tell you. Ask Hawke, I'm sure there's more I don't know about. But anyways," she wiped her eyes again from the laughter, "So to make sure Hawke minded his manors, old Joe strapped on his tool belt and helped with the renovation of this place."

"My Aunt and Uncle didn't trust me to be alone here, working, with Hawke?"

"No, no that wasn't it at all sweetie. The problem," she grinned, "Hawke couldn't keep his hands off you." Maude's carefree laughter turned serious, "See, Hawke never stayed attached long to any one person until you came along. You're the magic in him. I'm sure you've noticed already he can't get enough of you, Dove."

"I've noticed, Aunt Maude. I've really noticed." There was no hiding behind my fading smile the dilemma of me reconnecting with Hawke. "Why the fuss over him and I being alone? We were engaged." I switched out of the touchy-feely subject I didn't want to dwell on.

"Yes, yes, you were. Just satisfied Joe that he'd be able to keep an eye on you two, let him sleep at night." She chuckled.

"That's crazy. All this worry over the two of us being alone."

"You have to remember honey, to Joe and Phyllis you'd always been their little girl." As she stirred her coffee, Aunt Maude's smile grew. "Joe figured that if he was over here working, nothing was going to happen to you." Maude gave me a quick wink and we both started laughing. "They might not have been your parents, but Joe and Phyllis loved you."

"Please tell me I didn't give them a reason to be so protective."

"Not you as much as Hawke. After the two of you got together, Hawke's wildness just disappeared. Totally devoted and committed to you, Dove."

"I didn't know I had that kind of power." I giggled, but realized how right she was.

"Then the month after your twentieth birthday you two were married. Nothing too fancy. Just a nice service at the Ocean View Chapel. Neither one of you were big into the huge wedding scene. Jane and Fred stood up for you. And then we had a little reception at the diner."

"I do remember seeing the photo album of our wedding. My gown was just gorgeous."

"You wore Hawke's mother's wedding dress. It fit you like a glove. Seemed to be made just for the two of you."

"I wish I could remember all of this." I moped as Maude patted the back of my hand again and continued.

"You two weren't even married six months when my niece, Hawke's sister, Pearl and her husband Carl, were killed in a car accident. You and Hawke became instant parents. At the young age of twenty, a new bride, you had two babies to take care of that weren't even yours. Your lives were turned upside down and you both were running in a million directions. Emma just turned two and Amelia barely a year old. The boys' business picked up like a fast brewing storm. Hawke was either guiding hunts or out on the charters. That left you and the girls all alone."

"How in the world did we get through?" A second cup of coffee poured, I eagerly listened for more details of my life.

"Had lots of help. Your Aunt and Uncle, huge help." Aunt Maude tapped a polished nail on the picture frame in front of her. "They'd keep the girls while you worked the early morning and lunch shift. Tell you, we all enjoyed being instant grandparents to the girls. You're a wonderful mom to those two girls, they love you. Their hearts were smashed when all this happened to you."

"Every scenario thrown at us at once, I'm amazed our marriage survived."

Aunt Maude reached for the coffee pot, "You two are in it for the long haul, don't think anything or anyone could separate you. I'm sure Hawke has a few stories of his own about your Aunt and Uncle. Good people, but they made him tow the line. Ask him to tell you about the time Joe smacked him up along side the head. Sent him to the ER for handful of stitches. In a round about way, the story is funny." She chuckled and reached for the sugar bowl. "You got any of that fancy creamer?"

My mouth hung wide open as Maude's laughter filled the kitchen, "Creamer, I'll check. I appreciate all the details on me and Hawke." I rummaged around the refrigerator, "Found it. Amaretto flavor okay?"

"Perfect. Just so you know, you keep this stocked." I swear she poured half the sweet tasting creamer into her coffee. "You've got worry in your eyes, what is it?" She pushed the nearly empty container of creamer over to me.

I followed Aunt Maude's lead and emptied the remainder of the Amaretto creamer into my cup. "My memory wiped cleaned. So many things I can't remember, but things like cooking and music, I remember. My biggest fear," I played with my cup of coffee, "my memory of Hawke and me not returning."

"Oh honey, everything is going to be fine. You've already started to fit back into how life was. One day of devastation could take months to repair. Your body's healed, just a little longer for your mind to regain lost ground."

"I guess I'm asking too much of myself for wanting everything back right now." I met Maude's soft eyes of gentleness, "I want to know my husband again."

"You will, Dove. He'd wait for you until the end of time." She squeezed my hand, "Hawke was devastated, blamed himself for this happening to you. We could barely console him at times. The roughest, those first few weeks in the hospital. No one knew if you'd come back to us."

"The day I woke, it's still a little sketchy for me. I remember parts of the day, but not much." I brushed a stray hair from my eyes and smiled at Aunt Maude.

"And you woke up on my watch. Always will remember that day. Those beautiful blue eyes finding me. You remember?" From across the table, Aunt Maude held my hands.

"My vision was blurry, but you were the first person I saw. I heard you running from the room calling Hawke. I don't remember much about that day. The fog in my head, the pain medication, but I do remember seeing Hawke standing in the door way. His radiant smile, his hair, the smile he gave me." At this moment, I felt as if a warm hug just wrapped around me. Not like that day in the hospital, scared and filled with fear at not knowing anyone.

"We were all happy, Dove." She stopped to wipe away her smiling tears. "You're home, he's got you back. That spark of passion for you is burning in his eyes. See it in yours too. Life is good again, Dove. You need to rest honey, you're looking tired."

"No, no, I'm good Aunt Maude." I couldn't help the sign of helplessness, "I've missed so much. I don't know where to start or better yet, where I left off." Before Aunt Maude could answer me, I changed the subject. "Tell me about the girls. They'll be home at 3:30 from school."

"Emma and Amelia. Wonderful girls you've raised, but what a handful. Emma, all of eleven and Amelia is a solid ten. You might be their Aunt, but you're the mother they never got to know. Girls depend on you for everything. Poor kids, they took it hard when all this happened. Hawke wouldn't let them see you until the day you woke up. Jane and I took care of them as best we could, but it wasn't the same. Jane, she wrote you some notes on school schedules and a few other important things you might need to know."

"Now, Amelia, a little shy, she's extremely attached to you. Both girls cling to you. Emma, she's Hawke's little buddy. She'll go out on the charters fishing with him more than Amelia. High spirited like her Uncle. You'd never know those girls were your nieces. So much like the both of you, you've dedicated your life to those little ladies."

"I must have gotten the "mom" gene from you and my Aunt Phyllis."

"Believe you did, Dove." She smiled and sipped the last drop of her creamy coffee. "Can't wait to get you back at the diner. When you're ready, Dove. Know a lot of folks who've been pulling for you. Everyday someone would ask about you. Now, I can tell them pretty soon my main cook will be back." A smile of pride glossed over Aunt Maude's lips.

The roar of a noisy school bus interrupted my afternoon visit with Aunt Maude. Three thirty in the afternoon had magically appeared on the dot. The backdoor flung open with two excited screaming little girls. They nearly knocked me off my chair with their abundant hugs and kisses. The joyful duo sent Aunt Maude off into a tizzy as she broke into a long, but unheard, lecture about being careful of my fragile body. The trio of me and my clinging girls traveled into the living room while Aunt Maude gave up trying to peel them from my side. The old leather sofa groaned out a creak as the girls snuggled closer to me practically sitting on my lap.

"I've got to finish my errands before tomorrow gets here." Aunt Maude leaned over to kiss us goodbye. "Now remember Dove, if Hawke gets out of line, call me. Good luck with these two." She playfully tapped the girls on the nose. "Behave yourselves."

"Thank you, Aunt Maude, for everything. You've helped with so much." I found the warm motherly twinkle glowing in her eyes as she laughed heartily at the three of us.

"Stay comfortable with the girls, I'll let myself out. I'm so happy you're home, sweetie." Another round of kisses plastered on our forehead this time, and she went on her way. Aunt Maude was a force to be reckoned with, she ran a tight ship, and spoke her mind, but knew how to enjoy life. With a wink of her eye, she made sure I knew how much she loved me.

Preteen hands clung to mine as the girls snuggled in closer. The sweet smell of strawberry shampoo lingered in their ponytailed hair. In our quiet moment of snuggling, a flood of senses returned to me. I closed my eyes just to capture and enjoy the familiar sensation when I heard the softest giggling. I peeked at Amelia, then at Emma and the giggling session grew louder. Charged with the energy of knowing I'd be here when they got home, they shared their entire school day with me.

Four chimes rang from the grandfather clock in the living room corner. "Four o'clock already? Uncle Hawke will be home soon. Who has homework to finish?"

"Me, Social Studies," Amelia announced.

"Math and two pages of science for me," Emma added.

"Good, come keep me company in the kitchen while I finish dinner." Unable to release me, my giggling girls tagged along to the hub of our house.

"Aunt Dovey, does you hand still hurt?" Amelia picked at the special bandage around my left hand.

"Not as bad as it did. I just have to be careful for a little while longer."

"You made the dish," Emma's long sleek black ponytail bounced as she bobbed over to the stove. "The chicken peppy dish."

"I take it this is a standing favorite." I turned the burner to simmer under the skillet. "How about the homework?"

Pink and purple backpacks were dumped over the kitchen table while I put the last touches on my 'signature dish.'

In the kitchen, creating gourmet dishes, along with two beautiful pixies underfoot, felt so comfortable to me. But hanging at the back of my mind, I felt as if something was missing. A shadow of darkness tried to swallow me as I worked in my designer kitchen. A piece of my puzzled brain still hadn't been locked into place. Homework finished and a once over check by me, the girls fussed over who would set the table. Just hearing them babble on made my dark cloud disburse and a natural warm feeling of belonging replaced my doubts.

"Aunt Dovey, I hear Uncle Hawke's truck." Emma barreled out the backdoor with Amelia clipping on her heels.

Parked in the driveway, the chariot that brought me home from the hospital a few hours ago. In front of the kitchen sink I spied on Hawke from the open window. He didn't even get the truck door closed before the giggling beauties cheerfully surrounded him in hugs. He patiently absorbed every detail from the team of chatter boxes.

From my window view, I enjoyed the full view of my husband. The evening sunlight accented his thick black hair that skimmed beneath his shoulders. His smile pulled at my heart. Hawke's eyes captivated me and kept me drawn to him. All alone in the kitchen, only I heard my gasp of excitement tangled with a slight rush of visible nerves slip out as I noted how much more I need to learn about him. He hadn't even made it into the house and the fluttering of butterfly wings tumbled in my stomach from watching him in the yard with the girls.

An amazing picture unfolded in the backyard, truly this was my family. I didn't want to wake up from my living dream of happiness. I could hear the girls giggling and telling him about school and coming home to find me here. It wasn't a dream. This was real and I was a part of it.

"Aunt Dovey, look you got flowers." Amelia shouted as she shoved a bouquet of wild flowers at me.

Nearly knocked away from the sink, Emma dove into the cupboard below. I've got the vase."

"Thank you." Before I could even pull the cellophane from the bouquet, Amelia retrieved the flowers back out of my hands. "What are you doing?"

"Arranging them for you." Wide brown eyes smiled up at me.

"Of course." The fluttering in my stomach kicked into overdrive as I smiled at Hawke. No way could I hide my nervousness around him. For support, I borrowed the side of the sink as I watched him kick off his well worn snakeskin boots and hang his jean jacket behind the door.

"You look right at home again, Dove. How was the day?" His relaxed smile made my nervous flutter worse.

Curiously, I watched him as he placed a pack of cigarettes on the top shelve of the cupboard along side a fancy tin box of cigars. "Interesting to say the least. You didn't tell me we had a cat. I take it he's pretty much my pet." I caught the sarcastic roll of his eyes.

"Now that you're home, damn thing might stop hollering for you." The cat, who held on every word, had been perched on the edge of the kitchen counter glaring at Hawke, "Get you fuzzy ass off the counter." He swatted the table and Ebony ran for cover. "Maude come by?" He turned his surly grin on me.

"She did. I found out a lot about me. Got a recap on the basics, how we met, dating, married." Hawke laughed, I'm sure wondering what Maude had filled my head with. "I got a little insight on my Aunt Phyllis and Uncle Joe. Guess you'll need to fill in the details of them for me. And, what's this about getting wacked and stitches?"

A grinned cracked on his lips, "Your Uncle Joe, what a piece of work. Great man, though, loved him. And do I ever have tales to tell you about them and you."

"You'll have to fill me in on my curfew." Hawke's eye catching smile caught me off guard as I moved closer to the stove. His ogling session over me had my heart beating with wonder. He truly enjoyed the unspoken moment of my jittery nerves.

I felt it, the warmth flushed over my cheeks and I'm sure Hawke saw it. Quickly, I turned my back to him and pretended to check the simmering dish on the stove. Silently, he slipped behind me as I stirred the bubbling chicken dish. His chest brushed lighting against my tensed back. His long fingers played on my waistline, kneading gently. A breath of bundled nervous slipped from me when Hawke's right hand circled around my stomach. I hoped he couldn't feel the rapid butterflies batting their wings in my stomach. His warm breath tingled on my bare neck. He sent my heart skipping into a thousand beats as I felt his tender lips slowly kissing my neck. With my obvious staggered breathing, I closed my eyes as he continued to kiss my neck. The spoon I'd been stirring the chicken dish with dropped from my trembling hand and splattered over the stove with a loud clunk. I jumped at the sound and knocked myself slightly off balance and conveniently right into his arms that had gathered around me. A rumbling chuckle came from deep inside his chest as he rubbed his cheek on my neck.

Hawke's arms steadied me from falling as I barely whispered, "Sorry."

"I've got all the time you need to get used to me again, Dove." His sultry voice whispered in my ear as his fingers played deeper into my waist.

"I'm trying." My lump of fear was swallowed as I exhaled a deep trembling sigh and tried to relax in his arms.

Emma's voice broke the tense air from behind us, "Is dinner ready yet?"

Momentarily, I had been saved by a child's voice. Potholders covered my trembling hands as I went to pick the bubbling skillet of chicken paprika up.

"Better let me take this Dove." Hawke kissed my scarlet cheek as he carried dinner to the table.

"You sit here, Aunt Dovey." Emma pulled the chair out across the table from Hawke for me. A hush fell over the kitchen as the clanging of silverware to glass dishes could be heard while we filled our plates.

After several bites of the main course, Hawke wiggled his fork at me, "Dove, this is amazing. Memory or did you need the recipe?"

"All by memory." A contented smile eased from him to me.

"This is unbelievable," he savored another bite, "Glad your memory bank of cooking didn't get short circuited."

"Felt natural to be back in the kitchen." I tossed him a casual smile.

"You have this on when Maude showed up?"

"I'd just put it on a slow simmer when she got here. You would have thought I made a pot of gold by the way she reacted." I grinned back at him while enjoying my latest master piece.

Hawke glanced up from his plate, "Dove, you're using your left hand?"

I stopped eating and dangled my fork from my fingers tips. "I think all that therapy really helped." But I was slightly puzzled by all the questioning eyes that looked at me.

"Aunt Dovey you always used your right hand." Amelia pointed out to me.

"Really? I was right handed before the accident? That's really odd that I favor my left hand now." I shrugged my shoulders at Hawke and attempted to twirl my fork through my fingers. "I'll have to put this in my notebook. Please remind me to mention that to Dr. Thornton on my next visit."

"You keeping a list of things you remember?" Hawke asked as he heaped another helping of chicken on his plate.

"Had another one when Maude was here."

"And," In mid-bite Hawke waited for me to tell more.

"First date." The cat circled around my legs as Hawke's eyes met mine, "You took me to the theater."

"Right," he nearly dropped his fork, "but do you remember what we saw?"

"Cats," and Ebony hopped onto my lap. "Speaking of one." I petted the cat and returned him to the floor. "Maude said something about me turning eighteen and you on the doorstep with theater tickets."

With relief he eased back in the kitchen chair, "She's absolutely right."

"Kind of interesting putting my puzzle pieces back together don't you think?"

Hawke arched an eyebrow and flashed a smile at me, "I'm sure they'll be more pieces clicking into place before you know it."

Chatter from the girls filled our conversation as a harmonious joy floated through the air and happiness once again filled the old Victorian home.

Chapter 15 - Just the Jitter's

Nine o'clock had become the magic time to tuck two pretty little girls into bed. Bedtime snacks, bubble baths, and three stories all seemed to be second nature for me and the girls. The entire evening my little ladies showered me in their hugs, they barely had given me enough room to breath. Worry clouded their voice on the fifth and final time of saying goodnight. Emma and Amelia kept asking if I'd be here when they woke in the morning. Tears glossed their eyes and the distress in their soft voices nearly broke my heart. One more reassuring goodnight hug as I promised I'd be here forever lifted their shattered expressions into sleepy smiles.

Once again, I found myself back in my comfort zone, the kitchen. Cup of coffee in hand I found the natural flow in caring for the girls satisfying. My first day home, I had been saturated with so much information about me and my family, it left me happily exhausted. Fatigue edged at my tired muscles. As I rubbed at my nagging left shoulder, I stepped into the doorway of the living room. I found Hawke sitting comfortably with his feet propped up on the edge of the desk. He scanned the computer screen and checked over the paperwork in hand that he'd need for the morning. The same thought popped into my mind, I really wish I could remember more about him.

"I've got the girls' lunches packed, do I…should I," of course, I had to stammer over the simplest words, "do you want me to pack one for you?"

"No babe. You just make me coffee to go." Without even looking back to me, his answer short, but not abrasive.

"Just coffee to go." He grinned at my little sarcastic reply as I left him to his work.

Love the 'serve yourself' coffee pot. Simple to program, and presto, there'd be piping hot coffee brewed and ready for you in the morning. I had no problem remembering how things worked in my comfortable kitchen.

"Dove," the rasp of Hawke's soft voice had me and the bag of coffee whirling around.

"What?" Knowing he'd startled me, Hawke only grinned. "You scared me."

His grin only widened, "Heading up for the night, you coming?"

That confidence I'd been building all day, just fell to the ground and scattered around the floor, "I want to," after I took two deep breaths I managed to say, "coffee, I've got…" the bag of breakfast blend coffee squirmed in my fingers, "just want to preset the coffeepot."

"You need help with anything?" His offer to help was sweet, but I'm sure he was waiting to see if the panic in my eyes would erupt.

"No, no," thankful for the kitchen counter for support, "I'm fine." His eyes filtered over me, I'm sure questioning my response.

"Okay," his voice, soft, warm, even comforting. Hawke slipped from the room as quietly as he'd appeared. As the steps creaked under his footsteps, "Don't be too long, Dove," his husky voice echoed through the stillness of the house.

His carefree words instantly halted my coffee preparation. The open bag of coffee fell victim to my fingers tightening around its middle. The uncooked grounds surfaced around the edge of the bag from my tight squeezing hold. Somehow I managed to get the filter in the basket and with a shaking hand, the finely ground coffee nearly missed being placed in the basket. "Don't be long," I mumbled to myself as I set the timer on the pot.

Nighttime, it had come. The bedroom, where I'd be sharing the same bed with Hawke. Nowhere hidden in my deep dark lapsing memory did I even remember sleeping in the same bed with him. I had purposely locked this particular thought out of my head after finding the drawer full of the pretty lacy 'let's have sex' unmentionables.

"No, no, no, no. What am I going to do?" My knees weakened from the quivering or was it just plan fear? "Maybe I should call Maude? No Jane, she'd help." Talking out loud didn't ease my worry. "Who am I kidding? I'm on my own here."

Like a fire my thoughts ran wild. My head turned toward the ceiling to the sound of the shower running above where I stood. With my thoughts still racing, I felt the twisting flip flopping hit my stomach in full force. Somehow, someway, my feet managed to get my body over to the table where I plopped myself down into the nearest chair.

"What am I going to do now?" Subconsciously, I started to rub my forehead in an attempt to reason with myself. In one graceful leap, Ebony had landed softy on my lap to comfort me and my war of worries. "I wish you could tell me something, anything. Please pretty kitty, tell me what to expect. Should I run? Should I stay? Talk to me kitty." The beast who worshiped me only deepened his purring as I scratched his furry head.

Not knowing which way to run, I sat staring at the empty table. I'd occasionally glance up at the ceiling knowing Hawke would be waiting for me. I kept stroking Ebony's soft silky coat while his purring attempted to calm me. My thoughts were so focused on desperately trying to figure out what to do. I hadn't noticed that Hawke's shower had ended.

Through the quiet house Hawke's heavy foot steps stopped at the top of the stairway. "Dove, honey, when are you coming to bed?"

Flustered by his simple question my panic bolted. "I'll...I'll, I'll, be up in a minute." Breaking and cracking, my timid voice rattled.

Not budging from the table where I sat frozen, I continued to pet the cat. Each stroke harder and harder. All the while thinking Hawke just asked me to come to bed. With him. In the same bed. Next to him. Sleep with him. Be reasonable, I told myself. All he asked was when I was coming to bed. My mind played with me, just a torturing game of emotions running amuck.

"Ebony cat," I held him face to face with me as a relapse of panic hit. "What if he wants? Oh no." The cat's eyes popped the same time mine did. "He couldn't? I can't even remember. Oh dear God, no. Seriously, no, he couldn't." One hand cradled the cat closer to my flip flopping stomach as I rubbed my forehead with the other hand. My attempt to try and stop the wild wave of my own emotional mind games just didn't work.

As I pushed myself up from the table, the scraping of the chair over the hardwood floors had the cat leaping from my hands. He sold me out and ran for cover. The last light turned out, I managed to find my way to the base of the steps. Blankly, I stared up into the darkness. My heart pounded and the silky touch of the banister was no comfort.

Slowly, even hesitating, I began to climb each step. Quietly, I paused at the top of the stairs, still running my fingers over the smooth touch of the banister. I glanced down toward our bedroom. Instead of going to Hawke, I choose to walk to the opposite end of the hallway. My motherly instinct advised me to check on the girls. Both sound asleep. My emotional plea, that one of the girls would be awake and need me went unheard.

Guided by the dim nightlight in the hallway, I coaxed myself into walking the short distance to the only bright light left on. It shined welcomingly from the doorway of our bedroom. Apprehensively, I made my way to our waiting bedroom letting Ebony take the lead.

I could hear Hawke moving around in the huge walk-in closet. "Please be dressed, please be dressed," I whispered aloud, desperately wanting him to be dressed.

In all of my anxiousness, I soon found myself held up under the arch of the bedroom door. My eyes wondered around the spacious bedroom we shared. Carelessly tossed over the edge of the bed I found a green cotton jersey nightgown he had left for me. My movements were as silent as his as I made my way over to the bed. I did a double take toward the closet door, where I hoped Hawke would be getting dressed, or was dressed. As I held the gown up, my fingers soaked in the rich softness of the cotton. A simple flower print gown with a touch of lace had me smiling.

Startled once again by Hawke's fluent movements, he appeared in the doorway of the closet. "That's what you like to wear to bed." He flaunted his heart stopping smile to me.

"Really?" I could barely whisper my reply and kept examining the gown I held.

A sly chuckle came from his direction and my eyes drifted over to where Hawke stood. Instantly, I felt the warmth tingle in my cheeks. Hawke certainly didn't help with my insecurities as he stood there extremely relaxed with an arm propped on the doorframe. His sleek black hair, still wet from the shower, hung freely around his shoulders. Under the soft lighting in our bedroom, his russet dark skin glistened. His well defined muscles flirted with my emotions. Covering the rest of him, only cotton lounge pants that clung loosely to his hips and he topped that off with a teasing smile. My cheeks flushed rosier as I took in the full view of his muscular physique.

"Not exactly what I would like to see you in." Playfully, Hawke grinned at me and flipped a strand of his lose hair over his shoulder. "I'm sure you found,"

"The drawer...pretty, lacey," why did I invite myself into this conversation? "I found, I mean," my eyes closed, I could only shake my head wishing I hadn't even mentioned it.

"Dove," my eyes fluttered open at hearing him call my name.

"Guess I like to shop for those pretty things." I offered up as much as a hearty smile as I could and let the words barely escape my lips. Nervously, I clutched the plain nightgown in my hand, "I really like this one."

"One of your favorites. You got about five of those damn things."

"I do?"

"Yeah you do, why you're attached to those," he shook his head laughing at a memory I couldn't remember. "Only way I get you into," he nodded his head toward the dresser behind me, "is if I shop for you."

"You do what?" My eyes trailed to the drawer that had the naughty playful outfits hiding in them and back to him.

"All those girly things in your dresser drawer," he had the nerve to wink at me, "I shop for you." Speechless, I just clung tighter to the cotton gown in my hand. "I know what you like, even if it's that rag in your hands."

I nearly toppled over at Hawke's smooth reply to shopping. Saved by the corner post of the bed, I tried to steady my swaying. Mesmerized by the honey golden shade of warmth glowing from his eyes, I felt my cheek catch fire.

"Why don't you grab yourself a shower? It'll help you unwind." His simple rise of an eyebrow along with a grin had me blushing deeper. "I need to finish this paperwork up."

The cat protectively rubbed up against me as Hawke approached the opposite side of the bed. Still enjoying my tender nervousness of him, he reached for the folder lying on the bed. Across the romantic canopy bed stood my husband. My husband who I couldn't remember. I found the light in his eyes warm and trusting, but his smile, so inviting, so wanting, I could barely breathe, let alone move. Never once did he take his eyes off me and I begged my body 'please don't let me pass out on him.' Desperately, I fought off the light headedness that surged through my weakening body.

"A shower sounds great." Me and my 'rag of a nightgown' now clutched even tighter to my chest turned to leave the bedroom.

"Dove" I heard the softness in his voice behind me as I rested my shoulder on the doorframe. "There's no pressure, honey. When you're ready, I'll be here. You know I'm not going anywhere."

His caring words flowed like silk to my ears. The description and detail of what he said only sent a caressing, warm tingle twisting down my spine. Slightly, I turned my head to acknowledge him, managing a smile somehow, and whispered, "Thank you."

Before I could start out the doorway he just had to add, "I like that shade of blush on you," then his low chuckle of laughter followed me out of the room.

Fainting was not an option as I staggered down the hall to the bathroom. Groping around in the darkness, I finally found the light switch, right where it had always been. Flipping on the bright lights, I grabbed for the vanity to steady myself. I couldn't believe how rosy my cheeks were, the mirror's reflection wasn't lying to me. My heart still pounded as I stood there glaring at my glowing reflection in the mirror.

With more force than I anticipated, I yanked back the shower curtain frustrated by my own embarrassment, "Yep, he enjoyed my rosy glow, even said so."

Hot water shot from the showerhead as I returned the curtain to its natural place and hoped the massive spray would soon relax me. Peeling off my layers of clothes, I left them heaped in a messy pile on the floor. The steam from the shower had already started to fog the bathroom. Before I crawled in, I left the door ajar. The heat of the water soothed my edgy muscles and let my wild thoughts wash down the drain along with my "rosy" embarrassment. Lathered from head to toe, I felt a little more in control of my over-the-top emotions. Alerted by a meowing cat, the sound of a creaking door ended my self-confidence when I heard Hawke's voice, "Dove."

Not answering him, I clung to my soapy sponge and silently prayed, "No, please no. This can't be happening. He can't be in here with me."

Eyes tightly clinched shut all I heard was the pounding of my heart beating in my ears. Motionless, I stood in the steaming water and found that the wet sponge in my shaking hand didn't offer much coverage. The only thing that separated Hawke from me and my wet, naked, soap covered body…a plastic sea foam green shower curtain.

Hawke stifled my scream of panic with his smooth voice. "Dove, just poured you some brandy."

"Brandy?" I croaked out. "I…I like brandy?" I'm sure the hyperventilating in my voice had him laughing as I nervously asked from behind the security of the thin, non-protective shower curtain.

"Yeah honey, it's one of your favorite flavors. It'll help calm those nerves of yours."

Again a deep chuckle at my expense could be heard as he so politely enjoyed his moment of teasing. Without saying another word, he left me alone with my shower, my ragging thoughts, and my new best friend, the cat.

Saturated in the rushing hot water my body shook uncontrollably. Twisted in fear my tears smeared with the spray of water as I slowly sat down in the base of the tub. How could I be so scared of my own husband? Curled into a ball, I let the panic attack wash through me and prayed he wouldn't come back and find me like this. I found the hidden self-control I needed and pulled myself back together remembering his promise to take care of me. I had no choice. I had to trust him, he's all I have.

Panic attack over, with teary swollen eyes I peeked out from behind the shower curtain to make sure I really was alone. Relieved to find an empty bathroom, only the cat waited for me. Wrapped in a plush pink towel, I sat down on the closed toilet lid and propped my head against the wall. Covering my swollen eyes with a cold cloth I could smell the fragrant blackberry brandy next to me. The sweet smelling liquor sat patiently waiting on the vanity. The aroma of fresh blackberries filled my senses as I held the glass with trembling hands. The taste, unbelievably smooth, tingled on my tongue, but left a little bite on its way down my throat. Hawke used brandy to calm my nerves. How clever, he knows me so well, but why wouldn't he? Frowning at my reflection, I realized I had so much more to learn about him.

After another sip of his calming potion, I managed to find some lotions that didn't smell like cotton candy. Slipped on my new favorite nightgown, and dried my mass of curls. The pleasing look I saw in the mirror had my smile dancing. My unattractive "rag-gown" covered me perfectly. Loved the way it fell below my knees. Better yet, I felt good wearing it. As I tidied the bathroom, I took one last glimpse of me and my unflattering nightgown in the mirror. "Perfect." My reflection smiled back at me. With brandy in hand, I felt somewhat braver, until I headed down the hall. My quick pace slowed with hesitation seeing that the bedroom lights were still on. All I wanted, just to crawl into bed and tuck the covers around me.

"Get out of here you flea bag. Damn cat." Hawke's harsh voice echoed out the door as a slam of papers against the bed sent Ebony flying from our room when I walked in.

"Flea bag? That's not nice. What did that poor kitty do to you?" I tried not to laugh at seeing the glare in his eyes. Hawke just sneered at me and returned to his paperwork.

Thoughtfully, he had pulled the covers back for me. Thinking good thing for the brandy, I made my way to what I assumed to be my side of the bed. Ebony reappeared at the foot of the bed casting only a glare of what looked like death at Hawke.

"That cat really does not like you." I snickered at him and pulled the covers up as I crawled into bed. "What did you do to him?"

"You're the reason the damn thing gets to live." He smirked, not amused by the furry animal's glare of death. "You like to watch the news, the weather," and he flicked on the TV. Without looking up from his reading, he flipped the remote over to me.

Just close enough for my own comfort I could feel the radiant warmth of Hawke's body as I tried to curl up closer to him. Trying to be inconspicuous, I let my eyes wonder over his bare chest and thick muscled arms. His deep reddish tanned skin still held its bronze from the summer sun. Several deep and fine lined scars were scattered over his bare torso. A sudden urge had me wanting to trace each and every one of those scars with my fingers. Lost in my private picturesque view of his scars and hard muscles,

I soon found his arm draped across my lap. Hawke's unexpected and sudden touch, of course, made me jump and I nearly choked on my sip of brandy. I couldn't hide my curiosity, and my instant flushing gave me away. He'd caught me enjoying my quiet viewing of him. Afraid to move under the weight of his arm, my muscles tensed and I caught his side glance. Grinning at my flushed expression, he tried to hold back his laughter.

"You comfortable?" He shifted his body closer to me.

"Pretty much." I whispered, finally getting the chance to run my fingers over the arm that trapped me. "I like the brandy."

"Knew ya would, Need a refill?" Shaking my head no, he squeezed my knee playfully chuckling.

Relaxation and the brandy went hand in hand. Slowly my emotions calmed, I was drained, exhausted, and just tired. Bravely, thanks to a shot of brandy, I snuggled a little closer to him resting my head on his shoulder.

"I'm so glad I finally have you home." His kiss to the top of my head actually made me smile.

After he returned my empty glass to the nightstand, I daringly moved closer. Cradled in Hawke's arms I put my head on his chest and slipped into sleep by the beating of his heart. Deep in sleep, I didn't feel him move me to my pillow and wrap his warm body around mine.

A jarring awakening to my new surroundings struck me with panic. Freshly haunting my mind, the nightmare of dreams had followed me home. Always the same, always waking me with a heart pounding scare. Don't know why I thought they'd change or even go away. The young boy, his brilliant blue eyes, clouded with tears, he held his arms out to me, wanting me to hold him, comfort him.

Staring at the lace canopy above me, I couldn't shake the image of the unknown child from my mind. The silvery moonlight streamed through the windows and tried to calm my pounding heart. With Hawke's heavy arm wrapped securely around my waist I found comfort in his embrace as I played with the ends of his long hair that loosely rested on my chest. I couldn't move, literally. In the late hours of the night, I laid there listening to the deep breathing of his contented sleep. I found solitude in hearing his rhythmic heartbeat knowing he would be my security.

Not able to fall back to sleep, I finally managed to wiggle free of Hawke's hold and slipped from our bed, not waking him. At the foot of the bed I found his housecoat. Wrapping it around me, I quietly made my way to the sofa like chair in the corner of the room. In the shadows of our moonlit bedroom, I just watched Hawke sleep so peacefully. Wishing I could remember him, I slowly drifted back to sleep with the cat purring next to me.

Chapter 16 - Reacquainting With My Life

My first full week home, I spent reclaiming and relearning how I governed our old Victorian home by the seashore. Hardly missing a beat, I settled into my daily routine. Every morning at the dreadful hour of four a.m., the coffeepot perked life into Hawke's mornings. Emma and Amelia's school schedule kept me on my toes. It didn't go without notice from my family how my 'household' memory stayed intact.

Between piles of laundry, cooking, and adjusting to my surroundings, I enjoyed a deeper exploration of the house. Out of curiosity, I had visited Hawke's hideout. His "man cave" in the basement flat out scared me. Fully remolded to resemble a rustic cabin, the walls were covered with beautiful taxidermy animals. A variety of antlered deer, he said were either mule deer or whitetails, a moose, several elk, a fully mounted turkey encased in glass, and a life size bear decorated his manly room. In the right corner, a full size mountain lion, draped over a thick tree branch became my favorite. My husband obviously took hunting to the next level. In front of the wood burning stove laid a plush bear rug. Upon asking, I soon found the creature sprawled over the floor was indeed the animal that had brutally assaulted me. Seeing it turned into a fluffy rug, and lifelessly lounging around the basement, I still had no desire to touch or even pet its lush fur.

As I was still recovering, several evenings Hawk and I would enjoy the Indian summer nights on our deck. He'd offer me glimpses of our life together. Most devastating to me, how our marriage had spiraled out of control. He only offered limited information on the impact the miscarriages had on me. How his career had overtaken his life and his soul decision to make sure I'd never be put in the spot of living or dying over having a child. The only positive outcome I found was that before the accident, he claims he'd won my heart again. Any other questions I posed to him, he detoured them for another day when he was ready to talk about it.

Hawke had gladly given up the details on how he ended up in the ER because of my Uncle. The entire tale wrapped around the finishing of our bedroom. As told, Aunt Phyllis claimed to be redecorating her own bedroom. She'd have me browse through magazines filled with fully displayed bedroom groupings with her, then 'dog ear' every page I liked. As the story unfolded, Hawke forbid me to go anywhere near the bedroom project, even kept the room under lock and key. With the help of Uncle Joe, they reconstructed it to the glorious room it is now. What I didn't remember, Hawke had finished our bedroom as a wedding gift. The amusing part of the tale, included Hawke, Uncle Joe, a lecture on the value of marriage, a flying piece of wood, and a good ten stitches, all over Hawke making a comment of how he couldn't wait to get me alone in the new bedroom. He still sports the scar to prove my Uncle meant business.

An anytime discussion, Hawke's battle with Jane, or was it Jane's battle with Hawke. Either way the two of them could shred the other with just a glare. Even with the ongoing "feud" with my husband, Jane and I were still inseparable. Deep down, I think Hawke really does like her.

Mid September arrived and I felt the need to venture outside the comfort zone of our home. Reuniting with my family, the house, yard, and all I did around here, came naturally. As my mind healed, I got the itch. I needed and wanted more freedom. To be able to hop in the truck parked in the garage and go for groceries, pickup the girls, or run simple everyday errands without relying so heavily on Hawke or others for help. I hadn't been behind the wheel of my truck since the attack. Bound and determined, I started my daily practice of just backing up and down the driveway and easily another piece of the puzzle clicked into place. Still overly protective of me, Hawke wasn't so sure on handing over the keys. Instead, he coached me in a single driving lesson up and down Turtle Drive. Impressed that my mind allowed me to rattle off just about every single rule and regulation of the road, Hawke handed over the keys.

My first solo adventure, pathetic. Not even out of the door and I had to make a call to Hawke. Had no clue as to where my purse and the belongings, say like my wallet, could be found. Treated like a teenager, Hawke and Maude hit me with several curfews. Don't leave home without my cell phone. They needed a detailed plan of my adventures around town. If I stopped someplace not on the list, I had to call. I'd even been given time limits and if I didn't report in, my phone would be ringing. For some odd reason the GPS and I weren't on friendly terms. No matter how many times I programmed it, I got lost. Best yet, I gave in and called Hawke for help. After being treated to his abusive laughter, he gave me step-by-step details on how to work the not so complicated gizmo. Figured, if I got myself lost again, I'd just call Maude or Jane. At least they'd take pity on me.

Aunt Maude had carefully laid the groundwork for my return to the diner. Each visit, each telephone call, she proposed new ways of getting me back into her kitchen. Her plan, just start me off with maybe two days a week and build up from there. I agreed, but Hawke, still in that overprotective mode didn't budge until Dr. Thornton cleared me at my last checkup.

With my rapidly advancing improvements, physical and mental, the therapy sessions and visits with Dr. Thornton became far and few between. Getting good at picking peoples brains, I discussed my reoccurring nightmares with Dr. Thornton. He'd known me and my family for years. Nowhere could he remember or place a person who fit the description of the mysterious blond haired man in my dreams. He pointed out several possibilities for my nightly terrors. The trauma from the attack, my mind overcompensating for the memory loss, or while I was lost in the coma, subconsciously I'd picked up on another family's trauma. Encouraged by him, I kept two notebooks, one for the nightmares, when, how often, and if anything changed in them. The other, my mind healing, the more I did, the more memories flooded back to me.

I finally got all the photo albums from my hospital stay put away. Accidently, I knocked over a small box that contained pictures of Hawke as a child. Curiosity had me digging through the box of my husband's keep sakes, until I found a snapshot of two children on a sandy beach holding up a string of fish. The little boy was definitely Hawke, but the little girl with a toothless smile, resembled me. In smudged black ink, I could barely read Hawke's name, but the little girls name had faded away over the years.

What really caught my attention in the old colored photo the child's untamed curly red hair, and my own eyes stared back at me. This couldn't possibly be me. Hawke said we'd met when I was sixteen. But how could I've been fishing with him as a child? Delighted, I eagerly handed over the photo to Hawke. Along with asking for more information, I hoped it was me. To my disappointment it wasn't me, even though the freckled faced, curly haired little girl matched so many of my childhood photos.

The only feedback I got, Hawke had spent several summers in Michigan with Maude's sister and husband. The pretty little girl who had my hair and eyes was only a playmate for a few summers. Something about the old photo stuck in my absent mind, but once again, I couldn't place it.

My first month home, Hawke seemed to be on the back doorstep everyday around the lunch hour. Several times a day he'd call to just check in, more like checkup on me. I enjoyed the feeling of security with him.

In the short time I'd been home there was one major puzzle piece I kept stumbling over. Our one-on-one relationship that had once left us connected romantically wasn't flourishing. In my mind of forgotten memories, my husband was still a complete stranger to me when it came to being intimate. Frustrated at my own inability to reunite with him sexually I could only ask for his patience. I knew he needed more from me as I tried to adjust to his warm touch, his needs, and his desires. For a man who enjoyed the touch of my body under his fingers, he needed the mental connection we once held to come back. Patiently, Hawke gave me the freedom to reacquaint with him on my terms...slowly. Not saying he won't take an opportunity to push for more, and he did when the moment arose. My confidence slumped into a low when it came to me, him, and dancing under the bedcovers.

Chapter 17 - Hopeless

The early morning rays of the rising sun barely edged its brightness through the lacey curtains. A slight chill from the open window let the crisp fall air fill our bedroom. Curled on my side, I snuggled deeply under the pile of blankets covering me. According to the alarm clock, I still had time to curl tighter under my covers. A whole hour of sleep waited for me. I hadn't extended an open invitation to Hawke when his warm body sculpted around me. Hoping it was sleep he craved by curling up next to me. But I knew what he desirably needed, what he so patiently waited for me to say yes to. That same scared to death panic surfaced again as my body stiffened to his touch.

The heat from his body flowed along mine while his fingers ran through my tangled hair. The chill in the air was nothing compared to my increased heartbeats when he began to kiss my exposed neck. My thin nightgown didn't protect my back to his muscular chest brushing tightly up against me. I tried to ward off another round of self-induced panic when Hawke tugged my security blankets from my shoulder.

"Hawke, please, I don't think," when I reached to pull the covers up his hand stopped me. Close enough to me, his long silky hair draped over my exposed shoulder.

"Dove," I felt his whispering breath in my ear, "just try."

Unstable breathing rippled from me as I gripped my pillow tighter. I was thankful the dim morning light shielded my terrified expression. The quivering he felt under his touch, only encouraged him to keep trying, "Dove, it's only me. You know I won't hurt you."

"I can't, I don't, I'm…," another gasp of panic escaped me.

"Just breath, Dove," he quietly whispered to me, "Just try."

As if my fleshy side were his personal keyboard, Hawke fingers played out the tune he desired. When he reached the last key, his hand gently slipped under my "rag of a nightgown" I wore faithfully every night. My body gave way to the quivering and went into a full raging tremble. I'd slept next to him for nearly two months. Why was this so difficult for me? Why couldn't I return the same passion he offered me? Sheer panic flooded my entire pulsing blood stream as Hawke's hand glided up and over my bare thigh. He lingered over the curve of my hip and gently massaged the soft skin he'd found. Allowing no time for me to recover, he gracefully slipped his warm hand over my stomach. He continued the massaging technique my hip received but sculpted himself around my trembling body even closer.

"Hawke, I can't do this." There was no hiding my sheer terror as I grabbed for his hand to stop. My stumbling block of being intimate with him had been intensely taken over by my emotional heart and panicked mind.

With trembling hands, I threw the covers off of us and attempted to flee from our bed. Hawke's warm fingers skimmed lightly over my arm as I barely slipped through his hands when he reached to pull me back to him. No longer able to hold my composure, tears of real fear and embarrassment streamed down my face.

"Dove," his voice hard with frustration, "Dovey, stay with me," I felt his deep sigh of frustration as it stabbed into my heart, "You've got to trust me."

The doorframe held all the weight of my worry, "Hawke, I'm just not…"

"Dove, just come back to me." He held his voice steady, but it came out sharp, filled with disappointment as he pleaded with me to return to his waiting arms.

I couldn't go back to him, "I'm so sorry," I whispered and wiped away a handful of tears. Not looking back to him, "I'm sorry, I can't."

"Dove just let me hold you." When I didn't return to him, I could hear his deep growl of pent-up frustration as he fell back into the pile of cushioning bed pillows.

In another round of massive tears, I fled from our bedroom and blindly made my way down the stairs to the safety of the kitchen. On the edge of the countertop, Ebony, my guard cat waited for my arrival. Scooped tightly in my arms, I clung to the furry animal like a scared child. The vibrating purrs he shared with me couldn't begin to calm me.

Upstairs, I could hear Hawke moving around. His shower ran longer than usual, another cold one, I'm sure. The chiming of the grandfather clock startled me, five am. Hawke would be leaving for work and his patience with me was running out. Nervously, I ran my fingers through Ebony's thick coat and sat him back on the countertop.

Safety, that's what my kitchen meant to me. Out of habit, I started to make Hawke a cup of coffee. It was the least I could do. I did manage to get that much right. After drying my eyes on the dishtowel, I poured myself a cup of coffee and settled down at the table to wait.

"What am I going to do?" Question asked, but it fell upon deaf ears as I saw the cat disappear into the living room. The cat took pride in revenge against Hawke, especially sensing my sadness this morning. I knew Ebony would wait for the precise moment to launch an attack on Hawke all because of my tears. Legs pulled up on the chair, I tucked my security blanket of a gown around me and rested my aching head on my propped up knees. My shaking had stopped after a sip or two of coffee. There was no place for me to hide, not even in the safety of my kitchen. I still had to face Hawke. I held my breath as I heard each one of his heavy footsteps creaking on the staircase.

Like a furry bomb exploding, the angry hiss gurgled from the cat, "You son-of-a-bitch," not only did Hawke swear at the cat, but his fist slammed into the doorframe. "If I get my hands on you…" a black puffed ball of hissing fur ran and hid under the chair I quietly sat in. "Mother fucking cat," my cat hating husband announced as he entered the kitchen.

"Your coffee's ready." I managed to softly say from my hiding place at the table, "and leave my cat alone." Startled and shocked to hear my voice from the darkened corner, I thought Hawke would nearly jump out of his skin. "I didn't think anything could scare you."

"What the hell, Dove? Don't pull that shit on me." To recover, he held tightly to the doorframe he'd just accosted.

"Never heard you swear before." Guess there's a first time for everything, especially when nerves are frayed.

"You're as bad as that damn cat. How long have you been sitting down here?" His voice snapped as he whirled to face me and casted an annoyed glare in my direction.

Curled tightly on my chair, I chose to wash my fear down with a swallow of coffee and didn't answer him. My eyes still glistened with wet tears as I stared back into my husband's readable eyes. He edged on the state of frustration and didn't hide his disappointment with me. My heart broke knowing that the passion I once shared with him was lost.

Hawke picked up his coffee cup, blew the steam from it and took a long sip, all the while I sat silently under his watchful glare. It wasn't a hateful glare like he'd shared with the cat, just a basic "what the hell do we do now" kind of awkward moment. In the same fluent motion, he returned his half empty cup of coffee back to the counter and started to tie his hair back. Never once did he break his eye contact with me. Frustration ruled over him as he leaned heavily back on the kitchen counter. "Dove," he swiped a hand over his rigid jaw, then crossed both arms over his chest and heaved a sigh of irritation that I could feel. His glare had lightened, but my heart sank deeper as the disappointment clouded his eyes. "I get it. I get this is hard for you. In two months time, you've pieced a hell of a lot of your life back together. All but this."

No need to mention the word SEX, I knew what he meant, the three letter word had become a touchy subject. "I just can't," words failed me again, "I don't know why I can't…"

"When it comes to me, you, and the bedroom, you've got to get it together." Hawke didn't bother to sugar coat the hardness in his voice. "Don't get me wrong Dove, it's not just about sex. That's an added bonus between us."

Glad to be seated, my mind whirled. I tried to put what he'd said into prospective, even tried to respond with some kind of reasonable answer. All that happened, my head bobbed, not in disbelief, my lips moved, but nothing came out.

"I need your mind, I need your touch. Your soul. Your spirit. Making love to you is something I can't live without." Direct and to the point, when Hawke wanted something he made it perfectly clear. "You've got to let me back in to your world."

"I'm sorry I can't give you what you need." I patted the fresh tears from my eyes. "I'm trying Hawke. I'm trying so hard to find the connection back to you."

"Tell you one thing, cold showers," he gave me a half a grin, "it's not working for me." The sharp edge in his voice still held, "Dove, I don't know what else to do here. I've been trying to ease you back into what we had. You've got to meet me half way here."

"I can barely meet you a quarter of the way." Afraid of my own torture of hidden fear, I held my voice above a whisper. Dabbing my tears on the edge of my trusted night gown, I managed to put a little backbone into my whimpering voice. "Maybe I should just sleep in the spare room."

If I didn't already have Hawke's attention, I gained it in full now. He arched an eyebrow and let out a deep huff of what I thought was shocked amusement. By the scowl that grew deep in his narrowed eyes, I realized it was definitely the wrong thing to even suggest. To put me on edge even more, Hawke's familiar smirk appeared over his lips. "Like hell you'll sleep in the other room."

As my eyes popped wide open to his callus remark, "Didn't think that would work."

"No it won't, Dove."

Another raged breath exhaled as another tear fell from the corner of my eye. Not saying a word to his reply, I rested my chin on my legs and waited. Game playing wasn't his style. Hawke pulled the closest kitchen chair out and placed it directly in front of me. He straddled the chair, tugged it closer as he sat down until the edge of our chairs practically touched. So close, I actually slipped my bare toes under his warm, jean covered thighs. Moments ticked on the clock while he sat there and studied the complexity of my silent fear that I didn't attempt to hide from him.

"Dove, I've never forced you to do anything you weren't comfortable with. Never did. Never will." He tipped his head down to match me eye to eye. "May have coaxed you into trying things, but never forced you. Always let you come to me willingly."

"I'm sure...appreciate it." I didn't want to face him or my shattered fear of not being able to have the intimate relationship we once had, but somehow I still sat there hoping I could overcome this touchy subject between us.

"Dove," his fingers ruffled around my untamed mess of curls that helped to hide my agonizing pain.

"I heard you. Every word you've said. One puzzle piece that won't click in, me, you," I couldn't even say the word sex to him, "I'm sorry, I don't know why, but I can't..."

Hawke's sigh of raw frustration surrounded me. "You know how much I love you." He paused and gently surrounded my shoulders in his arms, "I need you emotionally as much as I need you physically."

"Hawke," I released the death grip on my legs and let my hands rest on his thighs. My eyes flickered with threatening tears, "Please be patient with me, I'm trying."

"I know you have been. You know I'll continue to pursue you." The soft rasp of his voice eased a little tension between us. Lightly, he brushed his lips over mine. "I just need all of you, Dove."

Not giving me time to think, or balk at his closeness, Hawke quickly returned to brush his lips over mine again. As the kiss deepened, my fingers tugged lightly at the end of the flannel shirt he wore. He let me ease back from his embrace and gently ran his fingers under my chin and leaned in for one last kiss.

"Promise me Dove, you'll work on this. I really need all of you." He patiently said as he stood to walk back to the counter. From under my chair, Ebony growled a hiss of snarled displeasure as Hawke opened the cupboard where he kept his cigarettes and cigars. "Damn animal of yours is lucky to be alive." Not looking back at me, he reached to the top shelf for the open pack of cigarettes that he hadn't touched since I'd come home. His nerves had to have been as edgy as mine. Smokes in his shirt pocket, he picked up his coffee and jacket. Half way to the backdoor he stopped to glance back at me. "I'll see ya at Maude's. Love ya white Dove."

"Love you too, see you for lunch." I offered him a broken smile as he shut the door behind him.

His glance to me, frustration, but yet I felt the love he had to offer. Motionlessly, I still sat at the kitchen table. As usual, the sound of the truck motor hummed to life. From the window I could see him backing out and down the driveway. He was gone and I was left in a bundle of untouchable emotions.

I stretched my legs out on his vacant chair and watched the early morning sunlight filter in the kitchen window. Sigh after sigh echoed in the quite of the morning. I knew I had to pull myself together. The girls would be up soon for school and I didn't want to explain my tear stained face. Not only did I not want to explain the tears, I certainly didn't want to share the reason for all of them.

The grandfather clock in the living room chimed out seven strokes. From my hiding spot at the kitchen table, I finished the remains of my cold coffee. I couldn't get my mind off the unnecessary fear I had of being intimate with Hawke. As I rubbed my pounding head, I wandered upstairs to wake my girls.

118

A morning with my sleeping beauties eased the tension from my headache. Easily, I slipped into mommy mode. My girls with sleepy smiles were slow to start our day. They'd chat to me about their dreams and what the day held for them. Mornings with Emma and Amelia had to be my favorite time of the day. Dressed and ready for school, I twisted a French braid into Amelia's hair.

"Aunt Dovey, can we go to October Fest this Saturday night?" Emma asked as she waited for me to braid her hair.

I looked around Amelia's head smiling at her. "An October Fest. That sounds like fun." I grinned.

"Do you think Uncle Hawke will take us?" My hands caught in Amelia's hair as she twisted around to ask me.

"I don't see why not. He's not out on the charters, so why not? When I see him, I'll let him know he has a date with three of us." The girl's eyes lit up. They were out the bathroom door giggling as I called after them to get their breakfast.

I stopped by our bedroom to change into my favorite sweats. As I pulled the covers so nice and neatly over the bed, the same bed where I couldn't let him make love to me in, I found a note on my pillow. In his own trashed handwriting short, sweet, and simple it read, "Love You".

Instantly my eyes filled with tears. I knew he loved me. Somewhere in my scrambled brain I knew my heart belonged solely to him. I grabbed a handful of tissues, they seemed to be an everyday item to have on hand for my emotional rollercoaster ride. Hawke had taken the time to once again reassure me of his love. Tissues in one hand, note in the other, I wondered why I couldn't accept his loving touch. Other than my lapse of memory, what could possibly be stopping me from joining him in the intimacy we once shared in this bed?

"Aunt Dove, it's almost time for the bus." Emma's voice drew me back to the time of day as I laid my handwritten note on the nightstand.

Chapter 18 - Girl Talk at the Diner

With the girls on their way to school, me and my maddening emotions took advantage of the pounding water of a long, soaking hot shower. So glad Maude didn't insist on a formal uniform, I threw on my everyday "diner" work clothes. Basically, anything I wanted to wear. A deep mauve t-shirt and jeans would do for the day.

I yanked, pulled, and tugged every loose end of my wild hair into a tight braid. "Good enough," I didn't like my reflection glaring back at me, she too questioned my thoughts. To add more insult to my injured ego, there wasn't a thing I could do to help the red puffiness that surrounded my swollen blue eyes.

Halfway down the steps I could hear the phone ringing. "I'm late. I know I'm late." I pretty much screamed at the ringing phone, "Why would they be calling to remind me?" I snapped at Ebony and roughly ruffled his furry head.

With a purring cat under my arm, I reached for the phone, then stopped. The caller I.D. didn't announce the diner's number, it flashed Hawke's cell phone number. "No. No. I don't want to talk. Not now. Not later. Just no." Again, I blasted my anger at the cheerful ringing phone.

I knew Hawke would be worried about me. How could he not, he witnessed and lived through my near death experience. With my emotions tearing me apart, I couldn't even pick up the phone to say "Hi" to him. In a mad rush to get out the door, I nearly forgot to put the cat down as I grabbed for my purse and keys.

"Sorry guy. Pretty sure Maude wouldn't approve," and I plopped him back on the counter along with a healthy dose of cats treats. Again, the phone started with the ringing, "Hey Ebony," he gave me a glance, but continued to crunch on the tasty treats, "take a message for me. Got to run, buddy." And I did, right out the backdoor.

With the way my morning had been rolling, I knew this just wasn't going to be my day. My means of transportation, the truck, it roared to life and I was glad to be escaping the house for a few hours. Only a ten minute drive to the diner, but it gave me ten more minutes to think about the promise I'd agreed to.

Lucky for me, I'd missed most of the early rush. I cased over the parking lot for Hawke's truck as I pulled in. Again, my luck held, only a semi-full parking lot of hungry customers. My usual spot next to Jane's outdated purple Ford Pinto was still unclaimed. The dashboard clock only proved I was nearly an hour late, really late for me.

"I hope I don't have to explain why I'm so late this morning." I muttered and took a quick look at my eyes in the rearview mirror. My still swollen eyes beamed with the brilliant shade of flaming red. "Great, just great." Even the cool morning air couldn't help with the puffiness. "How am I going to hide my latest anxiety attack from them?" These days, I couldn't get anything past Maude or Jane. I certainly didn't want to approach the subject of 'sex' with my husband's Aunt and my best friend. It just wasn't up for discussion. "Damn it." This time my cell phone rang as I slammed the door shut. With the contents of my purse's spread across the hood of the truck, I dug the ringing annoyance out, "Hey," on the other end I could hear Hawke breathe a sigh of relief.

"Been trying to call you." I expected to be greeted by his annoyed tone, instead Hawke's voice flowed with concern.

"Yeah, I know. Sorry. I got caught up in the shower. Didn't realize how late I really am. Do you think Maude will fire me?" I slouched over the hood of my truck gathering a few rolling items that had slipped from my purse.

"Nope, she won't let you off that easy. Just be prepared."

"Prepared for what? Hawke, I'm not up for a lecture on being punctual." I directed my nasty comment right at him.

"Not that Dove, I'm sure they'll be asking."

I cut him off again, "Asking what? What now?" This time my fingers drummed rapidly on the hood.

"Called looking for you. Maude knows something's up. You alright?"

"No," my sigh, completely pitiful, "I mean yes. Thanks for the warning. Oh damn."

"Dove, hate to tell you this, you're not one for swearing." He was right, the word damn usually wasn't in my monologue of creative words.

"Learned it from you this morning."

"Yeah, that," he ignored me and asked, "What has you swearing?"

"Jane's peeking out the door at me. I better get in there." Somehow my feet wouldn't give in to walking through the door yet.

"All I can say, good luck with that. Sure Jane will be all over you like a wet diaper."

"Hawke, that's just nasty, you're no help." I kind of inched my way up the sidewalk as he kept the conversation alive.

"Got a half day charter to run today,"

"So you won't be in to babysit me." The words just snapped out of my mouth and I'm sure left him reeling.

"Feisty, now aren't you?" The deep chuckle that vibrated from Hawke assured me he wasn't at all offended by my sarcasm. "See ya for dinner. You need me, call."

"I'll be okay, really, I'm fine." I paced my steps off slowly as I approached my place of work.

"Dove, still know when you're lying to me. Love ya."

"Love ya too." Phone back in my purse, I finally had my hand on the door.

With a questionable smile plastered on my face, I yanked the door open and read the numbers on the wall clock, nine thirty seven. From behind the counter, Jane eyed me with suspicion.

"Morning. Sorry, I'm so late," on purpose, I kept my red, puffy eyes glued to the floor and sulked past Jane. "Just...you know...couldn't get it together this morning." I found no need to lie. "Really sorry." Avoiding any possible eye contact or conversation with Jane or Maude, I brushed past the front counter in a hurry.

"Honey," Maude's voice called for my attention, "Hawke's been calling here for you. At least a dozen or so times. You forget that phone of yours?" I could feel her questioning eyes follow me as I slowed my pace and nodded my head no.

I did my best to slap on a happy smile as I barely made eye contact with her, "Just talked to him a few minutes ago," my feet didn't miss a step as they lead me straight for the kitchen.

"If Dove didn't think we wouldn't notice," Jane's glance of worry fell over to Maude, "she's sadly mistaken. Wonder what the hell Hawke did to her now. Think I just might make a call to him."

"Don't bother Jane. He's pretty rattled over whatever happened. Keep an eye on the counter for me. I'll see if Dove will say anything." Maude, with her feather like footsteps had followed me into the kitchen.

What a combo, my brighter than day red apron, tied securely around my waist, matched my deep red rimed eyes and I didn't hear Maude's soft footsteps sneaking up on me.

"Dove, honey," her soft motherly voice of concern reached my ears, "everything okay?"

"Sorry about being so late, it's just..." my eyes stung with an uprising of burning tears. With a little cough to clear my throat, "I'm, I'll be alright. Just..." And just like that, I stopped talking. If I said another word, I'd be on the floor in a pool of tears. I couldn't even turn to face her.

The warmth of Maude's gentle hands rested on my tense shoulders, "Just what, honey? Anything Jane or I can help you with?" She waited patiently for my response.

"No, no," my head shook out the rest of the no's, "Not now." All this talk about emotions, feelings and the dreaded word 'sex' had taken a toll on me.

"Everything okay at home, Dove?" She pressed on.

"No," again I just shook my head no, and hoped she'd let it die.

"Dove, honey you know we're here. When you're ready, let us help." Maude whispered as she hugged me then left me as silently as she found me.

Three order tickets hung in the window. I grabbed them with fury and slapped them down on the butcher block countertop. My frustration got taken out on the food order I was preparing. All my raging thoughts focused on the dishes I cooked. If my hands stayed busy, my mind won't wander off to the land of intimacy and the emotions tagging along with it.

On the griddle, a double order of hash browns and onions took a beating. "Just had to have another panic attack all because my husband wanted..." As I muttered miserably at myself, sausage links got rolled and the potatoes were flipped over and over. "Just wanted to be near me. Just wanted to have...stop thinking. Just stop thinking." I commanded of myself as I slapped the breakfast order on a plate. Another food ticket felt my wrath when I slammed it on the counter.

"Glad I'm not that order ticket." Maude chuckled as she planted her rounded bottom on a stool close to me. "Honey, maybe you should take a minute and give Hawke another call. He sounded pretty worried."

As if my swollen eyes weren't a good enough giveaway, I couldn't hide one thing from Maude. Not one. The order ticket in my hand started to shake, "Yeah, okay, I...I, he, said he's on a charter." Hot dish of breakfast food in my hand, I stopped and gave her a questioning glance.

"You know he'll call if you don't."

"I know. But, I don't," pancake batter sizzled on the hot griddle, "I already talked to him. He's working, I..." cakes on the griddle needed and got flipped, "don't want to bother him, again."

"Tell you what Dove, give me that phone of yours." She held her hand out wiggling her fingers trying to coax me to give it up.

"Why?" As she asked, I automatically pulled the phone from my pocket and placed it in her out stretched hand.

"He calls, I'll handle him." She winked at me. "How about when you finish that last order, you tackle that bread dough for me? Know it's not your favorite, but it could help relieve whatever has you in knots."

"Bread dough. No problem." I shot Maude a sly grin. Even I remembered how much me and bread dough didn't get along. But the loaves I created just melted in your mouth.

IPod in ears, I beat the helpless dough up one side and down the other. Had to hand it to Maude, she knew how to ease some of my frustrations. Had to give Maude a second hand, she'd kept Hawke's surprise visit under that grey hair of hers. Didn't even know he stopped in. This gave her the opportunity to drill him on why I was a basket case of rolling emotions. One of Maude's major concerns, she wanted to know if the sticky memory resurfaced of what him and I had been dueling over before my accident. After he'd reassured Maude that wasn't the case, he tapped danced around the real reason stressing me. Then again with Jane close on his heels for detailed information, Hawke only gave Maude enough details for her to figure it out. Maude knew both of us like she knew the front and back of her own hand. She sent Hawke packing out the door and back to work with the reassurance of letting her and Jane handle the new hurtle that crept into my life.

The morning rush trailed off and no customers lurked around the diner. "Jane, would you get three coffee mugs?" She called from her office. "Dove, could you come out here please?"

With remnants of bread dough clinging to my hands, I walked through the kitchen doors, "Did you call me?" I asked as the IPod cord dangled in my hand.

"Seriously, Dove, it's a wonder you can hear anything with that music blaring in your ears," Jane perched her skinny fanny on the stool at the counter and patted the seat next to her.

"Sit," Maude with her motherly concerned eyes darted to the stool next to Jane. She sat a bottle of her favorite Irish cream whiskey on the counter. Three deep coffee mugs that didn't even match were filled half full of the cream and topped off with a splash of hot coffee. "Have a seat, Dove."

Obediently, I did as she asked as the diner took on the sweet smell of the creamy whiskey blending with the coffee. Afraid to ask or say a word, I accepted the cup she handed me. Two sets of eyes had me squirming as I stirred the delicious smelling cup of coffee in front of me.

Maude took a drink of her coffee, "Drink a little Dove." Like a child in trouble, I did as she said and continued to squirm under her watchful gaze, "So what's going on?"

"Dove, did you remember something?" Jane rubbed my shoulder. "It's okay to tell us."

"No." Not up for talking about sex and my husband, I kept staring at my already stirred coffee cup.

"Dove, what's going on?" Maude inquired again.

I just kept staring at my coffee. I didn't even look up at them. "What do you mean what's going on?" I whispered and made no effort to make eye contact.

Both of them sighed in unison. "Well, there's something else that stayed the same. Try and get Dove to tell you what's bugging her." Jane sarcastically laughed.

As I bit at my lower lip, Maude lifted my chin so I'd be eye to eye with her. Once again, I found her soft motherly warm eyes as she held my hands around the coffee cup.

"Dove you need to tell us what's bothering you. We can help you. Now what happened?"

Just my luck, I started to shake, so I tried of few of those deep breathing techniques they taught me at the hospital.

"You're so pale." Jane's fingers feathered along my check, "Are you sick?" She touched my forehead with the back of her hand checking for a fever.

"Jane," I pushed her hand away, "No. No I'm not sick."

Jane's normally small circled shaped eyes just grew into the shapes of saucers. Her lips twitched into a glowing smile. "Are you pregnant?"

I just stared at her as a wave of nausea bolted and bounced through my stomach. "I think I'm going to puke." White as a ghost I trembled even more.

"Jane, we all know that's not possible," I flinched at the harsh words that Maude so softly spoke, "Drink it slowly, honey," Maude added as she topped off my coffee cup.

"Sorry Dove, but you never know, things could happen."

Obvious to Jane's kind words, the whitecaps of nausea settled into a calm sea when I sipped the sweet coffee drink. Maude waited for me to sit my cup down before she reached over to hold my trembling hands. "Honey, what's got you so upset?"

"Nothing, I'm…I can handle him." Still not ready to reveal my dilemma, I let out an agonizing sigh.

"Handle him?" Jane's eyes narrowed as she snapped, "Did Hawke hurt you?"

"No." My voice scolded and my eyes darted daggers toward Jane, "Why would you think that?"

"Had to ask." Her voice softened as she tried to coax what bugged me out, "You know you can tell us anything." Jane pulled at the back of my ponytail. "We can't help you unless you tell us. So spill your guts, girl." For once Jane didn't add insults to my already injured pride.

"It's…" I took another sip of coffee for courage, "it's more like what's not happening." I felt the glint of heat cross my checks, "I can't, you know, be…" Finally, I lifted my eyes to meet Maude's curious gaze.

"Hmmm," Maude evaluated my situation up and down, "private," I nodded my head yes as she continued to analyze me and my intimacy situation, "Don't think I need to guess here." Maude's smile didn't relax me, "You two haven't," she took a nice long sweet sip of her coffee, "this is all about sex, isn't it?"

The sigh that escaped me verified her answer to be correct, "Yep all about me, him and sex."

"He's got two hands. If I were you," Jane's top lip puckered with a twisted smile of amusement, "tell him to pick one and use it."

"Jane, how can you be so…I'm so done here. This so called chat is over. Some help you were." As I slipped off the stool and tried to stand up, I quickly found myself sitting back down next to Jane, "What is in that?" I pointed to bottle in Maude's hands.

"Jane, the goal here is to help Dove. Keep your snide-ass comments to yourself."

"So there you have it. We're not," I indulged in a long sip of coffee.

"By that response, I'd say Hawke isn't getting any now is he?" Jane snickered another laugh, all the while my face turned redder than the apron I wore.

"Is it that obvious?" A fast glace to Maude, "Forget I asked. It is. I know it. Things between the sheets, it's not happening for us." As I rubbed my forehead, Maude and Jane couldn't keep their giggling laughter contained. "Mark my words, it's not that amusing. I don't know what to do. It's so bad, Hawke, he's been taking ice cold showers when I can't." I didn't mean to blurt that small detail out. It just rolled right off my tongue as I half laughed and cried at the same time. "The two of you, you're not helping by laughing so hard at me." Glad to see my suffering had them howling with more laughter. Finally, I picked up what pride I had left off the top of the counter along with my flushed face. "Why are you two laughing at me?"

"We're not laughing at you Dove," Jane whisked a rolling tear of laughter from her eye. "It's the fact that Hawke's been forced into cold showers." Their tag teamed laughter soared.

"You've got that boy going crazy." Maude added to their hysterical laughter.

"But I'm not doing anything to him." Their screams of laughter even had me grinning.

"Dove, you don't have to do anything. You just being near Hawke…" Jane nearly doubled over with laughter, "You're killing me with the cold showers, Dove."

"Don't you dare tell him I said that," I grabbed Jane by the shoulder, "Promise me you won't say a word. Either one of you." I shot a death glare of "don't you dare" toward Maude.

"What goes on at the diner," Maude announced.

"Stays at the diner." Jane concluded

Without any warning, as Jane previously asked, I spilled my guts. "I can't remember his touch. His kiss." From soaring giggles our emotions turned serious as I proceeded on, "Worst part, can't even remember what it was like to make love with him. None of it has come back." One heavy sigh heaved from deep inside of my chest as I sipped at the coffee. "I can sleep next to him, in the same bed. Even accepted his arms around me. But don't touch me anywhere else." Neither one of them interrupted me, "I can barely touch him." Silently Maude and Jane took in every word I spoke and waited for the rest. I focused on the cup in my hands, "My panic attacks of being intimate," I did the little quote with the fingers in the air when I said panic, "I'm scaring myself and him. We all know, Hawke doesn't scare that easily."

"Dove," Maude tried to break my rhythm of flowing words, but I basically put her on hold with a simple "one more moment" hand gesture.

"Want to know how twisted I really am?" I didn't wait for either one of them to answer, "This morning, Hawke, all he wanted was for me to try…" I felt the wet tears fill up under my lashes, "when he slipped his hand under my "rag" of a nightgown, guess what happened?"

"You had a panic attack." Sympathetically, Jane answered for me.

"Yep, I sure did. Slipped from his loving arms and ran right out of the bedroom, in tears, and completely terrified of Hawke touching me. What's wrong with me? Why can't I get this connection back we had?"

"Dove, this is something that's just going to take a little more time," Jane handed me a stack of napkins. "Don't let yourself get all worked up over sex. It will happen when you're ready."

"You don't understand," between the so called deep cleansing breaths and warding off a river of tears I managed to continue, "not being able to remember the man I'd given my heart and soul to is the most isolating, depressing feeling I could have."

"Dove, I'm sure by now you're well aware you've got Hawke going completely and insanely crazy over you." Jane just couldn't keep her giggling laugh contained, "You don't have to do anything but breathe and Hawke has to have you. It's always been that way between the two of you."

"Thanks for the tidbit of info there. Wish I could remember it." Frustrated with myself, I rolled my eyes at Jane. "Nice to know that just breathing around my husband is cause for him to throw me in bed and jump on me."

For a moment, I felt like Ebony as I stretched my neck from side to side and arched my back. I found Maude's motherly eyes studying me deeply as I continued my contortion movements. She'd been the one to practically hold my hand through every step I took towards my recovery. I still depended on her and today was no exception.

"Dove," she carefully thought out her question before presenting it to me, "are you afraid of Hawke?"

"Yes," my bangs danced from the breath I let escape me. How could Maude hit the nail on the head when it came to everything about me?

"Why?"

Happy the cup of coffee relaxed me enough to talk, "I'm, it's not," I shoved the empty cup away from me, "pretty much completely terrified to be alone with him."

Jane's shoulder pressed into mine, "Dove, did something happen? I know he'd never force you, but…"

"No." I snapped harshly at her accusation, "It's not Hawke. The man has the patience of a Saint when it comes to my dilemma of getting naked."

"I get it, you're scared, why?" Jane, she didn't beat around the bush.

"It's not fair that Hawke knows every detail of my mind and body. For me everything is a blank slate. He pulls off his shirt, my heart starts into a thumping palpitation."

"That's a good sign, Dove." Again, I gave Jane another sarcastic eye roll.

"When he reaches for me, I stiffen like a board. I know he can feel me trembling. That can't be much of a comforting thought for him. And, if and when I'm a willing partner, what if our sex life isn't the same as before?" I bombard them with ample questions, "What if I don't like making love to my own husband? What if he's not happy?" A fresh panic attack nearly boiled over. "I don't know how to fix this."

"First off, Dove, you've got to calm down. This is a fixable problem." Jane wrapped her arms around my shoulder, "take my word for it, you're going to love having sex with him."

"How would you know?" I kind of shoved her off me and glared at her only to be met by a roar of laughter.

"Seriously??? Dove, we've sat up many of nights engaged in long, lengthy girl talks." She snorted another laugh.

"Oh good god, Jane," relief flooded over me, "the way you made it sound, like you'd slept with Hawke."

"Dove," Jane's turn to express an eye rolling, "that's gross. I'd rather take him on in a boxing match than ever sleep with him." As if a cold draft hit her, Jane shuddered.

126

"Enough you two," not overly amused by us, Maude broke into our conversation, "all this stress over the three letter word SEX. For starters stop dwelling on it."

"That's a little hard Maude, Hawke's kind of there. In the same bed with me. In the same house with me. Pretty much where I am, he is." I couldn't wait for her answer to that.

"Now just listen up, sure I mentioned all this before, but its worth repeating." Maude poured either a third or fourth round of Irish cream into our cups and topped it off with a touch of steaming black coffee. "When you two started dating, it took a while for you to warm up to Hawke. Your shyness only intrigued him more. Hawke new exactly what he wanted out of life and he wanted you with him." She winked at me, "Took things nice and easy. Not like Jane here," Maude's eyes darted over to Jane with a smirking smile. "Believe you me, I was fully aware of my nephew's shenanigans, but when it came to you," she gave me a wink, "that boy kept me worried."

Before I could even ask why, "Correction, Maude, we were all worried about her." With a gleaming smirk, Jane added her two cents. "Bad boy preys on pretty innocent girl," she tugged at the tail of my hair, "that would be you Dove. At least your story ended happily."

"You make us sound like some fairy tale romance," my eyes swung from Maude's then back to Jane's eyes.

"You could say that, Dove," Maude topped our coffee mugs off, again, "Don't want to say you were naïve back then, but you were so impressionable."

"Are you trying to say Hawke took advantage of me?" My ears perked up in interest.

"I'm sure he tried." With a wink from Maude, I knew it must've been true. "But you, Dove, you've got a free spirit about you that even Hawke can't bottle. Combine that with his obsession with you not only mentally, but..."

"Also meaning his physical needs," Jane interrupted by fake kissing the air, "and let me tell you, he's obsessed with you, Dove."

"I've already gathered that, but how is this helping me with my panic attacks of getting intimate with him?" I waited for my captain and co-captain to explain.

"Hawke gave you all the space you needed to get comfortable with him. I'm sure he still has a lot of that patience left for you, sweetie." Maude's words sounded so encouraging.

"Well let me tell you, that so called patience, it ran out this morning. I felt the full wrath of his frustration. I'm telling you, I'm even running out of patience with myself over this." After the fourth or was it now the fifth cup of Aunt Maude's special brew, the effects hit me. "I think I better slow down, won't be much help with the lunch rush if I don't." I grinned and tapped the cup.

"The magic, I see it in those free spirited eyes of yours. Honey, he's just so in love with you." Maude's eyes sparkled, "As you work your way back together, enjoy each other. Don't let your fears stop you."

"I know," Jane's giggling smirk gave warning, "Let's go shopping."

"Shopping? That's going to make me feel better?" I questioned suspiciously.

"We'll find you something so naughty, in black." Jane let her fingers spider walk up my shoulder.

"Are you crazy?" I brushed her spidery fingers away, "I found a drawer full of skimpy, naughty, lacey, let's just dress me up, things, that Hawke's bought for me."

"Always nice to have something new. I can never get Fred to go into those places with me. He'd die a thousand deaths if he'd have to walk into a place like that." Jane joked, "We've got a date, right?" Before I could answer with a flat out no, the bells on the door rang.

"Finally, I've been saved by the bell." Relieved, I wasn't so quick to make a mad dash to the safety of my kitchen. Instead, I grabbed for the counter top, "Maude,"

"You'll be fine honey, just stay away from the knives." Like the little girl I really was to her, she led me by the hand to the kitchen.

"Maude," I swayed a little, "I think I need straight black coffee." Instead of letting go of my hand, she just wrapped her arms around me. "Maude, do you think I'll ever be my old self again?"

"You are your old self. Do you realize how lucky you are to still be here? It's just a plain miracle. That mind of yours needs a little more reconnecting, that's all. Honey, listen to me. When it comes to Hawke, don't be afraid of him. He's crazy about you, always has been. You've had to handle a lot in a short time with a fuzzy memory. But the two of you have the magic. I can see it bubbling in you." I looked over my shoulder at her with questioning eyes. "It's there sweetie. Deep inside of you, the passion is just waiting to explode." Her hug tightened around me. "Just let those scared feelings go and see what happens. I'm telling you, it's magic. I'll go make us some strong black coffee." Another hug, I think more to steady herself, and she left me to the cooking and milling around with my new thoughts.

Chapter 19 - The Pretty Pink Box

October Fest weekend left the diner overflowing with hungry customers. With all the people coming and going you'd have thought we were in the height of our summer vacation season. The festival drew people in from all the neighboring towns.

Like clock work, the local sheriff had a permanent stool at the counter everyday for lunch. The only exception today, he had to take whatever stool came free.

"Hey Sheriff," I greeted him with my usual happy smile, "How's the day going? Find any crazies or does that happen after midnight?" As I poured him coffee, I turned my head to make sure he was still there. The local sheriff usually had some kind of snappy comeback for me. "Sheriff, you alright back there?" When I glanced at him again, I found my friend silently staring directly at the backside of me. "You okay?"

"Dove," he gulped a swallow of air down, "I'm sorry. Shouldn't have been staring at your," he pointed a pudgy finger in my direction, "your scars like that. Sorry, Dove."

Nearly all of my scars that the bear permanently tattooed to my body were exposed. The heat from the kitchen had me cooking in a tank top and shorts. I completely forgot the impact my unsightly designs could have on someone. Sympathetically, I smiled at his awkwardness and handed him the cup of coffee.

"Do you like my fancy "designed by a bear" tattoos?" I flashed the unsightly side of my left shoulder and rolled my eyes at him.

"Dove, you amaze me. You get your ass kicked by a bear, and I'm not talking about that husband of yours," he chuckled knowing better, "and look at you, smiling, like nothing every happened."

"You know for a fact, my ass-kicking husband wouldn't lay a hand on me, and truthfully," I did a second glance over my lined with designs body, "I'm glad I don't remember any of it happening. Best part, the worst of the scars stay behind me. I don't have to look at them."

"Hear most of your memory made it back. Guess that's a good thing for Hawke." The sheriff actually picked up my left hand and examined my healed skin.

"Can't say everything has flooded back, but I've been able to piece things together." I giggled when he ran a finger along the purple lines on my lower arm. "You're tickling me."

"Oh, sorry, Dove. Do you remember me stopping by the hospital to check on you?"

"No, not really. Just remember Hawke being there day in and day out."

"Never will forget the sight of you all bandaged up from head to toe. You gave everyone here one heck of a scare." He shuddered at the memories I barely could recall.

"No need to worry anymore. Besides look who I'm married to. You know I'm in good hands." Before he could comment I asked, "Usual for lunch? Or are you going to live dangerously? Come on let me fix you something with a kick to it?"

"No, no, just the usual Dove. Got to keep this figure in shape." The Sheriff, a jolly, round, extremely tall man flexed his arms into a bodybuilder's pose.

"Have it right out for you." Small chef salad, tomato soup, and a grilled cheese, Monday through Friday, just the usual for the Sheriff.

Knee deep into the lunch rush orders, I did notice Jane attempting to tiptoe her way in behind me. From the corner of my eye, I saw the brightly wrapped package along with her silently contained giggling.

"Fred got you something special there Jane?" Gooey cheese landed on my apron as I wiped my hands off. "You going to open it?" I gave her a seductive wink, we both knew there was only one place in town that sold things all wrapped pretty in pink and black.

"Don't be absurd, Dove, you know Fred wouldn't dare buy me what's tucked inside this box." Her giggle squealed out more like a high pitched scream.

She had my full attention, "What's in the box? It can't be that bad?"

"And you know Fred," she dismissed my questions, "he'd just die a thousand times over if he stepped foot into one of those stores." Sassily, Jane smirked back.

"What store?" Even though I knew, I kept playing right along with her.

"You know. Those kind of stores." She lip kissed the air at me and winked again. "This isn't for me," she toyed with the pretty box, "it's for you." In the palm of both of her hands, Jane extended the box toward me.

"Me? It's not my birthday or anniversary. What did you get me?" Playfully, I shook the box, no rattle, things only slid back and forth.

"Let's just say it's your lucky day." She inched closer to me, waiting for me to pull the ribbon off the frilly box.

"Lucky day?" My eyebrow perked with a dozen or more questions.

"Yes, lucky. Maude and I decided to do a little shopping for you. You know, set the mood."

"Set what mood, Jane?" Now in my hands, I shifted the gift box around.

"Something to make you feel, you know, feel like a woman." She sung out the last few words. "Something enticing." The harder she giggled the more I began to worry. "What are you waiting for? Open it." Jane oozed and the excitement dripped from her voice.

No need to ask where she'd gotten the pretty pink box from. There's only one place in town that carried a designer package like the one I held. After I studied every square corner of the glittery box, I glanced up to Jane who waited with anticipation.

"Will you just open it already?" Her giggle, more of a demand then request.

Keeping Jane humored, I plopped the box onto the countertop, "See," I swirled my fingers around the top, "I'm opening." One pink and black ribbon slipped off easily. As I hesitantly lifted the lid from the top of the box, Jane clutched her hands together and I swear she all but jumped into a cheer.

"You being over excited won't make me move faster," I gave her my best scrunched up prune face and sorted through the layers of pink tissue paper. "You did not? Jane, what...what did you do?"

"Do you like it?" I'm not sure if it was my stunned expression glowing on my face or the fact she'd totally taken me off guard that caused Jane to squeal into another round of high pitched laughter.

"Like it?" A little edged on the frantic side, I hissed my reply back at her, "Jane? You? Maude? You went shopping?" The new treasure to my wardrobe, an emerald green stain bra trimmed in black lace, dangled from my fingertips. "Jane...why?"

"Why not? There's more goodies. Pull them out." This time, Jane attempted to dig into my little box of privates.

"More? Are you kidding me?" I wore the frantic picture on my face well by the way Jane snickered out another laugh.

"Yes, there's more. Keep digging." She pushed the threatening box toward me.

"No, there can't be more," riffling through more tissue paper, I located all the accompaniments. To match my new bra of course there'd be emerald green panties trimmed with black lace. If that wasn't bad enough, I located the black silky stockings. All items draped over my arm, "What no garter belt?" The tone of my voice dripped in sarcasm.

"Well it better be in there." Jane leaned over the box double checking to see if I'd forgotten anything.

"Are you kidding me?" No my best friend wasn't. I found the so called garter belt all curled up like a pretty lacey snake waiting to make me turn red. "Jane?"

"You like it don't you?"

"No. Take it back." All of the sexy items, I shoved them into Jane's hands. "No, I can't wear this."

"You're going to look so great in this." She draped the unspeakable satin bra over my shoulder, "Maude's right. The dark green, with your hair," she held the panties up next to me, right where panties would go.

"Jane stop. You're taking this back." I pushed her hands away from my body.

"You're going to look so sensational in this. Hawke's not going to know what to grab for first."

"Jane? No, stop. I can't wear this! What are you two trying to do to me?" My mouth flapped open and closed so many times I lost count. Plus, I kept gasping for air as my own horrified thoughts ran freely through my shocked mind.

"Dove," Jane yanked my hands out and put the skimpy, let's talk about sex, outfit into them, "don't think we haven't noticed how you and Hawke have been getting touchy feely with each other. Just thought we'd help you along. Fresh and sexy lingerie can always set the mood."

"Mood? Are you crazy? What am I going to do with this?" Instantly, my fingertips tightened around the unmentionables that Jane insisted on talking about.

"I'd suggest you wear it. Let Hawke decide want he wants to do with it."

"If I can manage to get myself into this," I twisted my hands around examining the lacy goods I still held, "I'm sure it will shock the hell out of Hawke." Every level of panic wedged its way in between me and my present.

"Shut your mouth and listen up Dove." Jane commanded instead of hitting me with another fresh outburst of laughter. "You're going to wear this tonight," she wiggled the bra at me, "and you're going to like it!"

"Do what? Tonight? No, I don't think so Jane. You're asking the impossible." Wave number one of trembling just kicked in.

"Sit down, Dove. Now breathe. Fred and I are going to take the girls after we go to the October Fest and you're going home."

"Home? No girls? I don't think so Jane."

"Yes, Dove, you're going home alone with your husband."

"Wait a minute, I didn't...." glad for the wooden stool under my butt, "Jane, I don't know if I can..."

"Dove, just enjoy time alone with your husband. See where it goes. I'm sure this will help." She tapped the garments I still clung to.

"Jane," another round of trembling crept its way into my stomach, "I don't think I'm ready."

"Breath Dove, Breath." Deep breathing techniques with Jane as my coach was an experience all in its self. "Dove, you're more than ready. Take the leap. Just relax, enjoy. Hawke will handle the rest, you know he will."

"Diner's filling up girls, especially with your two husbands," Maude popped into the kitchen, "nice little gift you've got there, Dove."

"You were in on this?" I pointed to the tell tale box on the counter.

"Sure was. And you know what Dove?"

"No, but I suppose you're going to tell me," never could leave up on the sarcasm.

"Had fun picking it out for you. Now get that ruby red glow off your face. You know as well as I do Hawke's going to know something's up. Jane, need you in the dining room."

"I'm moving," but she didn't budge an inch.

"Maude," I shot her the nastiest dirty look, "I can't believe you were in on this. It's so not funny. The two of you," I shook the bra and panties at them, "you two have way too much time on your hands."

"That we do my sweet girl. That we do. Now get the frilly thing back in the box and hide it in my office. Move!"

Instead of obeying Maude's hand clapping commands, I crammed the sexy, lacy garments back into the pink and black box with a punch and glared at Jane. "I can handle Hawke, really didn't need all of this." This whole situation bugged me, and not in a good way.

"Like I said Dove, just a little incentive to help you get things rolling under the sheets." Jane had the nerve to laugh as she started to walk away from me and the annoying box of today's conversation.

My hand found the closest spoon in a simmering pot of spaghetti sauce. As Jane swayed her hips with attitude toward the dining room, I threw the metal spoon, dripping with red sauce across the kitchen at her back. My aim sucks, missed her by a mile. Instead, my weapon of choice collided with the wall not only with a splatter, but an awful thud.

Drops of spaghetti sauce shimmered off her left arm as she flew around to face me. "Dove, what the hell are you doing?" For a brief moment I enjoyed the sheer terror that filled her unsuspecting face.

"Payback Jane. It'll happen. When, don't know. Where, don't care." I squeezed the crazy designer box in my hand, "but it'll happen."

"Bring it on sister." She pursed her lips at me and welcomed my challenge. Being the nice person I really am, I tossed her a wet towel. "Still can't hit the broad side of a barn, can you?"

"Nope, but I'm just warning you." Jane pounced before I could say another word.

"And I'm warning you Dove, Hawke's like three steps from entering this kitchen. I'll let you explain." She pointed to the box in my hand, then to the sauce splattered wall. "See ya," she blew me one of her sarcastic kisses of knowing she had one up on me, again.

Not even bothering to worry about Hawke seeing the infamous box, I started to wash down the wall. I was more afraid of what Maude would do if she saw her starched white wall swimming in staining red spaghetti sauce.

"Hey," I basically said hello to Hawke's gnarly boots before I glanced up to him.

"Sauce explode?" He offered me his hand, then yanked me to my feet.

"Kind of." After I double checked the white tile for stains, Hawke followed me over to my work counter. "Needed to get Jane's attention." His eyes darted down toward the annoying box that I never got hidden in Maude's office.

"Take it you got her attention," I moved my body between me, him, and the taboo item waiting for me to explain its existence to him. "I missed."

"Kind of figured." He glanced back at the now clean wall, "Dove," Hawke circled his hand around my waist and rested it on the small of my back. "What are you hiding?"

"Nothing," with no escape and no one willing to rescue me, I shoved the box out of both of our reach before he could pull me closer to him.

"So tell me Dove, the pink box, it belongs to you?" His velvety smooth eyes began a silent interrogation.

"Kind of," easily he held my hands behind my back and I let him, "I guess."

"You guess?" His lips scorched with heat over mine. "Want to tell me about it?"

"Hawke, I don't," again our lips danced into a sizzle, "the orders, I've got to…"

The sharp slapping sound of a plastic menu hitting Hawke's back broke us apart, "Hawke, get the hell off her." Jane wacked him again when he didn't bother to let me go. "How the hell is Dove going to get these orders ready if you're back here lip locked with her?" In her usual Jane pose, hands on hips, she waited for us to separate.

"Jane," I could see Hawke reeling in every sarcastic, horrible thing he wanted to say to her, "believe Fred's out at the counter. Why don't you go service him?"

"Smartass, took care of him this morning. Why do you think he's so happy?" She wacked him again with the menus. My best friend wiggled her thin body between mine and Hawke's. "You only think with that brain in your pants," as she began to chastise him, Jane poked him in the center of his chest with a perfectly painted fingernail, "Do you think you could just possibly leave Dove alone? Just this once?" She backed him out of the kitchen with me following.

"Little pushy today now aren't you Jane?" Ignoring her and all of the comments babbling from her lips, Hawke chose to tease me with a playful grin, "Dove, we'll finish this later." All he had to do, wink at me and the scarlet flush painted itself over my cheeks.

"Go play with Fred," Jane pointed one of those polished nails toward her husband sitting at the end of the counter. In a flash she had me by the hand and escorted me back into the kitchen, "Stay. Now cook." Didn't know who was worse, her or Maude, at bossing me around.

Back to filling lunch tickets and happy to have Hawke's playful quest for knowing what I kept hidden in the pink box over, I slid another order into the pickup window. I couldn't help taking a moment to enjoy the view of my husband.

"Dove," Jane's voice pulled me from my enticing view.

"Did I mess an order up?"

"No," she glanced out to where Hawke was in a deep conversation with the local sheriff. "He's always had some kind of hold over you. You just melt in his presence. Always have. I think you always will. Look at you, you're still blushing."

"Jane, why do I feel like I'm going on my first date with him? Why am I scared of him?"

"You're not scared, sweetie. You're in love and just now rediscovering it." She gave me one of those hugs only a true friend could give.

Chapter 20 - The Magic of an October Night

October Fest meant one thing...fabulous old world Bavarian style food. Bratwurst, Frankfurters, Knockwurst, Pork Roast, and Wiener Schnitzel were top on the list to sample. Potato dumplings, potato pancakes, potato salad, red cabbage and sauerkraut were just a few of the side dishes. Who could choose? But the desserts, to die for. Apple Strudel, Black Forest Cake, Plum Cake, Lebkuchen, Pretzels and the endless list of tasty temptations went on.

Encircled in a halo of manly cigar, cigarette, and even pipe tobacco smoke that lingered in the air, Hawke kicked back with a smooth icy cold German beer, and of course, his favorite brand of cigars. While hanging out in the beer garden he'd become oblivious to his buddy's conversation of "who could out do who" and focused his full attention on his wife.

She'd become particularly jumpy this evening all over a little gift box he'd seen her with earlier in the day. He enjoyed teasing Dove, even taunting her about what was in the box as she tried so desperately to keep him out of their bedroom while she got ready.

He'd finally found Dove in the kitchen dressed in a cotton dress that accented her curvy figure. Unaware of him, Hawke caught her adjusting the sheer black hose on her long, sculpted legs. He wasn't about to interrupt a show he wasn't suppose to see. What really aroused his curiosity, when Dove gently tugged at the neckline of her dress. He grinned to himself as she glanced down inside and whispered what he thought was some kind of a prayer for later that evening. Seeing her fingers skim over the emerald green bra straps as she fussed with the top of her dress, Dove had given him yet another preview of what she kept hidden.

Through the crowd of people Hawke continued to enjoy his view of Dove. She moved freely in conversation with Maude and Jane as she kept a watchful eye on their two girls. He could only image what the topic of their so called 'girl talk' could possibly be about this evening. Most likely one topic he was sure they'd be covering, why Dove was so anxious over the gift she wanted to keep hidden from him. He chuckled aloud, and took a long inhale of his cigar. Before her accident, Dove would chastise him for smoking. Wiggling a slim finger as she lectured, reminding him about smoking his dreaded cancer sticks. Back then, deep down he'd known she enjoyed the scent of his flavored cigars, but she'd never admit it. That all changed, everything about Dove had changed in a blink of an eye.

"Hawk, she's fine." Lance noted how his friend had been lost to their surroundings. "Dove's with Maude and Jane. Nothing's going to happen to her. She's safe."

"Yep, I know." Hawke propped his feet up on the adjacent chair and let his cigar rest in the nearby ashtray. "Still can't believe this is the same woman who was on death's doorstep a few months ago." His eyes never left the glowing figure he'd been keeping tabs on.

"Think the big guy upstairs wasn't ready to keep her." Lance pointed to the darkened sky above and snuffed out his own cigar.

"Not one for being over religious, but I thank God everyday for not taking her."

"Everyone does Hawke, everyone does." Lance abruptly rose to his feet, "See ya guys in the morning. If I'm late, don't hold it against me." He waved to the pretty blond walking toward him.

"Where ya going?" The only reply Fred received, a sly smile of none of your business. "Would you look at that," Fred dared to point in the direction Lance headed, "did you know he'd been seeing someone?"

"Yep. Fred, my man, you really need to stay in the circle of female gossip. Jane told Dove. Who, of course, told me."

"Told you before, all that female bonding shit scares the hell out of me. You need a refill?"

"I'll take another." As Fred left to sample another brand of German beer, Hawke's view drifted back to Dove.

She'd been willing to let her guarded emotions flourish just by accepting his touch. A loving hug no longer had Dove jumping into a mere panic attack. More than once he'd found her curled tightly next to him during the midnight hour. Freely she'd been willing to engage him in lingering kisses. His favorite moments came when Dove slipped in the shower behind him. Her naked body curved so close into his back as the heat of the water cascaded over them. Each time she chose to join him, the longer she'd linger.

"Dude, what's got you smiling like that? What gives?" Fred handed him a refreshing cool ale. "I see the females are deep into," he shuddered, "whatever girl talk."

"Dove, seems she's been given one of those fancy boxes from the "Naughty and Nice" shop." A ring of smoke circled in the air as Hawke grinned.

"Yep. Heard all about your Aunt and my wife planning to get Dove back into the grove of L O V E." With a heavy emphasis, Fred spelled out each letter. "You ever been in one of those stores?"

"Guilty." Hawke winked at him. "Purchased many of those so called 'naughty lady' items for Dove."

"Holy hell, Jane drug my ass into one of those places," Fred slurped at his beer, "thought I'd just die of embarrassment."

"Fred my man, you're one of a kind." With a beer in one hand, favorite brand of cigar in the other, Hawke continued to enjoy the view of his wife.

xoxoxoxoxo

After receiving another round of goodnight hugs and kisses, I watched my girls trot off hand in hand for their slumber party at Jane and Fred's house. On that cue, Maude and Harry had also offered up their goodnight wishes and strolled on off into the moonlit night. Not even nine o'clock and I'd been abandoned by everyone, even my girls. A cool breeze circled around Hawke and me as we sat silently on the wooden bench together.

"You alright?" Hawke flipped the tale of my hair over my shoulder.

"Yeah, fine." I didn't need to wonder why he asked, I already knew. "The girls certainly enjoyed themselves."

"You spoil them, Dove." He lit yet another cigar, the scent of smoky cherry circled around us.

"I know, can't help it." Hawke conveniently stretched his arm comfortably around my shoulder, "Need to ask you about a memory."

"You have another slice of your life reappear and you forget to tell me?"

"No." I shot him a look of "are you serious?" "With all the commotion at the diner today. Getting the girls ready and," without any hesitation, I curled myself into the side of his warm body before I gave up the memory I hoped would be true.

"Want to share what clicked in that mind of yours?" With an exhaling breath, I could hear Hawke empty his lungs from the cigar he'd been puffing on.

From the curled position I'd cuddled into, I bolted straight up, my hand landed on his chest as I stared him in the eyes, "First date." My whispering voice startled him.

"First date. You mentioned that before. Took ya to see Cat's." By the smile that appeared on his lips I had him intrigued by my memory. "Something else pop into place?"

"I saw me with you," as if in a dream I could see the memory even with my eyes open.

"Dove," his hand circled around mine, "what did you remember?"

"Yellow colored house. Dark green shutters. Large front porch, steps in the middle." I took in another breath as he shuffled me around from where we sat so we faced each other. "Flowerpots both sides, going up each step. I stood on the second step from the bottom."

"And?" The only emotion he gave me, his honey amber eyes reflecting the carnival lights.

"You kissed me." Both of us consumed by my memory, the carnival atmosphere around us no longer existed. "Did it…did it happen?" On the edge of suspension I waited for him to say something. Anything about what I hoped to be a real memory.

"Nice memory, Dove," by this time he had my hands interlocked in his, "You just described the front of your Aunt and Uncle's house."

"But what about," I searched his eyes in hope. It had to be true, "kissing you."

"Happened every time I brought you home from a date. You'd purposely stand on the second step from the bottom."

"Why the second step?"

"So you were as tall as me. Made kissing you easier." I loved the way he'd just wink at me, "Plus, I knew your Uncle would be watching out the window. Wanted to make sure he saw where I rested my hands. I didn't keep them on your hips."

"You didn't?" I let a giggle slip free and I found exactly where Hawke's hands went. Even sitting on a bench he managed to squeeze the fleshy side of my bottom. "I take it my Uncle waited up on date night."

"Every time I took you out he'd be waiting up. I could see the curtains move. Knew it wasn't your cat in the window. Even heard your Aunt yell at him a few times for spying on us." He chuckled harder at the memory.

"Finally, I remembered something with you." All too pleased with myself, I coiled my fingers around his, "Kiss me." There was no need to ask, his lips sealed over mine.

"Comfortable?" Hawke asked as he lightly tugged at a stray curl of my hair.

"Yes, I'm…" That nagging voice barked at me, *'You realize you're going to be alone with him? All alone.'* Clearing my throat my voice held crisp, "Very comfortable."

"You ready to head home?" Through Hawke's eyes I could see his rambling unasked question, "when is she going to snap?" "We can stay longer if you want."

"No." For once I felt secure with my emotions, wants, and a burning desire for the man next to me, "Let's head home."

Hawke didn't think twice as he snubbed out his cigar, "Have your fill of German food?" He offered me his hand and in one tug had me on my feet next to him.

"I did. Made a list of mental notes for the dishes I want to try." The lights from the carnival danced under the full moon and the aroma of delicious German food followed us to the parking lot.

"Got to say, Dove, you make one heck of a mean dumpling." He eased my festering nerves with a familiar kiss to the top of my head as he helped me into the truck.

With all the grace I could muster, I climbed into the front seat of his big 4x4 truck. My comfortable dress with the flowing skirt did exactly that, flowed right up my leg. The cotton material slipped its way up my thigh and revealed the silky stocking attached to the edge of the lace garter. Hawke's eyes glistened in the moonlight at the view I gave him.

"What else have you been hiding from me, Dove?" Without warning, Hawke ran his fingers lightly over my exposed leg.

"Just a few...nothing." Avoiding eye contact with him, I tried to push the edge of my dress down along with his hand. "It's a...really it's..." His grin widened as I fumbled to say anything else. The warmth of his hands tingled on my bare legs, "Hawke, please," with my composure slipping fast, I playfully pushed at his hands in our game of tug of war over my dress. As my hands clasped his, his lips closed on mine. The cool crisp night air that circled around us couldn't chill the rush of warmth that flooded between him and me. Breathless, I found myself easing back from his kiss and eye to eye with him.

"Dove," his soft whisper tickled as he kissed my lips again, "better get you home." As he climbed into the driver's seat he just had to mention, "You're blushing."

"I know." I picked at the edge of my dress that now covered my knees as Hawke started the truck. "Who told you?" Nervously, I patted the edge of my dress.

"Told me what?" Puzzled he glanced over at me. "Dove, one thing about you, known it from the first time I met you," he offered me a sultry grin, "I've always been able to read you."

"You can read me like a book?" Would love to hear his thoughts on what I was thinking, but I didn't ask. "How did you know? You better keep your eyes on the road." Countless times his eyes drifted over at me even before we made it out of the parking lot.

"The box. I know where it came from, Dove." He rattled my emotions with a simple smile. "It's not a secret. I've bought you many of things from that store."

My heart pounded remembering the drawer full of sexy, silky items he'd bought for me, "Did Jane or Maude...did they say..." Just looking at him and knowing he knew what I kept delicately trapped under my dress. "Who told you?"

"No one, Dove. Figured it out. Little heads up, you might want to watch what all you mention to Jane."

"Jane?" The tension of our sexual arousal in the truck shifted into low gear at the thought that Jane would have sold me out.

"Fred, Jane, she tells him everything." Hawked laughed as the surprise literally jumped from me, and it didn't feel good. "She tells Fred just about everything."

"So what else do you know?" I asked, a little peeved at my bestfriend.

"Could use superglue on the woman's mouth and she'd still find a way of spilling the beans."

"Tell me you're not serious." Skeptic of what Hawke told me, "Really don't think Jane would tell all."

"Lucky for you, most of that girly shit you and her gab about, your secrets are safe." I couldn't tell if he was playing with my emotions or if he was serious.

Like the air deflating from a balloon, my lungs exhaled in relief. All I could think of was the day we drank Irish whiskey and talked about cold showers.

"Nice to have the house to ourselves tonight," Hawke moved to what he knew would be a touchy subject with me, "We haven't been alone for awhile." He accented the word "alone" with a soft smile as he pulled onto the street where we lived.

"Guess overnight stays at the hospital don't count." He slowed the truck to a near crawl as he turned into our driveway. The beast of a truck, parked, and Hawke pocketed his keys, "Home already."

"Yep, home already, Dove." Hawke, he wasted no time as he leaned over the console of the truck that separated us. His gentle touch still amazed me as he outlined the edge of my jaw with his fingertips.

Hawke wasn't the only one who could read minds. Again, I saw it in his eyes, the burning question of the evening, "When will she break?" The closeness between us should've had me hitting my well known panic mode. The nasty pit of nerves that harbored deep in my stomach evaporated. My own calmness startled Hawke when I initiated the first move by kissing him.

"Dove?"

"Just kiss me." The tips of my fingers dug deep into his forearm as I moved closer to him. The emotions that toyed with me, it just heighted the passion I felt for him. I shifted my weight in the seat and practically crawled over the console still lip locked with him.

"Dove," the warmth of his hands drifted over the bodice of my dress, "need to take this inside."

"Yeah, okay," neither one of us attempted to exit the truck, probably because his lips were searing down my neck.

"Might be more comfortable for you in our bed," suggestion made, but again, neither one of us acted on it.

"Hawke if you want to get me into the house, why is your hand roaming up and under my dress?" As I pulled back from him he tugged at the neckline of my dress revealing, again, a hint of my emerald green bra. "You want to..." I pointed to the backdoor, but Hawke's hand wrapped around the back of my neck and his lips crushed hard onto mine.

"I'm not messing around here, Dove." His words came thick with need.

"Neither am I." Freely, he let me slip from his grip and out of the truck. Before I closed the door I asked, "Are you joining me?"

The clicking sound of his door shutting behind me echoed in the still night. Hawke cocked his head to the side questioning me as I waited for him. "I'm not kidding, Dove, don't start something you can't finish."

"If I were having any doubts, I would've told you by now." The pattern of shadowy moonlight filtered between us as he cradled me in his arms. Our bodies nearly sculpted into one being from our closeness. Lost in my own emotional need, I couldn't help but breathe in the scent of him. The scent I had grown so familiar to. So attached to. The smell of his cologne mixed heavily with his distinctive masculine essence drew me in deeper as I held the deep lingering breath I took of him. Content with his caressing hugs, I didn't want to accept the slight movement of our bodies separating. How we landed on the deck without falling over each other I'd never know. Comfortably pinned under the weight of Hawke's body, the support of the locked kitchen door held me upright. My knees felt the need to buckle and he left me light headed just from his over powering kiss. I lunged back into his arms for another round. My lips lingered longer on his as he pushed me back into the sturdy door. My fingertips led me on a tour of his defined shoulders, the sway in his lean back, and the ripple of muscles down his arms.

"Keys? Do you..." A gasp of breath escaped me as Hawke's hand rode high up under my dress outlining the hidden lacy garter.

"Got them." He jingled them in his free hand and blindly poked at the locked door knob. "Dove..." the ring of keys clanged as they hit the wooden deck, "you've got to stop kissing my neck if we're going to get inside."

Finally, my supportive backdoor sprang wide open. Twisted and tangled in each others arms and legs, I stumbled at his quick guidance of moving me backwards. Caught and cushioned by the coats hanging on the wall, Hawke met my inviting wide eyed expression with another lustful kiss. Conveniently trapped by him, and half a dozen coats, he enjoyed my squirming under the weight of his warm body. As he continually tried to free me of my dress, I kept yanking the material up and over my shoulder. My syndical thoughts of being incredibly terrified of him for months vanished. My body responded to every wanting need he offered. Deliberately stopping, he eased back from me. Analyzing me, I'm sure he contemplated what my next move would be. I could feel his heavy breath covering me and I'm sure I totally amazed him at how far I let him go without a panic attack. Still caught between the coats, Hawke lingered over me. He tugged at a wave of cascading curls that dangled around the base of my neck.

Lost in his thoughts, I slipped out from under him and the cozy nest of coats. Left standing empty handed, Hawke watched me as I neatly tossed my purse on the kitchen table. My own sly grin of suspense graced over my lips. For a little extra support I clung to the kitchen chair and slipped out of my shoes. The hush whisper of a "whoosh" let me know he'd just kicked his boots off. The cupboard door clicked behind me, a gurgle of something wet and fragrant splashed into a glass.

"Dove," He held out a glass of my infamous brandy. "Care to join me?"

A magic calming potion Hawke often used to calm my anxiety, I accepted the crystal glass he offered, but didn't drink it. Instead, I offered him an enticing smile and quietly left the surrounding comfort of my kitchen. Hawke's motions were as silent as the name he'd been give, I never heard his footsteps as I began to climb the staircase only to be stopped by him tugging at the edge of my waving dress.

"Last time I'm asking, you sure you're up for this?" Anticipation sparked in his eyes as he waited for me to reply.

A sip from the crystal goblet I held only made me smile at him, "Believe I've answered that question before. I haven't changed my mind." Another sip and I licked the sweet mixture off my lips and started my own game of seduction with him. No panic attacks lurked. My heighted fears disappeared and I was free to play back.

The intensity of arousal grew between us. No words offered, I leaned into Hawke making sure not to spill my brandy, and just kissed him, then teasingly licked the brandy I'd left off his lips. "Thanks for sharing the brandy with me." Free from his hands, I finished what I'd started, climbing the stairs and praying I won't trip and fall. Still in disbelief, Hawke waited at the bottom of the steps. Would I trip and fall? Would I break and fade into a panic attack, or would I give him what he'd been longing for?

Safely, I arrived at the top of the steps, "I'm waiting," I reminded him as I slowly turned to peer down to him. Another sweet taste of the blackberry brandy eased down my throat as I waited for his response.

Hawke clinched one hand to the rail and braced his other hand on the wall. Was it disbelief that shot from his eyes? His desire of heated moments in the past had only been crushed by my insecurities. "Don't be playing with me, Dove." My playfulness only built his burning passion. "Dove, I'm not kidding." His rough voice of need and want held my attention.

After another sip of brandy, I gracefully ran my fingertips over the polished edge of the banister, "I'm not kidding. I'm willing to play." With a pink tipped fingernail I motioned for him to follow me.

As quickly as I turned towards our bedroom, Hawke's low familiar chuckle followed me as he took two steps at a time. Under the threshold of our bedroom door my body froze. In my sight, the bed I've always shared with him. Hawke's chest brushed lightly over my back. The small of my back was treated to the warmth of his hand resting there. Easily he rolled the palm of his hand over my back to my hip. No nudge, no push, he waited for me. Just for a moment I closed my eyes and enjoyed his touch and the sound of his pounding heart. Less than five steps to the dresser and my empty glass of brandy wobbled on the edge.

"Hawke...what are you..." Without any warning, he'd swept me into his arms and carelessly tossed me into the center of the bed. With a few laughing bounces, I steadied myself, sat up and enjoyed the view of him peeling off his shirt. Still a little stunned by Hawke's fast growing aggression, he moved to the foot of our bed.

"Your turn, Dove. The dress, it really needs to go." Hawke arched a questioning eyebrow as I slowly crossed my legs with the well exposed garter and black hose teasing him. With a sly grin he patiently waited for me to stop swinging my long exposed crossed legs.

Hawke leaned forward and grabbed at my swing leg, pulling me to a halt, "Dovey, I'd be more than happy to help you with your dress."

Butterflies, they danced inside and outside of me at his touch. My heart surrendered with anticipation and a warm glow slowly whispered over my cheeks.

"I got it." With trembling fingers I fumbled with my dress. "I've been dressing and undressing myself for how many years?" Frustrated with myself, I couldn't get the soft cotton material off my body.

"Dove," he motioned for me to come closer to him. In an unflattering crawl I inched my body from the center of the bed to his waiting hands. "What have you been hiding from me?"

"I take it I'm not a very good striptease act for you?"

"Prefer to strip you myself." With that, Hawke yanked at the top of my loose dress, stripped it down my arms, over my waist, and it just crumbled at my bent knees.

"Hawke! Don't tell me you ripped my dress." The palm of my hand met the thickness of his muscular shoulder with a cracking smack that he only laughed at.

"Finally," Like a Christmas package Hawke had me nearly unwrapped. Exposed for his eyes only, me in the silky emerald green trimmed with black lace outfit. Wanting to hide myself from his view, "Don't Dove," Hawke held my hands in his.

"Okay," I actually bit my bottom lip, "Now what?"

Hawke's eyes slowly drove over the paleness of my road mapped, lacy designed body. As he enjoyed his scenic view, I struggled a little with pulling his hair free of the tied ponytail. A mass of thick raven black hair finally threaded though my fingers. He eased back to let me explore his half naked body. His tight skin warmed my fingertips as I glided them over his broad shoulders. He didn't sport a six pack washboard stomach. Only well defined hard muscles met my touring hands. Slowly, my fingers played the back and forth game along the waistband of his jeans. On my part, I showed an incredible amount of boldness when I grabbed for his belt. Easily, I had it open along with the top button on his jeans.

"Feeling brave, Dove?"

"Yes." My own confidence elated his desires as I let my tongue trail over his moist lips. With ease I silenced him while unzipping his jeans. The element of surprise radiated over his weathered face at my forwardness. Just for fun, I proceeded to slip my now warmer hands between his jeans and body hugging boxers. Only the fabric of our clothes kept our heated bodies separated. The base of his spine became my target of enjoyment. With a swirling, massaging pattern my fingers danced up his rigid spine.

The braveness I'd been fronting didn't even slip when I heard his husky whisper, "Dove, I've waited a long time for you." With a griping pull to my back, my milky white fleshy body smashed hard into his rugged frame.

"Hawke," he felt the nervousness rise in my voice, "easy, please." In a small teasing plea, I batted my weary eyelashes at him.

My request, taken to heart, he stopped to caress the details of his fascination. Hawke made sure I felt every sensational touch he offered while he skimmed over the lacy material that still kept me somewhat hidden.

"Remind me to thank Maude and Jane," the pressure of his pleasing touch deepened.

"Can't promise to…" Thank Maude and Jane, sorry but that was the furthest thing from my mind.

The snap from the elastic garter pinching into the back of my leg brought me back to here and now. The roughness of his fingers slipped under the lace trim of my panties and outlined the curve of my bottom. Gently he persuaded me to follow his lead and lay back on the mound of pillows behind me. Under the lacy canopy bed, I attempted to make myself comfortable on all the decorative bed pillows. Hawke enjoyed toying with my tender uneasiness while he unhooked the silky hose from the garter belt. Inch by inch, he slipped the silky stocking from my leg.

"You didn't snag them?" When I went to set-up, Hawke only pushed me back into the comforting pillows.

"Dove, done this before. Got it handled." In the same gentle way, he peeled the other stocking free of my leg.

The arousal heighten between us when Hawke placed one delicate kiss to the inside of my thigh. We hadn't even begun to remove anymore clothing and he'd left me trembling and breathless. Far from being finished, he disregarded my earlier plea for gentleness and planted a teeth nipping kiss to my left hip. The garter belt that once held my silk stockings in place now became a violent game of tug and war by his teeth.

"Hawke," Gasping for breath, my fingers grabbed for the soft comforter under me, as he wiggled the small black lace garment down the length of my lower body, "when did you turn into some kind of wolfhound?" Then with the garter still dangling in his teeth, he just tossed it aside.

On his return to my body, I prepared myself for another delightful assault of lustful kisses as he began his attack above the edge of my lace panties. I melted under the slower, more controlled line of smoldering kisses he delivered. Under the pleasing dance from his lips and tongue I giggled and couldn't stop. Slower, more controlled, Hawke kissed a direct line of kisses from the center of my stomach to the valley between my breasts where he lingered longer. Not quite relaxed, I felt the intensity of my body quivering when his finger ran down the imaginary line of kisses he'd just placed on my bare skin. Spontaneously, a chill rose over my soon to be naked body as I reached for his thick dangling hair. My lips trembled under his when I felt the release of the bra. A little squirming and my pretty lace bra found its way to the floor.

"Your jeans," I tugged at the open waistband wanting him to remove them.

"Best be doing something about that." His grin had me giggling as he ran both hands over my creamy full breasts.

A private party striptease was out of the question for me. Hawke simply peeled away his everyday navy blue boxers in one smooth move.

"Dove," with a light touch of his finger he drew a line down my stomach, "panties," his fingers tugged at the silky material, "they just slow me down."

"Slow you down?" Not rushing me or anything, but Hawke barely gave me time to lift my hips as he practically yanked the satin panties down my legs. My last article of surprise clothing dangled from his left hand as his eyes scanned over the package he'd just unwrapped. His hand was skimming over my smooth bare legs when the soft light footed padding of the cat stole center stage.

Ebony strutted over the comforter, and I swear if a cat could smirk, he did at Hawke. "Fur bag, she's mine." Hawke's eyes narrowed at the intruding feline. "Get off the bed." With a shove, none the lightest, pussycat fell to the floor along with my panties. An angry hiss welled back at us as the cat thumped to the floor.

"And you wonder why the cat doesn't like you." My attempt to edge to the side of the bed to check on my beloved pet got halted.

"Don't care, Dove." Hawke's whispering light touch only aroused me, "You're the only one I intend to be playing with." With that he straddled over top of my body.

Hawke stopped my wondering hand from tugging down the plush comforter. There was no hiding under the protective blanket and sheets. I wiggled my body under the weight of his trying to find my own comfort. His bare skin smoothly rubbed over mine filling my mind with an erotic sensation. His feather light touches over my sensitive skin tingled with delightfulness. As the weight of his body rested on mine a sleeping desire awoke in me. The sheer silkiness of his untamed hair slipped through my fingers. I struggled to keep breathing under his heated fury of our passionate kissing.

"Dove, open your eyes. I need to see everything you're feeling." He never demanded anything from me, only a simple request.

Obeying his single wish, I opened my eyes to find his. Hawke gently guided my hands from his loose hair and secured them in his. He thrived on my eager willingness for him as he made the first thrust, gentle deep, sending a riveting thrill through my trembling body. He left me sweetly moaning for more as I wrapped my legs around his already heated body. His endless rhythmic movements of gentleness left me breathless. A deep, low rumble of excitement left him as I nipped at the edge of his earlobe then left a pattern of scalding kisses over his bare neck and chest as he slipped deeper into me. Freely, my chilled fingertips massaged down his spine. We both panted for breath as Hawke rolled to his back taking me with him. My scream of surprise basically went unheard as my limp and heated body sprawled out on top of him.

His heart pounded with the beat of mine, "Hawke," I could barely speak, "we need to…" His hand slipped behind my neck and guided me back to his waiting lips. Instead of answering me, Hawke choose to show me his answer in detail. The stillness of our bedroom echoed his delighted pleasure of the uncontrollable obsession of passion he held for me. The moment seemed to be endless as our bodies continued to intertwine with each other. His frustration and my insecure fears had turned into a sensational connection of intimacy and an irresistible unending bond of love and trust towards one another. His long awaiting hunger for me had been met and satisfied over and over to the point of exhausting both of us.

xoxoxoxoxo

With our bedroom still filled with the darkness of predawn, I awoke to a quiet house and a cat curled next to me purring. Five in the morning peacefully displayed itself on the clock as I rolled over to find an empty bed. Where was he? Hawke was always next to me when I woke. My panic surged as I grabbed the covers of the empty bed. My head snapped toward the open door as the sharp clatter of keys landing on the wooden kitchen table echoed in the empty house.

"Hawke?" The panic slipped through my voice as I heard his heavy footsteps climbing up the stairs. My heart raced when I received no answer. Quickly, I turned the lamp on beside the bed as the steps halted in the doorway to our bedroom. "Hawke." Relieved to see him, he greeted me with a smile of comfort.

"Morning beautiful. Thought you'd still be asleep." Under the arch of the doorway, Hawke stood holding two cups of coffee in one hand. The other a white paper bag filled with freshly made donuts. From his smiling lips dangled one of his other pleasures, a lit cigar. The powder white smoke circled in a cloud around his head. "Sorry, ran into the guys." He grinned and let another puff escape.

With my eyes, still blurred by sleep, I happily accepted one of the cups coffee. He plopped the bag of donuts on his nightstand. The lush aroma of fresh brewed coffee, donuts, and cigar smoke circled through our bedroom.

"Why does this smell so good to me?" I asked breathing in the flavorful scents of all three blending aromas.

"Which one babe? The coffee," sipping from his own cup, "or this?" He wiggled the cigar between his fingers at me then carefully laid it in the ashtray.

"You did this a lot," my blurry eyed sleep left as my eyes popped wide open, "didn't you?"

"Yep. I did. You remembering something?" He asked while tugging off his shirt.

"The smell of all three. This...this is..." I enjoyed another sip of coffee. "Every Sunday morning. You'd bring me coffee and donuts." Hawke's eyes sparkled with pleasure at what I'd just remembered. "You, we, sugar, coffee...sex." I said the last word sultry and wanted to blame the heat rolling over me from drinking hot coffee, but I couldn't. A full body flush just woke up all of my senses.

He laughed harder at what I just realized, "Even if we didn't have Saturday night sex, I'd still get you coffee and donuts." Clothes completely discarded, Hawke found his way back under the covers with me. "Dove, you just had another piece of your brain puzzle snap back into place."

"Amazing. Coffee, donuts, cigar smoke, and sex. That's a keeper of a memory." He kissed my bare shoulder and dumped the bag of donuts in my lap.

"Donuts." He offered up another grin, "For your sugar rush."

"My sugar rush? Why would I," I rolled my eyes at him, "you're good. How many did you get?" Giggling as if I were a ten year old, I dug through the bag to find a glazed cinnamon roll. I kissed him with sugar covered lips, "How did you know I would need this?" Hawke rumbled with a deep laughter as I kissed him again between bites of my sugary heaven.

"Dove, you're the only person I know who needs sugar to survive."

As I reached for my coffee, I felt his warm fingers tracing down the middle of my bare spine. His touch, always warm, tingled as his fingers traced over the permanent tattoo of claw marks. Hawke left his fingers linger longer on the flowered birthmark that had been sliced in half by the swipe of a vicious claw. With a warm and inviting smile, I glanced back over my shoulder to him. His velvety brown eyes were filled with the magical passion I came to love. A passion I wanted to keep in my heart and soul forever.

BOOK II

Chapter 21 – Time Flies

"Criminal Forensic Majors." Neatly and extremely carefully, I tore the mega dollar check from our personal checkbook. "Or is it Forensic Criminal? Both of them." The girl's college tuition check got stuffed into the University of Portland's return envelope. "Both of them. Why?"

"Why what?" As always, I didn't even hear Hawke enter the kitchen all the while he stood by the sink filling his coffee mug.

"It's your fault. All...your...fault." I announced the last three words at him sarcastically.

"Dove," he glanced at the watch on his wrist, "it's five thirty in the morning. What the hell did I do already?" Kindly, with a skeptical grin, he topped off my cup with questioning eyes. "You were all smiles a little while ago." With a free hand, he tugged at a curl that went astray and enjoyed how my cheeks turned pink at remembering the morning roll over the bed. "Been enjoying having the house to ourselves now that the girls are off to college."

Hawke had to wink at me and make my cheeks go rosier. He could always distract me with one single topic, sex. Even with the said subject on his mind, I managed to get back to my topic. "The girls. Both of them, Criminal Forensic majors." I slapped a stamp on the fancy brown colored envelope after sealing it.

"Not making the connection here, Dove."

"If you wouldn't have shown them how to gut fish and skin deer," I tapped the edge of the rather expensive tuition envelope on the edge of the table and let a heavy sigh ring out. "They wouldn't have picked such a dangerous career."

"It's not as dangerous as you think. Besides, they're both together. Can't separate either one of them. Makes sense they'd pick the same subject to major in." He joined me at the kitchen table.

"And what did they both minor in," my eyes brightened, "accounting. There, a nice safe profession."

"Got a birthday coming up don't you?" He side stepped my morning drama. "Someone's hitting the big forty."

"Well just aren't you so charming to remind me." Forty, not so sure how that would be settling in with me, "At least the girls will be home for the summer."

"Damn straight. No free ride this year. Promised to pay for at least a fourth of their tuition."

"Stop that." I shook the pricey envelope at him, "Let me remind you of your conversation. No, the promise you made. You told them if they kept an A-B average, we'd pay for college." I buttered another slice of homemade banana bread. "Believe the Hawthorne beauties are pulling a four point average."

"You know for someone whose mind got scrambled, you sure can remember the damndest things." Hawke swiped the buttered bread from my hand. "You got anymore of this?"

"Yes," He sat in my warm chair as I went to retrieve another loaf and more coffee.

"Noticed you've been restless the last few nights. What's troubling your sleep?"

Coffee slopped over the counter at his mention of my restless sleep. "You know, with the girls up in Portland," I kept talking to the coffee pot instead of facing him. "Just, you know, I'm missing them."

"Dove, this is their third year at Portland. You've been fine," I glanced over my shoulder to him, "until recently. Care to tell me what you've been dreaming about?"

"Maybe," my cup filled to the brim, the loaf of bread waited to be escorted over to the kitchen table. But, I didn't move. "Dreams, there…" the few steps to the table seemed like a mile to walk, "something's there," the bread and coffee got a spot on the table before I managed to sit myself down across from him. "The images, they're getting clearer. The voice, it's stronger, I can feel the intensity."

"How many?" Hawke studied my new disturbed disposition as our eyes meet.

"Let's just say the dream catcher Maude gave me, it's been working overtime."

"How many, Dove?"

"Snippets of the dream started about a few weeks ago. But, I was awake. It happened in the cooler at the diner."

"Why didn't you tell me?" He took a long drink of his cooled coffee. "How many more, Dove?"

"It's really picked up this week." I slid another piece of buttered banana bread over to him, "something's going to happen." Eyes locked, he didn't dismiss my premonition. "Same one. The man with blonde curly hair and the little boy. Still can't make out who they're searching for."

"You're awfully pale, something else you're not mentioning?" All these years together and like he'd always said, he could read me like a book.

"Just one other," my hands gripped tighter than usual on my coffee mug, my voice even cracked, "just why I hated you so badly."

A somber expression fell across Hawke's well lined face. The small sentence I stated struck him in the heart. That chunk of tasty bread he held in his hand, tumbled right into his cup of coffee. For a man whose skin was already summer bronze, he nearly turned as pale as my pasty complexion. "Who told you?" He fished the drenched piece of bread out with two fingers, "Who Dove?"

"Confirmed is more like it." My fingers slipped across my lips, did I want to further this conversation so early in the morning. Hawke wasn't angry, but I've never seen fear sear through him so fast.

"You should've come to me." His tone didn't snap, but his eyes swayed with worry. "Why didn't you come to me Dove?"

"You were gone." I blinked back the tears. "It happened when you were away with Fred and Lance. Had that group in for the weekend hunt, in the mountains." Hands on my lone coffee cup gave me support. "Puzzle piece hit me at the diner."

"And?" He waited for further details of my snap memory.

"Lunch rush had ended. Cleaning up the kitchen, I dropped a pan and…" napkins, not the softest but they'd do for tears. "My mind split wide open with a terrible memory of me and you."

"Tell me." If you could hear someone swallowing a lump of fear in their throat, I certainly heard his.

"You never really filled me in about the babies we lost." A chill crept over me so fast I shivered and bunched my robe closer to my chest.

"Oh God Dove." He ran his hand over his tied back hair. "I prayed that would be one memory that would never, ever surface. Why didn't you tell me when I got home?"

"Wasn't ready to bring it up. Guess the dreams forced me to." With shaking hands, I tried to sip my coffee for a distraction.

"One of those topics…you really never asked about." The color in his face, still a pasty white. Nothing rattled Hawke, but this did.

"Yeah, I know. But…" again, I tried to ward off the tears. "Maude found me in tears, you know," I gave him one of my well known helpless expressions, "had to tell her."

"And Jane?" He frowned. "What'd she have to say about your discovery?" A rage of color flashed into his rugged face. I knew all to well of their love hate relationship.

"Nothing, Maude made her stay out in the dining room." Visibly, I could see him relax.

"The flash came so fast. All I got, a baby was missing from my stomach. Crying in Maude's arms. And the worst, begging her to let me die. Then you walked in. That's all I got, but…"

"But what, Dove?" He reached for my shaking hand and I gladly took his.

"It wasn't pretty. I wish I'd never remembered it."

"You promised me, if you remembered anything, you'd come to me." His voice echoed the hurt feelings.

"I know, and I'm sorry. It'll be ten years this summer since the attack happened. And all of a sudden my mind opens up to this. Did we fight a lot before this happened?"

"Yes," I didn't expect him to confirm my answer so quickly.

"Why?"

"The business grew. We grew apart. I was gone weeks at a time, leaving you to tend to the girls and everything around here. We managed, but you weren't happy with me. I wasn't there when you needed me." I could see it wasn't the proudest moment in his life. "You could say the icing on the cake, the last miscarriage. Third one took a toll on you mentally and physically." He took a long pause, collecting his thoughts before he went on. "If you conceived again, carrying a child to full term, it could've killed you. Wasn't about to take the chance. I made sure you'd never get pregnant again. When all was said and done, you hated me and the air I breathed."

"So the happy story you told me about getting away for my birthday…" Paper napkins make the worst tissues.

"I took you away in hopes to save our marriage. It was our last chance."

"Did it work?" My memory bank, of course, didn't offer any information.

Hawke's lips curved into a wild smile, his eyes brighten, I swear the gold specks danced with excitement in his brown eyes, "Yes. Took me a few days to win you over. We patched things up. You even let me back into your bed again."

"I hated you that much that I wouldn't let you sleep in the same bed as me?" This was news to me.

"Wouldn't even let me touch you. I'd only get a tiny kiss. Slight hug, if the girls were around."

"Wow. That's pretty serious." I couldn't picture anything so drastic happening like that.

"You remember anything about the trip we took?" Information on my locked brain didn't come on demand, but Hawke always asked questions.

"Only what you've told me." To me, it seemed there was something more he wanted to ask, but didn't. "No recollection of it. Nothing."

"Good. Hope you never remember it." Hawke sliced another piece of banana bread.

"Would've rather had the memory of us making up than the one that slapped me up along side the head."

"I'm sorry, Dove. It's just part of our past." Gently his fingers circled around my palm as he continued, "You made me pay dearly for not being there that day."

"Good to hear." A weak smile of satisfaction graced my lips. "I'm sorry I didn't tell you. It felt like I relived the whole thing with Maude." I whispered. "It's just one more piece of finding me. A sad piece, but now I know."

"Now you know." He held tightly onto my hand. Nothing or no one would interfere with this moment.

The silence circled around us. There was no tension to be cut with a knife, just a new finding for me. The birds chirped outside as the early morning sunshine attempted to make this day bright.

"Girls will be home by mid-June." He cleared his throat and winked at me. "Just in time for your birthday."

For once I was thankful for his change in conversation. "And our anniversary. I'll be married to you for twenty years." My gasping giggle caught his attention.

"You realize we're in trouble, Dove."

"Why?"

"Emma and Amelia, you know they won't let either of those dates slide." His mood lifted along with mine.

"No wild surprises for my birthday. Just keep it here at home." I didn't need to bat my eyelashes at him, but I did, "please. Nothing over the top."

"Can't promise. Your girls," he pointed his finger right at me, "they're just like you."

"Thank you," I kissed Hawke as the grandfather clock chimed six times. "You're going to be late."

"What are they going to do, fire me?" He smirked as he put his cup in the sink. "When's your appointment with Dr. Thornton?"

"Yearly 'test my brain' appointment," I tapped the side of my head, "in a few more weeks. You'll be there?"

"Like always." Hawked grabbed for the ties on my housecoat as a soft purring circled below us. "Whose brilliant idea was it to get another cat?"

Burt the cat intertwined his furry body between our legs. "Your girls. They felt I needed a cat after Ebony died."

"Figures. Burt, you're a damn pussy." Ignoring the cat who wanted attention, Hawke planted a kiss to my lips. "Going to be out all day on a charter." His lips sizzled over mine again. "Can take this back upstairs," he pulled at the belt to my tied housecoat.

"You're already late." I wasn't protesting, I was leading the way to the sofa, forget going upstairs.

"Damn it." The phone in Hawke's back pocket buzzed an unhappy tune of interruption at us. He glared, even swore at the number blinking on his phone, "I know I'm not there Fred. Just calm your self down. I'm on my damn way."

I got dropped like a hot potato. Hawke practically dumped me on the sofa, "Hey what about me?" All I heard, Hawke's snarling four letter words back to Fred. Wrapping myself back in my housecoat, I trailed behind Hawke as he carried on his conversation.

"Walking out the door now. Just tell them I had an emergency." He gathered his jacket under his arm, coffee in the free hand and stomped out the back door without a goodbye to me.

"Don't forget to mail the girls tuition check." I ran out the open door waving the glossy envelope in the morning sun. Slick dew from the night and bare feet made sliding into Hawke like hitting a brick wall. "That hurt." I sucked a breath of cool morning air into my lungs to replace the air that escaped me from plowing into him. In his arms, again, Hawke's hands skimmed over my terrycloth covered body.

"You really make it hard to leave in the morning." His lips closed hard over mine, lingered longer, add a few more seconds and we surfaced for air, "that should keep you warm until I get home."

Chapter 22 - Visitors

A premonition should never be taken lightly, especially when it belongs to me and my mysterious dreams that had remained dormant until recently. Restlessly, I tapped my fingers on the metal counter waiting to flip the dozen or so pancakes frying on the griddle.

"Another order Dove," Maude called as she loaded her tray with three hot off the griddle orders. That would be the fifth one and I had four more in front of it.

"Orders seven, eight, and nine are ready for pickup Maude." The tourist season descended down on us like a rainstorm blowing in off the ocean. Early June showed us a sneak peek of what summer had in store. The bells on the door to the diner jingled nonstop the entire morning.

The early morning mad rush finally slowed down with just a few stragglers enjoying their breakfast. "Packed morning," Maude leaned against the counter as I finished the last order for the couple sitting at the breakfast counter.

"Have a seat, Maude, got this one covered." Into her waiting hands, I passed her a steaming cup of coffee. "You look beat."

"Thanks honey." Maude planted herself on the stool next to me and the sizzling griddle.

"Can't believe we had people sitting on the steps at five thirty. I didn't even have the lights on and they were banging on the door." Six more hotcakes got flipped to a side of golden brown. Three eggs scrambled to a perfect buttery yellow and bacon crisp to perfection for the last order.

"Had a line out the door by seven. You slammed the orders today, girl." Maude wiped at her brow, "tell ya what," her sigh was long and heavy as she took another sip of coffee, "I'm beat. Would you take the floor until Jane gets here? I'll cook for a while."

"I dread playing waitress." My eyes rolled with a dramatic flare, "you know that." Frowning didn't help either, but I knew she needed the rest. "Hope Jane's okay. She's never this late." Before I trotted off to the dining room, I pulled my dirty food soiled apron off and replaced it with a crisp clean one. "Should we call her?"

"It's Friday. Don't know what's going on with her and Fred, but the last few Fridays, Jane's been late. Hasn't been happy and she takes her nastiness out on us." Maude, I'm sure, hoped I had gossip to share as she wiped the counter down. "Good gads girl, you make a mess back here."

"That's my job," I chucked a kiss onto the side of Maude's cheek and blew by her with the tray stacked with plates of comfort food...breakfast was about to be served.

Maude peered out the window of the backdoor. "See Jane's about to grace us with her presence. Glad I'm not the person on the other end of that call. She's looking mighty ticked off."

"Wonder what Fred did this time? He called Hawke at the butt-crack-of-dawn this morning."

"Sure hope they get it worked out." Maude tied on an apron and braced herself for one of Jane's impacting moods along with her entrance.

"I want my kitchen back, Maude." So not like me, I stuck my tongue out at her and hustled myself and the last order out to the dining room.

Jane, along with her unhappy mood, appeared behind the counter. She wrapped her neon yellow apron around her tiny waist drawing the ties tighter and tighter. "I need a cigarette." Pen in hand, Jane, subconsciously pretended to inhale the smokeless pen.

"Morning to you too, sunshine." I patted her skinny behind as I passed by. "Take it going cigarette free isn't working so well?"

"No. No it's not." She snapped like a dragon breathing fire at me. "Had Fred on my ass all morning. Haven't had one damn cigarette in a week."

"You've been doing great, why's he giving you grief?" We cleared a table together when it dawned on me, "Jane you didn't agree to some kind of weird deal with Fred did you?" Jane and Fred, they always made off the wall deals with each other.

"You make too much sense for someone whose brain can't remember what she did yesterday." Jane slammed a few dirty dishes down on the tray giving cause for the remaining customers to nearly jump out of their skin.

"Easy on the glassware. They didn't do anything to you." Under the crunching of glass I examined a dinner plate, all was safe.

"Anyone ever tell you you're too damn perky in the morning?" Her boney fingers rolled into a ball, I knew she wouldn't sock me, but then again.

"Yes, you." This time I whispered, "Jane, what did you agree to?"

"If Fred catches me smoking I owe him," she glanced around the diner, leaned across the table motioning me to move closer to her, "deal is, every cigarette he catches me smoking, I give him a blow job."

"You didn't?" My lips snickered into what should've been a curving twist of disgust, but went into the biggest "oh my gosh" smile. Never try to suppress a giggle that could bust your chest wide open with laughter. Practically nose to nose with each other, "You hate doing that. Why in the world did you agree," quickly I glanced at the remaining customers, no one cared about our whispering, "to something so, you know sexual?"

"Fred suggested it. Knows I hate sucking. Thought I could handle it." I shushed Jane so loud I thought Maude heard us, "Thought Fred left this morning. Swear I heard his truck leave. So I lit one up, damn if you didn't know it, there he sat on the back porch. Busted my ass big time."

"So that's why you're late?" I hoisted the tray of dirty dishes up, "and pissed off?"

"Yes, he wouldn't let me leave until I got on my knees." She rolled her eyes as we started toward the kitchen.

"Jane, that's just too much information even for me."

"Rat bastard, he called to tell me he left a fresh pack of cigarettes and cinnamon hot licking lotion on the kitchen table for me."

I nearly tripped with a loaded tray of dirty dishes, "You've got to renegotiate the terms of the deal." Only a few eyes caught my misstep. The true friend I am to Jane, I did my best to be helpful between gagging and laughing at the same time. "Cinnamon hot lotion, sorry Jane." I gagged again.

"I detest the taste of cinnamon and he knows it. The prick, he's watching me like a hawk." The bells on the front door bounced to life with a jingle announcing the arrival of a trio of sun drenched men. "Will you take this one for me?" She tugged the heavy tray overflowing with dirty dishes from my hands.

"Sure thing." I couldn't help giving Jane a seductive wink, even dared to lick my lips as she walked away. "Morning guys." I tossed a smile of welcome over my shoulder to the three men who'd stepped in, "Grab a table, be right with you."

Dressed in typical fishing gear, the three men didn't budge an inch. Seemed as if the "Welcome" mat they stood on had wrapped around their feet like a thick weaving vine.

"Guys, would you like to have a seat?" I nodded my head toward the corner booth as their sun burnt faces drained to a noticeable shade of pale. "Can I get coffee for anyone?" That saying about seeing a ghost, yep I sure felt like one as they stumbled over each other trying to get to the table.

"Coffee, yes, all three. Sounds good." Salt and pepper hair peeked out from under the older man's fishing hat, "Guys, come on. Let's have a seat." He finally gathered the attention of the two younger men and found their seats.

Not used to being dumped on the floor to wait tables, I kept glancing back at the trio, who seemed to keep one eye each on me. Three empty mugs laced through my fingers and a pot of streaming coffee in the other hand, I drew in a deep breath and wished I'd still been tucked away in the kitchen.

"Weird, don't you think?" Jane immediately picked up on the unusual behavior of the three men. "It's like them watching you is like seeing a ghost. You know them?"

"No. Never seen them before. Kind of creepy." I took another glance over my shoulder. Only to catch their eyes darting back down to the menus.

"I can take the table if you want." Jane offered.

"No. I can handle it, but thanks. You get your attitude back in check." I mustered up a cheerful smile and turned to face the three. The trio shuffled around in their seats as I approached. Kind of like being caught by the teacher, they squirmed under my watchful gaze. What I didn't like, the way their eyes darted a secret code or message to one another. I reminded myself, one, I don't waitress, two, I was tired and beat from the early morning rush, and three, my imagination was probably playing tricks on me. "Morning. Who needs coffee?" Me with a cheery smile tried to ignore their purposeful stares. Personally, I was ready for a "cup of Joe" with some of Maude's Irish whiskey mixed in it.

"Coffee, for all three. Thank you." The older one, who I assumed to be the father, answered as I sat the cups down.

"Here on vacation?" I tried to keep the conversation light and poured the hearty roasted blend of coffee into their cups.

"We are. Heard about this LHF charter service," he slid the pamphlet over for my inspection. "Know anything about this place?"

I sat the coffee pot on the edge of the table, "I sure do." Relieved, a relaxed smile came with ease, "My husband is one of the owners. Their place is about ten minutes from here. If you book with them, you won't be disappointed. They've been in business well over twenty years."

"Looks like we've got another charter to checkout guys." Barely nodding their heads in agreement, the younger men kept stealing sneaky "peeks" at me while pretending to be interested in the menu.

Coffee poured, I pulled out my order pad, "Ready to order? We've got the Hungry Man's Breakfast platter, four hot cakes, three eggs, hash browns, bacon or sausage, looks like it could fill you three up." As I made eye contact with them, I noticed how the trio's eyes took in my presence. "Also have the fried wedged potatoes, sautéed with green peppers, mushroom, and onions, topped off with cheddar cheese, choice of meat and a side of homemade biscuits with sausage gravy. Both will stick to you until the dinner hour." Pen to pad I waited for a least one of them to order. But it didn't happen.

"Ma'am, I'm sorry to be so fixated on you, your…" the man with a fishing lore dangling from the brim of his hat stated.

"I've noticed." Patiently, I waited for the order.

"Yeah, really sorry about that, but you're the spitting image of my late sister. When we walked in, I could've sworn you were her." Crystal blue eyes swam with tears as the older man tried to hold onto his smile.

"Late sister?" With my best breakfast spill delivered, I really just wanted to run for the cover of the kitchen. Completely thrown off, I didn't know what to say.

"Again, so sorry, didn't mean to startle you. My sister passed away a few years ago."

"More like ten this summer." My eyes darted to the young man with matching blue eyes and tight curly red hair.

"I'm so sorry to hear that. You know they say everyone has a double." I quirked my lips into a semi smile. How do you keep a pleasant smile on your face after being blindsided by that? And the words ten years ago jumped out grabbing my attention even more. Ten years ago, I suffered a life threatening attack of my own. Moments passed as we all just looked at each other. So I went back to trying to get an order from them, "Have you decided on breakfast?"

"How about the Hungry Man's Breakfast for all three," relieved for the father of the groups decision, I jotted down the order.

"Bacon or sausage? And how about the eggs?" Almost there, I'd soon be back in the kitchen.

"Bacon and scrambled for me," the youngest of them answered. "You could be her twin." Again, I'd lost their attention for food.

"Whose twin?" Really not wanting to be a part of this conversation, I glanced back to the boy whose eyes and hair matched his brothers.

"Our Aunt Chloe. Seriously, you could be her twin." Without hesitation, he pointed it right out to me.

"Chloe, pretty name. Like I said, we all have a double someplace."

"Dad," the other boy interrupted, "don't you have a picture of Aunt Chloe and Uncle James with you? You always kept one in your wallet."

"Guys, let's have some breakfast and check out this fishing charter." He tapped a finger on one of Hawke's flyers still laying on the tabletop.

"Come on Dad," the youngest boy pressed, "you've got to show her."

"If you don't mind," he glanced around the next to empty diner, "we're not holding you up or anything." From his back pocket he retrieved a tattered black wallet.

"Only thing getting held up is your breakfast." I tapped the pen obnoxiously on the order pad. My diced up mind offered only one warning to me…RUN! Too bad I didn't listen to it.

Slowly, this man, who I had no clue of even his name, pulled a photo from his wallet. He smiled at the wearing around the edges of the photo in his hand, "My sister Chloe and her husband James." His fingers trembled as he offered me the photo.

"What a beautiful couple." My voice stilled as I took in the family photo. I even tried to hide the light shaking of my hand as I held the color faded photo. On closer examination I found, "We kind of do look alike. It's the hair." I offered them a warm smile. "Maybe she was my double." Shocked at what I saw, it really could have been me in the photo. My eyes fell heavily onto the man whose arms were snuggly wrapped around my so called twin. Mounds of blonde curly hair framed his sharp features. His eyes of sparkling blue smiled widely back at me. My heart nearly stopped beating as I stared into the eyes of young boy who clung happily to his mother's hands. "Beautiful family." I barely was able to whisper. Not sure how I managed to even say that and I couldn't tell who had turned that creepy shade of pasty pale first, me or them. "I'm so sorry for your loss." As I returned the photo back to its rightful owner, the oldest boy ran his finger along the faded purple scars on my left arm.

"Ma'am, your arm, what happened?" Softly, he continued to run his fingertips over the roadmap-like lines on my lower arm.

Startled back into reality by the stranger's touch, "Bear attack," the words flew from my lips so fast I didn't have time to take them back if I wanted to.

"My sister," the pain twisted into the older man's face, "she," he fought to control his own voice, "she died from being attacked by a bear," his face grew to a grayish shade of grey, "ten years ago this summer."

"Ten years ago?" The order pad in my hand became a free flying agent as it fell to the tile floor with a flopping plop sound. "Where was she?"

"Dove." I knew the husky voice that called my name so clearly. Felt the flooding warmth as Hawke's hand circled around my waist. "You feeling alright?" His rough to the touch fingers gingerly swept along my cheek. Hawke's unexpected presence had perfect timing. Temporally, just his touch calmed the fear that rattled deep inside of me.

"Fine." From his touch my color returned as I fed him a bold faced lie. "When did you sneak in?" He handed me my order pad. No need for an answer, I should have been used to Hawke showing up on his own schedule, "I need to get their order in. And," I still hadn't recovered from the jaw dropping photo, "just so happens these guys are in need of a fishing charter." Hawke didn't buy my nonchalant smile as I held up one of his flyers. "Have your breakfast right out."

"Be with you guys in a minute." All business like, Hawke excused himself, his footsteps clipped close to mine as he followed close behind me. "Dove," again I found the warmth of his hands circling around my waist. Cornered at the edge of the counter, Hawke's hands planted down on both sides of me, "What happened to you?" Trapped by him in broad daylight, he left me no chance for a graceful escape into the kitchen.

Sidestepping him, I slipped the order back to Maude, "They're watching," my eyes flickered over to where we'd been standing. My hands shook as I poured a cup of coffee and turned my back to the trio.

"Need to get you out of here," Hawke moved within inches of me ready and willing to set me free of the trio who claimed I could be their dead relative.

"You can't," He took the shaking cup from my hands, "my nightmare finally has a name." The concern from his eyes burned into me.

"Come on, let's go to Maude's office. You can tell me what the hell is going on."

"The man in my nightmare," I borrowed Hawke's thick bicep to steady myself as he watched what little color of pink I had on my cheeks rapidly drain away and my haunted blue eyes held the secret, "he has a name."

"Aunt Dove." Little girl giggles screamed from my two college aged young women who bounded from the doorway of the kitchen. "Surprise!" Both Emma and Amelia rushed me into a group hug.

"You're not to be here until next weekend." I embraced another round of the hugs, "I've missed the two of you so much." Hawke, only a footstep away from me, "You're behind this aren't you?"

"Yep," He leaned between our girls and I felt the warmth of his lips brushing over mine, "be finishing this later." No further questions asked, I knew he'd make good on that promise sooner than later. As my girls talked at once about their plans for summer, Hawke joined the three men in the corner booth to discuss a fishing charter and I'm sure I'd be another topic they brought to his attention.

xoxoxoxoxo

From the kitchen window Hawke's gaze fell intently over his wife. Barefooted, she wondered through the ample flower gardens coming into full bloom. With the one sided conversation he'd been sure that played in her mind, Dove settled her worried mind and curvy body on the wooden swing at the edge of the backyard. Just reading her composure through the open window he'd take the gamble that she'd been struggling with whatever kept her mind prisoner. In his hand, a burning cigar to ease his own nerves, a bottle of beer for him, and a crystal goblet filled with the potion he'd been able to calm her with for nearly twenty years.

"Dovey," she'd been completely unaware of his presence as he crossed the neatly trimmed lawn of the backyard to where she sat in silence. "You hiding from me?" He handed her the goblet filled to the edge with blackberry brandy.

"No." She turned her worried eyes to meet his, "Just," she avoided the topic he wanted to bring up, "don't think we'll be seeing the girls until tomorrow." Not like Dove to change any subject on him. "Can't believe you snuck them in right under my nose."

The old swing cracked, groaned, even dared to squeak under the weight of his heavy frame as he sat down beside her. "Looked like you needed the distraction. Mind telling me who has a name?" Hawke, never one to sidestep an issue in Dove's life, waited for her answer.

"I'd rather talk about how you managed to get the girls home without me knowing." Not even conversation of their girls eased her troubled mind.

"Easy, those phones we pay for, they called. Made arrangements. Picked them up this morning. Your turn, Dove."

"Prefer to hear some details. Like say, how long the three of you've been planning this?"

"Dove," he drew in a deep steady breath off his cigar. Smoke filtered over him as he exhaled, "I booked a charter with three guys who claim you look just like…"

"Their dead sister and aunt. I know. Who did the charter?" She didn't flinch, didn't even move.

"Dove, I'm not up for games." Was she testing his patience?

"Just tell me, please. I know it wasn't you. You've been in and out all day." Her eyes slightly swollen from the tears he wished never happened, but they did.

"Lance took them. Seems you were the topic of the day." Disturbed, even annoyed at how three people could turn his wife into a semi-basket case, he took a long slow drink of the icy beer he held.

"Hawke, no please tell me..." Dove's eyes flashed with the threat of fresh tears.

He waived her plea off, "You know Lance, he wasn't about to offer up anything on me, you, the bear attack. Nothing."

"Thank you." Relief swallowed her fears. Or did they?

"Back to you Dove. What's got you so wrapped up? Could hardly pay attention to the girls. They noticed."

"They did?" Mixing with today's episode of fear, add a little guilt.

"Don't appreciate getting asked what the hell I've done to you this time." At least she giggled at his harsh comment. "They're your girls."

"They are, aren't they," Dove's smile faded as fast as it had flared with happiness. "James," she sipped the blackberry cocktail he'd given her. "Headlining my nighttime drama, James," Hawke wanted to dive into a million unanswered questions, but knew if he dared to interrupt her, she'd never finished. "The trio from the diner," she stared into her goblet at the liquid that reflected her image back, "They showed me a family photo." She leaned away from him, her eyes held on the bright globe slipping into a setting sun. "The man with blonde curls, he's the one who creeps into my nightmares calling for his lost wife." Vertebrae by vertebrae, Hawke eased his warm fingers down Dove's tensed spine. "James is who I'm seeing in my dreams, with the crying little boy. The woman they lost, can't find," the goblet half filled with brandy tumbled right out of Dove's grip, "Chloe. He's searching for his dead wife in my dreams." Tears took their toll on her emotions. "Why? I don't understand why. Or how this is happening. I don't know these people."

"Dove," Hawke wrapped her into his protective arms, curling her tightly into his chest. "It's over honey. They're gone. Hopefully they've taken your nightmares with them. Just a freak coincidence."

She shoved her body away from him, but grabbed the hand he offered for comfort, "Coincident? No," vigorously, Dove shook her head no several times, "I think not. I'm a dead ringer for this woman who's dead. In that photo, it could've been me Hawke."

Chapter 23 - You Only Turn Forty Once

Emma and Amelia feed me a daily helping of sarcastic grief for not wanting any kind of celebration for my fortieth birthday. Each spoonful they feed me, the choking memories only reminded me of my tragedy our family suffered exactly ten years ago. For my thirtieth, I'd been swept away for a romantic weekend. The worst of it, I really did knock on death's doorstep. My jumbled mind was kind enough to spare me of the detailed memories. Each time someone mentioned my approaching mile-stone birthday, I flashed back to my lost days confined to a hospital bed. The painful recovery my body endured for months. My memory of our life before, to this day left with gapping holes. Never ever did I wish or want to travel beyond the safety of my home town again. After I'd made it perfectly clear for the umpteenth time, my double-trouble of girls decided a twentieth wedding anniversary party would be a better choice. I learned to never underestimate the determination of my now adult nieces.

"You've been moping around all week, Dove. What gives?" Patiently waiting for me to fill our coffee cups Hawke's so called "reading of my mind" didn't work.

"Why am I always serving you?" I snapped tighter than a twisted rubber band. Two cups of steaming hot coffee clinched in my hands, "Sorry, didn't mean that."

"Got to be in early today?" Noting my nasty comment with an arched brow, he glanced at his watch, "What's got those lacy panties of yours bunched up?"

"Not wearing lace, just the white ones you hate." I couldn't even pull off a decent threatening glare as I planted myself in the chair beside him.

"Spill it Dove." Hawke slide the entire poppy seed roll in front of me.

"I asked if I could escape work today. Asked two weeks ago. Maude called late last night with some lame excuse for needing me in by six." I whined, I pouted, I just down right ranted.

"Bet ole Harry's got Maude tied up in a neat little bow between the sheets this morning." He gave me a sly wink, "Man's been good for her."

"He's definitely good for her," I snorted a giggle, "but Maude claims she couldn't open. Had a delivery scheduled for six thirty."

"I've got to hit the road." He gulped the last bit of coffee down, "taking a charter out by five-thirty."

I glanced at the clock above the sink, barely four-thirty. Why was I up? It was my birthday. I should be in my bed with the covers over my head.

"You'll be home for dinner?" I whined pathetically watching him stretch into his jacket.

"Hopefully. All day charter." Coffee mug in hand, he headed for the backdoor without any sympathy for me.

My heart sank, "But it's..." my whining didn't impress him, "Thought you'd spend the day with me."

"Dove, I know it's your birthday. You're the one who said no celebrating." He planted a fast kiss on my lips before his escape. "I've got to go. Call ya later." Hawke left me in my own self-pity as the backdoor clicked shut behind him.

"Well just isn't that a Happy Birthday to me." I sulked back into the hard wooden chair at the kitchen table. Coffee in hand, I finished off the giant piece of poppy roll not feeling an ounce of guilt. Then I found comfort with the candy dish filled with assorted chocolates. "Got my wish, now didn't I? I'd hoped they'd at least have cake with me." Another three pieces of candy had been unwrapped in lighting speed. "May as well get ready for work. This is going to be some day." I had a good hour before needing to report in for the early-bird shift. Certainly hoped a steaming hot shower would help with my moping mood.

xoxoxoxoxoxo

Barely crawling at a snail's pace, inch by inch Hawke maneuvered his massive truck back into its original spot in the driveway. Engine silenced, he slipped from the truck only to quietly click the door shut behind him. With a glow of light shining from the bathroom window, he knew Dove would still be in the shower. His timing, perfect, Dove always lingered long in the shower. Her indulgence for a hot shower would give him the extra time he needed.

"Damn if you didn't know it," Hawke jiggled the door handle, "she actually locked the door." Keys in hand he let himself in through the backdoor.

Above him on the second floor of their home, the waves of water from Dove's shower kept running. Quickly he freed himself of his jacket, kicked out of his "tale telling" boots and headed for the staircase. In his hand, a gift for Dove's birthday, all wrapped and pretty. Bathroom door standing wide open, Hawke contemplated grabbing his wife's curvy silhouette figure freely moving behind the shower curtain. Radio blaring some song from the eighties, he watched her naked shadowy figure thinking how he'd enjoy being in there with her.

"Hisss," from its perch on the vanity, Burt the cat let it be known that an intruder had entered Dove's domain. Again the grumpy cat hissed a warning at him.

"Shut the hell up," Hawke mouthed the silent words at the annoying animal. As he left Dove's sanctuary along with his desiring thoughts, the thumping of paws landing on the floor and feet padding after him could be heard.

Both men in Dove's life had successfully made it into the bedroom without her knowing. In the center of the bed Hawke laid the brightly wrapped gift box, while Burt cozied up next to it with a coy look on his furry mug.

"Don't eat the ribbon, ya damn animal." Alerted to the fact that Dove's shower had ended, Hawke slipped into stealth movement. His footsteps, unnoticeable as he passed the open bathroom door while Dove wrapped her wet hair in a towel. Slipping inside Emma's bedroom doorway, he waited to spy on his wife. Dove's body securely wrapped up in his housecoat, Hawke enjoyed the view of her swaying hips as she walked into their bedroom. With Dove out of his view, Hawke inched his way back down the hall.

"Burt where did you get that box from?" He could hear Dove asking her pride and joy of a cat. "There's no way you put this on the bed." As he slipped behind the door to the spare bedroom, he could hear Dove's footsteps approaching. "Hawke? Honey are you here?" She practically ran down the hallway to the top of the stairs, "Hawke, are you down there?" Nothing greeted her but the ticking of the grandfather clock.

From his hiding place, he could see her anticipating what to do. If she went down the stairs, she'd find his coat, keys, and boots right in the middle of the kitchen.

"Hawke?" She called for him again. "Pretty sneaky mister." Happily she headed back to their bedroom. "Wonder what's in here?" At the corner of the four post canopy bed, Dove unwrapped the gold foil package. "Look how pretty," between her fingertips, Hawke could see the slim gold chain dangling from her fingers. "Amazing, he never buys me jewelry. This is so pretty." She ran her fingers over the gold chain. The excitement beamed from his terrycloth covered wife as he saw her picking up the phone. He was sure it'd be him she'd be calling.

The silence in the old Victorian house erupted into floorboards creaking and heavy foots steps flying up directly behind Dove before she could complete her call. Burt, her trusting guard cat, flew into a round of horrifying hisses as Hawke's massive hands grabbed a hold of Dove's body.

"Nooooooo! Get off me!" The wet towel wrapped around her head now covered her face. Hawke loved the way her body fought under his gripping hold. Dove's screaming only had him, her pretend attacker, tightening his grip. "Get off me!" She fought to remove the towel and he had to love her brave attempt to fight him. Legs kicking, but connecting only with the air, she even punched wildly in hopes to connect with the human's flesh that held her captive. "Let me go!" Another scream, another punch missed by Dove. Hawke, using more strength than needed, took over Dove and her house coated body.

With a grip so tight, he easily flipped Dove like a pancake and slammed her into the softness of their bed. Posed as the assailant she thought he was, his wild, long hair pooled around her face covering his identity. "Get off me!" She bucked her body into his, but this time her clinched fist connected with his hard muscular bicep. Holding back a laugh, he knew there'd be no mark left on his arm from her willful punch. Helping himself to her fighting body, Hawke straddled his heavy frame overtop of Dove's. Pinned to the fluffy comforter by the weight of his body, his lips attacked hers relentlessly. He held her wrists prisoner with his own hands, but Dove kept fighting him. She managed to grab at a glob of his dangling hair. And did she ever yank with all her might. Annoyed with Dove's struggling, he wasn't about to give up. Without hesitation, Dove assaulted his bottom lip slicing it with her teeth.

"Damn it Dove! What the hell?" Hawke cursed in agonizing pain from the crippling move she made on him. "What the hell are you doing?" The attacker, aka known as her husband, still straddled over her with blood dripping from his bottom lip. His wild mane of black hair tossed around like a windstorm just blew through it.

"Me? What the hell are you doing attacking me like that?" Instantly, Dove's eyes filled with tears. Her expression changed rapidly from scared to one pissed off woman. Better yet, those flaring blue eyes of hers just told him she wanted to kick his ass for scaring her to death.

Hawke wiped the trickle of blood from his lip on the back of his hand. "Surprised you didn't hear me when I came in." Still not happy with her revenge attack, he poked at his swelling lip.

"Hear you? Why would I hear you? You left at four thirty." She protested, still pinned under his body. "I was in the shower."

"Any clue register in your brain when you found fluff ass guarding a present?" Still miffed at her he rubbed the side of his head.

"Hear you? Think not," she sneered at him. "Went to the top of the stairs and yelled for you, but no answer. You're really mean. You know that don't you?" She spat out at him more hurt then angry that he'd scared her like that.

"Saw ya, and," he wiped at his torn lip again, "just bided my time until I had a chance to spring." He snapped back at her like he wanted to continue the rough romp they'd just shared.

"It's not funny, Hawke. You scared the hell out of me. Thought someone was really attacking me." Dove actually pouted as he leaned back but kept her pinned firmly between his jean covered thighs.

"Kind of like having the upper hand with you, Dove." Quickly, Dove became his personal playground. His terry housecoat she'd been so tightly wrapped in conveniently slipped open from her struggles.

"When don't you?" She let his finger slip through the slit in the open housecoat and between her breasts. "Your lips swelling, better put ice on it." She suggested and didn't mind where his hand was roaming.

Before even thinking of releasing her, he tied the thick ends of his black mane back into a tight pony tail. "So much for those self-defense classes you and the girls took."

"Only to be attacked on my birthday by my husband. Where's the necklace?" A little panicked, Dove pointed toward the nightstand, "is it still there? I dropped it when you decided to pull your sneak attack on me."

"Here," he dangled the gold rope like chain before her eyes, "surprised?"

"In more ways than one," he slipped the chain around her neck closing the clasp. "Sorry about your lip."

"No your not."

"Yep, you're right, I'm not. Can't believe you got me jewelry." Her fingers feathered around the chain, "I love it, thank you. Can you let me up so I can see my present in the mirror?"

"Dove, not quite done with you." His husky sultry voice gave way to what else he'd planned for her.

"Early morning tends to make you aggressive."

"So does the taste of your lips." Traced by the tip of his tongue, Hawke enjoyed the taste of her mango flavored lip gloss. "Need to get you out of this," he pulled the lose ties free from her waistline.

Unimpressed with Hawke's attempt to disrobe her, "I'm going to be late for work." Dove yanked the edges of the housecoat around her naked body. He silenced her and quenched his taste with her lips. "Maude is going to kill me if I miss that delivery appointment."

"Not worried about my Aunt," he stripped his t-shirt up and over his head and fought to reopen the edges to the housecoat.

"But," his mouth smothered over her babbling lips, "I promised Maude..." Hawke managed to slip Dove's bare upper body free of the terry robe, "Honey, really, I've..." her mumbling lips went in the direction he guided her.

"You really want me to stop, Dove?" He knew she couldn't. The words "No" didn't even form on her lips.

"She's going to be so mad." Dove let her body sink deeper into the fluffy comforter, "She's going to kill me."

"I'm in good with the owner," he caressed her bare neck with smooth kisses, "for a fact, I know she won't kill you."

"You win, but make it quick. Don't need to get fired on my birthday." Her teeth grazed over his bare taunt chest muscles nipping at his exposed skin.

"No way she'll fire you." His rough bronze colored hands sculpted and covered her milky white breasts. "You'll be late today, birthday girl."

"But, but, I…" his lips took another dance over her breast he cradled in his hands. "I'm never late on a promise." Dove's wiggle for freedom stopped as she moaned with pleasure. "Really…oh…you've got to…" the more Dove protested, the harder he sucked. "Hawke, you're going to leave me black and blue." She gasped for a breath, "Hawke," Dove tugged at the ends of his tied back hair.

"Stop protesting," he popped up for air, with both of her silky wet breasts overflowing in his hands. "Dove, got a note in my hip pocket. Spelled out an explanation to Maude as to why you're late. She'll love it." His tongue licked over her fleshy pink perky nipples. "Need to get down to business."

"Really? A note? Explaining what?" Hawke hovered over her sensual body before he rose to his feet. The only thing Dove wore, the gold chain he'd just given her. She let her bare feet drift up and over his thighs, "if you want to play with this," his eyes followed as her legs fell open for him, "get your jeans off."

His jeans dusted over the floor along with his boxers. "Couldn't let you leave without a little birthday sex." The warmth of his body slid between her chilled legs.

"Birthday sex? That's what we do on your birthday." No more questions needed, she gasped with anticipated pleasure.

Hawke enjoyed taking his time slipping deep inside of Dove. Her radiant blue eyes sparkled with a burning desire for him. The early morning sun peeked quietly though the windows while their elements of urges, wants, and a dance of a teasing tango verged to fulfillment. But interruptions are always close at hand. The telephone beside the bed whistled out its demand.

"It's Maude." Dove's sweet moaning in his ear between gasps of breath, her way of begging him not to stop, "she'll keep calling until we answer."

Hawke growled under his breath at the ringing disturbance. Easing off of Dove's tingling body, "don't move," he snapped the phone from the cradle. "What?" He didn't care who received his rant.

"Morning Hawke." Not even rattled by his harshness, Maude greeted him.

"Maude? What the hell? It's not even five thirty yet."

"Just seeing why Dove isn't at the diner. She's always early. Suppose you got her all tied up to that four-poster bed of yours?" Maude's jovial laughter bolted over the phone line.

"Yeah, Maude. I've got her flat on her back, tied up. Legs spread…"

"Hawke," Dove grabbed but failed to pull the phone from him, "give me that." Again, Dove attempted to yank the phone free, only to be pushed back down on the bed. Hawke griped her wrists and pinned her hands above the wild curly hair on her head all while he clung to the phone.

"Better let her up for air. I need Dove in one piece this morning." Maude's bubbly voice bounced over the line. "When should I expect her?"

"I'll get her there, when I get her there. Face it Maude," he licked his lips at Dove and winked, "she's going to be late." Phone clicked off, he didn't even bother to say good-bye to her. "Back to business."

"You're so mean to your Aunt." All of Dove's wiggling couldn't free her from his pinning grip.

"She'll get over it." Hawke eyes examined and scanned over his wife's naked body. "Like I said," his grin left no mercy for her, "back to business."

While Hawke made himself comfortable between Dove's legs, he released the tightness on her out stretched arms. Her hands still out of commission he enjoyed the way she nibbled at his neck, the way her tongue stroked over his skin, he even offered her the other side to taste. Dove, intentionally, sucked harder, nipping his neck with her teeth.

"Dove, you don't want to play rough with me." His eyes flashed with a hint of gold. With his free hand he circled and cupped her exposed breast. His lips lingered longer, sucking sweetly. His taste deepened into her flesh and held tight.

"You win," her laugh combined with a scream echoed in the silence of their bedroom. "You bit me." A fine deep purple line had already formed on Dove's ivory skin. "That's going to hurt all day."

"Give you a rain check to continue this adventure later tonight?" Hawke offered and playful kissed her wounded breast.

"Thought you said we weren't doing anything for my birthday?" From under the pillow, the jingle of the phone rang. "You answer it."

"Let her think you're on your way." Causally, Hawke rolled off her heated body and returned the phone to the nightstand. "Come on, I'll drop you off."

"You're dropping me off and coming to pick me up? This your way of paying up on the rain check for sex?" Dove rolled to the side of the bed in search of her now rumbled clothes.

"Always said you could read my mind," Hawke zipped his jeans up, "Meet you in the truck."

"You're forty-five and still act like a sex crazed teenager." He heard her snickering laugh.

Hawke's head whipped around to meet Dove and her teasing comment, "Only for you Dove. Only for you." Navy blue t-shirt stretched over his chest he gave her one last wink, "Get a move on Dove, Maude's already pissed at me."

"Don't forget to give me that excuse note you've got in your hip pocket." Dove called after him as he bounced down the steps. As Dove tossed herself back together for her day at the diner, she caught a whiff of Hawke's cigar smoke through the open window. She spied on Hawke from the bedroom window that faced the backyard. Cigar and a mug of coffee in one hand, he waited for her as he held a full conversation on his phone.

"Got a feeling this isn't the only surprise he has for me," Dove's grin reflected back to her in the window as she patted the old cat good-bye and went to catch her ride to the diner.

"A Little Thing Called Parking"

No obstacles in getting me to the diner. Finding a place to park, no problem there either. Me getting out of the truck and into the diner…huge dilemma. A sweet simple kiss good-bye that's all I offered. Just pecked Hawke on the lips. That's all it took to stimulate and spark the raving romance of burning desire between us. Hawke's rough play, there wasn't any denying it. He planned to finish what he started at home in the front seat of the truck. Firm hands gripped into my arms. Hawke hauled my curvy body over the console that separated our seats and landed me right in his lap. A honk from the horn signaled that the steering wheel wasn't impressed with my butt cheeks being smashed into it.

"Hawke, what are you doing?" Of course I knew what he was doing and oh yes I was going to protest. He shifted me and the seat back simultaneously. One more move and he'd reclined the bucket seat completely back with me clinging to him. "Comfortable?" I sarcastically asked. Straddling a man well over six-foot four, in the front seat of a king-sized-super-cab truck was a new challenge. "I'm late. Like so late, Maude's going to kick my butt if I don't get in there."

Hawke hit the electric locks on the door and just laughed at me. "You're late. And I'm not done with you." The morning arousal from the bedroom displayed its want in the front seat of the truck.

"Hawke, really, I've got to…" Me simply brushing my cotton t-shirt covered breast over his chest only heighted his arousal as I pretended to try and escape. Fully aware of the bulge pushing up on the inside of his jeans, he yanked me back down to his waiting lips.

"Stop with the squirming, Dove." The sting of his hand felt worse than the cracking sound to my bottom side.

"You hit me!" I sprang back colliding with the annoying steering wheel again.

"Little love tap, Dovey." The smirk of pleasure on his lips told me there was no way I'd be escaping him.

"Love tap?" My eyes brightened as I struggled to free myself from his grip. He returned my attempt by holding my hips tighter and smashed my body back into his. Hawke's rough foreplay kept me on my toes. It didn't happen often, but when it did, he kept my attention. But today, today I played his game willingly. I slipped my hand down between our bodies, fondling the swollen bulge tightly packed in his jeans. Eyes locked with his, my wicked laugh slipped out. I rubbed my hand over the exterior of his jeans. I let him think, even wonder, if I'd continue to stroke him so gently. Between our lip-to-lip combat, I enjoyed hearing Hawke moan as I squeezed him tighter and tighter. He moaned in pleasure as I bit harder at his neck. My struggles to free him of his jeans didn't work so well in the cab of the truck. No room to shed clothing. Not getting my way or what I desired, I sampled his neck even harder. Hawke would be sporting a sizzling bite mark that he'd have to explain. Location, location, location, is everything. With Hawke, there'd always be a payback to follow. I felt the sting of his hand on the left side of my butt cheek. The cracking sound didn't startle me as bad as the force he put behind it. Before I could snarl a verbal assault, Hawke hooked his hand behind my neck. His other hand took a finger flexing tour between my legs. He expected my scream as his lips covered mine with a crushing kiss to semi-silence me. No place to move, I fell prey to his massaging fingers. Only a thin layer of cloth separated my tingling flesh from his touch.

"You win." I panted like a cat in heat. "Please, I'm begging you, take me back home." My wild lose hair tumbled and surrounded both of us as I tried to get comfortable on his chest.

"You never beg, Dove." His oh-so-full-of-himself laughter filled the steamed windows of the truck. His chest rose and fell with mine as we tried to catch our breath. "Always come willingly."

"A little too willingly today." He ran his hand over my hair, soothing me. "Should I be purring?" I kissed his lips and slipped back over to my side of the truck. Our hot round of rough parking lot foreplay now simmered. He held me captive as I stared breathlessly into his velvety eyes. "What got into you?" A quick smack to his shoulder, I wiped at my swollen lips. "Thanks to you," I fumbled with my shirt, trying to smooth the wrinkles, "I'm not going to be able to think straight."

Overly pleased with himself, Hawke gloated with a chuckle. "Me? You want to know what got into me?" Still reclined in his seat his finger tips touched my swollen lips.

"Surprised there's not blood for the way you bit me." I smacked his shoulder again as he repositioned his seat to up-right.

"Aggressive? Even a little rough. Think you were holding your own, Dove." Hawke rubbed at the so called love bite I left on his neck. A purple line had already started to bubble under his sun-kissed skin. "What got into you?"

"You." I whisked away the remains of my frosty pink lip gloss left on his lips.

Gingerly, he kissed my finger tips, "You really want me to take you back home?" His fingertips circled around the palm of my hand. "Got the bed of the truck," he cast a quick glance toward the back window, "Dovey, you're blushing."

"Stop it." I whipped the visor down; the mirror reflected my steamy pink glow. "I can't go in there looking like this. It's your fault." Frantic at my appearance, still out of breath, Hawke laughed in approval knowing he had been the cause of my frazzled composure.

Nearly twenty years together Hawke could still melt me with his touch, whether it be tender or aggressive. With a spontaneous grin or the warmth from his honey brown eyes, he could get me to try just about anything with him. I never could get enough of him.

"Easy, Dove. Little on the light headed side?" The emotional twist he held over me really did leave me lighted headed and my heart pounding.

"How do you do that? Feel." I grabbed his hand and placed it on my thumping heart. My body swayed under his touch. It was no secret, I'd become a prisoner to his passionate needs. Still clinging to his hand, I wanted and took one last kiss before he freed me.

"You better get inside Dove. Sure I made Maude's shit list this morning." On a daily basis Hawke would end up on Maude's shit list for something. "Pick you up at closing." He sampled my lips one last time.

"See you at three." Purse in hand, I slipped out of the truck. One last wave, Hawke left me trying to catch my breath and composure. I couldn't walk into the diner in my rather aroused shape. I planted myself on the back steps and watched Hawke drive down the road. Still warmed by the sensational rush of lust, he left my body tingling for more. According to my watch, I wasn't too terribly late, just fashionably late.

"And the Birthday Celebration Continues"

My skin, once a sassy shade of heated pink, returned to the plain pale ivory everyone was used to seeing. I kept my hand resting on the frame of the backdoor and filled my lungs with several soothing deep breathes. Not only did I need to stabilize myself emotional, but add into that the physical factor. I couldn't believe how Hawke left my mind and soul wanting more from him. Mind cleared, but heart still erupting, I waltzed into the diner with a "good-morning" smile on my swollen, freshly glossed lips.

"Well good morning birthday girl." Jane greeted me with an "I know what you were doing" grin. She flicked her eyes to the clock above the sink then back to me. "Side tracked by something, or should I say someone this morning?" With a catty snicker she wanted an answer, "Do I dare ask what you two were doing out there?" Jane never missed opportunity to make me squirm. Her eyebrows twitched to an amused arch. She didn't even bother to let me answer. "See the time?" She pointed to the clock like an old school teacher ready to scold me. "Just a little early for that kind of inappropriate 'parking lot' behavior." No smile cracked as she musically tapped her Carney yellow fingertip on the counter top.

"Just chatting," ignoring Jane didn't come easy, "besides, I'm not all that late." The wall clock read six thirty. With my favorite, well stained apron tied around my waist, "Just got tied up. That's all." I pretended like nothing but idle chit-chat had been exchanged with my loving husband.

"Tied up?" Jane cocked a crooked smile at me, "that's all you can say? Details Dove. You know I live for details." Jane, at her best, tried to coax me into giving up the details of my morning parking lot romp. I swear the woman was compiling 'details' for some dirty novel she'd soon be writing. Not about to give up a single shred of information, I slipped a finger over my swollen bottom lip that Hawke had taken advantage of sucking on.

"Dove, just admit it." Whisper like, Jane circled behind me, just waiting for me to spill my guts of the front seat romp in a pick-up truck.

I'd been caught red handed making out with my husband in the back parking lot like two love sick teenagers. Couldn't deny it, his mating marks had barely faded. Then the total give-away package, a flush of pink spilled over my entire body.

"I knew it. You did. Didn't you?" Surprised Jane didn't have a note pad in hand waiting for play-by-play details.

"Morning Maude. Glad you were able to get that six a.m. delivery." My only hopes of safety strolled into the kitchen. Hopefully, she'd get Jane off my back. Not looking Maude in the eye, I grabbed for the first order. From behind me, I could feel Maude's sassy brown eyes surveying me. Feather like, I felt her slip in beside me as I tossed an order of hash browns.

"Lip gloss is all smeared, Dove." With the tip of her pinky finger she touched the edge of my perfectly swollen lips. Under her microscope eyes, she analyzed every inch of my rosy glow. "My goodness girl, what the hell did he do to you this time?"

Two eggs cracked and sizzling in the skillet, I twirled the flipper in my hand and smiled, "Hand job in the parking lot."

Jane, who'd been all ears, shot a mouthful of coffee over the prep-table. Creamy brown coffee dripped over the shiny surface and clung to the bottom of her chin. "You did what?" Not bothering with a napkin, she wiped her dripping mouth on the bottom of her apron.

Maude tossed her a towel still holding back her laughter, "Clean up your mess, Jane, and close your mouth. Not like you've never had sex in a parking lot." We all knew, Jane and Fred, they got it on anywhere, anyplace, anytime. "Boy always knows how to bring the glow out in you."

"He's in rare form this morning. Second time I had to escape from him." Eggs flipped, I worked on the pancakes with a smile. "Thanks for the phone call this morning."

"My pleasure. How pissed was he?" Maude took over the griddle as I worked on a salsa style omelet.

"Pissed. Maude, you should know by now how pissed your nephew gets when he's in the middle of getting a piece of ass."

"Dove, will you stop with the one liners? I'm losing too much coffee here." Jane now moped up the floor from her second spill.

"Check out my birthday present. Good reason why I'm late." Between slopping eggs and home fries on a plate, I pulled the gold chain out from its hiding place under my now "properly in place" t-shirt. "Oatmeal? Are you kidding? Who wants plain oatmeal?" I rattled off the next order.

"Hawke bought you jewelry?" Jane examined my birthday gift, "What did he do?"

"It's her birthday Jane," Maude pushed her aside and held my new present between her fingers. "Very nice."

"Impressive, don't you think?" Blueberries, raspberries, a handful of pecans and a pinch of brown sugar topped off the plain boring dish of oatmeal.

"Hold still, Dove. Can't believe he picked this out by himself." With a fine tooth comb, Maude examined my gift.

"You didn't help him?" My questioning eyes met hers as I handed her the now delicious dish of oatmeal.

"No. Not this time. Hawke didn't even recruit the girls for help." She garnished the oatmeal with a side order of sizzling crisp bacon.

"Complete surprise." I handed off my classic masterpiece, a salsa omelet, along with the blossoming fruit and oatmeal dish to Jane and tucked my pretty glittering present inside my shirt. "Take it you didn't need me here at the butt-crack of dawn."

"Nope figured that nephew of mine had other plans for you on his mind." Maude brought me another order ticket, "saw the two of you in the parking lot. Lordey me, lost count of how many times the sheriff would call complaining about you two parked in the back lot. And you were married."

"Really?" Another questioning piece of my puzzled mind left to the darkness of a stolen memory. "Me and Hawke? In the back parking lot?" I flipped six more pancakes before I caught Maude's eye, "You're serious aren't you?"

"She's as serious as that grease dripping off those strips of bacon," Jane piped in as I dapped a napkin over the freshly fried deliciousness, "Nothing new for you two to get busted by that old codger of a deputy. Think Hawke finally paid him off in lottery tickets to leave you two alone. Sure know Fred did." With that noted to my memory bank, Jane hustled another order out to the dining room.

"There's no talking to that boy when it comes to you, him, and getting those fancy panties of yours off. Gave him my last lecture on sex over twenty years ago." I handed

Maude two more completed orders, "He's your problem, Dove. Now, end of that subject."

"End of subject is right. Don't know how and why we're still discussing Hawke getting my panties off." I rang the pickup bell for Jane to glide herself over for another order. I'll keep my problem, thank you," grinning at Maude, I swiped the order ticket from her hand, "Wouldn't trade him for the world."

Just a hare before nine in the morning, I'd been caught and well harassed over the parking lot romp I'd shared and enjoyed with my husband. To top my morning off, here I stood, coffee cup in hand, celebrating my new age of forty. A smutty little grin flashed over my still swollen lips. My husband, he could still bring the rosy shade of blush out in me as if I were twenty again. Silly little grin plastered on my face, I prepped the daily special. Classic, and a known delight at our diner, "Baked Ravioli" choice of sauce, traditional sweet basil tomato or a white butter garlic sauce. Either of the two, heaven to the taste buds.

The early morning breakfast shift passed in a flurry with Jane and Maude quick to remind me of my "parking lot romance." As my ravioli baked to perfection, I welcomed my short break as the breakfast crowd cleared out. Soon the lunch rush would refill the empty seats.

xoxoxoxoxo

Up to my elbows in sudsy dishwater, I scrubbed fiercely at the crusted, baked on ravioli pans. A stirring breeze sent a chill over me and for an odd second I felt the rush of Hawke's present. A glance thrown over my shoulder, I cased the empty kitchen. Only to find nothing but me and the pile of dirty dishes in need of scrubbing.

"My premonition must be off today, he took the girls on a charter up to Astoria," I chatted away to my dirty dishes. "Won't be home until at least five, maybe even six tonight." My "feeling" shrugged off, I continued to scrub at the pan in need of my attention. "Crap. Double crap." Conveniently, I'd just drenched myself in mucky dirty dishwater. "I've got to stop my pathetic daydreaming." The protective apron I wore was completely soaked. I'd soaked myself all the way through to my t-shirt. Slipping across the wet floor, I scrambled for a handful of towels. Another handful of towels and I found myself on all fours mopping the slimy water up off the tiled floor. "I really hate," as my hand reached for an extra towel behind me, it found the soft texture of worn denim attached to someone's leg.

"Nothing like seeing my favorite woman down on all fours." Hawke's husky rasp took me off guard.

His familiar voice had me whirling around to confront him, "I'm your only woman." Instantly I snapped at his comment and quickly forgot about the wet floor I was trying to scramble up off of. Wet floors make for slippery tennis shoes. And slippery tennis shoes make for a fast spin and fall. "Hawke!" My panicked scream left him laughing as I grabbed for the hand he offered. Latched tightly onto him, "This is the second time you've scared the crap out of me today."

"And you've ended up in my arms both times, Dove." Easily, he popped me safely to my feet. "You ready to go?" Hawke's smugness shined as he offered me his famous 'let me win you over grin.'

168

"Ready for what?" Sarcastically, I eyed him up one side and down the other with a fresh glare of annoyance. "Thought you and the girls took a charter out?"

"Nope," a wink from his golden honey brown eyes set the stage, "had another date after I got stood-up by you this morning."

"Another date? Whom did you need to date so early in the morning?" Game playing, we enjoyed it.

"Met my girls," his smile broaden, "had some breakfast." He did it again, just winked at me and I felt myself melting like putty in his hands. "Made some plans."

"Plans? What plans?" Curiosity just struck me as Hawke's whole body composure shifted into surprise mode. "No. Hawke, no. You promised." That split moment flashback. Hospital. Waking up not knowing who, what, where. "Hawke, you promised. No party. Just simple. Cake at home." Panic did more than teeter in my voice. My emotions, scared, and unwilling to be tamed exposed themselves.

"Dove." Without protest, I let him take me into his arms. This time I needed his touch. "Just the girls. Promise, no one else. Nothing will happen."

Hawke's thick hair brushed over my shoulder as I clung tighter to him. His scent, I breathed it in and used it to calm my ragged nerves. "We're staying home, right?"

"Got it handled." He didn't answer my question. "You'll be safe with the three of us." He tugged at my loosely hair netted ponytail as I listened to the rhythmic beat of his heart. "You coming along peacefully, or?"

"Or what?" A quick step back on my part broke our secure embrace.

"I'll just toss you over my shoulder and haul you out." Amusement tickled in his voice as I stepped further back from him.

"You'll throw your back out tossing all of this," I fanned my hands in the air over the curves I rocked well, "Hawke, I don't know," I pouted like my girls when they were toddlers. "I think home…"

"Dove, trust me."

"More details, please." Sometimes my pouting lower lip could win him over. Instead, I got redirected to the dining room. It just became a no win situation for me. "Fine. You win. But the peaceful business…not happening." The tail of my freed netted hair slapped at Hawke's smiling face of accomplishment. My wet apron, crumbled and soggy, got slammed on the front counter. "Let me guess. The two of you," I poked a finger in the air towards Jane and Maude, "you knew about this."

As Jane examined my discarded apron, Maude's deep brown eyes filled with sentiment. "Jane, honey, do you remember way back when these two were dating?"

"How could I forget? Romeo there spent every waking hour here." Jane gave Hawke one of her well deserved evil-eye glares and a haughtily laugh. "He'd sit here and wait for you Dove. Just wait. Stalker in waiting." Jane blew Hawke an unwanted kiss through the air.

"Love you too, Jane." The love hate relationship between Jane and Hawke never missed a living beat of their hearts.

"And how you'd make him wait. Got to be an everyday game with the two of you." Maude broke up their taunted relationship, "Last pan dried and tucked away, Hawke, he'd drag you out the backdoor without even a goodbye. Just simply run off with you. Never knew where the two of you'd be off to." Glasses in hand, Maude rubbed at her tired eyes. "In all seriousness, Dovey, I gave up years ago trying to figure out what he's got planned for you. Wouldn't even drop me a clue or two." Maude's bright bouncing laughter turned sober. The wrinkles in her face creased with worry, "Hawke, don't you dare let anything happen to Dove." The fear in her voice triggered one too many memories from ten years ago.

"Maude," he rubbed his Aunt's aging shoulders, "Time to put those old ghosts to bed. We'll be fine."

"Promise?" Maude gently patted the top of her nephew's hands, "Promise me."

"Promise. I'll return her in the morning as good as new." Hawked winked at me and kissed the top of his Aunt's graying hair. "You're keeping me waiting, Dove." Stolen from the walk-in-closet, Hawke handed me one of my flower print sundresses.

His carefree attitude, the unknown plans, it just didn't sit well with me. "Why can't I go like this?" I gestured towards my water stained t-shirt.

"Would you please just get changed?" Again, he offered me my cotton dress.

As I snagged my dress from him, I felt Hawke's hand playfully smack my bottom side. "Ahhh, what is it with you and smacking my ass today?" With gritted teeth I sneered back at him.

"Maybe I like smacking your pretty little ass." There it was, his "I can get what I want" almighty grin. He knew it. I knew it. He could win me over with just one single grin. "Get changed. Don't want to be late."

Dress in hand I stomped off to the silence of the bathroom. My ego injured, and adding to it, a birthday surprise waiting some place for me. Too easily I gave into Hawke. Should've pushed the battle at wanting to stay home, easily he'd won me over. Still fuming at Hawke, I closed the door to the private bathroom Maude had off her office. Today's grease got scrubbed from my body as I hurried through my "spit shine" wash-up. Even helped myself to Maude's premium perfume she kept in the cabinet. Next up, hair. Most impossible thing to tame. I freed my wild curls from the captive ponytail. Only to smell the grease from the fryer lingering in it.

"Look it here," I held the bottle of shampoo up, "looks like Hawke's just going to have to wait a little longer." I shoved my head and mop of auburn curls into the sink. Five minutes later, I had management over my curls. A clip here, one there, and the decision to let it air-dry was made.

xoxoxoxoxo

"Dove? You fall in back there?" Hawke bellowed from the front of the diner.

"I'll be out when I'm good and ready." Two can play his game, and Dove dilly-dallied just a little longer.

"'Bout time." He smarted off as Dove approached the end of the counter. "You look good in pink, Dove." Hawke mentioned with a hint of pleasure building in his eyes.

"Thank you." She felt it, almost like the wings of butterflies tickled the inner walls of her stomach just from the smile he'd sent her. "Thought the girls were hanging with you today?" Still miffed, Dove did her best not to snap at him as they left the diner.

"Yep they were." Hawke wore his smugness well. "Dove, give it up."

"Give what up?" Innocently, she posed the question as he opened the truck door and offered her a friendly hand.

"You don't do nasty well. Worry, you do that well. Whatever it is, give it up. You know it doesn't work with me." Hawke served her his sarcasm with a polite grin and enjoyed watching her lose the "I need to know" battle to him.

"Please, won't you tell me?" With a quick kiss to silence her lips, he shut the door before Dove could spat anything absurd out. "You're not going to give me any nibbles? No clue? No nothing?" The hopes of a nice quite evening at home just got dashed. He turned the opposite way out of the parking lot and headed south out of town. She tried another play with him and let her finger tips skim over his bronzed colored arm.

"Dove?" Hawke actually squirmed when Dove's hand slipped between his thighs. "Dove, I promised to keep you safe." His fingers wrapped tightly around hers and he quickly put a stop to the game she tried to play. "Keep that thought for later." Another smile of affection and he kissed the tips of her polished fingertips. "What the hell color is that?" Change of subject, Hawke hoped would work.

"Ruby Garden," she flashed both hands up for him to see, "the girls got it for me. Why are we going this way? Home is back that way." With a helpful hint as to which way home was, Dove pointed back over her shoulder.

"Looks more like your nails are bleeding. Will you just relax? We'll be there soon."

"Your smile is getting annoying." With that statement, he broadened his grin back at her. Blinker on, Hawke turned left onto an overgrown sandy lane. "The beach?" From under her eyelashes she glanced at him, "Used to bring the girls here in the evening when you were out on a late charter. We'd sit on the dock and wait for you guys to go by. Harbor Cove, one dock, a few picnic tables, and an outhouse. A private sandy cove that most people passed by." As they bumped along the sandy road, Dove realized what she'd said, "Hawke did I just..." This time she turned her whole body facing him, "remember..."

"Yep, you did Dove." Amazed by the memory Hawke added, "Countless summer nights, I'd look forward to seeing you and the girls waiting on that dock for us to go by."

"That was nice." Her smile filled his heart with the memory as they rounded a bend into a clearing, "Take it we're here."

"Dove, promised you a nice quiet evening. Nice night to watch the sunset."

Her emotions finally agreed with his plan. The lane opened to the view of the Pacific Ocean. One lone, empty dock inhabited by a few sea gulls who enjoyed screeching to one another greeted them. The parking lot, all but empty except for a shinny blue Wrangler Jeep.

"The girls are here?" Seeing their empty car and she impatiently frowned at Hawke. "Something tells me, the three of you," she glanced his way then scanned the beach area for her girls, "the three of you, you've done something?"

"Ya know Dove," engine cut, keys pocketed, Hawke then twisted a lock of her long curls around his finger, "you don't need to know every detail. Just enjoy." His kiss to her lips lingered longer, easing her irritated mood. "Happy Birthday Dove."

"You win," she eased back from him, "I give up. No more questions." Dove slipped free of her strappy sandals as she inched her way out of the truck. Plum colored painted toenails dug deep into the warm sand as Hawke patiently waited for her to finish. "That feels so good." He couldn't help but enjoy her giggling smile.

The shimmering view of the ocean waves gently rocking back and forth had Dove forgetting why she'd been brought there. As the warm summer breeze circled around them, Hawke slide his hand around her curvy waistline. The sun hung low in the approaching evening sky as they walked down the sand covered path to the desolated beach. As the warmth of the sun played over the waves, they found arranged on a blue plaid blanket an over-sized picnic basket waiting, and their now adult girls.

"A beach party," her sigh of relief drifted in the ocean breeze, "how perfect."

"Got yourself all twisted in knots for nothing, Dove." As he finished leading her down the path to the waiting picnic, Dove was attacked by killer hugs and an endless bombardment of questions by Emma and Amelia.

"Aunt Dove, are you surprised?" Amelia started...

"What kept the two of you?"

"Uncle Hawke, how bad did she protest?"

"Did you really have to drag her out of the diner or what?"

"Aunt Dove, you smell like the perfume Aunt Maude wears."

"Please tell me you didn't eat."

"We took Uncle Hawke shopping...did you know..."

"Did you know he can grocery shop?" Emma, I'm sure not finished with the questions came to a halt by me.

"Amelia. Emma." My two adult nieces fell into their old routine of listening to me. "Hold those thoughts." For a split moment the only thing you could hear was the lapping of the ocean waves. "Do you really want me to answer every question? Or maybe we can just open the basket."

"Happy Birthday, Aunt Dove." Their chattering of questions, comments, and everything else kicked into full gear.

"And the two of them are studying Criminal Forensics." Hawke rolled his eyes as he watched his beauties deal out the contents of the heavily packed basket. "You sure Dove?" He asked her the age old question.

"Yep, I'm sure. They're ours." Hawke practically fell on top of Dove as she yanked him down to the blanket.

"Uncle Hawke open this." Emma demanded handing him a bottle of merlot. "Southern Point, supposed to go with everything."

"Everything? What else do you have hidden in the basket?" Like a deck of playing cards the girls dealt out a display of tempting delights. Sushi, slices of apples, grapes, figs, mixed with pecans and walnuts, all accompanied with a wide variety of cheese. Whole wheat crackers and a bag of my favorite chocolates were just a few of the items from the basket. "You two aren't old enough to buy wine." The mom in Dove pointed out as they arranged the tempting treats.

"No, but Uncle Hawke is." Emma had perfected her Uncle's wink of an eye. "He says you get all giggly."

Amelia joined the tale of their Aunt, "And what's all this crap about the wine gets you all nice and relaxed and..."

"And what?" Dove jolted upright trying to threaten Hawke with a failing glare, "what kind of conversation were the three of you having?"

"Oh please Aunt Dove." Emma rolled her eyes better than her Aunt, "we know you two still do it."

"Do what?" Dove, in a tempting teasing voice held her plastic, fake wine goblet for Hawke to fill, "To the top please."

Amelia popped open a can of orange crush, "We know you two are still hot for each other. Heard about the parking lot escapade this morning. In broad daylight! Seriously?"

"You told them?" With eyes popping wide in disbelief, Dove smacked Hawke in the shoulder.

"Aunt Jane did," Emma claimed as she passed the tray of sushi to her Uncle, "Aunt Dove you're turning the same color of the wine."

"Sunburn," a casual lie with no explanation needed, "What else are you hiding in the basket?" Without any warning, Dove changed the subject before anyone else could question her, including her husband.

"Just this." From behind the basket, Amelia held a familiar off white cake box in her hands.

Graciously, Dove accepted the box, "This has got to be one of Maude's famous cakes." It was no secret that Maude had a sweet reputation for her deluxe style cakes. "I can smell the chocolate." She passed her plastic goblet of wine into Hawke's hands and flipped the lid to the box open, "Heaven. It's real butter cream frosting." Swiping a finger full of frosting into her mouth, "oh to die for. Still can't believe the three of you did all this behind my back."

"Seriously, Aunt Dove? You were like totally surprised?" Emma passed her Aunt a cake knife. "We can't keep anything from you."

"Total surprise. I didn't have a clue until this one," she nodded her head over toward Hawke, "shows up at the diner. With my dress and a direct order to come along peacefully."

"Uncle Hawke hasn't learned anything from living with a houseful of females." Amelia handed him the bottle of wine, "Think Aunt Dove needs more."

"You guys are too much. Thank you. I couldn't have asked for a better birthday."

"You're so welcome Aunt Dove," Amelia pointed to her watch, "Emma we've got to go."

"Where?" Hawke's tone turned back to parental.

"Going to catch up with the old gang from school. You guys don't mind do you?"

"No. Go. Have fun. What time do you think you'll be home?" Dove asked as her girls began to repack the basket.

"We're not. Promised Aunt Jane we spend the night at her house. You know just like old times." Amelia giggled. "Maybe Fred will let us paint his nails. Or do his hair."

"God help poor Fred." Hawke snickered remembering what his buddy looked like after a slumber party with the Jane and the girls.

Double kisses landed on their Aunts cheek, "Happy Birthday Aunt Dove. Hope you enjoyed it."

"I did. Thank you for helping this one," Dove patted Hawke on the knee, "plan all of this." Arm and arm, Dove could hear her girls fading conversation as they disappeared up the sandy trail to the parking lot.

"Thank you," Dove turned her attention to Hawke, "You don't mind staying for the sunset, do you?" Knowing the answer would be yes, she asked anyways.

"Planned on it. You need help with all that?" In her own little element, Dove neatly wrapped and tucked the remaining leftovers back into the basket. "Need a refill?" He offered holding the half full bottle of wine up.

"I'm good for the moment," and a giggle escaped her as Hawke wrapped her in his arms.

In the mist of the rising night, Mother Nature at her best painted a memorable skyline. A blend of reds, pinks, and a touch of mauve splashed into the fading blue skyline.

"Happy?" Hawke asked cradling his wife in his arms as the ocean breeze tickled her bare legs.

"Perfect birthday." Dove nuzzled her face along his neck scalding him with her intriguing kisses. "But what are you doing?"

"Helping you." The zipper to her sundress slipped effortlessly down.

"What if someone else comes to the beach?" Playfully, Dove struggled against his advances. "What if the girls decide to come back and join us?"

"Dove," One navy blue t-shirt stripped free from his body. "We won't see the girls until tomorrow."

She tightened the grip around the bodice of her cotton dress with her arms, "But didn't you say the sheriff patrols here," instead of worry, she puckered her lips and blew a kiss to him, "just looking for lovers?"

"We've got 'til midnight." His warm hands massaged at her thighs. "You going help me get this dress off you?"

"No." She flopped back on the blanket exposing a little more of her curvy figure that Hawke loved, "figure it out for yourself."

An offer Hawke couldn't refuse, he straddled over her. The ocean air tangled his wild mane of hair. Long, sleek, and jet black, he let Dove take all the time she needed to filter his hair though her fingers. Strand by strand, she played until her heart was content. Dove's mysterious enthusiasm aroused another playful game of kissing and tugging at each other's clothing. The night stars popped into the sky as the rosy glow of daylight disappeared along with Dove's dress. As the cool ocean breeze danced between their heated bodies, a shiver tickled her exposed flesh.

"Cold?" Jeans stripped from his body, Hawke tossed them on top of her discarded, now rumbled dress.

"Isn't that your job, keeping me warm?" The warmth Dove craved, she received. His sculpted, hard body filled in along her curves. "You forgot something." She rubbed every inch of her creamy skin along his body.

"You and your damn panties…" Hawke parted her from the white cotton trimmed lace panties that held him back. The lacy treasure, now crumbled into the closed palm of his hand, "You like to make it difficult don't you?" Not bothering to give Dove a chance to answer, he covered her lips with a crushing kiss.

Under the rising moon, their bodies tangled and weaved together. Hawke felt the gasp of Dove's escaping breath as his thrust of burning desire met her craving need of all of him. Openly, she pleaded with him, offering her rising hips for his taking. Passionate request met, Hawke firmly grabbed her hips diving deeper, harder, and lasting longer inside of her. Dove's whimsical moans of delight kept him aroused and grinning. With her fingertips, she delicately traced his popping biceps down to his wrists. In a sweep, faster than the rocking ocean wave, Hawke had Dove's hands pinned above her head. Eagerly, she tightened her legs around his waist. Delighted in pleasing him, slowly she continued her tempting flirtation of lightly letting her tongue slide over his lips sending him into another erotic arousal. Dove's continuous play brought out a harder, deeper stimulating thrust from Hawke as their bodies glided effortlessly together repeating over and over the enthusiastic eagerness that had been waiting to erupt all day. Reaching his final climax, his deep release of pleased laughter from Dove's screams of pure delight was carried off by the roar of the ocean.

The ocean breeze's smooth rush of air tangled around them as Hawke collapsed on top of Dove. His heartbeat matched the wild beat pounding inside Dove. Contented, she curled closely into his still over-heated body. Hawke's long tail of dark hair splashed over her shoulder.

"I can't get enough of you." Dove's whispering voice trailed softly into the night air. She loved touching every single inch of his well defined, muscular body.

"Makes two of us, Dove." The summer night air had her shivering as he pulled the throw blanket over them. "Dovey, look at the skyline." Another arousing kiss fell on her lips as she stared into the universe. Above them, in full display, an endless canopy of brilliant twinkling stars sparkled in the black as night sky.

Chapter 24 - Nightmares do Come to Life

My highly, well educated, soon to be college graduate girls demanded their Uncle and I renew our wedding vows. My argument, it would only be our twentieth. You save celebrations like that for the twenty-fifth. There was no appeasing Emma and Amelia. At the mention of the brilliant gala to be thrown, Hawke would conveniently disappear on me. There we had it. Our girls had taken it upon themselves to plan, with specific details from Maude and Jane, the whole upcoming anniversary party. Complete with renewing our vows at the Ocean View Chapel all the way down to having our reception at the diner. Just like we did twenty years ago. I protested every chance I got but, like usual, my darling beauties had me jumping through hoops. They drove me nuts with their constant whispering behind my back with Maude and Jane. The clincher, who worried all of us…Hawke. He detested any lavish, frilly, girly type affair where he'd have to hang a tie around his neck. On several occasions, when he'd been pinned down, Hawke reminded his grown Princess's of his displeasure for the upcoming festivities. He enjoyed romance with me only. Hawke never cared being the center of everyone else's attention.

The wedding/anniversary weekend arrived in full bloom. And, like a mushroom, I'd been kept in the dark and was pretty clueless to what they had up their sleeves. Today's list of duties I'd been strapped with had me running late for the diner. After closing, my highlight, a long evening of overdue pampering. A rumor of facials, hair, nails and a much needed massage even had Maude intrigued. For our pre-wedding celebration, Maude had planned to close the diner for the entire weekend.

Late August and the summer tourist season showed no signs of slowing. The diner hopped with late-in-the-year vacationers and we welcomed the summer long help of Emma and Amelia. My kitchen under control, I desperately needed a refill of coffee.

"Dove, did you decide on today's specials?" With bifocals perched on the bridge of her nose, Maude inquired.

"Leftovers." My smug sneer smiled back at her. Wet towel in hand, "Yes, got it planned. Plenty of chicken to work with. And of course, meatloaf," I wiped off the specials board. Scribbled in my best handwriting, "Meatloaf Surprise" and my personal specialty "Chicken Paprika" along with dumplings and another side dish to choose from. Each entrée included a slice of homemade pie, Coconut Cream, Cherry Crum, or Peach. Finishing the last line, my hand cramped in pain. Crippled in brief agonizing pain, the flare-up would never let me fully forget the hideous bear attack of yesteryear. With a few simple therapeutic massage techniques my hand relaxed and was ready to assist me with a cup of the ole standby…coffee. As always, I needed a refill.

The jingle of the cheerful silver bells dangling freely on the handle of the door announced the arrival of more customers. Coffee pot still in hand I turned to greet them with a friendly smile. From off the busy street, the two traveler's had found their way into Maude's diner. And for me, my rock solid world began to crumble.

From under the age-old weathered doorway, my own eyes reflected back at me. With a whispering click the door had been shut by the apprehensive young man who mirrored my eyes. Same shape. Same sparkle of blue. He had my wild curly hair, only blonde tresses dangled around his pale thin face. Even taller than the man who stood to his right, who I slowly became aware of.

Beat by beat, my heart sputtered to keep its pulsing rhythm. Captivated and held motionless by this young man's appearance, I felt the vibrating pulse of my heart climb its way into my throat. My eyes flickered with a budding fear along with disbelief toward the older man who accompanied him. His think blond hair, tinted with aging grey. His fair, pale coloring identical to the younger man's. Are they father and son? Edged lines of worry creased deeply into his excited face. But his matching blue eyes held a sadness that aged him well before his years. A gleaming smile plastered over his worn, tired face and he directed it to me. This couldn't possibly be happening. Before me, the strangers who'd been caught and sealed tightly shut in my nightmares waited for me to welcome them with open arms.

Unnoticed by the clinging and clattering of customers, time had frozen for me along with the new arrivals. In our isolated silence the three of us were fixated on one another. My eerie consciousness made way for a haunting awareness. Every inch of my flesh chilled, not a single finger twitched. Not even a blink of an eye. Not one muscle dared to move.

"It's me, James." His excited words whispered around the small crowd in the diner that paid no attention to us.

His voice, steady, even, and light rang in my ears. Just hearing his three simple words sent a jagged stab that penetrated deep into my heart. My skin prickled from the sound of this man's voice. The pain packed a punching force that nearly doubled me over. My heart screamed "NO" but my mind demanded answers. Who are they? Why are they here? Why am I so incredibly scared at the sight of them? An agonizing spasm of truth attacked me when I fully realized this had to be the man who haunted the deepest depths of my nightmares. Unlike my tormenting dreams, I could always awake. Not today. Fully wide awake, the visions from my late night vault of dreams stood in front of me...they were alive and breathing. No breath to scream, I gripped the coffee pot tighter. My knuckles glowed white and my frozen silence never wavered. Distorted snips from my nightmares flooded my awakened conscious. Reality, it snapped with a force.

"Why? My nightmares...they can't be alive." I mouthed the words, not even hearing my own voice. "This can't be happening." In the flesh, the horror of my nightmares stood. Right before me, here in the diner...father and son, so I thought, breathed the same air as me.

The spinning vortex of the diner drifted slowly around the explosive pounding in my temples. My pulse raced in hopes to find a place to hide. My brow beaded with droplets of perspiration. My body swayed in a rhythmic circular motion from the spinning diner. I clung to the coffee pot for any kind of support as I heard his deep, soft voice again.

"Honey, it's me, James. I've come for you." He turned to the younger man with my eyes, "Jason, it's her."

"Come for me?" The spinning kicked up a notch or two. The ghostly softness of his eerie voice, the one that called out to the missing woman...it all matched. "Oh no. No, you're not real." Not real? Who was I kidding?

"Chloe, we've come to take you home." The man calling himself James informed me.

A new fear shot down my spine and my skin prickled with goose bumps. A ghostly form had always appeared in my dreams. Today, a real flesh and blood human stepped forward and called me the woman's name from my nightmare, "Chloe."

"Chloe." James inched his way closer to the front counter. "It's you. You're really alive. I'd know you anywhere." Delighted by my appearance, his eyes burned with a passionate fire for the love he thought I was.

"I'm," my voice barely above a whisper, "I'm, I am not Chloe." Scared didn't cover how I felt as I protested back. "Don't…stop calling me…"

"Chloe, honey it's okay. I'm, we're here." Tormenting me with his happiness, "We've finally found you. I knew you couldn't be dead." Like a child opening a gift he always dreamed of, James oozed with a whimsical joy. He stood inches from the counter that protected me from him.

"Dad," the young man who accompanied this James person, reached for his father's arm. "Dad, remember this lady," his jeweled eyes met mine, "she might not be mom." Again, he tugged at his father's arm.

"Jason, of course," sympathetically, he glanced at his son, "We'd just like to talk with you. Please, Chloe." With a sparkle of hope in his eyes, James pleaded with me.

"If its okay, we can sit right here." Jason pointed to the empty seats at the counter, now I knew his name.

"Okay?" I questioned, not asked, but the words never left my mouth.

"Maybe we can sit down at the booth, you don't look so good." Jason suggested politely.

"NO!!!" Those silent words that couldn't leave my lips just found their voice. My single word "no" slammed into them with an abrupt harshness that neither of them expected, but protected me like a shield. The remaining blood drained from my already pale complexion. "NO! NO! NO!" I screamed again. An added new twist began to torture me. An abrupt shortness of breath seized my lungs. The coffee swirled in the pot as I clung to it for dear life. Spinning faster and faster the walls of the diner circled around me.

"Get away from her!" Jane's curdling scream couldn't stop the fast paced spinning for me. At least by hearing Jane's scream, I knew help was on the way. Her empty tray hit the tile floor and bounced along colliding with an empty chair. "Dove!" Desperately she ran to me dodging tables, chairs, and customers. "Dove, are you alright?"

To me, everything hit in slow motion speed. She looked so funny running in that frame by frame spin, I almost laughed, almost. Those small beads of perspiration now dripped along the side of my face. Automatically, my eyes closed from the nauseating swirl of motion. The creeping tremble feeling pinched in my knees giving me warning I'd be going down soon. The sturdy grip I once held on my trusted coffee pot weakened. In another slow motion slide show, finger by finger, I set the scorching pot free.

"Dove!!!!" Was that Jane's voice? Why can't I find her? Round and round the room took me on its carnival ride of spins. Tables, chairs, even people spun by me.

I should've flinched. I should've jumped when the coffee pot hit the floor with a tremendous crash. By now heads were turning as the hot liquid splattered over my legs and the floor. The reel of slow motion timing kept me standing, but for how long?

"Chloe!!" James screamed the missing woman's name from my dreams at me. Was he trying to inch closer to me in my spinning vortex? His arms flailed like a flopping fish as I attempted to grab for the edge of the counter. As always, my luck took a vacation today. I missed the counter and my hands could only find empty air to grab at.

"Get back!" I heard Jane's voice shouting. Why is she running so funny and slow?

That warning my knees gave me a few minutes ago, it caught up to me. The floor was coming up faster than I expected. As I went down, the surrounding dishes came with me. Everything in front of me got knocked to the floor and smashed. Glassware landed with a smashing crash as pieces of glass flew over the tile floor. Any hopes of catching myself…it just didn't happen. A painfully loud crack interrupted all the screaming and yelling as my head collided with the silver edge of the frost swirled blue countertop. To greet me and my new found pain, the smashed glass and coffee soaked floor didn't exactly cushion my fall. With another bounce of my body on the scattered mess that caught my fall, a new set of screams scorched the air.

"Aunt Dove!!!" My girls? I heard them but between the spinning room and my eyes begging to close, I couldn't find them.

Left helpless, my contorted body finally came to rest behind the counter. Within minutes the movie likeness of my daytime drama kept playing. The reel kept spinning, just like the ceiling of the diner.

"Chloe!!! Oh my God, Chloe!!!" James, screamed at me in his panic stricken voice.

"I'm not her. I'm not her. No, I'm not Chloe. Someone please make them stop." My lips trembled as my words went unheard. "My name is Dove. Where are my girls? Where's Jane and Maude? Why aren't they here?" Frightened and feeling as if I'd been left alone with the intruders, I asked myself. The ceiling circled and circled making the nausea in my stomach worse. What senses I had left reminded me my name is Dove. Dove Hawthorne. I wasn't and never was this Chloe person, the mysterious missing woman he called for in my nightmares. My head throbbed, beat by pounding beat as the horror unfolded further. Had my body been over come by the pulsing pain and left me in the awkwardness of protective sleep? Only the hum of the freezer unit could be heard in the diner full of patrons.

"Emma, call 911!" The panic of Maude's ill stricken voice rattled the brief silence no one had enjoyed. A flutter of fast paced rubber soled footsteps squeaked along the wet floor. I barely heard the faint, quivering voice of Emma as she relayed the detailed message to the 911 dispatcher. "Amelia," again, Maude's terrified voice echoed in the stillness, "call your Uncle."

"He's on his way," Amelia's timid voice shook with fear as she held the line with her Uncle, "Fred and Lance are with him."

While all the commotion danced around me, I just wanted to close my eyes. Slip into a deep sleep. Blood pooled around me from the gash on my head. Washed over in pain, I wished for sleep to come. If sleep came, I could surely wake from this nightmare. My eyes chose not grant me my wish. The rotating circling that floated in my head kept me intrigued. My peaceful resting spot of pain was shattered by his voice.

"Chloe! Oh my God!" In a hysterical panic, James invaded my painful space of peace. "She's my wife. Chloe! Chloe, it's me James. I'm here. I've got to help her."

The sound of his voice, it sliced into my painful thumping head. Why is he still here? Where's Hawke? Why am I laying on the floor? The deliriousness raided what was left of my mind.

"Chloe, I'm here. Just hold on." James, dared to make a desperate move, he attempted to rush behind the counter to save me.

He met his worst nightmare…Maude. She stopped him dead straight in his tracks with her well rounded figure and blocked any access to me. She only moved her "gate blocking" figure inches to let Jane by. "She's not Chloe." The power of Maude's voice went from tearful to pure jagged anger. "What's wrong with you two? Who the hell do you think you are?" she demanded and inched her womanly frame towards them. "Don't take another step closer." The power of Maude, she sneered with a howl that would stop any living creature.

"She's my wife. My Chloe." James pathetically preached as his son tugged him back from "guard dog" Maude.

"Dad. Step back. Let them take care of her. This isn't how it's supposed to be." Jason, visibly alarmed, but in control, tugged harder at his father's arm.

"Jane, Jane is that you? You're spinning." Her shaking hands unfolded me from my safe, cradled position on the wet, glass riddled floor.

"Dove! Oh God Dove! Look at me. Focus on me." From behind me, she rested my blood soaked head on her knees. "Dove, stay with me. You can't sleep." Her voice, hollow, scared, incredibly scared. Applying pressure with the palm of her hand, Jane covered the deeply sliced cut that continually oozed blood from my forehead.

"Jane." Rolling my eyes backwards to find her, "Jane." Dazed, confused, barely conscious I felt the shreds of sharp glass beneath me pierce my skin.

"Don't talk, Dove. Just breathe and keep your eyes focused on me." My rock of strength was breaking. I saw the tears flowing down her cheeks. "Hang on. Just hang on, honey. They'll be here soon." My beloved friend's tears dripped on me as she held me tight next to her own shaking body.

"You don't understand. Please, you've got to let me help her. She's my wife." Again the voice from my nightmares spoke.

Absurdly brave, James attempted to maneuver past Maude. I'd have to say that wasn't the brightest thing for him to attempt. Maude, just like a gnarly old guard dog, went into protection mode, even barring teeth. From the burner, she yanked a steaming hot pot of coffee and shoved the heated liquid at James.

"Back off! You hear me?" She snapped in defense as coffee slopped over the edge. "My Dove is not your wife."

James flinched hard with confusion as Maude threatened him again with the steaming pot of coffee. Unwilling to comprehend the woman's name the hostile coffee slinging lady said, "Dove? No, she's..." James staggered back from the commotion playing out behind the lunch counter. "She's my Chloe," he whispered in denial.

"Jane...Ja-neey...my girls. Where..." Breathing had become labored and talking had become difficult, "where are my girls?" Clutched in Jane's arms my tears mingled with the blood steaming down my face.

"Standing guard with Maude." She freed a blood-tangled scrap of hair from my face, then applied a dirty dishtowel to my open wound. "Hawke's on the way. So is the ambulance. Stop talking. I've got you." Jane, once the pillar of strength melted with fear and worry.

"My head. It hurts." The overhead bright lights weren't helping with the pain. "Jane, please don't let that man near me." I begged her in a whispered breath. "Dreams. Nightmares. Jane," I gulped for a breath, "it's them, it's them." Violently, I felt my body begin to shake. Helpless, scared, and in agonizing pain, at least I wasn't alone. I clung to Jane's arm like a lost child being reunited with their parents. "Jane..."

"Dove, no one, and I mean no one is getting near you. Please just keep breathing. Look at me Dove. Stay with me." In her best scared, hysterical voice she hushed me. "Stay still. Stop moving." Her voice shook with fear. "Hawke's on his way," she whispered reassuringly and applied pressure to the dirty towel on my bleeding head.

"This is a freaking small town. Where the hell is the rescue squad?" Amelia settled to the right of me. Another dirty dish towel covered my bleeding wound. "For once Aunt Dove," I heard the shielded panic hinging in her young voice, "listen to Jane. Stay still. Uncle Hawke is on his way."

I allowed myself to drift into an insecure relaxation. Sirens wailed in the distance, but in my shaky calmness, I knew Hawke would be here first.

"He's here." I let my eyes flutter open catching the worry in Jane's. She didn't flinch or ask questions, she knew what I felt. Perceptively, I felt his presence before his appearance. I could've counted the seconds of his arrival by the beating in my pounding heart.

The front door of Maude's roadside family diner smashed into the brightly colored white wall. The glass, amazingly still in one piece, vibrated with a hum. The happy jingling Christmas bells that always announced new customers, flew from the antique brass door handle. As if they were miniature bowling balls, they rolled along the tiled floor looking to make a strike. The man behind all this brute force stood calmly in the doorway. Rattled to the core I knew, he knew, but Hawke would never show it. I counted down his footsteps as he approached the counter. Crumbled and broken, laying on a coffee and glass covered floor, he'd soon find me.

"Where is she?" Hawke, visibly shaken, stopped short of Maude, who still clung to her weapon...the coffee pot. With an intimidating glare that would send any soul running, he stared down the two men she'd kept at bay.

"Behind the counter. She's, oh honey, Dovey, she's on the..." Maude, not even taking her eyes off the unwanted company, pointed a shaking finger over her shoulder. "Janey," she took a shaky breath, "Amelia, they're with her."

"I got you Maude," Lance released the weapon of choice from her hands and wrapped his tattooed covered arms of comfort around her. "It's okay Maude. Dove's a fighter. She's going to be fine."

"Jane?" In a panic, Fred searched the diner for his wife.

"Freddie! We're down here," Jane, in need of security herself, called to him from our hiding place, "Freddie, I'm fine. It's Dovey. Hawke, what the hell kept you?" Jane, instead of lashing at Hawke with her serpent style harshness, she batted a tear from her eye, "Don't move her. She took a direct hit to her head."

"What the hell happened?" Broken glass crunched under each footstep he took. As Hawke knelt down beside me, through blurred eyes I saw the twisted panic kneading deeply into his rugged face. He lifted the dirty, blood soaked towel from my head. A mass of crimson red escaped and drained over my cheek, "Oh God Dovey." Fear, it wasn't something he wore openly. Today...today all bets were off. "How the hell did this happen?" His question demanded an answer. Carefully, Hawke removed the blood soiled towels, winching in his own pain from seeing the open gash.

"Uncle Hawke," Amelia huddled in beside him, "Clean towels," she examined my exposed, lacerated wound. "Keep the pressure here," she placed his hand on my forehead. "Everything was fine until those two wondered in." Her eyes darted to the strangers. "Don't know what he said to her, but she kept getting paler and paler. And the fear," Amelia swallowed the collected lump in her throat. "Uncle Hawke, I've never seen her so scared by a total stranger. Not even you could've scared her this badly. It got worse when that guy kept calling her Chloe."

"What?" The stare in Hawke's eyes shouted disbelief, "Amelia..."

"He kept calling her Chloe. Adding in that Aunt Dovey was his wife." Eye to eye with her Uncle, Amelia tipped her head toward the nervous man being held back by his son.

"Son of a bitch. The demons are real." Not only did I suffer from the nightmares, so did Hawke. "Dove," his voice silky smooth, "open your eyes." Hawke whispered loud enough for me to hear.

On his command, I did as he asked. The shining light of the diner blurred my vision, but easily I could see him.

"Tell me your name." Funny time for a pop quiz I thought.

With a murky smile I weakly answered him, "Dove. Dove Hawthorne."

"What day is it?" He asked another simple question.

"Day before our anniversary." My eyes closed, but not before I saw the smile spread across his worried lips.

"Dove, you got it right. She's ours Amelia. All ours." A shadow of relief eased over his intense, rugged face.

"Uncle Hawke, who's Chloe?" Before Amelia's question was answered another outburst erupted.

"You assholes!" Emma went on a verbal attack. "Who the hell do you think you are coming in here slinging your bullshit lies? She's not your wife. She's not this Chloe woman. Get the hell out of here!" Strong words from a strong young woman. With a short pause, just enough time to refill her lungs, "Look what you creeps did to my Aunt!"

A strong, masculine hand circled around Emma's trim waistline as she turned to attack this man named James. "Emma," Lance swayed her back a few steps. "We'll deal with them later. Put your focus on your Aunt Dove." A calm voice from a man she trusted.

The sound of everything happening to me magnified. James, his voice, I'd heard it over and over begging to help. Emma snapping back at him, pointing out the damaged he'd caused. As if I weren't present, Hawke, Jane, and Amelia discussed my situation overtop of me. But, I am here. The wet, coffee soaked floor had cooled and left me shivering. At least the warmth of blood trailing down my cheek had slowed.

Willing my eyes to open, "Hawke," the whisper of my voice gathered his attention. With a vague smile, I reached for his hand. Through blurred eyes I found him. Always my security. Just feeling the warmth of his touch left me with a guarded relief. "Please, get me out of here." A slight shifting from Jane's lap, I found the embrace of his warm arms wrapping around me.

"Careful with her." Maude's worried voice rang in my ears. "Watch her head."

"I've got her, Maude." Effortlessly, Hawked picked me up and cradled me into his massive arms. Limp to his touch, I was nothing more than a rag doll cuddled close to his steady beating heart. Quickly, Amelia arranged another towel on his shoulder for my throbbing head to rest comfortably. "Don't you dare leave me now Dove." His silky voice clearly commanded.

"Clear the way people." Fred's voice. I'd know it anywhere. "Backup. Give them some room." On crowd control, he motioned for everyone to get the hell out of the way then reached for his own wife and held Jane tightly in his arms.

Safely wrapped in Hawke's arms, I curled tightly into the warmth of his body. Hawke's bold heartbeat calmed my fear. My link to safety had come for me. The strangers who turned my world upside down no longer held my mind captive. Calmly, quietly, Hawke carried my limp and bloody body through the diner. As he rounded the counter, cradling me closer, he acknowledged the intruders. The glare he cast to James and his son held only one meaning, a sure fire of death.

Gravel flew in the parking lot as the rescue squad came to a rocking halt. Sirens deactivated, the paramedics scrambled to take me from Hawke's secure arms. In the silence of a perfectly good sunny day the eerie echoes of James' voice rang in my muddled mind, "She's Chloe. I know she's my Chloe."

Chapter 25 - A Hospital Room...Again

A thick haze circled in and through my throbbing head. Without even opening my eyes, I knew where I was, again. I knew the smell. Recalled the tedious sounds. I knew it all too well. My wish, to stay in this hazy dream, relishing in the quietness. I just wanted to listen to Hawke's steady breathing. Even in my wave of dreams I knew he was there. I could feel him without even touching him.

My peaceful land of dreaming abruptly ended. Emotions crashed down so hard from the voices echoing down the hall they jolted me from my peaceful serenity. An unfamiliar, frantic woman's voice interrupted my dreamy affair and shattered the stillness.

"James listen to me, Chloe died ten years ago. That woman, it's not her. Please stop this crusade. You're upsetting me. You're upsetting yourself. And why in God's name do you want to torment this family any further?"

"Sarah, you don't understand. I need to see her again." Snapped the voice I recalled hearing at the diner. "I need to see her for my own peace of mind!"

"No, James. This is absurd. Stop asking to see her. Honey, she has a family. They don't want us here. We really need to leave them alone." Her pleading voice could be heard with overflowing tears of distress.

"Sarah, you're my wife now, I know that. But I've got to be sure this woman isn't Chloe. Please, Sarah, we have to talk to them." His ghostly image intruded on my dreaming and I couldn't shake the sound of the immense pain coming from his broken voice.

"Dad you've got to calm down! Get a hold of yourself!" A completely drained voice of another male now interrupted. "Dad, think about it. That man, the one who gave us the glare of death. It's obvious he's her husband. We're not getting near her. That guy wants to kick the shit out of us. Those girls, remember them? Good chance they're her daughters. Dad those two girls nearly attacked us before those men grabbed them. Face it Dad, we did this to her. We put this woman in this hospital. You saw her. Covered in blood. Would you want anyone near Sarah if this happened to her?"

"James, please, I'm begging you, listen to Jason, you know he's right. Honey, you're only setting yourself up for another heartache." Some common sense verbalized from his wife.

"Just because Uncle Phil was lucky enough to snap those pictures of her, it doesn't mean she's mom. She just looks like her, that's all. Dad, we made one hell of a mess here. We really need to leave. We just need to leave them alone." The son seemed to be the reasonable one.

An array of delusions casted their shadows in my wishy washy sleep. One voice continued to haunt me. I've heard it before, well before today. Finally, their conversation slowly drifted away from me. Once again a serenity of peace surrounded me.

As I aroused from my drowsy state of mind the familiar odor of disinfectants that all hospitals have, pasty stale white walls, and the annoying sound of a beeping machine flooded my awakening conscious with an awful memory. Ten years ago, I'd awoken in a similar state with my memory wiped clean. And here I lay again, in a hospital bed, unsure of what had just happened to me.

I wanted to wrap myself into each and every heavy breath Hawke breathed as I slowly opened my eyes to this all too familiar place. "Not again. This can't be happening to me again." I mumbled aloud and rubbed at the bandage stuck to my throbbing head.

With clearing eyes, I searched around the overly bright white hospital room. In focus, I found my two beautiful nieces. There terrified eyes met with my gentle smile of reassurance. Not ready to move, I allowed my eyes to drift to the end of the hospital bed. Immediately, I recognized the "reptiles" the pet name I had fondly given Hawke's battered snake skinned boots. They were propped up on the edge of the bed as if they wanted to say, "I'm still guarding you." Drained with worry was the expression Hawke wore. The stress of the day had taken its toll on him. I'm sure with a patient agony, once again he waited for me to wake-up from yet another disastrous accident. The years from the rugged outdoors showed in every well defined line edged into his worried features. My heart melted for his smile which was unable to conceal his fears. Returning his warm smile, I closed my eyes breathing deeply in relief knowing my guardian was really here. This time I wasn't dreaming.

"Please tell me you remember me." The silkiness of his husky voice had recaptured my dreamy thoughts bringing me fully to all of his needed attention.

"Yes. Oh God yes." Tears, I was well known for them and they didn't fail me. "I really do know you." Grinning at my outburst of tears, he removed the "reptiles" from the edge of my bed. Now by my side he whisked away the straying tears like he'd done so often in the past.

"What are all these tears for?" Softly, he asked and pulled me into a closer embrace.

"Scared. Worried. My head hurts." I burrowed my tear stained face deeper into his chest. Our arms tangled tighter and tighter around each other. I never wanted to let him go. My familiar security blanket in every sense truly was Hawke. He knew it as well as I did. Just the warmth of his body next to mine held the calming comfort I craved. The smell of heavy cigarette smoke lingered on his entire being. I'm sure he'd been chain smoking to calm his own nerves. It only reminded me of the psychotic event from earlier today. The disastrous day weighed heavily on both our minds.

"You're safe, Dove. No one's going to take you from me." Not sure of whom Hawke wanted to reassure…me or him, possibly even both of us.

Safety, I needed to know I was safe. I kept drowning in the vast memory of waking to the fear of hearing the stranger's heightened voices. The horrible fall I'd taken at the diner. And of all places to be, back here in the hospital. I clung to him tighter not wanting to relive any of it. My steady stream of tears dripped like a leaky faucet and the flow was softly interrupted by Emma.

"Aunt Dovey, please don't cry. You're safe Aunt Dovey, we're all here."
Gently Hawke pushed the tear soaked hair out of my face as Amelia kept handing me a supply of fresh tissues.

"What, what happened to me this time?" Sniffing though tears, I managed to sob out.

"You tell me," Hawke couldn't hide the annoyed tone that hinged in his voice, "falling for another guy?" He cast me a thin lipped smile.

"You're not funny Mr. Hawthorne." I half heartedly snapped in disgust at him. "My head hurts. Don't make me laugh."

"Dove, think."

"I don't want to think. My head hurts." I pointed to the new decoration taped to my head.

"Got some guy claiming you're his long lost wife." Did a jealous side of Hawke just flutter to the surface? A side I wasn't used to seeing? "Tell me what you remember." Softer, gentler, he asked of me.

"Uncle Hawke, give her break. She just woke up to a splitting headache." Amelia stepped in.

"Honey," I slipped a smile to Amelia, "I'm okay...I think." As I tried to collect a morning's worth of memories, "Just wish the pounding in my head would stop."

"Her name." Hawke pointed to Emma.

"Emma," I flashed a smile to her, "Amelia," I pointed to my other niece. "Both study Criminal Forensic at the University of Portland. And you sir," the smile on my lips danced, "And you, you've been my heart throb for the last twenty years."

"One more," Hawke picked my injured memory...just wasn't up for it, but, "tell me how you make that chicken dish."

"Chicken Paprika?"

"That'd be the one." He waited and my mouth watered for a bite of the delicious comfort food.

"Stick of butter melted, onions sautéed to a golden brown, add chicken, cover it in paprika. Let it simmer in a bath of chicken broth. When done, remove chicken and onion pieces. Gravy, turn the heat up so the broth boils. Add a flour water mixture and of course more paprika, stir continually, add a pint of sour cream. Reduce heat, add chicken, lower heat and simmer while you make the egg dumplings. Need more description or am I cleared Dr. Hawthorne?"

"No one can create Chicken Paprika like Aunt Dove. She could do it blind folded." Emma bragged just a little.

"You're you." Tension drained slightly from his broad shoulders. "Back to what happened," he had the nerve to tap my bandaged head, "tell me."

"It's not much. Stopped for a cup of coffee. The bells rang on the door." I knew what Hawke wanted me to say, but I didn't want to believe it. "They stood there. Staring. They kept staring at me. You would've thought I was the dead that came back to life."

"Who Dove?" Today, Hawke's patience had been put through the ringer. "Who are they?"

"Them." A tear flickered from my eye. "Tissues please. Thought I'd tucked those nightmares in a graveyard for dreams. It should never be alive." Amelia's hand covered mine and the half empty tissue box. "Curly blond hair. Just like in my dream. That man, he matched the man from my dreams. The young man with him, my eyes...the boy has my eyes." Awakening today's terror drained my already frayed nerves.

"This really isn't necessary Uncle Hawke." Emma interrupted my re-encounter. "She's been through enough."

"Emma," shot down by her Uncle's glare, "Go on Dove."

"My nightmares, you remember?" I'm sure Hawke recalled the endless nights of hell I had, "They really came to life today. Right in off the street they waltzed. Wanted to have a seat right at the counter. Wanted to talk with me. The man, he insisted on calling me Chloe. Said something about he knew she wasn't dead." Fresh tissues, I couldn't be without them.

"Just breathe Aunt Dove. Take your time." Emma planted herself on the edge of the bed as my details unfolded.

"The older man, he started to come unglued with a bouncy happiness. Inched his way closer to me, kept calling me Chloe. About that time the diner started a slow motion spin. My mind started flashing those nightmares from years ago, but there they stood in real life form. It just got creepier and creepier." Fingers laced through Hawke's, I took a moment to regroup my thoughts. "Felt like a knife stabbed me in the heart. I couldn't breathe. I couldn't move. The diner kept spinning. The coffee pot went flying. Then the counter came up to greet me. It certainly didn't break my fall." Lightly I padded the wad of gauze taped to my head. "Why do they make counters so hard?" I rolled my eyes at the question I'd just asked.

"You sure this guy..."

"Wasn't in dreamland this time, real life." I held Hawke's 'unsure of me' but steady gaze.

"Real life?"

"You know human, flesh, blood, breathing, real person." Pretty good description I thought.

"You're losing me, Dove."

"Dreams. The dreams. It's him. It's them." If an alarm could blare for attention, I just set them all off. "And the boy...he has my eyes. My eyes," I pointed directly at my own hazel blue colored eyes, "has all my curls but blonde. Even my pale as white skin coloring."

"Dove, honey, try to stay calm." In a failed attempt, Hawke slowly lost control of my emotions.

"Anyone have any info on these two diner crashers?" Emma asked in an attempt to derail my boiling emotional outbreak.

"Yep, I know who they are." Hawke answered her, but kept his focus tuned into my panic. "As soon as we get you and your emotions under control..."

"Hawke, you're not getting it. Those nightmares from years ago...they're real. Hawke, they are human, breathing, real. And they're here. But why? And who's Chloe?"

"Girls, go find Dr. Thornton." He jerked his head toward the open door and my two beauties disappeared.

I clutched his hands tighter, whispering, "Those two. At the diner. Hawke it was them." My panic escalated to pure hysteria. "This can't be happening."

"This guy, he's just some deranged nutcase. Dove..." my muscles weakened under the grip I held on him, "Dove. Dovey, you know Thornton won't let you out of here unless you're calm. Hate to see what your blood pressure is." This time, he didn't joke.

"Uncle Hawke." Amelia appeared in the open doorway of my room, "We've got a problem."

"Where's Thornton?" Hawke glanced past her to see Emma practically fly into the room.

"You're not going to believe this. That jackass is back. He's got Dr. Thornton cornered at the end of the hall." Emma, one never to keep her voice pleasant when perturbed announced with a full rage burning in her eyes. "His name is James Morrison."

"He's here? He's back? Why? No, no, no, no, no." My last nerve had just been stomped on like sour grapes. "I'm not feeling so..." Slipping from Hawke's arms of protection I melted into the pillow waiting to cushion me. My head throbbed in pain. Subconsciously, those ragged nerves of mine begged my brain to shutdown. All it wanted, just to protect me from the torment of the newest drama unfolding. "No, Hawke. No. Please don't let him near me." The wild ride of panic had geared up for another round.

That particular deep, but low rumbling growl of annoyance rang from within Hawke. His retaliating frustration applied itself on me, "Damn it Dove, calm down. If you don't get yourself under control, Doc will knock your ass out."

"Knocked out, that could be a nice warm and fuzzy welcome. Then I won't have to deal with my own hysteria anymore." My sly sarcastic grin that Hawke new all too well played over my lips. Slightly moving my aching head to the side, I peered around Hawke, "What are they doing?"

The scraping, scratching sound of two woodened chairs being drug across the spotlessly clean hospital floor interrupted my thoughts. I cocked my head to the side getting a better view of Emma and Amelia. My two raven haired beauties perched themselves on the stiff woodened hospital chairs directly outside the door. Two perfectly poised guard cats sat side by side. I'm sure their claws were extended waiting for a fight. A double set of honey golden brown eyes glared a warning at the intruder standing at the end of the hallway.

"Now will you relax?" Grinning at his beauties, Hawke asked.

"Now will you tell me what you know?" Perfect calmness tried to wash over me.

"Your new buddy, name is James Morrison. Wife, Sarah. Son, Jason."

"Jason, the one sporting my eyes," my own eyes flickered wildly at the statement, "What do they want with me?"

"Think about it Dove. Flip your mind back to the beginning of summer. Three men show up at the diner. All of a sudden you're their topic of discussion. Questioned you about," he picked up my arm and ran his finger lightly over my scars.

"How I reminded them of someone who was dead. She died from a bear attack." A double shiver of fear laced over my body.

Hawke roughly rubbed the bottom of his chin, "Guess those visiting relatives, they managed to snap off a few pictures of you. Explains why Morrison and company are in town. Dove, apparently you're a dead ringer for his dead wife, Chloe."

"Dead wife?" A flash from my personal nightmare cleared it all up. The woman's name the stranger in my dream called for, who he frantically searched for...Chloe. "Oh God, no! He thinks I'm his dead wife?" That familiar shaking I should've been used to surfaced. So much for calmness, "Please tell me this is some twisted nightmare."

"Dove," I found myself in comfort as Hawke's arms circled around my shoulders, "No way in hell will I let that crazy ass bastard get near you."

The creep's still at it," Amelia sneered, "He's really giving Dr. Thornton an earful. He's got balls showing up here again." Not only did my head snap at Amelia's choice of words, so did Hawke's.

"Personally, I'd prefer to just kick his ass now." In all her refined so called lady like boldness, Emma hissed. "Should've finished the dickhead off at the diner when we had the chance."

"Ladies?" Hawke cleared his throat. Temporarily amused by his girls, smugly he glanced over his shoulder grinning as he exhaled a dark sarcastic chuckle. "Believe I raised them well."

"You?" I questioned, watching my defenders ward off the evil spirits of the day.

Our moment of peace ended as Hawke lost his edge of composure, "Can't fucking believe this whack-job blows into town and claims you're his wife." Hawke's anger boiled over as I flinched back from his attacking words. "Bastard really thinks you're his damn wife."

"Hawke, honey, I think you need to stay calm." Nice attempt on my part but...

His acid flaring tone chilled the air in the room. "I'm beyond pissed Dove. Look at what the hell happened to you." Overly protective was an understatement at this point. "Better hope I don't come face to face with him." Aggravated, not by a jealous side, but by a dark side that I rarely ever saw in him.

"Uncle Hawke, stop it. Stop blaming Aunt Dove. It's not her fault." Both guardians left their posts in hopes to rescue me. The three of us waited and wondered with uncertainty for his next explosive reaction. Mindlessly and blindly I tried to change the subject on him. His fingers twined around the hand I offered him.

"When can I go home? Or am I stuck here for the weekend?"

"If Doc wasn't detained," Hawke snapped, "he'd be down here now." I weaved my fingers around his hand and tried to ignore his cold sharpness.

"Just remember you carrying me out of the diner. Was I out of touch for long?" I whispered and tried anything to redirect his anger.

"A few hours, you woke during one of the scans." Slowly, with a delicate touch, I drew a lineless design on the back of his hand. With the hope I could derail his anger, but it was useless. The day's twisted affair had finally caught up with him.

"You've got everyone pretty damn worried. Again." His voice edged with worry. "Maude fell completely apart. And Jane, little Miss Tough as Nails, damn good thing Fred was there to put her back together. They had to close the diner after we got you out of there." All of Hawke's sarcasm, bitterness, and anger hit me.

"Hawke, I didn't," he waved his hand to silence me, which didn't sit well with me. "Don't you dare..." His lips silenced mine. I needed the kiss of distraction as much as he did.

A few shades of relaxation filtered over his rugged face when we surfaced, "The best, I get a call from Lance." This time a smile eased over his tense lips. "These two," directly he pointed to the girls, "seems a few dishes went flying along with a few punches. The guys had a hard time keeping hold of the "Glamour Girls.""

"At least all the money you paid for the karate classes paid off." With a snarky smile, Amelia blew her Uncle a kiss."

"I think I bruised Fred's ribs. Didn't mean to hit him, but he grabbed me." Emma pressed a smile of happiness to me. "Just inches and I would have..."

"Emma?" Hawke interrupted her, "Sorry to hear I missed a pretty damn good cat fight." He winked at his beauties, left out another pleased chuckle, and they left me speechless.

"What can we say Aunt Dovey, he taught us well." Emma's smirk, vicious joy.

"No one messes with you, except for him," Amelia rolled her eyes toward her Uncle.

Our little fun and game timeout period ended abruptly. Hawke's next breath drew heavy, his attention, once again, back on me. His calmness, nearly believable, but kept me at bay. He tucked a strand of my loose curly hair behind my ear. His fingers ran along the white bandage that tightly concealed the ugly accident. The tip of his fingers gently followed down my tear stained cheeks. With all his gentleness I'd grown to know he outlined my lips. His feathery touch slipped down my neck and finally his hand rested firmly on top of mine. Easily, he had me swept up in his emotional calmness. Wishing and wanting to enjoy the moment of tenderness, just a little longer, I knew better. His harshness flared. Reborn in his smothering brown eyes, anger peaked. His jaw tightened. My emotional high just crashed as the anger he harbored only a few minutes ago returned in full force.

"Now what?" His glaring eyes pierced me and I couldn't help but squirm under them. I wasn't a naughty five year old who just got caught with the bag of forbidden candy. "What is it?"

"You scared the hell out of me, Dove." Fear, anger, worry, confusion, it all just boiled over.

"I didn't do this. I'm not the one who..." Hawke had my hands pinned under his, the grip tightened as I struggled for words. "You're scaring me. Stop it." My weak demand met with his icy glare.

"I won't lose you again, Dove." Fragile words mixed with angered emotions.

"Not planning on going anywhere." Firmly, I made my statement clear.

"Uncle Hawke," Emma quietly whispered and clung to me.

"Please, Uncle Hawke, you've got to calm down. It's not going to help us if you lose it. We need you." Amelia's hug and meaningful suggestion barely phased him.

Gently, he drew my hands to his lips lightly kissing the back. I felt the familiar cycle pattern gliding on my palm. Who was trying to calm who here? The cold hard silence in the room spared no one's nerves, especially mine. Restless, ragged breathing filtered around us as my tears slowly dripped down my already tear stained face. Both girls waited for one of us to say something...anything.

Drained and trying to survive his own exhaustion Dr. Thornton stumbled into the room. "What a day from hell this has been." He ran a hand through his salt and peppered black hair. "I take it things aren't going well in here either?" Sarcasm oozed from him as he nailed Hawke with a harsh glare. "Dove, I expected to find you looking better. What's the problem in here?" Chin raised high, arms crossed over his chest; Dr. Thornton glared at the two of us over his bifocals.

"I'm fine. Just tired." It was like trying to lie to Maude. Doc knew better.

"Hawke, I really hope that temper of yours is in check." Dr. Thornton's sharp tone turned everyone's head. "You're the last person I need flying off the handle." Sternly, using only words, he reprimanded Hawke without missing a beat. "One of you two better start talking or I'll be clearing this room. Dove I suggest it be you." Authority had spoken.

"Really, we're fine." Again, I tried to cover it all up.

"And did anyone tell you, you can't lie?" I got the fatherly stare and I'm disappointed in your attitude from the good doctor.

"My head hurts. Been a long day. Stress factor is way over a hundred." No way could I win a dueling match with Dr. Thornton, but I gave it a shot. "I wake up to hear the voice of the man who caused this and…and, he's just down the hall from me. He's fighting with you to see me. How could you even let him on this floor?" My scared but yet snapping attitude took Dr. Thornton by surprise.

"Mr. Morrison and company are gone." His reassuring words, I didn't buy it.

"Gone? He made it to the floor again. What the hell is next? Will Mr. Morrison and company be waltzing right through the door at anytime." The day's hysteria opened and poured out of me.

"Dove, I need you to keep calm. You've got to relax. There's no need to worry. Let's focus on you and your injury." His voice of reason didn't reach me.

"Relax? Stay calm? That nutcase is the reason why I'm here with my head bandaged. And, just how the hell do you know he won't show up again? Everyone in this room is over the edge and you want me to stay calm?"

"Dove, no one is getting near you but me." Dr. Thornton tried out his best smile as he walked closer to the bed. "Just take some deep breathes with me. Lord knows I need to."

Nothing doing. I yanked my hands free of Hawke's hold, "Take me home. Please, just take me home." A fast shove to move Hawke out of my way, I attempted to get out of the hospital bed. "Let's go. I know I'll be safe at home. Girls help me. Find me something to wear other than this damn gown."

"No you don't, Dove." Dr. Thornton's hands pinched at my shoulders, "Hawke don't let her up."

"Aunt Dovey, get back in bed, you're going to hurt yourself." Great time for my guard cats to gang up on me.

Out numbered by four bodies and eight hands I found myself secured back in the hospital bed. A new decoration to match my ugly hospital gown, a blood pressure cup just got slapped around my arm.

"I just want to go home. Please, Hawke, take me home." Reduced to tears, I begged him as the blood pressure cup tightened around my arm.

"Be still Dove. I need to get a good reading." My dear Dr. Thornton was not in the mood for anymore crap today, even from me. "Dove, this is terribly high. Too high, I can't let you go home. What the hell's been happening in here?"

"What the hell do think is going on? My wife is laid up in the hospital. Again. I don't think I need to remind you." Sarcasm sprouted wings and started to fly right out of Hawke's mouth. "You've got Morrison running amuck. And guess what, the bastard's just feet away from Dove. If I get my hands on him…"

"Mr. Hawthorn, this is my only warning to you. I'll toss your ass right out of this hospital. The tension between the two of you is unbelievable." A forceful side of Dr. Thornton surfaced. "Dove needs to stay calm. She needs you. Improve your attitude or you're out of here. Understand?" The depth of Dr. Thornton's rush of seriousness silenced everyone in my room.

"If I stay calm and relax, please, can I just go home?" I was more like one of Dr. Thornton's daughters than a patient.

"Sorry, Dove, you're staying overnight." Short and to the point came his words. "I need you here under observation."

"No, I don't feel safe here." A fresh round of tears flourished and I collapsed into my own self pity.

"I'm sorry, honey." There came the fatherly voice I'd grown to love, "With your pressure this bad and head injury, I can't let you go home yet." Long thin fingers felt over the well padded bump on my head. Dr. Thornton continued to shine the pin light in my eyes and study my reactions.

"Please." I tried one more time. My heart sank at the frown on doc's face.

"If, and only if, you stay in this bed, and follow my directions, I'm sure you'll be free first thing in the morning. I don't want to be the reason why you missed getting married to this ugly soul." Dr. Thornton snorted a laugh at Hawke's expense as he rechecked my blood pressure. "Still not good enough. We've got to drop these numbers." He reached into his lab coat pocket. "This will help take the edge off and let you relax and rest."

"No. Don't you dare. Don't knock me out." Between my pleading scream, I found I was no match for Hawke. My husband easily grabbed my arm and pinned me down. I felt the needles pinch and the burn from the medicine slip free flowingly into my body. "Ouch, that hurt. Get off of me you trader." I directed that statement at Hawke as I attempted to shove him off me.

"This should kick in with a few minutes. Dove I need your blood pressure down. You need to just rest." I rolled my eyes at him like a disgruntled teenager. "Don't make me give you something stronger." Over the past ten years Dr. Thornton and I had our share of sparing over my health.

In the tug and war over my comfort, Hawke tucked an extra pillow behind me. Me, I could only scowl at his thoughtfulness. It felt like Dr. Thornton hit me with a heavier dose than said. It kicked in faster than I wanted. I didn't want to sleep, but I had lost the battle thanks to Dr. Thornton. Quietly, my body and my mind relaxed. All I could do now, just lay in bed as Dr. Thornton and Hawke's conversation about me faded in and out.

xoxoxoxoxo

"You better keep your shit together." Doc didn't mince words with Hawke.

"Got it handled, Doc."

"I meant what I said before, Hawke. Dove is my top priority."

"Understood, Doc. She's mine, too." As the two continued the conversation, Hawke securely tucked the covers around Dove, "Close your eyes."

"Maybe," sleepily her voice whispered.

"She's one tough lady, Hawke. Dove's in far better shape than she was ten years ago. Amazing, just amazing."

"Other than this blood pressure issue what's the hold up? Why can't we take her home? This Morrison guy, he has open access to her. I don't like it." Anger peaked in Hawke's voice.

"Hawke get it in check. I've got security watching the floor. I need Dove to stay. There's one more set of tests I'm waiting on. I had a PET scan ran. Results, as usual, still pending. Other than that Dove's doing great. You need to keep her resting."

"This Morrison guy, the whole damn family of them, Dove totally flipped out. Doc, she said Morrison matches the man from her nightmares. Understand why I don't want any of them near her?" Quietly, but blunt, Hawke made his case known.

"She had a flare-up last summer from those nightmares, didn't she?" Doc asked.

"Yep. Seems Morrison, he's the brother-in-law to the guy who agitated Dove earlier this summer."

"Don't think we have anything to worry about, Hawke. Notified security, they're on top of it. Believe we have this strange problem handled."

"Not impressed with your security team, Doc. Just how are you going to handle them?" With a dry smirk, Hawke asked smugly. "They've been able to hit this floor twice."

"Got that one handled. Told Morrison I'd be more than happy to have the pretty girls who were sitting in the doorway come on down and have a heart-to-heart chat with him." Dr. Thornton grinned at the girls. "And as for you two, I don't want any 'ass kicking' in my hospital. If your Aunt stays calm, there's no more trouble from anyone, I'm sure she'll be out of here in the morning." He cast one more warning glare at Hawke.

"Just can't close your eyes can you Dove?" All tempers had calmed, "you need to rest."

"Please don't leave me alone." Dove's groggy voice pleaded with him to stay.

"I'll be here when you wakeup." Relaxed, even calm, Hawke reassured her.

"Promise?" She fought the medication to stay wake.

"Promise." Last word given, Hawke settled himself beside Dove on the bed, as she finally slipped into a peaceful sleep.

"Dr. Thornton, the scans are back for Mrs. Hawthorn. I've got them at the desk when you're ready."

"Thank you Nurse Jenkins." He acknowledged her and checked Dove's blood pressure one last time, "Excellent. Hawke, you up for checking out what we might find inside Dove's head? He grinned motioning him towards the door as Dove slept.

"I don't know Doc, promised her if she woke up," wrapping his finger around a daggling curl, Emma eased in beside him.

"We're not leaving her Uncle Hawke. Go with him. You need the break, even for a cigarette. If she wakes up, we'll find you."

"If she wakes up…"

Amelia held up her cell phone, "We'll find you, immediately. We'll take care of her."

Before leaving his wife's side, "God, I love you," gently Hawke wrapped a wild loose curl through his fingers, "If she wakes."

"Would you just go? Let her sleep." Emma whispered, and pushed her uncle towards the door to go with Dr. Thornton.

Chapter 26 - Face to Face

"She's amazing Hawke. Literally amazing. Ten years ago, Dove should've been dead from the bear attack. The woman has a will to live." Another profile of Dove's famous skull lit up on the screen as Dr. Thornton grinned at Hawke. "Dove lives for you and those girls. Never seen a woman so devoted to a fool like you."

"I'll take that as a compliment Doc. We all know how lucky we are. Tell ya, I couldn't live without her." Hawke finally left his guard down, "Thank God everyday that he didn't take her from us." Underneath it all the rugged outdoorsman really did have a soft side to him.

"Amen to that son. Here, here look at this. Right there." Dr. Thornton's fingertips tapped at the image. "This is what I needed to see." Elated by the discovery, he ran his finger over the bright screen. "Fabulous. Just made my whole miserable day."

"Doc, not a clue as to what I'm looking at here. Little out of my field." Lost and out of his elements Hawke stared at the digital images.

"Let me show you my boy." For a moment, Dr. Thornton slipped back into his days of teaching and Hawke had just become his new student. "This here," he tapped at the screen again, "right here on the screen…full three-dimensional scans of Dove's, beautiful brain and skull. You following?"

"I'll do my best to keep up with you." Hawke moved closer to the illuminating image as Dr. Thornton ran his finger along the scan.

"This line," he pointed at a faint shadow, "today's injury…fresh injury. Just love this 3-D imaging." Delighted by the scan, Dr. Thornton went into excessive detail for Hawke. "Dove took a clean hit to her head, but…" he took another breath, "no breaks, no cracks, not even a blessed hair line fracture. She has no structural damage to the skull. Just extremely bruised."

"Explains why Dove can be so hard headed at times." The smile seeped over Hawke's lips.

"This, my friend, is the best damn news of the day." Dr. Thornton flipped over to the computer for another set of images.

"So I can take her home?" Hawke ran his hand over his sturdy jaw and grinned.

"Not yet Hawke, not yet."

"But, you just said her skull is fine." Disappointed, his smile slipped from view.

"Dove's got swelling right…here." Dr. Thornton outlined with his pen the swollen section of Dove's brain. "It's not much. But with everything she's been through, it's best to keep her for observation."

"Observation? The girls and I can do that from home. Doc, you know she'd be happier in her own bed."

"Like I said before Hawke, Dove's been through a lot today. The best thing we can do is keep her off her feet. You know as well as I do Dove won't stay in bed at home. She's got to rest. If Dove has a good night, she's all yours in the morning."

"I'm going to hold you to that Doc."

"I expect you'll be spending the night with Dove?" Dr. Thornton recalled the nights he found Hawke sleeping next to Dove's bedside so many years ago.

"I'll be staying. Pretty sure I'll be able to get the girls to go home." Hawke ran his finger over the last images, "Can't believe we're here again."

"Mr. Hawthorne," the stranger cleared his throat, "I really need to speak with your wife."

In unison, Hawke and Dr. Thornton abruptly spun around to face the voice who called for their attention. To Hawke's unimaginable horror, he found himself face to face with the man who was responsible for putting Dove back in the hospital. Gurgling in the pit of his stomach, a fury of hate boiled as he glared at the man standing within steps of him. Automatically, he clenched his fists into a hard ball. His sturdy jaw tightened. The veins in his neck popped as he fought back the surfacing anger. But his cold, hard brown eyes spoke a tongue of bitter coldness towards the intruder. For the second time today Hawke had found himself being confronted by James Morrison. The violent growl that vibrated deep from inside Hawke had Dr. Thornton grabbing to restrain him.

"YOU! What the hell are you doing here?" Hawke didn't even bother to shake free of Dr. Thornton's grip.

"I'm very sorry to intrude. Please, if I could…I just want to…"

"You've got a lot of fucking nerve showing your face here." Not even a flinch of worry crossed James' face from Hawke's vicious, deep cutting words.

"You can't believe how sorry I am for what's happened. Please accept my apologies. I'm begging you," he continued to plead his case, "please just let me talk to her." Head held high with pride James didn't budge from where he stood.

Like lightening flashing, a bolt of anger flew from Hawke's eyes, "Like hell I'm going to let you get near my wife. She's scared to death of you. How the hell did you get past security?" Two steps towards James Morrison, Hawke dragged Dr. Thornton and his pinching grip along with him.

"Mr. Hawthorn, please let me explain." In a polite, reasonably calm manner, James continued on with his intrusion and demand to see Dove.

"Explain? Let me." Determined to keep James Morrison from his wife, Hawke closed the small open space between them, "Go near my wife and I'll kill you. Explanation enough for you?"

"I'm so sorry," James asking for a plea of forgiveness held his hand up, "If I'd only handled this differently."

"Differently? You have no business near my wife, Morrison." Hawke, trying to remain in control, spat his razor sharp words at James.

The chart in Dr. Thornton's hand tumbled to the floor as he secured a position between the rising of a volatile situation. "Think about Dove, Hawke. She needs you." With a failed attempt he tried to maneuver Hawke back a few steps, "Remember, Dove can hear you."

"Mr. Hawthorn, please, I'm asking," James rustled with the photographs in his hand. "Please, just look at these. You'll understand why I need to speak with your wife." James extended a shaking hand, fingers still gripping tightly on something he loved. "Please, Mr. Hawthorn, just take a look." James admired the second photograph in his hand, then slowly offered it to Hawke. "This is my late wife, Chloe. She died ten years ago. The other, our wedding." With unsteady legs supporting him, James stepped forward extending the photos to Hawke. "Please, all I'm asking is just look."

From the outstretched hand of James, Hawke sidestepped Dr. Thornton and reluctantly took hold of the two photographs. James, barely holding his own emotions together, waited and watched as Hawke studied the woman in the pictures.

In curiosity Dr. Thornton leaned closer to Hawke to see who the mystery woman was in the pictures. "Oh good Lord," he gasped at seeing the strong resemblance to Dove. Speechless, he could see how visibly shaken Hawke had become.

Lost in his own concentration of hate towards James, Hawke repressed each and every draining emotion he felt as the realization of the woman in the photographs soaked in. Chloe Morrison could have been his own beloved wife in the pictures.

Slowly lifting his eyes from the photos, Hawke's harden glare of disgust reflected to James. "My Dove is not your dead wife." The venom spilled from Hawke's jagged edged words as he handed back the pictures to James.

"Two women were attacked that day, Mr. Hawthorne." James stated with a shaky voice.

"And I'm the one who put the bullet into the son-of-a-bitch that attacked them." Hawke's memory would never allow him to forget that day.

"All I'm asking, please let me meet her. She's got to know," James glanced at the pictures he held secure, "There could be a chance," his lip trembled, "she could be my Chloe."

The snake in Hawke coiled, ready for attack. "Dove is not your wife." He ran his hand through the lose ends of his hair barely able to keep himself in check, "I don't want you near MY wife or MY family. Do I make myself clear?" Anger fueled his erupting temper.

"Please try to understand. You'd be asking the same if you stood in my shoes." James clutched the pictures in his hand.

"Morrison, I'm giving you one last chance to walk out of this hospital," Hawke's grin turned gravely sour, "in one piece. You go near Dove...you'll end up in a bed on the psych ward."

Acting as a buffer, Dr. Thornton again placed himself between the pending battle. On the horizon he felt the heat of Hawke's enraged anger and noted how James barely waivered under the pressure. Fast to put a plan into gear, he had to keep James out of Hawke's reach. The more distance between them, the better.

"Mr. Morrison you've been escorted from this hospital twice in one day. I'd be more than happy to arrange for a police escort this time." Dr. Thornton braced himself for the fallout.

Completely ignoring the doctor's instructions, James rallied with his own anger, "You've got to take what happened ten years ago into consideration. Your wife could be Chloe. I need some kind of proof she isn't." He no longer toted his polite calmness.

Tension from the bitter meeting escalated, "How stupid are you?" Hawke vented on the edge of volatile. "No way in hell are you getting a DNA sample of my wife. You're the damn reason why she's laid up."

"Security, I need security to the fifth floor." Before the fists started to fly, Dr. Thornton managed to call for backup. "Send everyone you have!"

"Morrison, I have no qualms with taking you off this floor myself," Hawke, now within reaching distance of James, warned.

With a mid-body tackle to Hawke's waist, "Hawke, damn it, stop fighting me." Dr. Thornton turned into a defensive linebacker, pinning Hawke against the wall.

"Get the hell off me Doc," anger vented from Hawke, "I've got it handled."

"Like hell you do!" Dr. Thornton tightened his grip around Hawke.

"All I'm asking for Mr. Hawthorne is the truth. I just want a chance to talk to your wife. A simple DNA test will tell us the truth about who she really is." James had to poke the already angered bear.

"You really are insane, Morrison. I know who my wife is." Easily, Hawke shoved Dr. Thornton out of his way.

"Where the hell is security?" Thankful for the two orderly's who now blocked James, Dr. Thornton scanned the hallway. "Hawke, stay put. I mean it. You stay put." One hand held firmly on Hawke's chest, he turned to James. "You, Morrison back away. For you own damn good get out of this hospital." Size wise, Dr. Thornton barely reached Hawke's shoulders, but he wasn't about to let fists fly.

"Why can't you understand," James yelled from behind the orderly's blocking bodies "I need to talk to her."

"Morrison, I'm done warning you." Hawke found himself smashed against the wall, again, by Dr. Thornton. He'd reached his breaking-point. Doc knew all too well the damage Hawke could do when it came to protecting his family.

"Don't be the stupid one here, Hawke." With what muscle power he had left, Dr. Thornton powered him back against the wall.

"Morrison, I'll kill your sorry ass if you go near my wife." Provoked beyond reason, Hawke overpowered Dr. Thornton and sent him tumbling to the floor.

On safety detail, the two orderly's fought to keep James in place. The gentle "dinging" of the elevator alerted everyone to someone's arrival. As the doors slid opened a crack team of only two security guards rushed the floor to finally assist Dr. Thornton.

"Two of you? That's it?" Prepared for a boxing match Dr. Thornton scrambled to his feet, "We've got a major situation on this floor. All I get is you two?" Disgruntled with the lack of security, he barked in anger at them, "Take him out of here." Irritated to the point of being unprofessional, Dr. Thornton directed the security team toward James. "Oh no you don't..." For a man in his early sixties, panting heavily, Dr. Thornton muscled up another defensive move on Hawke.

"Get the hell off me, Doc." Hawke shook free of the grinding hold Dr. Thornton held on him. "You're not the one I want to hurt." Hawke easily backed the second security guard off with an impressive glare of pure anger. "Morrison, I've had about enough of you and your shit for one day. Dove is MY wife! Only MY wife!"

"Well see about that!" A burst of antagonizing confidence glared from James. "If I have to, I'll get a court order to prove who she is." He practically spat the threat in Hawke's face.

"You're one deranged idiot, Morrison. Get it through your head, Dove's not your dead wife." Free from Dr. Thornton's death grip Hawke paced off the short steps straight for James.

"Noooooooo," A shrill scream filled the empty hall and temporarily halted the hospital brawl, "Uncle Hawke..." Emma's footsteps hit hard on the white tile floor as she raced toward him.

"What the hell are you two waiting for? Get Morrison out of this hospital." While security guard number one banged away on the elevator button, Emma flew into her Uncle's arms. Grateful to hear the slow sliding doors open, Dr. Thornton, along with the two security guards filled the opening elevator with the still-in-one-piece James Morrison. "Take him out. I want the Sheriff notified. Can you two manage that much?" Dr. Thornton snapped as the elevators doors clicked shut.

"Emma," panic and worry overshadowed Hawke's anger. "Dove, she's awake? Tell me she's not out of bed. Where's Amelia?"

"Amelia's with Aunt Dove. She's sound asleep. She's fine. We could hear all the commotion. When I checked to see what was going on…" Emma brushed a gob of hair from her eyes, "I saw you…I thought you were going to kill that guy."

"Everything's fine, honey." Hawke held his oldest niece in his arms, "Morrison's gone. Hell, I hope for good." Exhausted mentally, he caught a ragged appearing Dr. Thornton. "Doc, you okay?" Hawke turned his concern toward the rattled physician.

"I'm too old for this shit." He ran a hand over his standing-on-end salt and peppered hair, "You're damn lucky Dove managed to sleep though this escapade."

"Damn lucky I didn't get my hands on Morrison. See why Dove needs to be home? Bastard snuck right past your ace security team. Made it right to her floor."

"Had this talk with you before, you can't take Dave home." Dr. Thornton snapped at Hawke.

"And you can't keep her safe from that lunatic." He shifted Emma to his side, "Crack team of two security guards…lot of help they were."

"For God's sake, Hawke, Dove has swelling in her brain. I need her here tonight for observation." Eye to eye with Hawke, Dr. Thornton refused to give into his demand.

"Think we should go check on Aunt Dove," Emma nudged him to move down the hall, "we all know you'll be spending the night here."

"Suggest you listen to your niece," Dr. Thornton rubbed at his throbbing temple, "I'll check on Dove, right after I make a phone call to the sheriff."

"Doc," Hawke extended his hand, "Couldn't have made it without you."

Hand taken, "Go check on your wife ya grizzly soul. She's the one who needs you."

Right where he'd left her, lost in the well needed peaceful slumber of sleep, he found Dove. Covers still tucked in tightly around her curvy figure, "She's so pale." Hawke reached for one of Dove's stray wild red curls and ran it between his fingers.

"She's been asleep since you left with Dr. Thornton." Amelia glanced up to her uncle, "She stirred a little when she heard your voice earlier, but didn't wake. Why don't you stay with her?"

"You need a cup of coffee," Emma suggested.

"Could go for something harder, but coffee sounds good," Hawke offered a smile to his girls as they left the hospital room.

Gently, he picked up Dove's left hand and glided his finger over her wedding band, "Best thing I ever did was marry you Dove." She stirred slightly when he placed a kiss on her sleeping lips.

Chapter 27 - Just a Shower

Hospital beds were meant for only one. Not in Hawke's case. I didn't mind sharing mine with him. Comfortably positioned under a heavy leg, he had me securely locked with an arm wrapped around my waist. He meant what he said; he'd keep me in this bed one way or another. The rest I needed came easily with Hawke next to me. Still dozing in out of sleep, I would catch parts and bits of the girls chatting. The buzz of wedding details filled the passing time. All plans had been kept under wraps until today. The only inch of information my crazed bridal consultants would give up, the Ocean View Chapel we'd been married in twenty years ago had been reserved.

"You awake?" I played with the tail of Hawke's inky black hair. "Pretty sure your dates have arrived." Before the elevator doors even closed we could hear the commotion from Fred and Lance's arrival. From the opposite end of the hallway they made their grand entrance known to everyone. "Don't want to be late for cigars, burgers, and pool, do you?"

"I'm not going." Hawke wouldn't budge off of my chest. "You make the best pillow, Dove." He snuggled his face deeper into the flimsy hospital gown that concealed my fleshy breasts. "Comfortable right here."

"If you don't go they'll nag at you until you give in. Who'd want to miss playing pool and drinking a few brews? I could even go for that."

"Fine, but don't make me regret leaving." As he sat up, Hawke gave me the once over, "Your color's back. Feeling better?"

"Amazing, what peace, quiet, and sleep can do for a person who got their ass kicked by a countertop."

"Surprised the dream team over there didn't doodle another flower on your head." Small flashback from years ago had us both grinning. In a deep stretch he reached for the ceiling then ran a hand through his poker straight locks. Then hit the girls with a noticeable glare they completely ignored. "They're still at it? How long have they been on those damn phones?"

"All afternoon. Wedding plans, you know." I was amused by Hawke and it had me giggling.

"Let me guess, those hot little phones in their hand, I'm still paying for them?" He snarled at his girls.

"Yes you are dear. Along with the new upgrades. It's another reason why they love you so much." I cracked another giggle at his unimpressed mood. "Glad you slept through all their planning."

"You two," he shook a finger at them, "you're costing me money. Hang up already." His scowling frown went into a chuckle as the girls rolled their eyes at him in unison.

"Let my bridal consultants be." I poked my grumpy bear in the ribs, but his grin faded quickly when he took a hold of my hand.

"Dove, one warning," his eyes glinted with serious, "you better not get out of this bed. I don't want a phone call saying you did something stupid." A calm, stern warning, but this time I grinned. "Dove, I'm not kidding. Stop smirking at me like that."

"This is kind of fun, it's my turn to torture you." I couldn't help the playful sarcasm.

He planted a kiss goodbye on the bandage that covered my wound and I got one more lecture. "Call me immediately if anyone shows up. Understand?" With a catty nod, I kept grinning. "I'll be back after your little girly party. Love ya." Another kiss stolen from my lips, and he met the cluster causing commotion of Fred and Lance in the doorway. "You're in for in it now," Hawke ducked back into my room, "Jane and Maude just stepped off the elevator. Good luck." I blew him a kiss from the comfort of my bed "Remember what I said."

"Go." I pointed at the open doorway, "And don't forget to have fun." I had less than fifteen seconds to mentally prepare for round two of lectures. Maude perfected the 'motherly fuss' mode. Hands folded neatly in my lap, I prepared myself for the woman who I dearly referred to as my second mother.

"Oh my. My, my, my. Dove." Maude's well rounded figure filled the doorway to my room. "Oh Dove, my sweet girl." In her eyes the memories of ten years ago flooded from her mind. "Not again." Quickly, she whisked away a dripping tear from her eye.

"It's not like ten years ago, Maude," Jane pushed past her, "she remembers all of us. Even that rotten to the core nephew of yours." The sound of Jane's sharp tongue only made me smile.

"Maude, I'm fine. Memory is still intact." I tapped my head decoration, "If all goes well, I'm out of here in the morning." I met her outstretched arms for a warm hug.

"Can't help it, honey. Just too many scary memories boiling up today." Maude, famous for digging in her bra for a tissue, which she found, dabbed her eyes dry.

"Really Maude, Dove's a tough-old-broad for only being forty. Now let her up so she can breathe. How's the head." On the other side of the bed Jane poked at my white bandage. "No one drew a picture on you yet."

"Who's calling who an old broad, you're older than me." I welcomed Jane and her acid tongue whole heartedly. "Believe you were the one sobbing while I bled all over you this morning."

"I'm human. Just don't tell anyone." Hugs between best friends felt so right.

While Jane and I dueled in our specialized sarcasm, Maude examined my head. In her own fashionable style of medicine she thoroughly checked the well padded bump.

"Maude, what are you doing?" She picked at the tape fastened to my skin.

"Sit still. I know what I'm doing." She peeled back the end of the gauze. "Much better. Clean, don't think you'll have a scar." She tugged on the gauzy bandage, "It's going to leave one nasty bruise." Dr. Maude made her assessment. "Better than when I saw you last." With fingertips like a feather, she neatly replaced the bandage and kissed my head. "There, all better."

"Thanks mom." Like the child I was to her, I flashed her a loving smile. "Dr. Thornton says I'm doing fine. As long as I stay in this bed and rest. Just keeping me because there's a little swelling. Claims he can't trust me to go home. Something about me not staying off my feet, waiting on Hawke hand and foot." My joke made her smile. "Just for tonight. Observation and all. Besides, Hawke has already set up camp. He'll be spending the night."

"I remember those days like yesterday. He never left your side. Been so worried, honey. Hawke tried to keep us updated. Understand you had some unwanted company."

"Yep. Morrison showed up while Hawke and Dr. Thornton were going over all my scans. Wasn't pretty, got the full report from the girls. Lucky I slept through it."

"This Morrison guy, he's not playing with a full deck. Seems to be obsessed with getting to you." Maude pulled an extra chair over to the bed. "Never seen anything like it before."

"I know. Glad I've got someone staying with me around the clock." I tried to smile, but I couldn't hide my fear from her. "Can't lie, guy scares the hell out of me."

"Glad Hawke's spending the night with you." She patted my hand.

"Where did Jane and the girls go?" Deep in conversation with Maude we never noticed how they slipped out of the room.

As that very question left my lips, legs sprouted out from under a dozen or more shiny purple and yellow helium balloons.

"Surprise!" Amelia, the first to poke through the bouquet squealed. "It's shower time, Aunt Dove!"

"Don't say a word," Emma lined up over half a dozen frilly gift bags at the foot of the bed. "You're to stay relaxed and calm."

"Calm?" In Jane's hands one of Maude's famous cakes, "and we're going to feed her all this sugar."

"Chocolate cherry?" The child in me ran my finger through the dark chocolate butter cream frosting. "It's the real stuff."

"Only make the real stuff." Maude arranged the napkins and plates next to the cake. "Purple flowers look nice on all this chocolate." Maude, pleased with her latest design, opened her large flowered bag. "As promised." From the depths of the bag she pulled out a bottle of red wine. "You know, our family history claims we were pretty damn good at smuggling back in the day."

"Perfect. Chocolate cake and red wine to finish my day off. Maude, this is next to heaven." I licked off my fork, back and front, and gladly accepted another king sized piece of cake. "This hits the spot, haven't eaten all day."

"Here open these." Emma piled the pretty gift bags next to me.

Just like a slumber party everyone piled onto my bed. "Let's see what Jane tucked in here." From bag number one I pulled three sets of matching panties and bras. "Flower print, love it. Oh meow, check this out, purple leopard print. Thank you, Jane."

"Wanted to get you something naughty…black lace and all, but…" Jane shoved a bite of cake into her mouth while her checks turned rosy.

"Take it you saved the black lace to share with Fred?" Mouth full of cake all Jane could do…just nod her head yes.

Maude shoved her bag to me next, "You know I don't shop for," she glanced at Jane and her red face, "figured you'd be needing this."

"A bottle of blackberry brandy." I held up my favorite brand, "Perfect for sipping on the deck."

"Grab those Emma." Amelia rounded up the last few bags. Between her and Emma they just dumped the contents on my lap.

"What the heck did you two do?" I held up several barely there so called g-string panties, "you got me butt floss? Bubble bath, lip gloss, always need those." I sorted through all the lace bras and panties more to my liking. "Had fun shopping did we girls?"

"There's more." Emma held up a sheer peach colored lacey teddy. "We all know you and Uncle Hawke still get it on."

"Get it on?" Jane snickered, "should be asking her how many times they've been busted for getting it on."

"At least we haven't been busted by the local police." I snickered back at Jane.

"Aunt Jane, really?" Amelia turned to her, "Giving up any details?"

"Why don't you ask the "Diner Parking Lot Queen" here," she put the attention back on me, "Go ahead, ask her how many times she's been caught playing in the back lot?"

"When did this turn into how, when and where we've all been caught sneaking kisses?" I asked and slipped my hand under the next to nothing sheer nightgown. "He's going to like this."

"No way, the worst," Emma faintly grinned at me, "trying to sneak in after curfew and hearing your Aunt and Uncle getting it on down the hall. Totally gross." She actually gagged.

"When did you do that?" Did my ears hear right? "Wait a minute, how many times did you sneak in?"

With a grin of guilt, Emma just told on herself, "only a few."

"No way could I get that lucky. I get embarrassed nearly to death," Amelia slapped a hand to her forehead, "Never, never, and I mean never be five minutes late on curfew."

"What happened?" Maude never heard the dreaded curfew tales told by her great-nieces.

"Five," Amelia flashed five fingers with anger, "five minutes past midnight. Uncle Hawke. There he sat, smoking like a chimney on the back deck." She curled her lips tight, still ticked off, "With the shotgun resting on his knees."

"I remember that. Lectured you and that poor boy for a good half hour. You didn't get another date with him did you?"

"Would you want to date me with an Uncle like that?" Amelia groaned.

"Why didn't I ever hear about this?" Maude passed us all another piece of cake, "He's got a lot of nerve. Gave me so much grey hair," she touched her pinned up curls, "staying out all night, running wild with Fred and Lance. Until..."

"Until Dove turned eighteen." Jane poked me in the foot with her plastic fork, "Camped on Dove's door step all the time. You remember any of that?"

"Wish I did. Then I won't have to rely on you. Never know if the truth is leaving those luscious lips of yours. At least Maude tells me the truth." Like best friends, we just giggled at each other.

"Evening ladies," the floor nurse made her rounds, "sorry to break up the party. Oh these are nice," she held up my new thong underwear, "but, I've let you stay way past the regular visiting hours." Nicely, she slapped the blood pressure cuff around my arm. "Bride-to-be needs her sleep."

"Appreciate you breaking the rules for us." I packed all of my 'unmentionables' into one gift bag. "How's the pressure holding?"

"Excellent, Dove. Suppose that husband of yours will be sneaking down the hall?"

"Surprised he's not here yet."

My nurse glanced up at the clock, "Expect to see him by ten. This little party did you good Dove. But under Dr. Thornton's orders, everyone out, please." She gladly accepted the cake Maude offered her.

Less than twenty minutes later my bridal shower had been packed and cleaned up. The tales of 'who got busted, when and where,' had been put on hold for another girl's night out. Kissed and hugged goodbye, I waved goodnight to my four favorite women.

"Wish they could've stayed longer." I read the label on the brandy, "Better not open this, but it would really taste good." One last wish on my list, snuggling next to Hawke in the comfort of our over-sized bed. Tonight, my bedtime date would be strolling in soon. TV turned down low, I kept an ear tuned for the click-clack steps of Hawke's boots sneaking down the hall.

Chapter 28 Late Night Visitor

Alone, stuck in a hospital bed for the night, I flicked through all fifty TV channels. Not one interested me. By the light of the TV I could read the clock on the wall, only nine. Thought by now Hawke would've strolled back in. Better safe than sorry, I dialed his number. Conveniently, I'd been dumped into his voice mail. Message left, I figured he'd knocked down a few beers and smoked a cigar or two with the guys. Fred "Mr. Pool Shark" most likely had cleaned the table several times not only on Hawke, but I'm sure Lance lost a minor wager, too.

With my attention drawn back to a cooking show I'd finally found, I relaxed into the double layer of pillows. Home tomorrow morning, if all goes well tonight. Wedding also scheduled, I kept reminding myself. All I need, Hawke to be standing in the doorway. I'd welcome the smell of cigar smoke lingering on him and the taste of beer on his lips. To my surprise, the hallway light that filled the doorway, shadowed over.

"Chloe?" I recognized this particular man's whispering voice.

"You?" My dream of seeing my husband vanished when I flipped on the overhead lights to find James Morrison approaching my bedside. "What the hell are you doing here?" Simultaneously, I grabbed for my phone and the call button.

"Oh no you don't. Not this time." In calculated control, James jerked the cell phone from my hand. My hopes of signaling the nurse for help was dashed too. The call button and attached cord got yanked from my hand and thrown across the room.

"What the hell are you doing?" Left alone in an ugly blue hospital gown, helpless and pretty much defenseless, I screamed, "HELP!!! Someone help me!"

James put his premeditated plan into action. "You're as beautiful as I remember Chloe." His sizzling smile smacked the fear of God into me. "I hoped you would be more cooperative," he pocketed my out-of-date cell phone. Then, in hopes to conceal us from the outside world of the fifth floor, he shut the door to my room. "Chloe, honey you need to listen to reason." His voice calm, stern, and laced with psychopath.

"I'm not Chloe." Screaming, I prayed someone would hear me before the door clicked shut. "Don't you come near me." The ringtone from my phone sang from James' pants pocket. "Give me my phone!" I demanded and held my hand out for it. As if that would happen.

James sneered at the caller ID, "He's not your husband. I am. I've been secretly searching for the last ten years for you." Annoyed by the ringing phone, James whipped it across the room. The happy little tune it sang silenced when it smashed into the wall. "I've got you right where I want you...alone." The devil himself stood before me. Blue eyes shined with his achieving goal in mind.

In another wild attempt, I grabbed for the good old landline phone on the nightstand and dialed wildly. Immediately, dumped into Hawke's voice mail. "Help me!" I screamed the message, and hoped someone could hear me. "Get away from me!" James kept to his own sick plans. "Help!!!!" I screamed into the receiver again as he stalked toward me. Another phone wrestled out of my hands but not until I cracked James a few times with it.

"Chloe, please calm down. You're going to draw attention to us." My noncompliance gave way to his anger. "I'd hope you'd understand why I've come to take you home."

"I'm not going anywhere with you!" I shouted and screamed, "HELP!!" Someone on this floor had to hear me.

"You're going to make things worse. I don't want to hurt you. Please, Chloe, just do as I say." James sported a crazy eye glare, his mind set on one thing. Me. "You need clothes. What did they do with your clothes?"

"You've totally lost it. I'm not going anywhere with you. Someone...anyone...HELP ME!!" My voice nearly hoarse from screaming, but I kept my effort for help alive.

"I haven't lost anything. I found you. We'll be a family, again." Intently in control, James willed himself to remain calm. "With time you'll remember the life we had. Me, you, and Jason. They stole you from me ten years ago. I won't let that redneck backwoodsman keep you from me. We don't have much time." On a dime he spun around approaching the tiny closet in hopes to find my street clothes.

Why wasn't anyone hearing my screams for help? My head pounded to the rhythm of a scared beat. I fought the medication that should be relaxing me. I had to keep it together. Even if I wanted to I couldn't make a run for the door; James blocked it in search of my clothes. Beside me, on the nightstand, a lead crystal vase filled with pink roses from Hawke. My last ray of sunshine and hope.

"You can wrap up in this," James faced me, with a hospital style bathrobe. "Chloe," surprised by what I held, "what do you think you're doing? Put that down." I took aim, flower water slopped over me as I fired my weapon. "No. Don't." He actually took cover while the vase, flowers, and water went sailing through the air.

"For the last time, I'm not Chloe. Someone HELP ME!" I screamed again while the vase narrowly missed James's head. Instead, it smashed into the back of the door shattering into a thousand crystal pieces. A dozen beautiful roses scattered while shards of glass and water spilled over the tile floor. One way or another I'd get out that closed door.

"Chloe." That nice calm demeanor, gone. I'd provoked the evil in James.

On my feet, not sure of my next step, "My name is Dove. Dove Hawthorne," I reached back for a skinny vase with a single rose in it, "I'm not your dead wife."

"Chloe, please, don't make me hurt you. Come quietly or..." James closed the short distance between us.

Adrenaline kicked into overdrive, my head thumped to the pounding beat of my scared heart. My mind commanded me to stay on my feet and fight, my body wasn't willing to play this game much longer. Darkness spread in my eyes, while the swirling dizzy dance rushed me. "No, don't come near me," small vase gripped tight, I swung wildly as James made his next move to grab me.

Not hearing the door creek open and crunching foot steps, unexpectedly James found himself being tackled from behind. The impact sent him flying into me. Pretty sure I made contact into human flesh with the trusty vase as I found myself flying backward. The small sofa for two by the window broke our fall. Hitting hard, and thankful for the cushioning comfort of the sofa, I had the weight of James wrapped and clinging to the midsection of my body. My weapon of choice rolled over the white tile floor and landed at the feet of my hero.

"Dove. Stay still." I knew the voice. My friend, my medical confidant, and now my hero. Once again Dr. Thornton to my rescue. "Morrison, get the hell off her!" In his own rage, Dr. Thornton ripped James free of my body and flung him across the room.

"Sheriff Meyer, I want him locked up." James landed in the hands of two uniformed deputies. "Get him out of this hospital. I'm personally pressing charges."

"No!" Punches flew, but James had been outnumbered. "Don't take her from me." Smashed against the same wall my phone died on, the deputy slapped handcuff on James. "She's my wife. I've got to take her home." Dragged across broken chips of glass and tangled rose stems, the two deputies hauled a protesting James Morrison down the hall.

A breath of relief escaped my lungs. My eyes scanned my upheaval of a hospital room. My cell phone cracked to bits still laid on the floor. A dozen pink roses scattered over the threshold mixed with the smashed crystal vase. My gift bag of 'unmentionables' tossed over the bedcovers. Myself still sprawled over the sofa for two, "Doc, where's Hawke? I need him." My head bounced in pain as I tried to sit up. "Please Doc, I need him."

"Easy Dove, easy." By my side, Dr. Thornton wrapped his fatherly arms around me in a hug of comfort. "It's over honey. All over. Are you alright?" Immediately, he started to examine today's wound.

"I couldn't reach Hawke." Adrenaline drained, emotional me returned. My tears filled with fear, ran from my eyes.

"Can you stand, Dove?"

"I think so." On shaky legs I let Dr. Thornton guide me back to the bed.

"Are you hurt anywhere else?" Gingerly, with what grace I had while wrapped in an ugly hospital gown, he helped into the bed. Covers tucked around me, I almost wished he'd been reading me a bedtime story instead of the real life story we just lived.

"Didn't hit my head," we shared a smile of 'Oh Thank God,' "A little sore from where Morrison landed on me. All other body parts," I glanced down over me, "they seem to check out. I really need Hawke." Doc offered me the tissue box, "Did anyone find him?" Scared out of my wits I couldn't hold the tears back. From trying to play warrior to save myself, I slipped back into panic mode.

"For once Dove, I'm thankful Hawke went out with the boys. Glad he wasn't here."

"Wasn't here for," glass crunched beneath Hawke's reptile boots, "what the hell happened?"

"Hawke!!" My arms outstretched like a child begging to cling to its favorite stuffed animal, I wanted him by my side.

"Dr. Thornton, Dr. Thornton," a frantic male voice yelled down the hall, "Mr. Hawthorne's" the baby faced security guard plowed into the back of Hawke, "oh shit."

"Great security you've got, Thornton." Hawke glared at the young man who was practically plastered to his side, "What the hell happened in here?" The burn simmered in his coffee brown eyes as he took inventory of my topsy-turvy room. Less than five glass crunching steps away, his arms intertwined with mine.

"I tried to call you." Safe in his warmth, my emotions broke free. "No one came. I kept screaming for help. He closed the door and, and…"

"Morrison was here?" Those coffee colored eyes of Hawke's just boiled over worse than my emotions. "How the hell did he get in here?" Shoved into the protective crook of Hawke's arm, he glared at the junior security cop.

Dr. Thornton motioned with a flat hand for Hawke to simmer down, "Morrison must've been watching the hospital."

"Just great. Tell ya what Doc, I'll just take Dove home with me." Hawke's eyes still lazed on the timid security guard.

"James Morrison won't be back." Dr. Thornton handed me my age old smashed cell hone. "Went out in cuffs. Sure he's in a holding cell by now."

"You better hope to hell the bastard's in a cell or he'll end up in your morgue."

"Easy Hawke, been enough trouble today. Tony," mop, broom and bucket in hand, ne evening janitor arrived, along with another member of the security super team.

"I'll have the room back in order in no time." He nodded to Doc and went to work.

"Think you're good for her, Hawke." Dr. Thornton released my arm, "Dove, pressure s back to normal."

Subconsciously, I rubbed at my bandaged head. "Please don't tell Maude, or the girls. hey'll be so upset they left me. And Jane, she wanted to stay, but I told her to go."

Dr. Thornton's pager buzzed, "Sheriff Meyer." He frowned at the number, "better take nis. Stay put, Dove." He stepped away from us, "Nice work Tony, appreciate you." He atted the janitor on the back, but just before he exited my room, "And Hawke, don't hink of sneaking Dove out. Got my boys posted on the floor for the night."

"Like that's going to do any good." One sarcastic glare from Hawke and guard umber two staggered backwards. "What did I tell you?" He rolled his eyes at my young eam of protectors.

"Dove, you up for giving me the details?" Hawke had a simple way to relax me. On he palm of my hand, his fingers rounded in a slow circle pattern. "You rather wait for)oc to come back?"

"No. Glad you're finally here." Not even in relaxed mode, a huge sigh left my lungs. I'm so tired. Please don't tell the girls until after tomorrow." Why I worried about my our best friends instead of me, no clue. "I couldn't reach you." I melted back into the pile of pillows with fresh tears spilling.

"Be right back," Hawke kissed my forehead and left my side. "Out," he motioned for ecurity guard one and two to leave the room.

"But Dr. Thornton…"

"I don't give a damn what Doc said. Out." He ushered them to the hallway, "Don't listurb us." New orders given, he closed the door soundly behind him. "You okay?"

"Maybe. No. Not really." I practiced that deep breathing thing over and over and it vasn't working for me. "Everyone left from the shower. Promise you won't say unything to the girls, please."

"Promise. I'm not upset with them." He stood at the foot of my bed. Calmly, he eached down and grabbed my twitching foot. "Tell me what happened." Gently his massaging fingers glided over my right foot.

"Called you, got dumped into voicemail. Then," I did another one of those deep oreathing exercises, "there he stood. Proud as a peacock to find me alone." My voice rembled, my body shook. Even with Hawke's massage, I couldn't relax.

"Try this." He flipped a chocolate bar to me. "When all else fails to calm you…"

"Try chocolate." My lips rounded into a smile for him. "Thank you."

"You ready?"

"Got more chocolate hidden?"

"Dove, what happened next?" No kidding around with a husband who'd like to kick someone's ass.

"Took my phone, yanked the call button right out of the socket. Kept calling me Chloe. And how he's been searching for me..." In disgust, I tossed my hands in the air, "her for the past ten years. All the time I kept screaming for help." Hawke's fingers were like magic and put me at ease. "James kept telling me he was taking me home. That you stole me from him."

"What?" Anger flared, but he kept it in control, "Morrison is delusional." A thin line of fire ignited in Hawke's eyes and I felt the pressure deepen as he massaged my legs.

"I didn't know if anyone could hear me screaming. I saw the next best thing, a vase full of flowers. I threw it at him. Disappointed I'd missed. You're right, I can't hit the broad side of a barn." Finally after turning the chocolate bar end for end, I opened it. "This is so good."

The intensity from our conversation grated on both of what frayed nerves we had left. Slowly, Hawke walked around the corner of the bed and made himself comfortable next to me. Deliberately, he crossed his arm over my body leaning into me so I would be directly in front of him.

"What aren't you telling me, Dove?"

Hurt, even slightly annoyed by the way he phrased his question, "Hawke, I tell you everything."

"Only when it's on your terms, Dove." He could read the pages to my agonizing mind so easily. "Now, Dove."

"After I tossed the vase, with no success," deep breath in and out, "I jumped out of bed. James blocked the doorway, but I wasn't going to let him take me." With a little more control to my emotions I dabbed back a few tears. "Had one last vase. He kept coming closer. I kept screaming for help. James kept saying he didn't want to hurt me."

"Dove, breathe, just take a deep breath." This time when I looked into Hawke's eyes, I not only saw my pain, but felt his. "Should've never left you."

"We all thought I was safe." My padded forehead bumped his. "When he tried to grab me...me and my trusty vase went on attack." Resourceful of me I thought. "Dr. Thornton tackled him from behind. I ended up flat on the sofa with Morrison on top of me. You should've seen Doc in action. Even had Sheriff Meyer and two deputies for backup this time."

"Personally, I would've loved a piece of Morrison for myself." Anger, envy, and a little tarnished pride projected from my husband. "I'm so sorry I wasn't here."

"You're here now. That's all the matters." I ran his dangling silky hair through my fingers, "You'd been proud of me, got a few good whacks in before he flattened me."

"Least you learned something from me." Close enough to me, his kiss was effortless.

"You're not going home, are you?" A little panic in my eyes searched his for the answer I needed to hear.

He swung his body to the side of the bed. His pet reptile boots he wore hit the floor one after the other. "Planned on sharing this awful bed with you. This way I know you're safe. Move it over. No one but me is going to bother you for the rest of the night."

Covers pulled tightly around us, I snuggled deep next to his body. Safely wrapped in his arms I felt protected. Sleep clouded my mind as Hawke gently ran his fingers through my mess of curls. With each of Hawke's breaths I felt his tension ease, "Dove," his husky voice drew me in, "you're safe with me. Promise."

Chapter 29 - Wedding

"They're in bed! Together!" Shocked, maybe even appalled, Amelia gasped in horror.

"What are you two doing? You're not...you didn't?" Still standing in the doorway, Emma squirmed.

"Put money on it, they did." Amelia snapped at us.

"Please tell us you didn't. You're in a hospital." Emma crossed her arms close to her chest in the same disapproving style Maude would have used. "What did I tell you," she turned her appalled glare to Amelia, "they're worse than two sneaky teenagers."

"Should've taken your bag of treats home with us last night." Drama spilled from Amelia's lips. "You just had to show him, didn't you Aunt Dove?"

Awakened to the hyper-shrill voices of our chastising adult nieces, I found their display of judgmental emotions rather amusing. It's not like they've never seen the two of us in bed together.

"Uncle Hawke," Emma tossed his t-shirt and jeans on the bed, "you don't even have clothes on."

"Unbelievable." Amelia practiced another one of Maude's glares on us, "Aunt Dove, can't you ever say "NO" to him? You preached the "Just Say No," line to us." Perplexed by our togetherness in a hospital bed, their annoyed opinions ranted on.

How dare their Aunt and Uncle be caught in the same bed, in such a public place, like the hospital? Hawke, still draped over me, enjoyed the sheer delight of his niece's disapproval, maybe even embarrassment from catching us in bed together.

"Good morning girls." I couldn't control my snickering laugh. "Would you like me to answer those questions in alphabetical order? Or would you rather have the juicy details of last night?" They met me with a silent, harsh scowl only to have me egg the circumstance on. "What's the problem? You've seen us in bed before. So we spent the night in a hospital bed...together."

"You've missed the point," clearly Emma was about to point it out to me. "You're in a hospital. Sick people." She gave me the "duh" look. "And why is Uncle Hawke still in the bed with you?"

"The beauty squad must have missed their morning coffee." Not missing a beat Hawke planned to antagonize them further. "Tell me now, how long have I been married to your Aunt?" Hawke rolled away from our curled up embrace, "Any guess?"

"Twenty years," Amelia answered quietly, "but it's the..."

"In fact, twenty years today." He smirked at his girls. "I'd say that gives me the right to be in any bed with your Aunt at anytime I want."

"But Uncle Hawke, it's the hospital." Annoyed at the situation, Amelia ranted on. "You're not supposed to see the bride before the wedding." She blatantly informed us. "You're messing up everything." The truth behind their hysteria surfaced. We pulled a major "faux pas" to their fairy tale wedding plans.

"Emma. Amelia." I practically blinded my girls with a stern motherly glare. A loving affection I'm sure they hadn't felt in years. "Why are the two of you so surprised?" I wiggled back to the center of the bed. "You both knew your Uncle would be staying the night with me."

"Not like this." Emma pointed out.

"Morrison showed his ugly face last night." Well look who couldn't keep his promise...my husband.

"What? You mean that freak showed his ugly mug here again?" Emma's mood switched to defensive. "I knew we should've stayed last night."

"Aunt Dove, did he hurt you?" Amelia, grabbing Emma by the hand rushed to my bedside. "Are you okay?"

"I'm fine..."

"Bullshit," Hawke yanked yesterday's t-shirt over his head. "Morrison made it up here last night after everyone left. Thought he was going to take your Aunt home with him." He whipped the bedcovers off exposing his navy blue boxers to all.

"Uncle Hawke," Emma pitched his jeans at him, "do you have to do that in front of us?"

"Make up my mind for me. You want me out of the bed or back in the bed?" The boxers in question had now been covered and hidden on the inside of Hawke's faded jeans. "Which is it?"

"What happened with Morrison?" Amelia asked.

"He's gone." I said flatly before Hawke could fly into a rage.

"Family gathering I see, morning everyone." Subject changed by Dr. Thornton's cheery, booming voice. "So Hawke, I see you've skipped all that formal wedding hocus pocus crap and headed straight for the honeymoon." Behind him, muffled, disgruntled mumbles leaked from the girls. "You could've arranged for a nicer, maybe even fancier place than this old hospital. Dove's put up with you all these years, she certainly deserves better."

Hawke tossed a wink over his shoulder just for me, "Only the best for my babe, Doc. Got anything in your magic bag of drugs to slap these two into relaxation?" Unmercifully, he grinned at the girls' horrified expression.

Ignoring his request, "Dove, I take it you were well protected all night?" Dr. Thornton grinned at Hawke and flipped open my thick chart.

"Slept all night. I'm more interested in being sprung from here." All eyes turned to the good doctor. "Please, Dr. Thornton, after last night's escapade, I can't stay here one more day."

All the power revolved in Dr. Thornton's hands. He glanced up from writing in my chart, "Full moon last night, you know." He played the game of anticipation to the hilt.

"What does that have to do with me going home?" Skeptical of his answer I asked.

"You survived yesterday's back-to-back episodes. Be thankful those moon beams are on your side." Whether scientific or super natural, Dr. Thornton believed in every aspect of medicine. Finally he stopped writing in my chart. Sternly, over charcoal grey rimmed bifocals, his steely blue eyes glared in my direction. "The entire set of tests results are back, Dove."

Breath held I waited for a lecture, bad news, or good news. "Blood pressure has read normal all night."

"Thanks to having my personal teddy bear with me." My girls groaned and I giggled.

"Sure that helped, as for all the scans," bifocals pocketed, my chart folded and tucked under his arm, Dr. Thornton kept us waiting on purpose, "clean. Everything is reading normal. Swelling is down. Vitals are stable."

"She's ours? We can take her home?" The bridal consultants attacked with questions, "When? Can we take Aunt Dove home now?"

"Yes, ladies, you can take her home. Try to keep the stress level to a minimum." He reminded them. "Once again, Dove, you've out proven the medical world." He scribbled his name over my release forms, "You," Doc shoved the pink release form into Hawke's hand, "take care of her. Dove, routine follow up scheduled in one month. And have a good anniversary party."

"Thanks Dr. Thornton. See you in four weeks." My smile of relief said it all. "Did anyone bring me clothes?"

"Here," Amelia emptied the contents from a hot pink camouflage bag, "t-shirt, shorts, underwear, bra, sandals. Do you need help?"

"I've got it. Just gather up everything else for me." No privacy to be had, I stripped out of my lovely hospital gown and tossed it at Hawke. "Can't wait to shower." My clothes quickly arranged over the body, I found myself in Hawke's arms.

"Want to skip all this madness? We can make a run for it." Lip locked with him I couldn't give my vote on his questions.

"Will you two put a hold on all the kissing?" Amelia complained. "We've got a lot to do."

"Come up for air will you?" Emma tried to separate us. "Get off her. Schedule, remember, you need to stick to it."

"You can have Aunt Dove all to yourself after the wedding." Amelia smacked us with a pillow. "Get off her already. Move it mister." Another hit from the fluffy pillow had us apart.

"Enough already," an annoyed growl rumbled from Hawke, "You're driving me crazy."

"Keep your hands to yourself and head for the door." Emma pulled at his hand. "Why don't you have your boots on?" His reptile boots flew through the air at him, "Move it." She had him down the hall before I could ask for a kiss goodbye. Emma's lecture of wedding do's and don'ts to her Uncle soon faded along the corridor as she hustled him away.

"Time to move, Aunt Dove." Amelia checked her watch. "We have less than three hours. Come on, let's go." My charming niece, the sweet reasonable one, turned into the consultant drill sergeant.

"Is your Uncle going to be at Fred and Jane's?" I thought my question was innocent enough.

"Yes. Doesn't this elevator move any faster?" She snapped. "Jane's in charge of those two. God help her."

"Can I borrow your phone? I want to call him and..."

"You're not seeing or talking to him until we get you to the church." She shut me down before I could finish.

"But I need to..." Shoved into the front seat of the truck, Amelia gave meaning to driving like a bat out of hell.

"No, Aunt Dove. Uncle Hawke can sidetrack you with one of those melt your heart smiles. You fall for it every single time."

"That's not always true. Is it? Watch the bump!" I shouted while Amelia swerved at a high rate of speed into our driveway. "I believe that was record time." Flying in

211

behind us Emma screeched her car to a halt. "You both got your Uncle's driving abilities." Thankful to be parked in our driveway I really wanted to kiss the ground.

"Aunt Dove," her whole car rocked from how hard she slammed the door. "How do you put up with him?" She stomped passed us verbalizing how ticked off Hawke had made her. "He's such a bear today." The backdoor felt her fury as she swung it open. "A tie. He won't wear a tie. Aunt Dove, I know we just sprang you from the hospital, but please, please work with us."

I didn't offer any advice, or help, or even attempted to be reasonable about Hawke. I just filed through the backdoor like a good bride-to-be, then waited for the next set of commands.

"You really reek like sick people," Amelia pinched her nose, "you smell like the hospital, Aunt Dove."

"Thank you...I don't think so but..." again cut off by my bridal consultants.

"Plan of action, shower, then meet us in your bedroom." Amelia pushed me towards the staircase.

"Wait." I put my own screeching brakes on, "Coffee. I need coffee. Or," with an evil eye I glared at both of them, "I'll turn into your Uncle."

The coffee pot immediately received attention. On my way to the bathroom I swiped Emma's cell phone off the counter. Pretty pleased with my swift grab I bounced up to the safety of the bathroom. I hoped the shower would drown out my conversation with Hawke as I dialed his number.

"Please, please, please answer your phone." I hopped and prayed as I tugged off my clothes.

"Now what do you want?" Roughly, Hawke's voice filled the line.

"It's me," my rush of girlish giggles greeted him, "I stole Emma's phone."

"Dove," The calm, smooth silky sound of his voice returned.

"I don't have long. They didn't see me swipe the phone." On my own personal secret mission, my giggling erupted again. "I feel like I'm being held hostage. What are they doing to you?" I peeked out the bathroom door to find an empty hallway.

"Kind of comical over here. Fred's turned into the "Yes" man. Whatever Jane says he does. She's got the poor bastard jumping through hoops." He chuckled softly, "how's things over there?"

"I'm to shower and meet the bridal consultants in our bedroom. Not too bad, yet." I did another peek into the hall. "Coast is still clear. They haven't noticed. How's Maude with all this?"

"She's playing it pretty cool. Just laid my clothes out. Told me how to dress. Yelled at me for giving Emma grief over the tie. Maude, she's just like the girls, she's living for this moment. Hold on babe." 'Maude, I'm on the phone with Dove,' I could hear him as plain as day bellowing to her, 'Be down in a minute.' Still with me?"

"Yes, you should send her over here to help me." I couldn't stop giggling.

"You'll love this. She started to give me the lecture." His laughter got harder.

"A lecture? What did you do?" I cast another glance down the hall, the only soul moving my way, the cat. And he wouldn't sell me out.

"Maude and sex. She got all flustered when she realized I didn't need her sex talk." He howled with laughter.

"I'd rather have Maude's sex talk then be kept hostage by these two. I can hear them from the kitchen."

"Remind me, I'm cutting off the girls' tuition for next fall."

"Why would you do that?"

"Simple, for putting us through this." He snorted a laugh at his own deranged comment.

"I better get in the shower before...oh crap, I'm in trouble." Unannounced, Amelia walked right smack dab into my bathroom conversation with a cup of coffee. "Been busted big time, honey. Amelia's growling, even baring teeth at me."

"Glad it's you and not me, Dove."

"Thanks. Come save me." I joked, but Amelia didn't find me all that amusing.

"I'll be waiting for you at the church, Dove. Love you."

"Love you too." I could hear Hawke laughing as I handed the cell phone over. Thank you for the coffee, sweetie." Not a word from Amelia, just a speechless frown.

Privacy came in the form of a steamy hot shower. Until repeated knocking and asking Are you done yet?" spoiled it for me.

The Dress

"Aunt Dove, are you done yet?" Barely enough time to get toweled off Dove managed to slip her housecoat over her freshly showered figure. "Aunt Dove?" Emma pounded harder on the unlocked bathroom door, "We've waited months to show you this."

"What have you waited months to show me?" Dove yanked the bathroom door wide open to find no one waiting. "Where are you two?" As she stepped into the empty hallway, Dove found her girls guarding the bedroom door, "What gives?"

"We found your original wedding dress. It's really, really super old. Where did you get it from?" Amelia asked, but neither girl would move.

"It belonged to your grandmother on your Uncle's side. Why?" Dove couldn't help but wonder what her dream team had up their sleeves.

"That was Grandma Hawthorne's dress?" Amelia relayed a glance over to Emma.

"Yes. Aunt Maude had it repaired and fit to my size." Dove glanced down over her terrycloth covered body. "I don't think..."

"We tried to have it repaired, but you've gotten, well..." kind of lost for words, Emma continued, "you've gotten curvy over the years."

"Thanks for the reminder. I was as skinny as you two back in the day." Dove tried to take a peek into her bedroom. "What are you two hiding?"

"We didn't want to have anything happen to your original dress," Emma stepped aside, "We," she pointed to Amelia, "we got you a new one. Pretty sure we, well, we hope you like this one."

Dove stepped between her nieces to find the hidden secret surprise hanging from her oval dressing mirror. "Vintage? Has to be 1930's." Delicately, Dove skimmed her hands over the dress. The wedding gown shimmered in the sunlight glowing through the window.

"How did you know?" Emma slipped in behind her Aunt as she examined the intricate detail of the dress.

"Nearly as perfect as your grandmother's gown. Nearly the same pattern. Everything it really could be the same gown." Dove let her fingertips slip smoothly over the sheer fabric.

"This is why we kept measuring you all summer." Amelia laced her arm through Emma's, "we tried to find one like yours."

"When? Where did you...how did you afford this?" Stunned that her nieces pulled this off she continued to admire the dress. With a fitted bodice, soft fabric of creamy ivory cascaded into a tea length style. The entire gown had been trimmed in shear lace with hand crafted pearl beads sewn delicately around the edges, "Beautiful. Just absolutely, beautiful."

"Found it at an old heirloom shop in Portland. It screamed your name. We had to have it for you. Take it you like it?" Emma glowed with excitement.

"Love it." Dove felt the smooth silk under the palm of her hand, "Girls how in the world did you afford this?"

"Uncle Hawke," Amelia nudged Emma, "he floated us the cash, well his credit card. So you can really thank him."

"He knew?" Dove knew her husband could barely keep a secret, but he held tight to this one.

"He promised to keep his lips sealed. Come on Aunt Dove, time to get dressed." Amelia slipped the dress from the hanger.

"Is the gift bag on the bed for me or the cat?" Dove inquired as she questioned her girls.

"From Aunt Maude," Emma announced, "might want to put "that" on before this." She pointed at the gown.

"Think Aunt Maude's been walking on the wild side." Dove held up the champagne colored lace bra with matching panties. "She's been on a lingerie kick lately."

"It can be your 'something new,'" Amelia suggested as she helped her Aunt step into the vintage gown. "It fits you like a glove."

"Hold still Aunt Dove, there's like a hundred and one buttons back here." Emma carefully fastened each pearl button.

In a matter of minutes Dove's executive designers teased, sprayed and pinned the long flowing sheer veil into their Aunt's hair. Not a soul would've known that yesterdays slicing gash to Dove's head had been hidden under her freshly styled hair. Next up, the double trouble team turned into makeup artists. A sheer foundation matching Dove's complexion had been applied. Lips lined in plum, were topped with a deep wine colored lipstick. No fun bubble gum flavored lip gloss for today. Dove's eyes were treated to a soft pink rose petal shadow and lined with a shimmering blue eyeliner. Quickly, they'd transformed Dove from an everyday diner-cook into a vintage bride.

"Don't look until we're dressed." Emma unzipped another garment bag. "We know you like green, so...what do you think?"

"Emerald green, my favorite." Her girls had chosen an elegant simple style strapless gown. "Very nice. How did you two afford all of this?"

"Between working at the diner and well, Uncle Hawke." Emma finished zipping her sister's dress.

"I should've known. Can I look in the mirror?" With her back to the oval floor mirror Dove waited patiently for her girls to finish.

"Don't cry when you see yourself." Amelia suggested as the trio crowded around the mirror.

"Is this really me?" Dove questioned as she saw the beautiful handy work of her nieces. "I barely recognize me. You two are amazing. Are you sure this is really me?" She poked her finger at the reflecting mirror.

"It's really you Aunt Dove." Amelia fluffed the veil over her Aunt's shoulders.

"Hey! Why did you pinch me?" Startled by Emma's pinch, Dove simply pinched her back.

"Owww, Aunt Dove that hurts. Only wanted to let you know it's really you."

"I really need a tissue. Don't want to mess-up your work." Dove scanned the bedroom for the tissue box.

"No tears." Emma, tissue in hand, dotted her Aunt's watery eyes, "Save it for when you say 'I do' to Uncle Hawke again."

"Can't wait to see his face when he sees you." Amelia grabbed her phone and tossed Emma hers. "We've got the pictures covered for you. It's time." Amelia tugged her Aunt's hand. "No way are you going to be late. Please don't fall down the stairs Aunt Dove. We are so done with trips to the hospital."

"Aren't we all?" Sarcastically, Dove added.

Upon their arrival into the kitchen, the bridal party found the only man in the house, the cat, poised like a stone statue as he waited on the countertop. With a leap to the floor, Burt circled around Dove's trailing dress to give his seal of approval.

"Photo op." Emma, ready to snap a picture, "This will drive Uncle Hawke nuts." One last photo of Dove holding Burt the cat had been snapped and saved. "Here," Emma handed Dove a little beaded handbag. "Goes with your dress."

"Thanks. This is really cute." Dove took a quick peek inside the bag, "Tissues, I'll need those, my lip gloss." Thrilled they remembered the small things she loved, Dove hugged them both. "I still can't believe you two pulled this off."

"Glad you're enjoying everything. To tell you the truth we've had a great time putting this together." By the hand, Amelia led her Aunt out the backdoor.

"Where's Emma?" Car door opened, Amelia continued to help her Aunt, along with the flowing wedding gown, into the car.

"Probably stopped by the bathroom to make sure she got her face on right." Amelia snickered at her own lame excuse. "Everything taken care of?" Dove asked as Emma slammed the backdoor shut with a wide grin plastered over her face.

The Church

As Hawke drove to the edge of town, the Ocean View Chapel came into his view. He maneuvered his aging truck into the parking lot and parked in the shade of an old oak tree. Engine cut, he stepped out into the sweltering heat of the August day. "Fine time to hang a damn tie around my neck." He chastised the skinny piece of material as he tied it snuggly under his shirt collar.

Only a few recognizable cars were parked in a line before he arrived. The "Pinto-Mobile," the mark of Jane. Hopefully, Fred arrived in one piece. A 1968 Ford pickup, beat nearly to death, belonging to Lance sat next to the old Pinto. Sure Lance's steady girlfriend enjoyed showing up in the rattle-trap truck. And of course, Maude left well before him with Harry on her arm. Hawke laughed to himself. His crazy Aunt finally met her match in men with Harry. They made a great pair.

Not bothering to go inside the chapel, Hawke choose to wait on the front steps for his bride. Behind the closed doors he could hear the commotion kicking up between Jane and Maude. He wanted no part of it. Hawke counted the seconds on his watch as his girls pulled their jeep into the parking lot. No need to worry about them being late. He wasn't into the glitz and glamour of an elaborate wedding. Hawke would've rather celebrated alone with Dove, but his girls thought otherwise.

Hawke felt a rush in his heart as Dove stepped from the jeep. Her appearance alone stirred deeply inside his soul. The bond of love they'd shared for twenty years grew stronger everyday. The warm winds breezing off the ocean swirled around her satin and lace gown. To him, Dove was a living, breathing angel sent just to rescue him.

"He's here." He could read Dove's lips even under the sheer cover of her veil.

"And I hope Uncle Hawke's in a better mood." Emma snapped as she shut the car door glaring at him.

"Don't count on it." Amelia countered. "He's been cooped up with Jane. Even Aunt Maude bailed on him.

"He'll forget everything when he sees Aunt Dovey." Emma grinned at her sister.

"He already has." Dove's eyes fixated on her husband. She felt the familiar fluttering butterfly dance inside the walls of her stomach. The afternoon ocean breeze played with the long layers of her sheer veil. Freely it flowed beside her. She had captured Hawke's full attention.

Planted securely under the old arched doorway, well weathered from the sea, Hawke stood patiently waiting for the three women in his life. A gentle smile eased over his rugged face. Behind him, the midsummer's sunlight rippled off the stained glassed windows.

From the edge of the cobblestone walkway, Dove continued to admire him. A sage green dress shirt, freshly pressed by Maude, had been neatly tucked into a brand new pair of denim jeans. A forest green, leaf print tie hung neatly around his neck. Emma won the "tie" battle. And, of course, he couldn't leave home without the reptiles on his feet. His favorite snakeskin boots loved to the point of being wore thin. Inky black hair, tinted with a few streaks of grey, rustled around his shoulder in the breeze. Hawke's skin, weathered from years out on the open salt water, still held the darkened tan from the sun's rays. Eyes of honey amber brown returned the passionate moment.

"Aunt Dove you're blushing already." Emma whispered.

"Can't help it. Your Uncle has a way of doing that to me." As if it were their first date, Dove felt her heart pound with excitement.

"So this is what real love is." Amelia whispered as she clung to her Aunt's hand.

"Aunt Dove, you're the only one in Uncle Hawke's eyes right now." Emma held tight to her Aunt's other hand.

Steadily, Hawke rocked back on the heels of his boots as the trio approached him. "Dove," his hands rested on her narrow satin covered shoulders. Gently he skimmed her silky arms as he reached her hands. "You're as stunning as you were the day I married you." Gently, he kissed her fingertips and softly pulled her into his arms, "You're beautiful. And you're all mine." Removing the veil that helped to conceal Dove's lips, he let his kiss linger as if a feather had just dusted over their lips. The rosy blush deepened in her cheeks as he whispered, "You're trembling, Dove."

Inside the aged old chapel, a warm summer breeze circulated through the cathedral ceiling. A pattern of colorful designs flickered on the pews from the endless sunshine streaming through the stained glass windows. Just the roar of the familiar ocean waves crashing onto the shore with an occasional call of a seagull escorted them down the short aisle.

Tightly, Dove held onto Hawke's arm as they waited at the end of the aisle. "Just wish a memory from our first wedding would come flooding back."

"We'll just make new memories, Dove." Hawke reassured her, "I can promise you that."

On each side of them, their now adult nieces joined them. The minister, a young man, with a broad smile waited with the small group of family and friends. In a traditional ceremony, they exchanged their wedding vows. The simple words of pledging their love to one another had summoned Dove's forever falling tears. Before anyone could rescue her with a tissue, she once again found Hawke's fingertip gently wiping them away like he had done so often for her in the past. Their private wedding, now sealed with a kiss, as the minister happily pronounced them husband and wife, once again.

"Either you're a crazy fool or you really do love me." Hawke folded Dove into his arms, "You've just married me, again."

"I know. I'd do it all over with you, again and again."

Reception

Finally freed from our snap happy photographer, Jane continued to capture all the special moments as we celebrated at the diner. In full display, neatly arranged over the lunch counter, we found our original wedding photographs. At the very end of the memory lane display sat a replica of our original wedding cake. Maude had recreated the four layer cake with deep plum roses once again.

Activity flared from the kitchen which peeked my interest. Apron in hand, I slung my veil over my shoulder and went to see who and what had caused the commotion. "Can I help?"

"Stop!" Hand held out like a school crossing guard, Jane demanded, "Don't you dare take one more step." She snapped at me with a wicked smile.

"Hawke," At the top of her lungs Maude bellowed for him, "Get Dove out of here! For once in your life you are not touching one single thing in this kitchen. Out!"

"But you need help. The girls aren't here and...." I'd just been booted from my second home, the kitchen.

"Dove, just sit yourself down and relax with me. They don't need you." By the hand, Hawke towed me along and we settled into the round corner booth in front of the windows. We'd shared many dinners together in this booth. "Take this damn thing." With a sarcastic grin he handed me the cumbersome tie and unbuttoned the top two buttons of his shirt. "That's the last time you'll see me wearing it."

"I wonder what's keeping the girls. Weren't they right behind us?" I folded his strangling tie and gave it a home in my little clutch purse. No sooner than the words came out of my mouth did the double trouble team appear by the kitchen door. By the devious grins they cast our way, we just knew another secret surprise had been set into motion, but what?

"What the hell did they do now?" Hawke never missed the chance to try to intimidate them, but it didn't work. Not today. Their laughter won him over. A glass of champagne each, they huddled with us in the circular booth still giggling.

"Either of you giving up any details?" I asked, but only received shrugged shoulders and giggles.

"Just wait until you get home." Emma, with arms around her Uncle, laughed harder. Hawke's menacing growl gave way to even more laughter. "Oh stop growling Uncle Hawke. It's your fault anyways."

"My fault?" He rolled his eyes at both girls, "Really? How is whatever the two of you did my fault?" His brow beating glare didn't even begin to intimidate her.

"Wait until you see it, Aunt Dove. You're going to love it." Amelia giggled harder.

"See what?" As I glanced back and forth at them, I didn't know who to laugh at, my giggling girls or Hawke's scowl.

"Here's the deal, seeing as Aunt Dove won't leave the house tonight," Emma began...

"We know, Uncle Hawke, you lost the battle of trying to talk her into going anywhere." Amelia giggled harder and blurted out the surprise, "We turned your bedroom into a honeymoon suite. It totally rocks."

"Everything you can dream of. You'll love it Aunt Dove. Flowers, candles, candy, you name it we put it in there." Emma enjoyed the teasing moment of torment over her uncle. "And don't worry, Uncle Hawke, we got you a box of your favorite smokes."

Champagne in hand, I quietly sipped and listened to my two high flying bridal consultants. Hawke, with the last of his threatening glares to both girls only shook his head. Casually, calmly, with a smirk creasing over his lips, he rubbed his chin as he smoothly asked them. "Honeymoon suite? It rocks?" He scowled and glanced back to each of his girls. "What I really want to hear is an explanation on how the two you know so much about honeymoon suites."

Lost in a curious silence my lips pursed into a tight smile. A little nudge from my elbow to Hawke's rib cage, "Honey, our girls, well they're adults now."

"And..." My reflection flickered back to me in his so called stern, father-like glaring eyes. Hawke's fingers tapped the tabletop with a precise drumming.

"And," I squared my shoulder in an attempt to be the supportive Aunt/mother, "well what they do sexually is their own business." Biting my tongue I tried to hold onto the seriousness of the conversation. But, I couldn't hold back the giggling vibrating from me.

"Dove, they're only twenty and twenty-two." His argument fell flat. Hawke knew when he'd been defeated.

"Twenty, the age I married you, remember?" I pecked a kiss to his cheek. "And these two know more than I ever knew at that age."

"Forgot to tell you," Emma grinned, "Aunt Jane and Aunt Maude helped us."

"God help me." Hawke shuddered at all the tormenting thoughts raging in his head. "How many times have I told the three of you I don't want to know any of it? Just dealing with you," he pointed a finger at me, "is bad enough." On the receiving end of his so called glare, Hawke opted to kiss me.

"We're going to help Aunt Maude in the kitchen. And rescue poor Fred. Jane's been barking at him all afternoon." By the hand Emma pulled Amelia to her feet.

"Did you, you know have that," his cough, rather unsettling, "you know, that talk with them?" Cowardly, Hawke asked me.

"Yes. Matter of fact, they tell me just about everything." I patted his knee and grinned. "Didn't you?"

"Once."

"Just once? Lucky you, they still hit me up for answers." Proud of myself for the fact my girls could ask me anything. "When?" I asked. "They never told me."

"Before they went to college. Cornered me out on the boat. Talk about sweating, those two are something. Fired off questions I didn't even want to think about. Let alone answer. You raised two beautiful girls, lady."

"So did you." I loved the way his lips eased over mine, lingered, and just deepened the kiss to perfection.

"Dinner is served. Boys, pull those tables together." Maude directed with a spatula in hand and a bright green apron covering her new "Aunt of the Groom" dress.

On the menu, my famous Chicken Paprika dish, an Elk roast with fresh garden vegetables, catch of the day, salmon dressed in a brown sugar pecan glaze, and heavenly garlic mashed potatoes. At Maude's request we cut the cake and tried to duplicate the pictures taken twenty years earlier.

"Here honey, you'll need this for later." In Maude's hands a white box filled with the top layer of our handcrafted wedding cake. With a kiss to my forehead and a hug she whispered, "I'm so glad we still have you. Life couldn't be more perfect." She couldn't hide her tears anymore.

Tightly squeezing her back, "I love you too, Maude."

Hawke's hand wrapped around the silky bodice of my dress, "Maude, I need my wife back."

Tears filled her eyes as she grabbed Hawke into a hug, "Where did the last twenty years go?" she asked, wiping away her tears. "Go on. Get out of here you two. Just like when we sent you off before. Just wish Joe and Phyllis could've seen this day. Honey," she wrapped me into her arms for another hug, "your Aunt and Uncle would've been so proud of the two of you." She dabbed at her tears, "Go on. Don't you two have that honeymoon suite waiting for you?" One last hug and she pushed us out the front door of the diner.

Stay at Home Honeymoon

The heat from the boiling summer day had cooled into a shimmering summer evening as the sun slowly set over the ocean.

"What do you think they did to our bedroom?" Gracefully, I gathered up the satin fabric and attempted to get into the truck with Hawke's help.

"With those two," Hawke rolled his eyes in amusement, "God only knows." He handed me the box filled with cake, "Can you at least save me a piece for breakfast?" With a playful grin he knew it would be next to impossible for me to keep that promise.

As we pulled into the driveway, a warm welcome glowed from the front picture window. My fancy, fake Tiffany lamp lit the way to home. On the backdoor, flapping in the breeze, we found a note taped from the girls.

"Happy 20th Anniversary."
Enjoy your evening together.
See you tomorrow.
Love Emma & Amelia.

Kitchen lights flipped on, I surveyed the surrounding area. Everything in place. Nothing out of order. Nothing new, all except for another note left on the table. Addressed only to Hawke.

"From your girls." He kept the contents to himself. "They're good. You've trained them well." He laughed and pocketed the note so I couldn't read it. "Very direct instructions. Wait here. Be back in a minute."

"Where are you going?" He left me standing alone in the kitchen as I heard him climbing the staircase.

"Following orders, Dove."

I made myself useful in his absence. What else to do, but program the coffee pot for the morning. I gave up wondering how long this secret would take and dove into another piece of Maude's famous cake. I swear the cake called my name from inside the box.

"This is to die for," I licked the evidence clean from my fingers and went for another bite of cake.

"You're so busted." Caught big time, I didn't even hear Hawke coming down the steps.

"How do you do that? You just sneak in on me." I continued to nibble at the tasty treat, "Maude makes the best ever killer cakes. Want a bite?"

"Save it for a midnight snack. Come on." He swiped the fork from my hand. "You're not going to believe what the dynamic bridal consultants did this time."

Hawke's warm hands surrounded my waist and guided me toward the staircase. His fingers gently massaged through the silk fabric that covered me. Three clips undone and my hair tumbled to my shoulders. Nuzzling his face into my hair, his burning lips found their way to my neck under all my cascading curls. At the bottom of the steps I started to unbutton his shirt. Tug here, tug there, I nearly had it stripped off him.

"Are you sure we're going to make it to the bedroom?" Buttoned cuffs stopped me.

"Hum, you never did like having sex on the steps." Smirking, his lips kissed softly over my satin covered shoulders. "Dove," Hawke ruffled another layer of silk on my dress, "there's too much material here."

As Hawke tugged and pulled at the dress's fabric that kept me bound, I nearly tripped over the first step. Immediately, I grabbed for the banister and froze in place. With Hawke's hands around my waist I leaned heavily back into his chest for balance. Not moving from the first step, I let the uncanny sense of memory surround me. Eyes closed, breathing deeply, I embraced myself with the past memory as it restored itself.

"Dove?" Clearly, I heard the question of concern in his voice.

But I didn't answer him. I chose to continue letting the memory rush over me. Willingly, I absorbed it like a sponge soaking up everything that flooded back. I wanted more. Memory completed, I let out a breath of satisfaction and faced him.

"What just happened? Too much cake? Or too much champagne?" Hawke tried to make light of my remote distance.

"Not the cake." I whispered still aware of the memory of Hawke and I. "I've done this before, haven't I?"

Laughter filled the cavity of the stairwell, "Yeah Dove, we've climbed these stairs thousands of times."

"No. No, not that." Processing what he meant, it finally dawned on me, "No, you're not getting it. I meant I just remembered this moment. Right here on the steps."

"Sure it's not the champagne bubbling in your brain?" Still not believing me, he took the opportunity to kiss my lips.

"Did I ever tell you, I really don't like champagne?" Of course, my truthful moment of not caring for champagne didn't stop Hawke's nibbling at my moving lips.

"Yep, that's why I never buy it." With a gentle push, he encouraged me to take another step in hopes to get me closer to our bedroom.

"Hawke," this time I halted his wanting actions and cupped his rugged lined face in my hands, "Our first night together. We didn't go anywhere. We came back here to the house."

"We sunk every penny we had into fixing up the old place. Really couldn't afford to go anywhere. Didn't think you'd go for a camping trip in the backwoods for our honeymoon. So we camped out here." Finally, he caught the excitement in my eyes, "Dove..."

"You. Me. Here, right here at this point. The memory, the passion that flared between us. You, you just took me by the hand and, and we went..." my eyes fluttered toward the top of the staircase, "to the bedroom."

I placed my hand on his chest and felt the steady, even beat of his heart. "You really remember our first night, Dove?"

"Yes. It's not all that scrambled. Pretty clear." I breathed in the familiar scent of him. "You finished remodeling the bedroom as a wedding gift for me."

"Your gift to me..." His smile could've lit the world on fire.

"We never slept together until..." My memory had me giggling, "Until you married me."

"Yep, until I married you. Believe you me Dove, I tried to get those lacy panties off you. Many of times." He planted a hard lip locking kiss on me. "You have no idea how hard it was to keep my hands off you."

"Think I found that out over the years." Another step up, I tugged at his hand. "Was I as nervous as I am now?"

"Worse," He held me still on the third step from the bottom, "Why would you be nervous now?"

"Because I actually remembered making love to you." My fingers caressed the edge of his cheek, "and I never want to stop."

Step by step, hand in hand, we reached the upstairs landing, but I deliberately stalled on the top step. Delighted with the new found emotion I'd just shared with Hawke, I felt like his blushing bride from twenty years ago. An enticing warm glow welcomed us to our bedroom.

"The mystery note had strict instructions to light all the candles." He stopped me under the arch of our bedroom door.

"I can't believe the two of them did all this." Hawke's arms snuggly wrapped around me. Together we admired the detailed work of our bridal consultants. From every angle of the room candlelight flickered. Fresh velvety rose petals, generously tossed over the rolled down covers of the bed. Comfortably tucked between two pillows, a box of assorted chocolates waited. A single pillar candle accented the chilled bottle of wine on the nightstand. The lacey drawn back curtains to the canopy bed had been dropped for our private romantic evening.

"Hawke," A handful of yellow rose petals trickled from my hand onto the dresser. "I can't get out of my dress." As I looked over my shoulder into the mirror, it reflected the back of my vintage dress and the long line of pearl buttons still neatly fastened. No zipper. No easy escape. Layer after layer of silky material surrounded me. My girls had completely buttoned me from the back of my neck to my waist into the wedding gown. "You have to help me."

Hawke said nothing, he only watched me struggle from the doorway of the closet. "Got a pair of scissors up here somewhere. I'll just cut the damn thing off you."

I heard the sound of scissors snapping together behind me. "You wouldn't." Madly, I whirled around to find Hawke twirling the scissors around his finger. "Don't you dare."

"Hold still." Casually, with scissors in hand, Hawke eyed me and my restricting dress closely. Each step he took, he snapped the scissors at me. Horrified that he would even think of doing such a thing, I frantically shook my head no. "Just kidding babe."

Hawke turned me around a few more times examining his possibilities of how to remove the contraption that kept him from his desired pleasures. A light chuckle rose from him, "Your first dress was far easier to get off. One zip down the back and you were mine." He pulled me to the edge of the bed where he seated himself. "Unbelievable, there's got to be a hundred or more buttons." With a sigh of frustration, I felt his fingers fumble with each button as he started at my neck. "Can't believe there's no zipper."

"Vintage dresses of this time period were not made with zippers." I mentioned as he carefully unbuttoned each and every tiny button.

"Finally," Hawked gently moved the fabric of the dress across my shoulders.

The cool summer air drifting in from the open windows traced over my bare back as I clung to the bodice of my dress. I glanced over my shoulder as the tips of Hawke's finger ran down my exposed, scarred skin.

"When did you get this?" Hawke's hand circled around my flesh bottom feeling the silk material of my new lacy panties.

"Apparently your Aunt picked this out for me." A ruffle of satin rustled over my body as I let the dress slip to the floor. As I stepped free from it, Hawke carelessly tossed it to a nearby chair and sat me down on the edge of the bed's comforter.

"Tell me Dove," his fingers glided softy along my silky thigh high hose.

"Tell you what?" He heard the smallest of gasping whispers escape me as his fingers massaged the inside of my fleshy thigh. My heart fluttered, "I felt it," the memory rushed over me, "the feelings I had for you twenty years ago." Finally able to connect with him on a memory of love and passion I let the loose ends of his graying hair feather through my fingers. Smoothly, he brushed his lips over mine and gently laid me back on our bed filled with fresh rose petals.

hapter 30 - The White Envelope

On the calendar, circled in red ink, my reminder appointment with Dr. Thornton eamed at me. Exactly one month to the day of my accident that put me in the hospital gain. Just a simple routine checkup, that's all. Hawke had called to let me know he'd e joining me for my appointment. Not unusual, but it surprised me. Afterwards, he ven claimed he'd stick around to take me out for breakfast. All plans made, it sounded ood to me.

"Things been going well for you?" My favorite nurse asked as she escorted me to Dr. hornton's office.

"Feeling really good. Why am I here?" I pointed around Dr. Thornton's office, onfused as to why we weren't in the usual exam room.

"He's just finishing up with another patient. Asked for you to have a seat in here." /ith a smile, Nurse Jenkins left me alone.

"Doc's never late." I planted myself in one of his comfortable office chairs. The lock ticked, my fingers tapped. Twenty minutes floated by and no Dr. Thornton. No lawke, either. "This is really odd. He always sees me in the exam room." Randomly, I lurted out my thoughts. "Why am I in his office?"

Boredom struck with all the mindless waiting. My eyes scanned over a single file eatly lying in the center of Dr. Thornton's desk. "Well, well, well, what do we have ere?" My name, in heavy, thick blue ink, called for me to take a peek inside. Not once, ven more than twice, I eyed the tempting folder. It belonged to me. "Should I? Or houldn't I?" I questioned myself out loud. "What's the harm? It's all medical mumble nyways." Instantly, I snagged the file folder from his desktop. In all reality, the chart id belong to me. So why did I feel like it held some secret document. A document for)r. Thornton's eyes only. While my curiosity peaked, I kept the folder closed. Second loughts knocked at my brain. "Might find something I don't want to see. I'll wait." he reasonable side of me won. As I handed the folder back over to the desk, a white nvelope slipped from its insides. It dropped, face up, right into my lap. "What's this?" ly eyes froze on the two names listed on the outside. "Mrs. Dove Hawthorne and Mrs. :hloe Morrison."

"Morning Dove. Sorry for the wait. Thought Hawke would've been here by now." I adn't even been rattled by Dr. Thornton's sudden entrance. "Dove? Are you alright?" le hadn't seen what I held in my hand.

"What is this?" I knew the color drained rapidly from my face as I showed him the nvelope. "What's going on?"

Visually shaken by my horrified expression, Dr. Thornton didn't have an explanation. 'Where did you get that?" was all he could ask.

"You didn't answer my question." A small bead of perspiration bubbled on his brow vhile I mouthed off. "What the hell is this?"

"Dove, please Dove, tell me you didn't open that letter." Dr. Thornton, my other rock)f strength, teetered on panicking.

I flipped it over revealing the sealed side of the envelope, "No." My fingers traced)ver the bold and outspoken black ink on the envelope. "Did you read what's in here?" asked, still staring at the two names on the envelope.

"No. No, I haven't read the test results."

"Test results?" My anger perked up. "What test did you run on me?"

"A DNA test." Dr. Thornton's voice trailed off to a shy "I've been busted" whisper.

"You did what?" I shouted at him from my comfortable seat.

"Dove, Hawke's on his way." Desperately, he glanced out the doorway. I'm sure in hopes that my husband would be strolling down the hall. "Let's wait for Hawke. I'l explain everything that I've found out to both of you." Panic flew through his voice something Dr. Thornton never showed.

"Who gave you the right, let alone permission to run a DNA test on me?" On my fee this time, I demanded an answer.

"Please Dove, just sit down and, and..." again he took another glance down the empty hall, "I will tell you everything when Hawke gets here."

"When Hawke gets here?" Red flags darted over my questioning mind. How dare Dr Thornton take it upon himself to run a DNA test on me. "I'm not waiting for Hawke Either you tell me now or..."

"Dove, I don't even know what's in that envelope." He held his hand out, motioning me to fork it over.

"You went behind my back, Dr. Thornton." With the envelope clenched tight in one hand, purse in the other, I attempted to storm past him. Dr. Thornton blocked my route of exit.

Hands held up in a peaceful protest to keep me in his office, "Dove, Dove please wait here. Let me give you all the facts I found out."

"Facts? You found out? Please, just get out of my way." My angered stare bore through him and beyond. "I've trusted you all these years. Move now!" I demanded politely. "Please."

Unwillingly, Dr. Thornton stepped aside, "Please Dove, stay." He reached for the envelope, "Please don't open this without me." His degree of alarm rocketed. "Hawke should be here any minute. Just, please Dove, don't walk out on me. You've got to stay."

Without a second thought, me and my unread note pushed past him. Dr. Thornton didn't follow me at first. He knew it'd be useless. On a whim I stopped and glanced back at him. What did he know about me? He had his cell phone in hand. Pretty sure it was Hawke he'd be calling. My mind could only focus on the words written on the envelope. Again I read the boldly printed names on the envelope, "Mrs. Dove Hawthorne and Mrs. Chloe Morrison." What did I have in common with James Morrison's dead wife?

"Dove! Dove, please come back!" Doctor Thornton's pounding footsteps rapidly paced down the hall after me.

As the elevator doors slowly closed, my eyes were fixed on Dr. Thornton's frantic face. Blindly, I had made my way out of the hospital and into the parking lot. Surprised at the fact my own cell phone hadn't rang, I wondered how many times Dr. Thornton dialed Hawke's number. Alone in the parking lot I glared at the envelope still in my hand.

"Why is my name on here with that dead woman's?" No one but the pavement heard my conversation. "Now what the hell am I going to do with this?" More pissed at myself for taking the envelope than realizing I didn't know what to do with it, I unlocked my truck and crawled in. The ringing of my cell phone irritated me. Looking at the number, Hawke had found me. "No, no, no, I'm not talking to you either. Why was Doc so insistent that you be here?" Snapping at the innocent phone, I turned it off. Completely off. It hit a rough landing when I tossed it back into my purse. I had plenty of questions boiling over in my mind. Did I want to ask them? Better yet, did I want to know the answers to them? A moment of shock riveted through me. "What if...don't go there." I told myself.

My hands shook as I fumbled with the truck keys. Somehow I managed to start the engine. Even remembered to wrap the seatbelt around me. With a little wisdom left in tack, I headed towards the back entrance of the hospital parking lot, all in hopes of avoiding my husband. In my review mirror I caught a glimpse of Dr. Thornton frantically trying to wave me down. Again, I chose to ignore him and drove off. The bizarre envelope got tucked under my leg for safe keeping. It seemed comfortable to hide it from myself there. No longer could I see the dead woman's name next to mine, but it burned in my mind. Lost in my own town, I kept driving all the back roads until I found my favorite scenic park by the ocean. I used to bring the girls here to play when they were little. Today, I was the only soul parked in its empty lot. Collecting my rambling thoughts I sat in the warm truck. Just sat and stared out the windshield. Motionless, I didn't dare move the envelope...yet. Another deep breath, and I finally stepped out of my cozy truck. The cool September air greeted me like an old friend. For a moment I felt safe, welcomed by this old park, but then I looked at what I held in my hand.

"Why?" I asked, staring at the envelope. "Why in the world would Dr. Thornton have a DNA test ran on me?" Down the path I hopelessly wandered. A weathered bench by the rocky ocean front was where I dropped myself. My legs gave out and I hit the wooden seat with a hard plop. Alone with my mysterious white envelope, I kept it flipped over. I didn't want to see her name mixed with mine.

The results of what this envelope held certainly put Dr. Thornton over the edge. In all my years of being under his professional care, I'd never witnessed him so unnerved. My last head injury should have put him over the edge. Today, the white envelope nearly put him in the cardiac unit. DNA test results rested in my hand. But how did Chloe Morrison tie into this baffling picture? The seriousness of this damn envelope put me on edge. Not even comforted by the rocking of the waves, I just sat there. My eyes focused on the riding water. I wish I could've caught one of those waves and just drifted out to sea, just for a while. Amazing how a white envelope holding my name and a dead woman's name on it managed to scare the hell right out of me.

Close behind me I could hear the quietness of Hawke's husky voice. Concern for me clung in each word I overheard. "Yeah Doc, I found her. She's where I thought she'd be."

"See if you can get her to come back in. I need to explain this situation to her." Dr. Thornton urged him.

"Can't promise that. Wouldn't count on it, either. I doubt she'll come back in. Don't worry Doc, I'll try to explain it to her." Explain what to me? I asked myself hearing his voice. "I don't know how she's going to take all this."

"Do you want me to come out there?" Dr. Thornton asked hopefully.

"No. Don't think that's a good idea."

"If you need me, you've got my cell. Call me. Good luck, Hawke." The good doctor finally backed down.

"Yeah thanks, I'll need it." With a sharp cough, Hawke cleared his throat, with that I knew the conversation with Dr. Thornton had ended.

Hawke's footsteps crunched in the freshly fallen leaves as he walked closer to me. I didn't even turn to meet the worry in his eyes. Instead, I continued my grey stone cold stare right out over the wavy ocean water. With a gentle squeeze, I found his two warm hands resting on my shoulders.

"Thought I'd find you here." Rightfully concerned he kept his voice gentle. "Turned your phone off I take it?"

I didn't move. I didn't say anything to him. I had time to think about the two names on the envelope. It scared me not knowing what waited for me on the paperwork. After my short shoulder massage, Hawke came around and sat down beside me.

"Got a call from Dr. Thornton. He's pretty worried about you." Dr. Thornton wasn't the only one filled with a new running fear.

I still hadn't looked over to him. Didn't offer an answer. I just watched the waves rolling up on the shore, coming and going as they pleased.

"Said you walked out on him over an envelope you found." Politely, but carefully, Hawke continued. "That's not like you Dove. Just left his office with out saying a word." Velvety smooth, I could feel his eyes warm on me. He waited patiently for my explanation. "Dove, you knew I was on my way. Why didn't you wait?"

The motion of the ocean water had me mesmerized and deeply lost in my own thoughts. I knew he was sitting there beside me. Hawke waited for some kind of acknowledgement. He wanted an answer to his question, but I still couldn't look over to him. A single tear had escaped my filling eyes and gently rolled down my cheek.

"This the problem?" He pointed to the envelope in my fingers, "Dove, this time you really need to talk to me." I could hear his stress mixed along with his lingering fear, he couldn't hide it from me.

Over and over, I kept fingering the white envelope in my hands. I barely held myself together as I attempted to answer him.

"I got bored waiting. There it lay, a file folder with my whole life history. Wanted to see what my chart had to tell me. It was just sitting there on Dr. Thornton's desk." I exhausted a long sigh, still not looking at him. "When I picked it up..." finally showing him the names on the envelope, "this fell out." The bold print of my name side by side with Chloe Morrison's dug at the walls of my stomach as I sat there staring at it. I still couldn't look at him as my pooling tears dropped on the envelope. Hawke reached for it, but swiftly I pulled it away before he could take it and whispered. "Did you know Dr. Thornton ran a DNA test on me?" Instead of answering me, Hawke tried one of his old calming methods. My hand in his, he circled the palm of my hand with his fingers. "Answer me." Not so sweetly I yanked my hand from his.

"Found out this morning when he called but," Hawke searched for the right words to continue with, "makes sense now."

"What makes sense now?" My head flung up sharply to stare him in the eyes. "What aren't you telling me?"

"Last weekend, when Doc called, he wanted to go fishing." Hawke playfully patted my knee. "He had more on his mind than fishing."

"What does that have to do with this?" I waved the envelope in the air.

"Give me a minute Dove." His tattered sigh revealed more to come. "I've got to piece this mess together for you. Took me the whole damn week to wrap my brain round what Doc needed to get off his chest."

"Around what?" Lost, confused, my emotions rocked back and forth, just like the ocean waves.

"Doc wanted to make sure we were alone when he unloaded this."

"Unloaded what? What did he tell you? Why didn't he tell me?" My agitation grew along with more confusion.

"Dove, this is going to take a few minutes. Just bare with me." His hands shook as he patted my knee. "Did you know that you were adopted?" he asked as I met his eyes with an odd expression.

"Yes. Uncle Joe and Aunt Phyllis adopted me after my parents died. All the legal documents are in the safe in the basement."

"True honey, that's true. But your parents, they weren't your birthparents. They adopted you when you were three weeks old."

"What?" My mouth hit the ground as I stared at him in total disbelief. "No. That can't be true? My birth certificate says…"

"Say's you're adopted, Dove. I looked at it the other day. Just thought Joe and Phyllis had it changed when they adopted you."

"Why didn't any of this come up when we played 'let's rebuild Dove's memory?'" I choked a little on my sarcastic comment.

"I didn't even know. Doc just found out too." The painful truth in his eyes left me feeling hopeless.

Comfort, we needed it from each other. I inched closer to him and let my head rest on his shoulder. "What did Dr. Thornton have to get off his chest that he couldn't tell me?"

"Doc did some research after Morrison showed up. Dug a little too deep for my liking but…"

"But what? What did he tell you?" I slipped my hand under his.

"Your birthmother, a seventeen year old girl from California. She gave birth, twin girls. Gave you and your sister up for adoption."

At hearing those words come out of his mouth, I popped up off his shoulder filled with a little excitement. "I have a sister? There's a sister out there? Where is she? Hawke, why wouldn't Dr. Thornton just tell me all of this?"

"You're an identical twin. You know, you look a like, but you don't have the same DNA." He pointed to the envelope.

"Chloe Morrison," I stuttered her name, "she's, she's my sister?"

"Apparently so." He pulled a pack of cigarettes from his pocket.

"This isn't happening. No, Hawke, someone is playing a sick joke on us." My empty stomach flipped and flopped into my throat.

"Dove, let me finish." Sadness clouded his deep brown eyes as he quietly continued. "The adoption agency was out of California. You came home to Oregon and your sister was adopted by a couple in Ohio. Files were sealed back then. Papers were signed by the birthmother that she never wanted to be found by either of you." Hawke pulled a cigarette from the pack. Not lighting it, he subconsciously ran it through his fingers. One thing I knew for sure about my husband, he only smoked on a few occasions. An after sex smoke, when aggravated, or when something was completely out of his control. Today's choice for smoking, things were completely out of his control.

"How did Dr. Thornton find all this out?"

"After the encounter with Morrison, Doc called in a few favors. Said the wedding photo James had kept haunting him. Claims it could've been you standing there."

"Favors? What kind…from whom?" I asked, trying to piece the puzzle together.

"Seems our girls helped him." Disappointment clung in his voice.

"Our girls?" Tears and all I snapped back, "They helped Dr. Thornton?"

"What do you expect from two Criminal Forensic Specialists in training?" He smirked at me. "Do you know how easy it was for them? Got a few samples of your hair. Picked up stuff from your coffee mug. God only knows what else they lifted."

"When did they do all…no…please Hawke, tell me this is a mistake."

"Wish I could Dove. Practically ripped them apart for getting involved in this and not telling us." His frown deepened, "Our three-way conversation wasn't pretty with me doing all the yelling."

"I know they didn't do this to hurt me. Or hurt you. But why?"

"They were all in to help Thornton prove to Morrison that you are their Aunt."

"The girls, they, they," I stuttered over my question. "Do they know the results?"

"No one knows what's in that envelope."

"You need to get back to the point of this envelope." Now in my hand, the topic, the envelope, and I waved it in the air. "I'm barely hanging on here. I've got a sister. She's dead. I'm alive. And you…have you left out anymore essential information?"

"Dove, just bare with me. This isn't easy for me. I've got to…" his long hesitation scared me even more. "Dove, me, everyone, we've always told you the bear attack happened down the coast." Hawke, always calm, always in control, but at this minute, I never saw him over shadowed by nerves. "The bear attack," he finally lit the cigarette in his hand and drew in a long hard breath, "it happened when I took you to Michigan with me." He exhaled the tension from his lungs.

"Michigan? Hawke, why would you lie about that? How could you lie about something so devastating that happened to us?" Bewildered, frustrated, even mad by what he just enlighten me to, I hit him hard with the palm of my hand square to his broad shoulder. "How could you keep this from me?" His only reaction, slightly surprised by the punch I delivered to him.

"Well that's a first." He glanced at his shoulder then back to me. Hawke took another drag off his cigarette and cast his eyes towards the ocean in hopes of more answers.

Me on the other hand, I wasn't happy with his comment. I took my frustration out on his bicep. My fingers pinched deep into his flesh, "Why would you lie to me about that?" My anger screamed at him through gritted teeth. "Why?" I demanded, growling at him as the palm of my hand slammed back into his shoulder. "Tell me!"

He grabbed my wrist before I could hit him for a third time. My glare pierced deep into him as his fingers tightened around my hand. With a stern glare of his own, he calmly offered, "Don't hit me again, Dove. I need you to listen to every word I'm going to tell you. Do you understand?"

"What secrets have you kept from me?" The lump in my throat rose as I nodded my head yes. It was useless to yank my hand from him, he only held me tighter.

"The rest of this is pretty twisted, Dove. Pretty tricky to follow. You think you can handle the rest?" Obviously aware of my already tear stained face and shattered nerves, he waited for an answer.

As I fidgeted, I apprehensively asked, "It's going to get worse isn't it?"

"Won't lie to you, Dove, it's going to get bad." Distracting me, he reached for the envelope under my leg, "Why don't you give me that to hold?"

"Not until you tell me what happened to me." The turmoil in his sigh assured me that the lost chapters of my life were going to get ugly.

"That little memory you had," he drew a breath in and released it, "the one as to why you hated me?"

"Yes, but I thought we…"

"Just left out a few details Dove. Only told you what you needed to know at the time. I went to Michigan to track down a nuisance bear. Took you with me in hopes to save our failing marriage. You went under protest, but we both knew this was our only chance. We stayed with Maude's sister, Ruby and her husband Ralph."

"Hawke, that's a lot of information to leave out, but…"

"Dove, just let me finish." So I did. "A new walking path had been put in next to Ruby and Ralph's cottage. Searched the area over, found no trace of the bear. After that, every morning the two of you took off for a walk. My guess, both of you held some kind of female, womanly, bonding session. Cause you warmed up to me." His smile broke the tension. "Anyways, the day before we were to fly home, you went alone. You woke me up early, sun wasn't even up, told me you were going walking." He started chuckling, enjoying his hidden memory.

I had to ask, "You're laughing? Why?" After being so distraught, I too could use a pick-me-up.

"You wanted to make love with me." Grinning, he ran his finger down the bridge of my nose, "We had reconnected so much, that you came to me."

"Oh." Even under the extreme stress of our day, Hawke could still make me blush.

"Still remember how happy you were. How happy you made me. You kissed me, even hugged me before you got out of bed. You were beaming. I laid there watching you dress. Still remember, purple t-shirt and shorts. You grabbed that IPod thing and said you'd be back in an hour." His eyes fell to distant stillness. Silence. He breathed a heavy hearted sigh. Another cigarette lit, he tried to calm himself.

"Hawke, please tell me what happened next." I watched him agonize over his thoughts. Slowly he ran his hand through his loose hair. He filled his lungs by taking in a deep, long drag of the cigarette. Then he slowly exhaled.

"A couple of hours passed and you weren't back. Then we got the call." He shut his eyes to conceal the pain. "The call," he drew in his breath, "a bear had been spotted in the same area you were walking. The guys and I flew out of there packing guns and ammo."

"Lance and Fred? They were with us?"

"Yeah honey. You weren't happy about them going with us, but I needed their help with tracking. Lance went on foot down the path. Fred and I loaded up the truck and took off to the other end of the trail. I knew the spot where you'd walk to." He inhaled another long drag of the cigarette. In his next smoke filled breath, "Found the bear and…"

"And? Did you find me?" Hawke shifted his eyes to meet mine. "What did you find?"

"Got there in time to see the bear fling you toward the tree line. In time to hear your screams. Feel your agonizing pain as you hit the trees. The ungodly sound of your body smashing into the ground." Hawke rubbed at his temples. A vivid memory I'm sure he'd rather have forgotten. "Saw you lying there completely lifeless."

On the edge of the weathered pine bench I sat quivering as Hawke finished the cigarette in his shaking hand. With his other hand he reached for my arm. "You need to sit back before you fall off the bench, Dove."

I did as he said, but slid next to him sitting sideways. Still shaking, he rubbed my leg and started the horrifying nightmare again.

"The bear, it went on a rampage straight for you. I chambered one round. One shot. I dropped the bastard dead on the spot. Damn thing actually fell next to you. Landed with a paw on your chest."

There wasn't any blood left to drain from my face as I sat motionless next to him waiting. He pulled out his pack of cigarettes along with the lighter. He took his time lighting the next one. After a few long hits off it, he looked over at my drained face, shook his head, and continued.

"You were laying there in a broken pile of blood, torn flesh and exposed bones. I really thought you were dead. Amazingly, you tried to talk to me when I picked you up. Fred and I, we wrapped you in a blanket and started to the hospital. On the way we found out that another woman had been attacked down from where we found you." A long pause to steady himself, he took another long drag from the cigarette. "Thought Fred was going to drive right through the ER doors. You were barely hanging on by a thread. From my arms, you were taken to the trauma unit. The other woman, who'd been mauled, arrived right before us. Had both of you in one trauma unit. The hospital was a complete disaster. People were yelling. Running in and out of the unit. Screaming things no one should've ever heard. Covered in blood, all I could do was wait and pray. Worst part about waiting was the not knowing. A deputy came over and handed me your driver license. You had your ID on you that day. Then I heard them making the call for Life Flight."

"Why didn't you just tell me the truth?" He'd finished off half a pack of cigarettes, but who was counting? "I don't understand."

"Dove I never, and I mean never, wanted to relive or remember what happened there again. Closed chapter of my life. In the short amount of time we had there together, I had finally gotten you back. I got my wife back, my best friend. You let your wall tumble down and fell back in love with me. And then, then you nearly died on me. For me, it was just easier the way I told you."

Neither one of us could break the intensity of our gaze we shared. His dark tanned face paled, something I wasn't used to seeing. Never had I witnessed him so scared, shaken to the core of life. For a moment, time between us stood still. The breeze from the ocean swirled my loose hair around and he gently reached for a stray strand, tucking it behind my ear.

"Things went crazy wrong that day. From where we stood..."

"We, who else was there?"

"Fred, Lance, then Ruby and Ralph came down as soon as they heard. The place went uts when one of the machines flat lined. None of us knew who it belonged to. Minutes ent by with no answers. Next thing I knew a blood covered surgeon yelled for me. ushed me back into the trauma unit were I found you completely covered in bandages nd blankets. I swear every inch of you was wrapped tightly in the white, bloody andages. Told me they didn't think you were going to live. Their last hope, Life Flight. Needed to get you into a bigger, better equipped hospital."

"You think the other woman in the trauma unit..." I pulled the envelope out from nder my leg, "you think she was Chloe Morrison?"

"Sad to say Dove, the woman I carried in, she wasn't you." Hawke's tanned leather ace simply went ghost white. "I brought in Chloe. The Rangers found you."

"Oh God." My whole body swayed. "How, how," my words stumbled from my nouth, "how do you know that?" Tears didn't seep down my cheeks, they ran.

"Could've been the look in her eyes when I laid her on the gurney. Could've been the merald bracelet around her wrist. Never thought about any of it until now."

"Someone died that day...how did you know for sure I was yours?" The deeper uestion could only lead to what I know we both thought. "How?"

He brushed a stray tear from my check, "Before Life Flight landed, I stood there olding your hand. You squeezed my hand back. Tried to say something, but your eyes losed. They took you from me to board the helicopter. Dove, I don't know how you nade it. But you did."

"If Chloe Morrison, my sister, if she's dead," I looked at the envelope in my hand, why this?"

"From what Dr. Thornton found out, Morrison identified his wife's body all the way lown to the purple nail polish she was wearing."

"But why would Dr. Thornton have a DNA test run on me?" I shook the unsuspecting etter harder. "Why?"

"Apparently, at the hospital in Michigan things got way out of control. Two major raumas, two women who resembled each other attacked by a bear...everything got nixed up. The staff there, they just wanted to save you both. She died in the bed next to ou."

"My sister died next to me?" The nasty wave of nausea circled around in my stomach ind I curled up like a cat on the park bench resting my aching head on Hawke's thigh. His fingers continually weaved through my hair as I watched the ocean waves moving, ethinking everything he had just told me. The smell of cigarette smoke filled the urrounding air before Hawke spoke again.

"When Morrison blew into town and turned our lives upside down, Doc claims Morrison demanded a DNA test be done right then and there. He'd been so sure you vere Chloe."

As I lay curled next to Hawke, what common sense I had left, raced rapidly away. Slowly the realization popped into my battered brain. Am I really me, or could I possibly be Chloe Morrison. No one knew for sure who was who in that trauma unit ten years igo.

"This all boils down to one thing." Slowly, I sat myself back up and faced Hawke. 'There's a fifty-fifty chance that I'm really not your wife. I might not be me." Hawke grabbed me by the shoulders, practically shaking me, as I sobbed harder.

"Dove, you're my wife. I know every curvy inch of your beautiful body. Before and after it'd been scarred. I know the ins and outs of how your crazy mind works. I know what your fears are. Certain things about you, they've never changed. You're mine."

"But how can you be sure if I don't open this?" That white envelope, it wasn't so white anymore. The nasty thing now had my smudged fingerprints all over it.

"I know you're mine," he reached for the tattered envelope. Again, I didn't give it up. "Dove, you've remembered bits and pieces of our life. One most impressive memory you had..." his face lighten with a smile, "you stood on the steps and told me you remembered making love to me on our wedding night. Think about it, over the years you've been able to piece parts of your life back together."

"Give me your lighter." My voice whispered the request to him. Hawke watched the strange calmness glaze over me as I wiped away the last of my tears.

"Why do you want my lighter?" Left puzzled by my sudden change in moods, he didn't offer it up fast enough.

"Give me your damn lighter!" My breathing became erratic as I shouted the words at him. Not waiting for him, I started to search his shirt pocket. Hawke opened the palm of his hand offering me the bright neon green lighter. Lighter in hand, I watched the flame flicker as I held it up to corner edge of the white envelope. Instantly the results of who I could be went up in flames.

"Dove!" Hawke, shocked by my actions, yelled. "What the hell are you doing?" He reached for the flaming, not-so-threatening-anymore, envelope.

I jumped from the bench and out of his reach, "Hawke, no! Don't touch it! Let it burn! Just let the damn thing burn!"

The torment of the day went up in flames as we both watched the very private, very personal letter burn in the cool fall air. Nearly burning my fingers, I finally dropped the unreadable remains to the ground. There was nothing left of the letter, no one would ever be able to read it. As the final edges burned to a crisp, I joined him back on the bench.

"Dove..."

I shook my head not wanting to hear anymore. I simply looked into the eyes of the man who kept me captivated for years. "Hawke, I know who I am. I'm me. Your wife. Your lover. Your best friend. My heart belongs to you and only you." My day, a sucker punch of emotions, was finally over. "At who's request did Dr. Thornton have this test ran? For his personal knowledge, or did James Morrison antagonize him enough to go through with it? If Chloe Morrison is really my sister, we'll deal with that. But for now, I don't need, nor do I want to know what the results of the DNA test showed. All I need and want is to be with you. I want to grow old, wrinkly and grey with you. It's over."

"Dove, through all of this, never once did I ever doubt that you weren't mine." Rough hands that appeared to have worked over a hundred years circled my tear stained face. The stale stench of cigarettes lingered on his lips as he pressed them to mine.

Wrapped in Hawke's arms of love, comfort, my only security, I brushed my lips softly over his, "I'll be yours until my last dying breath and beyond."

The End

Epilogue

The highway going south out of Michigan long behind us, we now followed the rural routes along the Ohio farm country.

"Can't believe you remembered the way to Ruby and Ralph's cottage. You haven't been there since..." Hawke's voice trailed to another time. Another place from our life history, "Dove, your memory, it's amazing."

"Amazing? I amazed your Aunt and Uncle when I asked about the squeaky bed we'd slept in." My memory of making love to Hawke in the old bed drew a warm smile from him. "My memory, it's been like a jigsaw puzzle. Piece by piece I've been putting things back together."

"Over the last few years you've pieced together just about everything about our lives. Love when you just blurt out details, descriptions."

"It's kind of like being blindsided. Suddenly a piece slips in. It clicks. When we started planning this trip so many memories flooded back to me."

"You remember anything about..." Hawke slid the question in, "anything from the attack?"

"The lake. The cottage. Shopping in town with Aunt Ruby. Rekindling my love for you." Not only did I fall back in love with Hawke before the bear attack, but I fell back in love with this man who was so devoted to me. "That day, the bear, the attack itself. Nothing. Completely blank. I hope I never remember it."

"Would you tell me if you did?" Under his sunglasses I read the sadness in his well lined face.

"Maybe." The thought pondered around in my mind, "I'm sure, yeah, I would."

The GPS directed us to another road. "Well according to this thing," Hawke tapped the black plastic box barking out directions, "should be arriving pretty soon."

Hillside Cemetery came into our view sooner than I had expected. A jolt of uncertainty, even fear, jarred my entire body as the little machine announced "arriving at destination." Really, what could have prepared me for this day? Actually, nothing. Under the weathered, wrought iron archway that held the spelled out name of the cemetery, Hawke stopped the truck. From his shirt pocket he pulled out and unfolded a lined yellow paper that held the last of the directions. Under his dark sunglasses I felt his eyes on me. Simultaneously, I meet his covered eyes as I subconsciously picked at my pretty, painted fingernails.

"Says to follow the main drive until we come to row M." Hawked handed me the yellow ruled paper and proceeded.

With a shaking hand I held the directions and read aloud, "At row M, turn left. Continue until the first cross road. On the right corner of the crossing there will be an angel reaching toward the sky. Hawke, I'm..."

"Dove, I can turn around. Take you wherever you want to go." He slowed the truck to barely a crawl as the crossroad came into our view.

"No. We made it this far." I continued to read over the note, "says to wait for them here."

"Glad to see we're on time." Hawked shifted his old, favorite truck into park. After removing his knock off Ray-Ban sunglasses, he drummed his thumb repetitively on the steering wheel. He'd bagged his attitude for our two thousand mile plus cross country drive. "You okay?"

Barely noticing anything around me, even the sound of Hawke's voice. And how could I not notice that? We were surrounded by all shapes and sizes of granite headstones in the cemetery. My full attention rested on the angel reaching for the heavens.

"Dove?"

The cellophane wrapped white daisies fumbled under my touch, "Hope she likes these." Hawke cocked his head to the side analyzing my answer. I know he wanted to say something sarcastic to my not so coherent reply. But he spared me. "I'm okay." relied on every bit of his emotional support on this trip back east.

"See your Primroses made it. You dig those out of your flowerbed?" He shifted in his seat trying to judge my feelings.

"Yes, I did. They'll bloom in purple and yellow. I hope no one minds. Just wanted to leave a little of me with her." The tears I could no longer hold onto escaped.

"Dove," Hawks fingers tugged at my curly hair. "You just say the word and..."

"No, Hawke, I'm sorry. I'll be okay." A sniff, tears wiped away, I perked up my lips into what I hoped would be a believable smile for him. "Need to do this so we can move on with our lives."

"Ruby handed this over." Hawke slipped an old, faded photo from his shirt pocket into my hand.

"I know this isn't me and you." I said quietly and flipped the photo over. "Hawke and Chloe." I read allowed. "Hawke you..."

"From the age of five to fifteen Maude shipped my butt back to Ruby and Ralph's every summer. For a couple years this little girl was my fishing buddy." His voice soft as he reflected back on the memory, "She's your sister."

"You knew Chloe."

"Never put two and two together until Ruby gave me the photo."

"That's, it's just...do you remember anything about her?"

Hawke grinned at me and glanced down at the picture, "Wild red hair," he flipped one of my curls over my shoulder, "and a spirit that matches yours. Worse fisherman than you."

"This day's just been," I ran my fingers over the old photo and smiled, "just emotional."

The hot summer sun of July poured into the front windshield. Vaguely, off in the distance a dull roar could be heard from a grounds keeper's lawn mower. A monarch butterfly fluttered its way into my window. Could it be a sign? Maude would have said yes. I have to believe it is. I batted one last stray tear away knowing Hawke could read my thought pattern. Fixed and focused, I kept my eyes on the surrounding headstones as we waited for the others.

"Ohio's a nice state, don't you think?" Small talk wasn't like Hawke, but he humored me after dropping the last bombshell on me.

"I like it. Glad you got off the freeway and took the back roads, reminds me of home. Do you think she's close?" Again, Hawke cocked his head to the side. From his side of the truck he analyzed my thought pattern.

"Just like Maude, you can feel her." Hawke surprised me. "You've always known things. Never could figure out how you did it. Maude's the same way."

"Must have gotten it from her." The "feeling", been clued into it my entire life. Now I know what my missing piece has been. "Peaceful here, don't you think?"

"Most cemeteries are Dove." He rolled his eyes and didn't bother to hold back his smirk.

"Is it the girls?" I turned around to see the car rolling up behind us.

"Our personal tag team of forensic experts." Hawke didn't turn around. His glare reflected off the rearview mirror to the parked car behind us.

"You promised." I whispered and reached for his hand, "It's been three years."

"Yep. I know." His eyes never left the mirror.

"Thought you patched everything up with them." I unhooked my seatbelt and waited to join our girls.

"Dove, they went behind your back. Our backs. Never said one damn word. Came home, collected samples of your hair, your blood, even lifted stuff off your coffee mug."

"They're good. What did you expect from our newly graduated Criminal Forensic experts? And their cousin, Jason, all three of them with the same degree. Honey, it's over. Remember you forgave them."

"May have forgave them, but I didn't forget. Even teamed up with the Morrison kid. The whole mess could have blown up in their faces."

Car doors slammed behind us, "But it didn't. It all worked out. I'm yours. Always have been. Always will be."

"Aunt Dove," Amelia popped open my door. "Uncle Hawke, I can't believe you drove the old dragon all the way to Ohio."

Hawke cast his niece somewhat of a smile, "It's reliable."

"Thanks for making sure Aunt Dove got here." This time his weathered face gently filled with a warmer smile for Amelia.

"Let's go Uncle Hawke." His truck door flew open.

"Emma." He swung one leg out and glared at her. The two of them had always had a love hate relationship. But the love always out weighed the hate.

"Out." Reverting back to her childhood, Emma tugged at her Uncle's hand for his full attention. "Wasn't so sure you'd show, let alone bring Aunt Dove."

Uncle and niece stood face to face under the rays of the hot Ohio sun. With a peck to his cheek, Emma hugged her Uncle's still broad shoulders. "We're so glad you both came. Please don't be mad at us."

"I'm not. Had a little time to wrap my brain around what you two pulled. Or should I say the three of you." He yanked at the streaks of purple mixing in her raven black hair, "What the hell is this?"

"Are the two of you done yet?" Amelia snuggled next to her Uncle for a hug, as Emma slipped into my arms. "We always knew you were our Aunt."

"Believe in proving our point." Emma nodded towards the approaching car, "Is that Jason's car?"

The sleek black SUV snaked its way around the narrow cemetery lanes. A hand waved out the open window as they parked in line with the other vehicles. As uncomfortable as we all were, being here together seemed to be the right thing. I secured myself to Hawke's side. His hand wrapped tightly around my waist.

235

"Jason," my girls hugged their cousin as his father, with head held high, approached us.

"Hawke," James, with a manly hello extended his hand to his brother-in-law, "Can't thank you enough for bringing Dove and coming. Means a lot." Then he embraced me in a hug of comfort, "you're so much like Chloe," tears filled his eyes, "just wish she could've met you."

"Feel like I've known her all my life from all the details you shared with us." Easily, slipped back into Hawke's arms for the support I needed. "Hope you don't mind, brought a Primroses plant for Chloe. They're from my garden."

"I'm sure she'd love them." James, along with his wife Sarah gestured for us to join them by Chloe's headstone.

"We need to celebrate," Emma held up a bottle of wine, "It's our "Aunts' birthday.""

"Got your favorite kind of cake Aunt Dove," Amelia held a bakery box in her hands.

Conversation came easy as we shared the cake and wine. I placed a glass goblet filled to the rim with a sweet red wine on top of my sister's headstone along with a slice of birthday cake. "Happy Birthday Chloe. Wish we would've found each other sooner."

We hadn't had any contact with James until the truth about who I really was came to light. I'd finally given in to reading a duplicate copy of the DNA report. As I knew, was and still am Dove Hawthorne. The fallout from three years ago with James had been put to rest. Through e-mails, telephone calls, and text messages we blended our families together. Hawke still kept a guarded reserve to the family I never knew existed, but seemed to enjoy the time he'd spent on the phone talking with James.

As we leisurely celebrated mine and my late sister's birthday I left her one last gift. A handmade dream catcher from Maude. "Chloe's glass of wine," the crystal goblet sparkled in the sun, "it's empty."

About the Author

Independently published author Sharon R. Hunter, entered her first writing at the Y-City Writers of Zanesville, Ohio. It was not a writing of romance but an inspirational writing thanks to her special needs daughter, Lauren, which won her a second place ribbon.

A romance reader at heart, Sharon took up writing in her late forties, finally fulfilling her lifelong dream. Encouraged by her husband Jeff, and a handful of special girlfriends, she's developed into an inspiring romance writer. Most of her writings revolve around her dreams and she enjoys twisting and turning them into tangled webs to create a passionate love affairs.

Residing in Streetsboro, Ohio, Sharon is at home with her husband Jeff, daughters Meghan and Lauren, son Beau, and their furry feline children. Writing for Sharon is no longer a hobby; it is a budding career.

Current romance novels by Sharon are:

The Ranch Series: "The Rancher's Wife & Love on the Ranch"

"Happy Hooker's Bait & Tackle Shop, A Romantic Comedy"

You can follow Sharon on Facebook at Sharon R. Hunter, Author and Goodreads

All novels are available on Amazon, Kindle

65856414R00132

Made in the USA
Charleston, SC
04 January 2017